THESE LONLEY PLACES

R.K. KOMBRINCK

CONTENTS

"The whole neighborhood abounds with local tales, haunted spots, and twilight superstitions; stars shoot and meteors glare oftener across the valley than in any other part of the country, and the nightmare, with her whole ninefold, seems to make it the favorite scene of her gambols."

—Washington Irving

PERMANENT RESIDENTS

They caught sight of the motel from the bridge that crossed the highway. It squatted on a kidney-shaped plot of pavement, surrounded on three sides by trees and dark hills. There was nothing and no one else around for miles.

"There it is." Amanda reached out and grasped Wendy's hand, squeezing tightly. She was excited. They had done the silo facility in Chillicothe. They'd walked the three miles of track to the derelict rail depot in Hartwell. They'd explored the one room schoolhouse in Cleves, the old factory in Hyde Park and the deserted neighborhood off the highway behind Lookout Acres. All had been thoroughly boring, and Amanda wanted something more. A place with a rich, dark history. She'd almost given up on finding one when she'd overheard two girls in the University's common area talking about the, "Murder Motel." She'd asked some questions, done some Googling and discovered the thing she'd been looking for had been hiding in plain sight, right under her nose.

It had been something of a nine-days wonder back in the fall of 1983. News outlets across the state had run the story of how a man named Terry Loughton had come stumbling into the front office of the Royal Motel just after sunset waving a pistol. He murdered six employees and two guests before turning the gun on himself. His wife's body was discovered at the couple's home, a hunting knife jammed deep in her belly, her guts spoiling on the kitchen floor. Their seven-year-old daughter Jackie was never seen again.

The Royal Motel was shut down quietly and left to rot. No developers came to rehab it. No one bulldozed it to build something else in its place. It just sat, empty and waiting. People forgot the name Terry Loughton. Forgot the names of the victims. It was relegated to late night conversations in bars and truck stops, and even that eventually dried up. For years the story lay as dormant as the motel itself. Then, after some time passed, it found a second, vivid life amongst the kind of people who could really appreciated gruesome tales of blood and tragedy.

"All the kids say that a group of Devil worshippers started using the place for rituals. That they had orgies and called up demons and communicated with the ghosts of the people who'd died there." Amanda grinned as she spun the yarn. They'd left the bridge and turned onto a road rough from neglect and full of potholes. "Another story says a group of paranormal investigators went out there to stay overnight and study the place. They ran out screaming after only three hours. They disbanded the group and never spoke of that night again."

Clark leaned forward from the back seat, pushing his face between the two sisters. The sun was bright, and he squinted out from beneath his red knit cap. "Is that true?"

She shrugged. "Who knows? Probably not. The only thing that's for sure is that nine people died there. The rest are just rumors." She raised her eyebrow theatrically. "But there are a *lot* of rumors. Everybody at Bridlefield has a story about this place and there's a couple of websites that mention it."

They bumped along for another couple of miles until the pines suddenly swept back from the road, leaving a swath of unruly grass. A thick, metal pole reached up from the scrub, topped with a sign that proclaimed, *Royal Motel: Air Conditioned • Free HBO.* Just beyond that, on the right, lay their destination.

A sagging, two level affair, it sprawled in the shadows of the encroaching woods. Its yellow paint had faded almost to white. There was a check-in office at one end, and a tunnel which cut through to the rear of the motel. Every ten feet or so, were rooms. Closed white doors accompanied by large, naked, windows. Further down were two stairways to the second floor, and a glass enclosure where a long-dead ice machine hulked. Wendy pulled into the parking lot, stirring drifts of dead leaves. No other cars passed down the road. They had the place to themselves.

"Damn. This is legit." Clark's tone was hushed and respectful.

"Yeah," Wendy shut off the ignition. "But I wish it was closer to home. It's gonna be dark soon. We should've started earlier."

Amanda undid her seatbelt. "We can spend the night in my dorm if you want. It'll be quiet. Everybody's gone for the holiday." She opened her door and stepped out onto the pavement. A smile spread across her face as she drank in the squalid atmosphere. The chipped and peeling paint. The empty flowerpot outside the office door. The ghosts of parking space lines. She was in love. She pulled her pack from the front seat and began rummaging through it. Clark got out and stood next to her, stretching. He looked back in at Wendy.

"Yeah, that's a good plan. We can all spend the night together. In your dorm room I mean. Makes sense."

Amanda glanced over at him, amused to see his face had gone bright red beneath his scruffy beard, "Yeah, we can't use my roommate's bed so we're all gonna have to squeeze into mine." She pulled her camera from her pack and began snapping pictures.

Wendy stepped out and stood by the car. After a moment's consideration she wrapped her scarf around her neck. It had been unseasonably warm for late November, but it was cold in the shade of the motel. She sniffed the air.

"Ugh. What's that smell?"

The artificial click of Amanda's digital camera went off and the flash bloomed. "I don't smell anything." She was fascinated with the grime on the windows. It made patterns that looked like handprints.

Clark went around to Wendy's side and leaned against the car. "No, there's definitely a smell. It's like dead leaves, moldy carpet, and raccoon shit." His voice dropped to an ominous growl. "Or maybe it's the lingering stench of death." He chuckled and lit a cigarette.

"Don't be a dick. People died here." Wendy shut the driver's side door and sidled over to her sister. "Is this one creepy enough for you?"

Amanda kept taking pictures, her eyes on the viewscreen, but she spoke as she moved the camera around. "Another thing they say is that, sometimes, people driving by at night see lights on in the windows. And sometimes, they see shadows in those lit up rooms."

Wendy hugged herself and shivered. "Maybe people are staying here. Squatters or something."

Amanda looked up from her camera. "And who's paying the electric bill?" She slipped the camera's strap over her shoulder and hoisted her pack. "You guys ready to explore?" Without waiting for an answer, she strode across the parking lot towards the front office.

She stepped over a parking block onto the walk. Stubborn weeds clawed their way up between the cracks in the cement. She pressed her face up to the plate-glass that fronted the office and put her hands to either side, trying to see in. This was where Terry Loughton had gunned down four of his eight (*Actually, it was ten, counting the wife and little girl,* she reminded herself) victims. The night manager, the front desk clerk and two maids. She felt a morbid thrill knowing that blood had been spilled just a few feet away. The window was nearly opaque with dust and grit and it was very dark inside. She couldn't make out anything at all. She tried the door and found it locked, just as she'd expected.

No big deal. She had her lock-picking kit. She heard Wendy and Clark shuffling up behind her and turned to face them.

"I say we start with the rear of the building. Cut through the tunnel, see what's back there. Maybe try a few of the rooms then make our way back here. Finish with the office. What do you guys think?"

Wendy chewed at her lower lip. She looked uncomfortable. "How many rooms do you want to go through? We can't stay here too long. It's already three-thirty."

"Jesus Wen. We drove all this way, we're gonna check out as many rooms as we can. We've got flashlights."

"Sorry. I was just asking."

Clark tossed his cigarette to the ground and put his hand on Wendy's arm. "Don't worry about it. We'll be alright."

She gave him a withering look and shrugged his hand off. "I know. I was just asking."

Amanda left them behind. She went into the tunnel that connected the front of the motel to the rear. It was dark inside. An overlapping and confusing roadmap of graffiti spread out across the walls. She stepped back trying to take all of it in. A lot of it was the usual childish vulgarity. Depictions of huge penises, impossibly large breasts, pot-leaves and the names of heavy metal bands. She particularly liked the one that said, "April Priest + Beer =Blowjobs." Some of it, however, was quite strange. She took her camera and began shooting pictures. Each time the flash went off it illuminated a small piece of the chaotic puzzle.

flash

Eight small figures in silhouette holding hands, their eyes round, white holes.

flash

A crude drawing of a little girl in a dress and pigtails. Blank white eyes and her mouth drawn down in an exaggerated frown.

flash

"!!! La niña quiere comer su alma, salir y permanecer fuera hermanos!!!"

flash

A bouquet of thorny stems crowned, not with flowers, but with crescent shaped eyes.

flash

"Say hi to Jackie for me."

flash

Something that looked like a huge scorpion with human hands instead of claws. Beside it the words, "I'm sorry I came here."

flash

"Jacky ate my baby."

flash

"Jackie RULZ!"

flash

"Jackie sux dix." Below this the addendum, "Jackie EATZ dicks. Get it straight fucker."

flash

"Everybody up. Amanda's here," encircled by a chain of white eyes.

Amanda stumbled back, nearly dropping her camera. She leaned forward, so close her nose almost touched the wall. The circle of eyes was there but what she'd thought were words now just looked like a greasy black streak. Her mind had played a little prank on her. She smiled as she turned and examined the writing on the opposite wall. *This is exactly what I wanted.* She shouldered her camera and headed cheerfully to the rear of the motel.

She stepped out of the tunnel and into what had once been the Royal Motel's recreational area. To her right a small structure stuck out perpendicular from the main building. It had no windows, just a gaping doorway. Faded paintings of Pac-Man, Q-Bert and Space Invaders decorated the front wall. She wondered if any of the old games were still in there, shrouded in cobwebs. She doubted it. People had been out here. Someone would have spirited them away if the owners had been stupid enough to leave them in the first place.

A concrete courtyard spread out from the arcade across the back of the building. A few old weather-stained lounge-chairs were strewn here and there. To her left, a bit further back, was a small swimming pool surrounded by a low fence. The gate had been torn away and left discarded on the ground. Amanda could see that the pool was half full of dark water. A breeze blew across it, carrying an odor like drowned things. A child's deflated, pink inner tube floated listlessly at the surface. It was the only spot of color to be found. Everything else was gray and damp. She wrinkled her nose but was delighted all the same.

"Smells like dead fish." Wendy had come through the tunnel and Clark was standing behind her.

"I know." Amanda set her pack on the ground and hunkered down next to it. She opened it and began taking items out. She set a flashlight head-down on the concrete then placed a small plastic box next to it. As she did this, she heard Clark exclaim behind her.

"Oh shit, is that an arcade?"

"All signs point to yes." Amanda flipped the lid of her case revealing a set of small tools. "Why don't you go check it out. You can take my light."

"'S'alright, I've got one." He padded off to the arcade as she stood.

She saw that her sister wore an amusing expression of boredom mixed with unease. Amanda knew the only reason Wendy went on these excursions was because she wanted to show everyone, she was more than just a pretty face. She gamely clambered through garbage strewn trailers, rodent infested basements, and crumbling factories. She took photos and commented on blog posts, but Amanda knew she had no real interest in these lonely places. They were very different women. Wendy was tall, brunette, and gorgeous while Amanda was small, athletic and blonde. They were both intelligent, but everyone seemed to regard Amanda as the "smart" one and it rankled Wendy.

"You okay sis?" Amanda pulled off her gloves and stuffed them into her jacket pockets.

Wendy shrugged. "Yeah. Just tired. And cold. What happened to the sun? Feels like the temperature's dropped twenty degrees since we got here."

"Well, the trees keep it pretty shady. And it's breezy." Amanda started towards one of the rooms that faced the courtyard. "Wanna come in here with me?"

Before she had a chance to answer Clark came out of the arcade. His eyes sparkled. "You guys gotta see this. There's a bunch more of that crazy shit spray painted all over the walls and ceiling. Names, little nursery rhymes. Weird drawings. No games though." His tone was disappointed for a moment but bounced right back. "The creepiest part is that there's handprints in the dust all over it. Give me the camera."

Amanda placed it in Clark's outstretched hand. "I'll see it in a bit. I want to get into these rooms first."

"I'll come with you Clark." Wendy turned her back to the motel. Amanda saw Clark smile widely and felt a sting of annoyance. He was so predictable. She watched them go into the arcade and a moment later the flash of the camera began lighting up the darkness within.

She turned and walked past the iron stairway that led from the courtyard to the second floor. She stepped beneath the overhang and walked up to a door. Room 21. Through the window she could vaguely make out the shape of what was probably a bedframe. She tried the knob. It was locked. That made sense, all the doors probably were. She selected one of the little tools in her case and slipped it into the lock, wiggling it back and forth. After a moment there was a click and the knob turned in Amanda's hand. Her heart sped up as she pushed the door open and stepped into the room.

She switched on her flashlight and moved the beam across the room. The metal bedframe was there and that was about it. The room had been stripped of furniture and the carpet had been torn up in a few places showing bald cement. It felt empty (of course, why shouldn't it?) and disappointing. She gave it thirty seconds of attention before backing out of it and moving on. She pulled the door shut and then, on impulse, tried to open it again. It had locked automatically. She walked along to the next room and jimmied the lock without even trying it first.

In this room the bed came complete, mattress and all, with a filthy blanket scrunched up at the foot. A side table with two drawers sat beside the bed against the wall and a long, low dresser sprawled beneath the window.

She moved to the side of the bed and leaned over, touching the mattress. She had expected it to be damp for some reason, but it was bone dry. A cloud of dust puffed up around her hand. The springs screeched as she lowered herself onto it. She settled in and looked around the room.

Amanda had really hoped to find some personal items. Artifacts left behind by the last guests to stay here, or even junk that transients and squatters had forgotten. Anything that would connect to a human presence. She trained the flashlight's beam downward and swept it along the floor. More dust. More cobwebs. Nothing else.

She began opening the dresser drawers. The first two were empty. The third one contained a very large, hairy spider and Amanda slammed it shut with a gasp. She uttered a breathless little giggle and drew the last one open cautiously, shining the light in. A pencil rolled across the bottom. That was it.

With a disappointed grunt she leaned over and opened the top drawer of the side table. Inside was a thick, cheaply bound book. *Now we're getting somewhere*, she thought as she lifted the book out (giving it a good shake to dislodge any creepy-crawly stowaways). Someone had tried to blot out the title with black ink, but it was stamped into the cover and clearly legible. *Holy Bible.*

"Well shit." Amanda felt a queasy wave of excitement in her belly. She tried to flip through it and found all the pages were stuck together. Someone had glued them shut. She was intrigued and turned the defaced scriptures this way and that. She ran her thumb across the pages and found that it opened in the center of the book. She laid it open on the bed beside her. The original text had been pasted over with notebook paper and something was written on it in tight little letters. She held up her light and bent over. As she did, Wendy and Clark's shadows passed in front of the dirty window. She heard the door to the next room open as they entered. They thumped around, their voices muffled but loud.

So much for not wanting to explore the rooms. It irritated Amanda that the only reason her sister was rooting around in there was because Clark was with her. Somehow, he'd coaxed her into a room when Amanda could not. His crush was becoming unbearable. It had sneaked in and devoured a part of their friendship. It didn't matter, though, because Wendy would never give him what he wanted. Another part of Amanda wondered why it never even occurred to him to try and see if *she* would.

Because Wendy is the pretty one. That's why.

She shook the sour thoughts away and concentrated on trying to make out the writing on the pages pasted into the bible. The handwriting was cramped and seemed to be in a language that Amanda couldn't even guess at, though every so often English words and phrases were peppered in. She read aloud, pronouncing as best she could:

"Briiecxo gullis bub soom-neilsgh'h alarkcrit upharsin, mene-tekel bubb marked by its lividity shub gomthog Yoth Kamog sybl naahg bub-heilsgh'b aggrieved and unburied lesh coulerig sebs"

The thumping next door suddenly intensified. It sounded like someone was hitting the wall, just on the other side. *Ugh, is she letting him fuck her?* Amanda grimaced, disgusted at the thought. *God, they know I'm in here.* It was like they were doing it just to mess with her. Normally she would find the idea ridiculous but here, in this dark room with dust floating around her like dirty snow, it seemed completely reasonable.

She stood from the bed, snapped the bible closed and stuffed it into her jacket pocket. She explored the rest of the room, shining her light in every gloomy corner and crevice. The bathroom was empty, and the closets held nothing but a couple of theft-proof wooden hangers. It seemed this room had given her everything it had. The bible was a nice relic though, and she couldn't wait to get it home and start researching the writing on the notebook paper. Someone somewhere had to have an idea of what it meant. As she reached for the knob, there was another thump from the room next door, and she rolled her eyes impatiently.

"Jesus Christ you guys." She opened the door, expecting the sudden onrush of daylight to dazzle her but the sky had dimmed considerably. In fact, the sun had sunk low behind the hills and the shadows of the pines stretched out long.

Amanda pulled her phone from her pocket. The clock said 4:28. She stared at it for a few seconds and then looked stupidly back up at the sky, trying to reconcile the two. It couldn't have been much later than 3:40 when she'd gone into the room, and it seemed to her that she'd only been inside for nine or ten minutes at most. She moved slowly towards the next room, intending to ask Wendy and Clark if they'd noticed her long absence. *Of course, they hadn't.* She reached out and knocked on the door. There was no reply. No sound of any kind. She knocked again and called out.

"Guys? Hey. Guys. You in there?" Nothing. No more of the thumping, no more voices. She decided to just walk in and hope they'd finished. The doorknob was cold against her hand as she closed her fingers around it and turned.

It was locked.

She jiggled the knob, but it wouldn't budge. She leaned in close, putting her ear against the door. She strained to catch any sound from within. She swept her hair behind her neck and pressed more tightly. Was that something? A tapping? Just on the other side of the door? Maybe not. If it had been there at all, it was gone now. She pounded on the door and shouted.

"Hey! This is bullshit. It's not funny. HEY!" The sound of her fist rapping against the mute wood echoed across the pavement, startling some birds from the trees. There was no reply. She stepped away from the door. They weren't in there. She turned slowly and surveyed the courtyard. In the thickening shade, the swimming pool was black, the inner tube drifting listlessly across it, urged on by the breeze. The ruined gates that surrounded it were skeletal silhouettes. They offered no answers. She took one last look at the door and considered letting herself in with her pick. After a moment, she decided, instead, to try the next room down.

She picked the lock and entered. The dark of the room was thicker than the last two. She turned on her flashlight and swung the beam around. She felt hurried now. Less genuinely curious, and anxious about being caught there after sundown. She didn't need to see the bathroom and there was no dresser or table in this room for her to explore. Just a bare bedframe. She was turning to the door when something on the carpet caught her eye. It was small and bright, startling against the dingy gray nap. It was a business card. She knelt and picked it up, shining her light on it.

N.O.P.E.
Northern Ohio Paranormal Examiners
"Getting to know the unknown"

Matt Lauritsen M.S.
Bridlefield University

So, a paranormal group really had come out here. Shit. She shook the thought away with a jerk of her head. *So what?* She stood and shoved the card into her pocket next to the bible. Not bothering to take a last look around, she stepped out of the room, pulling the door closed behind her.

"Guys?" Her voice was small. Where the hell were they? Amanda went back to the arcade, very aware of how quickly the sky was darkening. "Wendy? Clark?"

She stepped through the doorway into the quiet. She switched on her flashlight. Dust swam in the air. She looked around the room and her breath caught in her throat. There *was* graffiti on the walls and ceiling, as Clark had said, but he'd gotten it wrong. There were no words, no obscene pictures. Just hundreds, maybe thousands of eyes. All shapes and sizes, some detailed, some simple. All staring at her.

She backed away from the wall and tripped over something in the middle of the floor. She landed hard on her rear and dropped the flashlight. It spun a few times and came to rest with the beam trained on what had tangled up her feet.

The camera.

She snatched it up by the strap and stood. She thumbed the power button, and the little green light came on with a mechanical whine. She couldn't understand why Clark would leave it lying there. She turned on the "view" mode to see what the last picture he'd taken had been.

It was a shot of Wendy in the doorway, framed by gray daylight. She wasn't smiling. There was a strange smudge in the background over her shoulder. Amanda pressed the little plus sign, enlarging the picture and scrolling it slightly to the right. It wasn't a smudge, but a shadow.

A person standing behind her sister.

The sun was almost gone, a fading pink glow behind the silent pines. She stepped out into the shady courtyard and yelled as loudly as she could.

"Wendy? Wendy *please*!" She desperately hoped they were messing with her. She wouldn't even be mad. She was ready to leave now. Her footfalls were loud as she hurried across the pavement. She turned and went into the tunnel, calling for her sister as she went. She had never wanted to see Wendy as badly as this before in her life. A knot of dark worry bloomed in her chest. She needed her sister. Needed to wrap her arms around her beautiful shoulders and feel her *rightness*.

Amanda could see the car out in the front parking lot. It was running, and the headlights were on. The front doors were thrown wide open, but no one was inside. She was about to step into the parking lot when she realized, with a start, that something was wrong with the tunnel. She shined her flashlight across the walls and gasped.

All the writing had disappeared, replaced by more mute, indifferent eyes. She remembered chuckling at the silliness of the adolescent graffiti (*April Priest + Beer =Blowjobs*). She knew it had been there. A scream crawled up her throat, but she struggled fiercely to keep it inside. She did not want to lose control. She turned away from the eyes (*what if they started blinking?)* and rushed to the car.

The heater was running. Amanda stuck her head in the driver's side and glanced in the back. It was empty. Only Wendy's scarf, lying abandoned on her seat, gave any indication she'd been there. There was no sign of Clark at all.

Amanda's heart was pounding. She turned and looked back at the motel. Where could they be? They had to be fucking around with her. They *had* to be. She sat down behind the wheel and switched the ignition off. No sense wasting gas. She pressed down on the horn, letting it blast for a long time. She slammed her fist down on it in a staccato beat. Why weren't they coming out, laughing at her for being scared? This had all been *her* idea. This had been what *she* wanted. A spooky location to explore. A bad place. It would be hilarious for them to turn the tables on her. Mean, maybe, but funny in a dark way. Teach her a lesson. She knew now that she needed one. About showing respect for the past and the places that still reeked of it.

Minutes passed and the cold crept in. The only sound was Amanda's breathing. She'd pulled the doors shut, and the windows fogged up. She'd tried calling Wendy's phone, but it went straight to voicemail. She thought about dialing the police, but what would she say? That she and her friends had been trespassing on a piece of property where a bunch of people had been murdered, years ago, just to poke around for laughs, and now her sister and friend had somehow disappeared? That maybe they were playing a cruel joke on her, but she was terrified that they weren't? The longer she waited in silence with the dark drawing down, the idea seemed less and less crazy.

She had just pressed the "9" and the "1" on her keypad when a voice called from out in the gloom.

"Amanda! Hey!"

It was Clark.

She flung the door open and jumped out. At first, she couldn't tell where his voice was coming from. She scanned the front of the motel and was startled to realize he was leaning out the open door of the office.

How the hell did they get in there?

"Asshole! What's wrong with you?" She tried to sound angry, but the relief in her voice was impossible to hide. She almost wanted to laugh. "Come on. Let's get out of here."

"Not yet. Come in here. There's something you've got to see."

Amanda rolled her eyes. She had lost all desire to explore the Royal Motel. She'd seen enough. As far as she was concerned, it was time to maybe look for a new hobby altogether. She shook her head and called back.

"No, come on. I'm cold. Where's Wendy?"

"She's in here. She wants you to see this. Hurry up." His small form, barely visible in the dark, disappeared back into the office, letting the door snick shut.

Amanda was annoyed all over again. These two were real pieces of work. She left the car behind and strode to the door. They were acting like mean little kids. Bullies. They were probably hiding in there, waiting for her to enter so they could jump out and scare her. She wasn't going to give them the satisfaction. She would steel herself for the shock and show no reaction. She reached out and pulled the door open. She stepped into the heavy darkness and readied herself for whatever they had in store for her.

She realized too late what a horrible mistake she'd made.

The door closed behind her, enfolding her in darkness, but she could still see well enough to know the room was full of people. Arms, legs, bellies, eyes and feet swam in and out of the shadows. With a choked scream, she threw herself back against the door. It wouldn't budge. The people in the dark didn't move. They just watched as she flung herself over and over against the unyielding glass, pounding her fists uselessly. She cried and called for help. Called for Wendy and Clark and beat at the door. It wouldn't open. She tried to punch through the glass, but it was too thick. No one made a sound behind her. Not until she slid to the floor, tears streaming down her cheeks, sobs turning to exhausted dry heaves. Then a voice spoke up. One she'd never heard before. The voice of a little girl.

"No time for that now, Amanda. Everybody's here." There was a childish giggle and sudden light filled the room.

Amanda didn't want to turn around. Every instinct she had cried out against it, but of course she did. Ancient, dead bulbs in the ceiling glowed with phantom power, revealing the small crowd who stood watching her. Five men, three women, their clothes filthy and tattered, stained with age and blood. One of the women was missing her right eye along with most of the right side of her face. Her hair was a matted bird's nest that hung over the dark wound like a curtain, and Amanda could see bugs squirming in it. Another, a man wearing a loud sport-coat and jeans, had a ragged hole in his shirt, just above his belt. Something was hanging out of the tear. Something that looked like gray-black sausage clotted with dark sludge. He regarded her from behind lightly tinted glasses, unperturbed by her scrutiny. She looked from face to face. They all watched her wordlessly. Their eyes were sad. Flies buzzed everywhere. She could feel them lighting on her cheeks and brows and flitting away again. And there was a smell. Thick, rank, and horribly sweet.

I am sharing a room with ghosts.

"I *wish* I was a ghost." The gravelly voice came from a corner off to her left. Against her better judgment, she turned to look. Sitting against the wall, his knees drawn up to his chest, was a broad-shouldered man covered in dust. A spray of maroon spread out across the wall just above his head, stark in the sallow light. The revolver he'd used to kill himself and the other eight people in the room lay at his side, garlanded with cobwebs. "Ghosts don't know they're dead."

"Oh, stop being so grumpy." It was the young girl's voice again. Amanda snapped her head around and found herself face to face with its owner.

She was seven or eight years old (when she *died*, a merciless part of Amanda's mind amended), with long blonde hair pulled back in a ponytail. She wore a Strawberry Shortcake t-shirt with frilly sleeves over a pair of red gym-shorts. The shirt was a bit faded but clean, as were the girl's hair and skin. Her eyes were bright, her face fresh. She was in complete contrast to the other things that shared the room with her. It was perhaps in deference to this distinction that their dead eyes glowed with adoration as they gazed down upon the little girl. She drew very close to Amanda and smiled. Her teeth were white and perfect, but her breath—oh, her breath was vile. Like the wet, clogged odor of the swimming pool out back but much stronger, much closer.

"Jackie." Amanda had known the moment she'd heard the girl's voice, but now, looking at her, breathing in her foul reek, it seemed necessary to say out loud. "You're Jackie Loughton."

The girl's face lit up. Delighted, but not surprised. "Yep. And you're Amanda Corcoran. I'm glad you came."

From the corner, the dead (but not ghostly—he'd been very clear on that) Terry Loughton moaned miserably. "I'm so sorry. I thought they brought her here to kill her. I didn't know."

The mirth drained from Jackie's eyes and she spoke through suddenly clenched jaws. "Daddy, I told you to stop. Being. So. *GRUMPY.*"

He sobbed, or maybe he chuckled, it was hard to tell, but words kept spilling from his spoiled lips. "They brought her here, but that's what she wanted. It's what she was waiting for. How could I know? Oh Sharon, I'm sorry. I'm so, so sorry. I didn't know she had that knife. I could've stopped her maybe..." His voice gurgled and rasped.

Jackie's face suddenly snapped away from Amanda. It flew back towards her father's body, carried on a neck grown suddenly long and thin. Her ponytail flew out behind her head like a poisonous comet's tail and the sound of her teeth chomping together was hideously loud as she spoke.

"Shut up! Shut up! Shut up! I told you never to talk about Momma. Never, ever, *ever.*"

Now it was clear the man was laughing. It was an awful sound. "Or what? You can't make this any worse. I'll say what I want. You're the one who killed her. You were a terrible daughter." His words dissolved into a series of wheezing coughs that in turn lapsed back into sludgy underwater gurgles.

"I spared her this." Jackie's voice was no longer like a little girl's. It wasn't like anything human at all anymore. It was as if the buzz of cicadas in high summer had formed into words. "Because I loved her best. I loved her *only.* I spared her, so you would suffer this. *DADDY.*" The head pulled back on the serpentine neck, a triumphant sneer wrinkling her lips. "I'm leaving you here. My flock is coming with me, but you'll stay behind with the new residents."

Terry Loughton's face crumpled with fear and terror. "No! I'm sorry sweetie, I take it back. Please don't leave me here with them. *Please.* Jackie. Please!"

With horrifying speed, Jackie thrust her head forward and clamped her open mouth over her father's. For a moment it looked like they were sharing a deep lover's kiss, but then Jackie pulled back violently, Terry's brown tongue dangling between her teeth. She tossed her head back, letting it slide down her gullet like a pelican swallowing a fish, and then smiled.

"I told you to stop talking." As if this pronouncement had some other significance, the other dead people in the office all raised their hands above their heads in unison and chanted in low, hissing tones.

"Medhor chogro lor shub Kamog."

Jackie swung her head back to Amanda, hovering above her like a Jack lantern. Her eyes had become huge empty sockets that glowed bright white, and her teeth had grown long and sharp, but when she spoke, her voice was that of a little girl again. "I'm sorry to leave you with him but he should be quieter now."

Amanda had no idea she would ever be able to speak again, but she surprised herself by responding. "What do you mean? Where's my sister? *Where's Wendy?*"

Jackie's grin spread to an impossible width. Even in this form, childish glee capered on her face and it was abominable. She sang in her high, sweet voice. *"Wendy, Wendy, her arms and legs are bendy ..."*

Before she could stop it, Amanda's hand flew from her side and struck the monstrous face hanging in the air before her. It was like striking warm, wet clay. She recoiled with a gasp but couldn't contain her words any more than she could her open palm. "Where's my sister you fucking *whore*?"

Jackie's crooning abruptly ceased. She closed her mouth and regarded Amanda solemnly. It seemed like a long time passed. Minutes. Hours. It was hard to say. Silence crept in. The dead watched impassively. Terry hadn't moved in some time. He just sat in his corner with his head cradled in his arms. Amanda got the idea she was dreaming, maybe sick with a terrible fever, and relief began to flood through her but then she caught a strong whiff of the room and of Jackie's breath and knew it was no dream. Finally, Jackie spoke.

"My flock ...my *friends*, picked this place because they were waiting for me to be born. They knew I would be special. In fact, they helped bring me here. To this world." Her human voice had been left behind for good. Her words buzzed and rattled. "They spent years reading books, learning languages. They hurt people. They killed people. They watched for signs and when I was born they found me. My daddy didn't know what I was, but I think my momma did. She knew, but she didn't care. She loved me anyway. That's why I let her die free."

At that, Terry moaned , but Jackie didn't waste even a glance on him. She just looked deep into Amanda's eyes, droning like the voice of madness.

"They didn't expect Daddy to show up here with his gun. He thought they killed her. Killed her and kidnapped me. He followed them back here. They thought he spoiled their plans. The ritual. But I knew it was going to happen that way. It must. There always has to be a sacrifice. I told them we'd walk out of here in darkness and glory, but I never said they would be walking out alive. This place has to be *fed*. Guarded, tended and fed. Always. Someone always has to stay behind. I'm sorry, that's just the way it is." She stretched her tiny hand out, so far beneath her floating head, and reached into Amanda's jacket pocket. She grasped the defaced bible and pulled it free, clutching it against her chest. "People have come and gone before. Some of them sensed us, some of them saw us. We could always show little bits and pieces of ourselves, aspects. Whispers. Visions. No one ever stayed very long, though. Not even the ones who came looking for us. But you pressed on and you found this. Our absolution."

Amanda's thoughts were a muddy swirl of fear and confusion, but the memory of reading the words from the bible cut through the haze with cold clarity. Fresh tears began to spill down her cheeks. She'd never felt so lost before in her life. "Wendy." She just wanted to see her sister. That was the only thought that seemed to have any light to it. If only she could see Wendy, then maybe things could still be alright.

Jackie nodded, her ponytail bobbing joyfully to and fro. "Yes. Maybe it's time for you to see your sister, and your friend. Would you like that?"

The words sounded like poison in the demon's mouth, but Amanda nodded vehemently. She didn't care what came next. The idea of seeing Wendy at that moment had become everything. Jackie reared up off the floor. Her neck had retracted, bringing her head closer to her body, but the rest of her had begun to change shape. Her arms and legs had multiplied while she'd been speaking with Amanda; six, eight, it was hard to tell how many limbs she now had, and they'd grown longer and many jointed. Her back was bowed inward and elongated, tearing free of the Strawberry Shortcake shirt, and she seemed fuller, plumper. Amanda saw these things and understood somewhere deep inside that she should be screaming and pounding her head against the glass of the front door until she lost consciousness, but her love and concern for Wendy would not allow that to happen. Not yet.

The Jackie thing, now standing six feet above the filthy floor, skittered with arthropodal grace across the room. Her retinue of dead worshippers stepped to either side to allow her passage and she disappeared into the room behind what had once been the check-in desk. Amanda waited, trying not to think about the flies crawling in her hair, the chill of all those lifeless eyes upon her, or the way Jackie's abdomen had undulated between her spindly legs as she'd moved away. She tried to think about nothing other than seeing her sister.

She didn't wait long.

A few minutes after Jackie had disappeared into the back, two shadows came shuffling into the room. They shoved past the small, silent congregation that huddled beneath the fluorescent ghost-lights, and stopped in front of Amanda, swaying gently.

Amanda took one look at her sister Wendy—whom she'd built tents out of blankets with when they were little, who'd been the first person she called when she lost her virginity, who she'd confessed her stupid, useless crush on Clark to—and began to scream.

Wendy's face had been smashed in. Her jaw had been wrenched horribly to one side and crushed. Her lips were split wide, exposing shredded gums and a jumble of teeth. Her beautiful dark hair was matted to her face with dark, tacky blood. Her nose had been obliterated, reduced to a red, wet channel. Her eyes were bright though. Bright and aware and staring at Amanda with dull hate.

Beside her, Clark stood with his head twisted nearly around backwards, his skull crushed above the right temple. One eye socket had been fractured and his eyeball had sunk into it, caught in the oozing crack. Blood and brains leaked from the gash in his head and down onto the collar of his coat in pink and red lumps. His good eye was also trained on Amanda, sad and afraid.

Jackie reappeared behind and above them. She was huge now, almost filling the room. She had sprouted long, dragonfly-like wings that shimmered in the sick light. She'd shed her clothes and her body had become segmented. Eyes like white toadstools opened up all along her sides, lidless and glistening. The worst, though, was that her face was still, more or less, that of the little girl she had been.

Amanda, summoning the last bit of sanity she possessed, howled angrily at the creature towering over the bodies of her sister and friend.

"You killed them! Oh God, you killed *Wendy!*"

The thing that had never really been a little girl named Jackie Loughton at all opened its mouth and laughed in its nightmare drone. "*Me*? Don't be a silly-silly. I've never killed anyone. You did *that*."

Amanda rose up off the floor, her fear and grief buried under an avalanche of cold fury. She could stand no more lies. She would beat this monster into the floor with the heavy, blood-soaked flashlight she held in her left hand before finding a way to…

When had she picked up the flashlight?

She remembered leaving it in the car, with her pack. Didn't she?

How had it gotten bloody like that? Whose hair was matted to the front plate?

She looked back up and the room was empty. Jackie was gone. Her dead acolytes were gone. Terry Loughton was gone. All was dark. But she still had the flashlight in her hand. She thumbed the switch, and it came on, the light filtered through a red haze. She shone it around the room. Not everyone had gone. Wendy and Clark lay on the floor in pools of drying blood. They didn't move. After all of that, it was strange to see dead people acting dead. She aimed the beam of light around the room. One other thing seemed to have been left behind. Terry Loughton's pistol. She crawled over to where it lay and sat up against the wall, drawing her legs up to her chest. She set the flashlight down and picked the gun up. She wondered if it had any shots left. She pulled the hammer back and heard the chamber click into place. Her curiosity grew. She wondered how the barrel would feel in her mouth. After a moment, she put it between her lips to find out. It was cold.

She sat that way for a while before she realized someone else was in the room with her. She looked up and in the light cast by the flashlight saw the silhouette of a young girl just inside the door. A voice that reminded her of summertime and mosquito bites whispered to her.

"This place feeds on tragedy."

Amanda nodded. She'd finally figured that out. Sometime later, she realized she was alone again. The batteries in the flashlight died. She didn't know if her eyes were open or closed, but the gun was still in her mouth. With a sigh, she leaned her head against the wall and pulled the trigger.

****

They caught sight of the motel from the bridge that crossed the highway. It squatted on a kidney-shaped plot of pavement, surrounded on three sides by trees and dark hills. There was nothing and no one else around for miles.

"There it is." The older boy said to the younger one from astride his bike. "They found the bodies of her sister and her boyfriend in room 23. Their heads were busted open. She beat 'em both to death with her flashlight and there were brains *everywhere*."

The younger boy paled. He'd begun to regret coming along on this trip. "Brains?"

"Yeah. *Everywhere*. And more brains where she killed herself in the front office. That's where we should go first. Dibs on any cool stuff we find like bullet casings."

"Alright." The younger boy had no qualms giving up dibs on anything they might find in the Royal Motel. It had gained a nasty reputation in the couple of years since the murder/suicide and he couldn't for the life of him, remember how he'd let himself get talked into this excursion. His goal now was to get in and out as quickly as possible, but he knew that his friend had come along bearing tools for breaking locks. It would not be easy to dissuade him from exploring every room.

"Last one there eats dogshit!" The older boy stood on his pedals and began his descent to the deserted road below. No one had passed that way since they'd caught sight of the motel. After a moment, the younger boy shook his head, and followed, hoping they'd be done before dark.

THE VISITOR

From the November 3rd edition of the Tusc Valley Times-Reporter:

Small Town Celebrates Mythical Being—It's time once again for the greater Tuscarawas county area to cast a bemused eye down route 77 to Griffithstown. It's the weekend after Halloween and their annual "Autumn Harvest Sasquatch Festival" kicks off this Friday at dusk. Far from a typical, small-town festival, Griffithstown's celebration revolves around the area's notorious reputation as a hot-spot for sightings of the legendary creature known as Sasquatch.

For decades Griffithstown (along with the nearby town of Eastchurch and the adjacent Ami Pierce Township) has boasted frequent "sightings" of what eyewitnesses claim is Ohio's version of the infamous ape-man. In the last thirty-five years, nearly seventy of these accounts have been reported to the Tuscarwas County Sheriff's office. Also reported are strange howling sounds attributed to the creature and occasional sets of over-sized footprints, one set of which was photographed in 1979 and published in a book about U.F.O's and other strange phenomena.

Far from keeping their notoriety hush-hush, the citizens of Griffithstown celebrate their status as Ohio's cryptozoological epicenter. Each year since 1980, the town puts on their "Autumn Harvest Sasquatch Festival" the first weekend of November. The festival's activities include arts and crafts, games, rides, and a large parade, among other things, all in commemoration of their (alleged) hairy, outdoor neighbor. The festival atmosphere is one of high spirits and good cheer. Many of the festival-goers boast having caught glimpses of the elusive beast themselves-but no one fears for their safety. They regard the creature as a town treasure.

"I've seen him four or five times in the last fifteen years or so" says Merton Squibb, 51, of Ami Pierce Twp., "The last time he was out at the back of my south field standin' at the fence. He's got no reason to hurt nobody. We all want to keep him safe."

(Article cont'd on page C-4)

****

It was Thanksgiving and the children watched the snow with squealing delight. The family was spread across three round tables in the dining room at the back of the house. It was comfortably warm and lit by lamps that cast a cheerful glow. Conversation at the kids' table turned quickly to the impending Christmas vacation, Santa Claus and what presents they expected to find under their trees.

Cliff sat at his table, nibbling on a buttered roll and looking out the window at the whitewashed scenery with disquiet. He did not share the children's enthusiastic opinion of snow. Brooke, sitting next to him, was talking to her cousin Libby about something, laughing occasionally. In his own world, Cliff stared out into the gloomy afternoon and sighed inwardly.

He was considering getting up to grab another cup of punch when he realized that Libby's husband was looking at him expectantly. Cliff suddenly wondered if Mark had been trying to talk to him. Mark was a small, timid-looking man with thinning hair and a growing beer-gut. He seldom spoke to anyone, and Cliff had sort of forgotten he was with them at all. Now he flushed with embarrassment. It was clear from the look on Mark's face that he had said something to Cliff and was awaiting a response. "Sorry man, I was off in Oz. What'd you say?" Cliff asked.

"I said, it's gonna be a rough ride to our place if this snow keeps up."

Shit, Cliff thought. *He's right*. Cliff and Brooke had made the four-hour drive that very morning, heading straight to Aunt Mindy's but were staying at Mark and Libby's new house which they had only just moved into the weekend before. They had been remarking off and on all day about how far off the beaten path it was. "We've hardly seen more than a couple of cars go by all week long." Libby had said. She'd meant it to be a boast about the peace and quiet, but Cliff was a city-boy and wasn't as charmed by the stillness of the country as his wife's cousin.

"You guys should be careful when you're comin' out that way. There ain't no lights or anything." Mark nodded and took a sip of punch. "It's *real* dark."

"Oooh and spooky too!" Libby leaned forward and turned her attention to Cliff. "We live right up the road from the Warlock's grave. Has BeBe ever told you about the Warlock's Grave?"

"No," Cliff cast a sidelong glance at Brooke and smiled crookedly at the nickname she hated. "BeBe sure hasn't."

Brooke rolled her eyes at him. "It's just a story the kids around here scare themselves with." She turned to Libby. "Jeez, you guys moved all the way out there?" She shook her head. "That really is the boonies."

"I know it is but I love it." Libby nodded, her tall, teased bangs swaying back and forth. "Anyway. Cliff, there's a little graveyard off the side of the road, not even a mile up from our new house. It's very old; in fact, I think it's a registered historical site. In the very back of the cemetery, near where the fence meets the woods, there's a grave back by itself away from the other stones."

"And this would be 'The Warlock's grave'?" Cliff asked.

"Yes. The name on the stone is worn away, though everybody thinks it says David something, but the dates you can read."

There was a space of seconds where the room was quiet. Everyone was listening along with Cliff even though they all knew this story well.

Libby surveyed her audience with a grin and continued. "Born October 31st 1781, died October 31st, 1906." She paused for a heartbeat or two to let the information sink in and then went on. "Underneath that it says, 'May He never wake'."

Cliff felt an unexpected chill slip down his neck and along the backs of his arms. He mentally calculated the age that the dates on the supposed gravestone suggested. Then Brooke was standing behind him, her hands resting on his shoulders. She picked up the thread of the story, speaking in a low, breathy voice. "At some point, people started saying it was a Warlock that was buried there and that his ghost haunted the cemetery and the woods around there. People don't like driving past there at night and sometimes say they can see a tall, white figure standing at the wall waving to them as they passed by. Sometimes people even disappear out there."

"Wow." Cliff leaned back in his chair. "Let's stay at the Motel 6 instead." He chuckled and the spell was broken. Brooke and Libby burst into giggles and Libby's two little boys did the same. Aunt Mindy smiled broadly and asked who wanted some pumpkin pie and everyone raised their hands.

Mark sat quietly, looking out the window into the gathering dark. "Damn. It's startin to snow again." He said it out loud, but no one was listening to him.

****

Sometime after dinner, the gentle snowshower that had been falling so gracefully earlier became a swirling haze of white. The local newscasters on TV warned people to stay off of the roads and batten down for the night, especially in the rural areas.

Libby and Mark had a Jeep and decided to brave the storm to go visit Mark's family. Cliff and Brooke had stayed behind, not wanting to risk it in their little car, but around eight-twenty the clouds broke up some. The snow slowed, and it seemed that this might be the time for anyone visiting family to make a run for home. They bid everyone a goodnight and a happy Thanksgiving and said they were going on to Libby and Mark's.

Cliff and Brooke set off through the center of town and after a few twists and turns they finally found their way onto Gimlin Road, which led to Libby and Mark's new house. They drove for what felt like a long time and the landscape became desolate. As far as other houses, they had only passed two in the last ten minutes and these looked dark and not well kept, maybe even abandoned. The scenery was pretty, though, and Cliff watched it go by from the passenger seat. On one side of the road, the ground climbed up a gentle rocky slope. Short, stout pine trees grew in sparse little patches near the bottom, giving way to their taller cousins as they marched up and away. On the other side lay winter-barren fields, stamped flat by the cruel weather of late November. These fields sprawled from the edge of the road until they gave way to dense woods,. A sparkling blanket of snow covered the fields marred only by the sporadic tracks of animals that had passed by.

"Oh my God I'm so full. I'm not sure I can stay awake." Cliff took one last drag on his cigarette. He opened his window enough to shove the butt through, and a whistling blast of cold air snatched it from his fingers.

Brooke grinned, "Yeah, I feel more stuffed than the damn turkey." It was very cozy inside the car with the heater going full blast and Nat King Cole on the radio. Still, Brooke was driving cautiously. The road seemed to have been hastily plowed a couple of hours earlier, but it was still slick with moisture and a stiff wind was blowing skirls of snow everywhere. "I kind of wish I'd known they were going to Mark's Mom's house to eat again. We could've just stayed at Aunt Mindy's."

"Oh well. No big deal." Cliff sounded casual, but also wished they had stayed at Aunt Mindy's. They could be playing Euchre with Brooke's brother right now, or in their room, fooling around quietly. Instead, here they were feeling their way along this slippery back road trying to find a house they'd never been to.

"I'm sorry." Brooke sighed.

Cliff reached out a hand and put it on Brooke's leg. "It's not your fault. They're the ones that—holy shit, what is *that*?" He sat straight up in his seat, putting both hands on the dashboard.

"What's what?" Brooke's eyes didn't leave the road.

"Slow down, slow down. You don't see that?"

"Well I'm trying to watch the road so we don't die."

"Seriously, slow down and look over here." Cliff pointed out of his corner of the windshield and rolled his window down letting in a sheet of cold air that smacked him across the face, making him wince. "Jesus."

Brooke slowed them to a crawl and looked out the windshield between the swishing wipers where Cliff was pointing. A good distance down the road, silhouetted against the white of the snowfall, was a large someone or something standing at the side of the road.

"That is one really tall guy." Cliff had his head out the window. He squinted his eyes and cupped his hand over his brow to keep errant flakes out of his face. "What's he doing out there?" He shook his head. "Damn, that guy looks as tall as our living room ceiling."

They were barely moving now as Brooke pulled off the gas and eased on the brake. The softly frozen crust of snow crunched under the tires as they crawled along.

"Clifford, that's an optical illusion. Nobody's that tall." She continued to look from the road to the figure hulking beyond the reach of their headlights.

"Yeah, I'm sure you're right." On the radio Nat King Cole had given way to Elvis trilling through "Blue Christmas" and Cliff turned it off. Visibility had been greatly reduced as the storm began to rev up again and everything outside the car seemed to be swaying and shimmering. "It looks pretty goddamn big to me, though, and I think it's moving."

The car was now inching along at barely ten miles an hour as Brooke lightly tapped the gas every few seconds to keep them moving. They hadn't seen another car in either direction since they'd pulled onto this road and it was like there was no one else in the world besides them and the strange visitor up ahead. Despite their slow progress they were getting closer to the thing, and it appeared to be wearing a fur coat. It was still unlit by their headlights, but both of them had the impression of a shaggy, wind-blown outline.

"Are there bears out here?" Brooke asked suddenly.

"Well," Cliff paused and licked his lips, contemplating. "I mean, I don't really know. I didn't think so, but I guess it could be a bear. I don't know how long they can stand up on two legs like that."

"But it could be a bear, you think?"

"That would be one big-ass bear but yeah, maybe." There was a long pause. "Makes more sense than a man, right?" Cliff pulled his head back in the window and glanced at Brooke.

Brooke shrugged. "I mean some kind of animal. It's obviously not—*Whoa!*" Her nose wrinkled as a foul and powerful odor swept through Cliff's open window on a gust of air. It was a smell that reminded her of rotting garbage mixed with spoiled meat. It was a hot, wild smell out of place on a cold Autumn night. "Ew God, that's *awful*." Her voice sounded as if she'd suddenly come down with a bad cold.

Cliff's face seemed to collapse in on itself as he recoiled from the stench. "God, maybe the bear is guarding a kill or something. I don't know what else would smell like…"

His voice trailed off as their headlights finally washed over the thing and reflected back at them from its enormous silver eyes. It turned its shaggy head and shoulders to look right at Cliff.

It was definitely *not* a bear.

Suddenly it seemed as if time was speeding up and slowing down simultaneously. When it turned its face into the light they saw it very clearly despite the screen of falling snow. Beneath the outrageous shining eyes was a flat, leathery nose and a wide, jutting lower jaw. Cliff's eyes weren't sharp enough to pick it up, but Brooke could see long teeth or tusks thrusting out of its mouth. Moonlight glinted off of them. They looked sharp. It was covered in long, thick, dark hair, with slumped shoulders and huge arms ending in hands that hung down almost below its knees. Not paws. *Hands*. Hands that were tipped with very dangerous-looking, thorny claws. They looked like they were made for opening up the bellies of elk or moose to spill blood and steaming ropes of guts upon the cold ground below.

"Cliff, what *is* it?" Brooke's hands were clenched around the steering wheel, the skin pulled tight around her knuckles.

"Jesus, I don't know." It came out in a breathless whisper. "But I think we should turn around." Cliff began pushing himself back against his seat. That smell was even stronger, a thickening blanket of stink. "Brooke. Turn the car around."

Brooke nodded curtly, not needing to be told twice. She pressed the gas and yanked the wheel to the left, her eyes squeezed tightly shut as she attempted an immediate U-turn.

As the car turned, it hit a slick spot on the road and began a wild, shimmying fishtail. "Shit!" Brooke screamed. "Shit! Shit! Shit!" The car did a full 180, catching more wet, slippery snow and continued to spin, threatening to toss itself off of the road. The front end swung, the wheel steering Brooke instead of the other way around. As she fought for control they flew right past the spot where the shadowy figure lurked. For a moment the strobing headlights illuminated it clearly, but in their panic neither Cliff nor Brooke noticed.

Cliff slid over till he was pressed up against Brooke's side. He reached out and grabbed the wheel. "Hit the brakes and let go of the wheel!"

As Cliff grabbed the wheel, Brooke let her hands fly away and shoved her foot down onto the brake as hard as she could. The front end jerked and Cliff pulled the wheel hard to the right. The back end swung sharply to the left, tires screeching, half frozen sludge and snow flying up from beneath the back wheels and the car came to a rough, stuttering halt.

After taking a few ragged breaths, Cliff realized that they'd stopped and scooted back to his seat. He leaned his head against the head-rest and draped his hand across his eyes. "Holy shit, you ok? I mean…" He stopped abruptly and in a frenzy of flailing arms and legs, spun around in his seat to look out the back windshield.

The car had finished at a point past where the open field ended and small plots of trees and brush made their way up to the gravelly shoulder. The trees were tall and thin and reached their branches out and over the road and ticker-bushes crouched amongst the trunks. From where they sat the long white field was still visible, glowing with moonlight and Cliff saw that the gigantic, dark shape had shambled out into the road and was heading towards them. It pulled itself along in a disconcerting, loose-boned shuffle, its knees bent, its arms reaching out for them. Its eyes gleamed like stainless steel and Cliff watched, hypnotized, for several seconds as it dragged itself after them. Then its lower jaw dropped open like a trap-door full of upward thrusting spikes, and it screamed.

The sound filled the cold Autumn air and seemed to make it colder. Cliff grimaced, transfixed, sudden tears forming at the corners of his eyes and spilling down over his cheeks.

With a jerk of his head Cliff shook off his paralysis and turned to Brooke. She was also staring out the back window, mouth agape, a puzzled look in her eyes.

"Brooke." Cliff tugged gently at her arm. "Hey. Hey, come on babe, we've gotta go."

Brooke closed her mouth, turned back in her seat hurriedly and hit the gas. As the car leapt forward into the shadows beneath the overhanging trees, Cliff looked out the back window again. A small hiss of air escaped his lips. The thing on the road had reached the spot where the car had been just moments before, and was still following them. It was not far behind them and Cliff finally got a really good look at it. Its fur was matted, long in some spots and much shorter and coarse in others. Powerful-looking muscles flexed under the dark hair as it moved. Cliff knew that those arms could rip a man to shreds with very little effort. But it was the eyes that he kept coming back to. Huge ovals with no visible pupils or irises, just protuberant, reflective silver orbs, motionless and expressionless.

They were picking up speed now and Brooke gave it more gas. "Hey, turn around," she tapped Cliff's hip. "You've got to help me look for Libby's house." Her voice was shaky.

"Jesus, Brooke, it's following us." Cliff still knelt on his seat facing the back of the car. "*Chasing* us."

"Okay Cliff, that's why we need to get to Libby's."

Cliff finally tore his gaze from the back windshield and looked at his wife. "Are you crazy? We're not stopping." He turned back to look again, but they'd pulled too far ahead for him to see it clearly anymore. He finally turned around and sat in his seat. He pulled a cigarette out pushed the car's lighter into its slot. Tall trees lined both sides of the road now, forming a dark archway. Underneath this canopy the snow couldn't fall as thickly. There hadn't been a street-light or a house for miles. "Call them and tell them they should take the boys back to Aunt Mindy's. Tell them…" The lighter popped out, fully charged, and Cliff lit up. He took a long drag, opened his window a crack, and exhaled, getting ready to finish his thought.

"Tell them what?" Brooke realized she was rocketing along at what was becoming an unsafe speed and eased on the brake a little. A leaning yellow sign came up on the right warning of a bend ahead. "Should I tell them we just saw a monster and that it's chasing us?" As if it had heard, the creature let out another blood-freezing scream from somewhere in the darkness behind them. Both Cliff and Brooke winced as if they'd been struck.

They rounded the bend in the road and the headlights picked out what seemed to be a derelict building on the left-hand side of the road. A rusted out car, broken chairs, a lot of crumbled cement littering the lot,. It was the closest thing to a house they'd seen.

"Yeah, I think maybe you should. It might follow us straight to them."

"Mmm-hmm. Okay." Brooke sounded a little hysterical. She took one hand off the wheel and mimed holding a phone to her ear. "Hey Libby, it's Brooke. Yeah, um, just wanted to let you know that me and Cliff just saw Bigfoot and he's on his way to your house to eat us all for dinner. Yeah. Oh, you *invited* him? Oh well that's fine then. Bye." She put her hand back on the wheel. "Like that?"

"No, not like that; smart-ass." Cliff giggled shrilly. "They wouldn't have invited him, they've already had two dinners."

Brooke smiled despite her fear. In a moment they were both cracking up and a moment after that they were laughing uncontrollably. She slowed the car to a stop in the middle of the road to let the wave of terror-fueled hilarity pass.

As soon as the car stopped and they were motionless in the dark, the mood sobered quickly. Their laughter trickled to a series of hiccups and sighs until there was nothing left. Brooke's eyes searched the rearview mirror for signs of anything coming up the road behind them. Cliff finished his cigarette and dropped it out the window.

"So, you're right." Cliff rubbed his hand across his mouth as he considered their situation. "We can't tell them like that." He shook his head and looked at Brooke with one eyebrow raised. "Have I ever told you that I fucking *hate* the country?"

"You and me both. I can't imagine why they would move all the way out here."

"Probably because monsters and warlocks really bring down the cost of property."

"Get my phone out of my purse." Brooke checked the mirror again.

Cliff reached down between his feet and into her purse. He fished around for a moment and then pulled out her cellphone. "What do you think I should tell them?" He flipped it open. With his thumb he began pushing buttons, searching her contacts list.

"Well," Brooke said, coming up with an idea on the spot, "Let's say that there was some crazy guy with a gun who ran out on the road and started shooting at us. We'll say he started chasing us down the road and that he might be headed their way. How's that?"

"Yeah, that's perfect." Cliff studied the screen of Brooke's phone with squinted eyes, his face glowing blue in the light it cast. "Jeez, where is she in here?"

"She's under LB. Here, hand it to me." As Brooke started to reach for the phone another yowling scream rang out across the night. It didn't sound very far off. Brooke gasped, her face twisting into a mask of terror. "Cliff?"

"Shit," Cliff shot a look out the back window and then turned back to the front. "You just drive, I'll call them."

Brooke turned, started up the car, and a moment later they were on their way. As they sped off down the blacktop another shriek pierced the dark.

Cliff found Libby's number in Brooke's contact list and pressed "send." He held the phone up to his ear and frowned. "Hey Libby, its Cliff. Me and Brooke were on our way to your house when we ran into…well, into some trouble. We think you guys should take the kids and head back to Aunt Mindy's. We'll explain when we meet up there. It's pretty urgent so give us a call back when you get this." He pressed "end" and rested the phone against his thigh. "Voicemail."

"Maybe they're still at Mark's Mom's house."

As they sped past, the trees on the right-hand side of the road dropped back, letting the moonlight fall through once again, brightening the snow-frosted scenery. Lying, gray and ominous in this illuminated gap, was a cemetery. It looked very old. They caught a momentary glimpse of

flat, weathered stones jutting from the ground, penned in by an ancient stone wall.

"Libby said their house was the next thing after the graveyard. Brooke started slowing the car. "On the right. Help me look for it."

Cliff was trying the phone again. When he got Libby's voicemail once more, he snapped the phone shut. "They better be home and just ignoring our calls." He opened Brooke's phone one more time and hit "send."

After they passed the cemetery, the trees came back up to the road in thick and Brooke almost drove past Libby and Mark's house. It was set a good fifty yards back off the road and was walled in by the woods around it. An uneven, gravel driveway led up and around to the back of the house.

From what they could see, the house was as dark inside as the yard was outside. It was a one-story brick box with a sagging roof. There were two large windows at the front of the house on either side of the tin storm door. Both had screens that were riddled with rips and holes. The whole place looked defeated.

Brooke pulled the car up to where the front walk curved around to meet the driveway and stopped. There was no way to see through the windows because the curtains were drawn but there didn't appear to be any lights on behind them. Brooke and Cliff sat silently for a few moments, considering what to do next.

Cliff sighed. "Alright. Now what?"

Brooke bit her lower lip. "Well, should we go up and knock? See if they're in there?"

"I'd really rather not get out of the car if possible." Cliff's tone was matter-of-fact but his eyes looked haunted.

Brooke looked back up at the house. "Hold on, let's call Aunt Mindy. Maybe she knows where they are."

Cliff nodded. "That's a great idea." He held the phone out to his wife.

She took the phone from him, scrolling through her recent calls till she found Aunt Mindy's number. She sent the call and held the phone up to her ear, pulling her long hair back behind her neck with her other hand. A moment later she looked to Cliff and gave a thumbs-up

"Hey, Aunt Mindy. No. No, not yet, hey listen, do you know if Libby and Mark are still at his mom's house?" She listened, her smile fading. "Uh-huh. Well because we're at their house and they're not here." Suddenly her eyes widened with realization. "Wait, their Jeep's not here. They must be out. Libby just wasn't…what? They do?" Cliff watched her expression fall again. "They did?" She heaved a heavy sigh. "Okay, well we'll check. Yeah, you try to call her too, okay? Alright. Bye." She set the phone on the dashboard and looked up at the house.

Cliff waited for her to say something. After ten seconds had gone by he spoke. "So, what did Aunt Mindy say? I hadn't even thought of their car not being here. Does she know where they' are?"

"They park up around the back of the house. They go in through the kitchen door back there."

"Right. Okay."

"Libby called a few minutes after we left to let Mindy know they were home and to see if we were still there. They'd just put the kids to bed. They were worried we might not be able to find the place."

"Huh." Cliff pondered this and picked Brooke's phone up off the dashboard to look at the clock. Eight forty-

two. "So, did they *all* decide to go to bed or something? Why aren't the lights on?"

"Cliff I'm scared." Brooke was still staring out the window, her fingers tapping on the steering wheel. "I think we need to go around back and see if their car's there."

"Okay. What if it's not?"

"We leave them a note on the back door telling them to come straight to Aunt Mindy's."

"Why don't you just text her?"

"I'll do that too but she's not answering her phone. Maybe it's dead or she has the ringer off. We need to leave a note just in case."

"Alright. And what if the truck is there?"

Brooke looked at him. "I don't know. Knock I guess."

"Alright here," He picked Brooke's purse up from the floor and handed it to her. "Find a pen and something to write on."

Brooke turned the interior light on and dug through her purse. She pulled out an old receipt and set it on the dashboard. "What are we doing?"

"Write your note. Just, 'come back to Aunt Mindy's immediately!' and sign it. I'm going to take it and go around back. If the car isn't there, I'm gonna put the note somewhere near the door where they'll see it." He looked out the passenger window into the dark outside. "And if their truck does happen to be there then I'll go up and pound on the door a couple of times. If no lights come on and nobody answers, then we're booking it the hell out of here back to Aunt Mindy's and we can all talk about where to go from there."

"Can't we just drive around to see? I don't want you getting out of the car and walking around out there any more than you do. And it's windy out. What if the note blows away?"

"Well, Brooke...I mean, it's the best we can do. You know?" He blew a long breath between his lips. "And I'm afraid of getting stuck back there. This isn't a Jeep, and this driveway is terrible. God knows what it's like back there and I don't wanna stick around out here. That thing could be anywhere..."

Brooke looked out into the night. "Okay. Do it fast then." She leaned forward, holding the receipt against the center of the steering wheel, and wrote the note. "Here," she handed it to Cliff, "I love you."

Cliff took the note from her, leaned forward, and planted a quick kiss on her mouth. "Love you too. I'll be right back."

Cliff opened the passenger door and stepped out onto the drive. The sound of gravel beneath his feet seemed very loud to his ears. It was grave-quiet and very cold. The only sound was the wind sighing through the trees making the branches clatter together. He walked up to the house and passed around to the side and hurried on around back.

He turned the corner and frowned. Libby and Mark's old Jeep was sitting as silent and dark as everything else. He could also see the back door of the house laying discarded in the snow next to the truck. It had been violently torn off its hinges. Splintered wood from the door hung in the space where the door had been. Pieces of lath lay on and around the short steps that led up to the kitchen. He took a timid step towards the yawning doorway and then another till he finally reached the steps to the back door.

The damage was immense. He could see the way the metal hinges had twisted and buckled where the door had been yanked free. "Oh, Jesus." He leaned against the outer wall for a moment. He breathed deeply a few times and crept into the silent kitchen.

A strip of moonlight fell through the doorway behind him, but it was very dark inside. Snow blew in and clung gently to Cliff's back and shoulders. It had piled up on the floor. He moved along very slowly and very deliberately. With great reluctance Cliff stepped out of the triangle of light the moon provided and went into the shadows. His eyes began to adjust to the gloom, and he was able to discern the shapes of furniture out in the living room beyond.

"H-Hey," he whispered hoarsely. "Is anybody here?"

He moved another few inches into the deepening shadows. "Libby? Mark?" He began to take another step when a sound, loud and strident shattered the stillness. Cliff cried out in surprise and threw his hands up in front of his face. The sound continued for another couple of seconds and then stopped. He realized it was an electronic sound. In fact, it was a sound he recognized. He'd heard it several times earlier in the day. It was Libby's text alert sound. It had come from somewhere very close to him. His heart was beating hard as he moved through the kitchen trying to pinpoint where it had come from.

He came around to the side near the sink and was feeling his way along the counter when he stumbled over something lying on the floor in front of him. He grabbed on to the edge of the counter, loudly knocking over a box of cereal, and managed to keep his feet. He turned, leaned down and peered at what it was he'd tripped over.

It was Libby's ankle. She was lying face-down on the floor. Cliff's mouth dropped open as he took in the shape of her. In the semi-darkness it was tough to make out details, but he thought that her right arm was missing. As his eyes continued to adjust to the low light he could tell that whatever she was wearing had been mercilessly shredded and torn. He felt his thanksgiving dinner begin to rise. He turned away from her and vomited loudly. The sound of it splashing against the floor caused him to do it again.

When he'd finished retching, Cliff stood up and looked around wildly, trying not to hyperventilate. That's when he heard a sound from somewhere beyond the unlit hallway that separated the kitchen from the living room. He wasn't sure what it and he strained to listen for anything that disturbed that silence. At first, there was nothing but as his ears adjusted to the quiet he thought he could just make out the sound of breathing, very slow and deliberate. Like someone out there in the dark was trying to be just as quiet as he was.

Cliff took a step back, being careful not to step on Libby. His eyes never left the room ahead of him. Without bothering to whisper he called out. "Mark?"

There was a shuffling sound and then the painful squeal of a floorboard as something very heavy moved. Without another moment's hesitation, he turned and bolted for the door.

***

When Cliff came running around the house and down the drive Brook turned the key in the ignition and started the car. He threw a look back over his shoulder towards the house and then slid along the side of the car to his door. He yanked it open, fell into his seat, and slammed it shut again.

"Go."

"Cliff, what happened? Was the truck…?" "Go!" He shouted. "Just go."

Brooke threw the car into reverse and backed down the driveway, watching through the rearview mirror. She reached the end of the driveway and backed out onto the road, turning back the way they'd come.

"Cliff, I texted Libby. I haven't gotten an answer back yet though."

"I know." Cliff shut his eyes and rubbed them with the backs of his hands. "Come on, we gotta go."

"What does *that* mean? How do you know?" Brooke turned her head and looked at Cliff. "What happened back there? Is she okay?"

Cliff looked out the back windshield. "Never mind. We've gotta get out of here. Now."

"Not 'never mind'. You tell me what you saw." Tears formed at the corners of her eyes. *"What happened to Libby?"*

"Drive faster," Cliff said as they pulled away from Mark and Libby's house. He grabbed Brooke's cell phone from the dashboard and opened it up. "We'll talk about it in a minute."

Brooke stepped on the gas, and they shot forward. With tears streaming down her cheeks she began to sob. "Fuck you, Cliff. We'll talk about it *now*." Her eyes flicked from the road to Cliff. "Who're you calling?"

"911."

Brooke grimaced and squeezed her eyes shut, her foot still pressing on the gas. "Oh *God*." She snuffled back snot and tears and looked at Cliff again. "You tell me what happened!"

Cliff looked up from the phone in his hand to respond but anything he might have said was cut short. "Brooke! Look out!" was all he had time to say.

What happened next only took only a few seconds.

Brooke looked out the windshield. They were approaching the decrepit old graveyard, bouncing along and still accelerating when a giant black shadow came running out from between the crooked stones. It stepped easily over the four-foot stone wall and darted out into the road in front of the car. It turned its massive bulk to face them, its silver eyes implacable and flat and it let out one more ear-splitting scream that went on and on.

Then, the collision.

The airbags deployed and everything became shattering glass, screeching tires, and crunching metal. The force of impact was like hitting an oak tree. There was a blur of dark hair and huge arms flailing against the hood. Claws shrieked against steel as the unending scream reached an unbearable crescendo.

The force of impact shoved Cliff and Brooke forward hard against their seatbelts, their heads slamming into the rough nylon of the airbags before they bounced back into their seats. Neither of them heard it happen but both front tires had been blown out.

Then it was over.

Neither Brooke nor Cliff moved for a while. The car was making a hissing sound but neither of them noticed. Brooke had been knocked unconscious, her head lolling on her neck against her window. Cliff, meanwhile, began to stir. He sat up with a wince and a hiss as a spasm of pain shot all the way to his shoulder.

"Oh Goddammit." Using his left arm, he reached out and grabbed onto Brooke's headrest and pulled himself upright. He squirmed, turning himself in his seat so that he could reach the doorhandle with his left hand. His hurt arm got squeezed between his body and his seat and he gritted his teeth. He reached out and pulled the handle, pushing the door open with his foot. He leaned forward, putting his feet on the ground and gingerly stood up. He shuffled around to the front of the car, his earlier fear muted by shock.

The damage to the front end of the car was amazing. The hood and grille were deeply crimped inward where they'd hit the thing, as if they'd run into a telephone pole instead of a living being. The bumper was hanging, twisted out of shape, and a plume of steam rose into the air from the crushed radiator. Long, ugly grooves reached from the windshield to the headlights. Cliff saw that the tires had exploded, tread hanging off the rims in rubbery strips. The windshield had a spider web of cracks radiating out from the lower right corner where the hood had pushed back into it. Incredibly, the headlights were still shining but something was obscuring the one on the driver's side. Cliff limped around and knelt down. A patch of coarse, dark hair was matted against the light by a wet, red smear of blood. He reached out to touch it and then thought better of it, pulling his hand back. There was more hair and more blood spread across the destroyed front end and all over the ground. This reminded Cliff of what it was they'd hit. He stood up hastily and spun around. He looked out into the road where something huge should have lay dying or dead, but the road was empty.

He was confused. The car had pounded into that thing at nearly forty miles an hour. He took a few uncertain steps forward, searching the road for more blood and hair. He walked as far ahead as the headlights illuminated and saw no further trace. It was like they'd hit an invisible force-field. He stood out in the road a moment longer, looking right and then left off into the dark trees. He scanned the old cemetery from which the thing had come running. It was filled with black shadows and revealed nothing but gravestones.

Cliff dragged himself back to the car and gently settled into his seat. He searched the dashboard for Brooke's phone, but it wasn't there. He leaned carefully over, trying not to move his right arm too much, and reached down between his legs. After a few moments of scrabbling around on the floor, his fingers closed over the phone. Next to him, Brooke was starting to regain consciousness. She was moving her head back and forth and murmuring.

Cliff reached out and tenderly stroked her face with the back of his hand.

He held the phone down in front of him and dialed, holding it up to his ear, and waited for the response.

"911, what is your emergency?"

"Hi. My name is Cliff Morgan and I need to report an accident"

****

(from the November 29th edition of the Cincinati Enquirer) **Local Couple Disappears in Bizarre Missing-Persons Case**—A Cincinnati couple was reported missing last weekend in the city of Connington, Ohio, two hours southwest of Cleveland. Cliff and Brooke Morgan, of Mt. Healthy, had been visiting family over Thanksgiving when their black Volkswagen Jetta was discovered wrecked and empty of passengers on a heavily wooded, back country road Thanksgiving night.

At approximately 9:07 pm, 911 received, what the dispatcher called, "a very strange call for help," from Mr. Morgan. He reported that he and his wife had hit a large, unidentified animal with their car and that they needed assistance. He also reported that there was some problem involving family members that they had been visiting and that emergency medical assistance was needed.

When law enforcement and Emergency Services arrived on the scene, they found the battered car but no sign of Mr. or Mrs. Morgan. Upon investigating the home of Mark and Elizabeth Welker, the family members they'd been visitng, it was discovered that they too were missing along with their two sons, Dylan, age 6, and Garrett, age 4. There were signs of forced entry into the Welker residence as well as signs of a struggle within including blood and torn clothing.

A large-scale search has been mounted by the Tuscarawas County PD and has been widened to include the area surrounding the nearby towns of Eastchurch, Dover, and Griffithstown. This is not the first time that disappearances have been reported along this particular stretch of road.

(Continued on Page A-11)

MRS. LUMLEY'S MASKS

The dining room table must have been beautiful when it was new. It was made from good, solid oak and had to weigh upwards of two-hundred pounds. The legs were stout and immovable, and the beveled top was inlaid with a rich cherry panel.

Chrissy thought you could probably drop a bowling ball on this table, and it wouldn't tremble. Even a little bit. Only the scratches and gouges that crisscrossed its surface betrayed its age and use. She wondered how many generations of dinnerware must have been dragged across it to have left such deep, ugly grooves.

"Would you like some more coffee, honey?" Mrs. Lumley smiled across the scarred table at her.

Chrissy smiled back and shook her head, her ponytail bobbing from side to side. "Oh, no thanks." She patted her empty mug. "I'm all set."

"Alrighty." The old woman slowly stood from her chair with a groan. "Then I guess we should go ahead and get started. What do you say?"

"Sounds good to me." Chrissy bounced to her feet as the old woman shuffled out of the dining room and into the shadowy front hallway. Their footfalls echoed off the granite-tiled floor.

"So, Mrs. Lumley, when does your sister actually move in?"

Mrs. Lumley tottered past the front door to the other end of the hall where a staircase huddled against the far wall. She stopped at the newel post, which was nearly three inches taller than she was, and turned to look back at Chrissy.

"She'll be coming up this evening." With a grunt she heaved herself onto the first step. "Later today I'm having the medical supply people come in and install one of those motorized chairs that go up and down the steps." She continued up the stairs, waiting till both feet were on a riser before ascending the next. The old wood creaked and sighed with every step. "I'd love to have one for myself, even though I'm sure having to do all this walking has kept the rigor mortis away." She cackled and went on.

"Come on now," Chrissy mock scolded, "None of that rigor mortis talk. You're still a young lady." She was climbing right behind Mrs. Lumley, forced to adopt the old woman's gait. *Step-step wait, step-step wait.* She'd begun to feel a burble in her stomach which was unsurprising considering the strong coffee she'd just had. She knew she would probably need to use the restroom soon and willed the old woman to move faster.

They finally stepped into the upstairs hallway, darker even than the one below. Only the gray Autumn daylight, spilling through windows at either end of the hall, gave any illumination. It fell through the spindles of the second-floor railing, spotlighting the dust-covered strands of old spider-webs.

There were four rooms upstairs, all with old-fashioned, paneled doors, each one closed except for a bathroom at the far-right end. The walls were painted a dark brown with ornate crown molding along the ceiling. The molding had probably been a gleaming white once but now, like everything else in the house, was dark with grime.

The two women padded along the carpet and Chrissy looked around, her heart breaking a little at the sad state of neglect that had befallen the lovely home. She told herself that after helping Mrs. Lumley get these upstairs rooms cleaned, she would work on the rest of the place as well. She wanted the elderly sisters to finish out their time together in clean, pleasant surroundings.

Mrs. Lumley stopped at the last door to the left of the stairway. "This is going to be Ginny's room." She turned the cut-glass knob and shoved her weight against the door. It popped open with a wooden shriek. She stepped inside and Chrissy followed.

The room was large, the wallpaper covered with vertical lines of dark blue leaves running from floor to ceiling. A window at the back of the room looked out, presumably onto the backyard. It was hard to say for sure what it looked out on because a wall of junk stood between it and anyone who might want to look out of it. This junk blockade wound its way into the center of the room where it crumbled into a loose pile of debris. Cardboard boxes overflowed with papers and photographs. A small hutch piled high with costume jewelry, makeup kits, and compacts crouched below a gilt-edged mirror. Several different kinds of lamps had been shoved into corners and towers of stacked books leaned against the walls. Two different bureaus held many years' worth of magazines and there was an old writing-desk that looked like it may have been used by depression-era schoolchildren.

Chrissy let her gaze sweep from one side of the room to the other, trying not to be overwhelmed, but her face gave away her apprehension. Mrs. Lumley saw his and her eyes fell with shame.

"Yessir, this is quite a mess. I don't know why I let it get so bad in here." She picked her way over odds and ends to a straight-backed wooden chair that was partially hidden under some discarded drapes. She pushed the curtains aside and sat down. "After Gordon died, I just started putting things in here that I couldn't find a place for anymore. I don't think I ever expected to need this room again."

"It's not that bad." Chrissy lied. Her thoughts were much more honest. *This is going to suck so bad. Some of this stuff looks really heavy and my head's starting to hurt.* She wanted to ask for an Advil or aspirin but didn't want Mrs. Lumley to have to go all the way back downstairs to get one. She decided to just try and fight through it and get the job done. "Where are we going with all of it?"

"Well," Mrs. Lumley looked around at her belongings sadly. "A lot of it will go in the trash."

"Oh, are you sure?" Chrissy felt a flutter of distress. She didn't feel good about helping an old lady throw her memories away.

"Yes. Quite sure." Mrs. Lumley managed to paste a smile on her quivering lips. "I don't need most of this old junk. Anything I keep will go in the next room over. With the masks."

Chrissy wasn't sure she'd heard that last part right. "The masks?"

Mrs. Lumley looked up, her false smile suddenly becoming genuine. "I forgot to tell you about my collection, didn't I?" She hopped up from her chair and scrambled through the maze of junk to the door. Her sudden flurry of movement caught Chrissy off-guard since, coming up the stairs, Mrs. Lumley had seemed very frail and slow. Now she scuttled around the room like an agile crab. "Come on, I haven't had anyone to show this to in a while." She stepped out into the hallway and Chrissy followed.

"Actually, you can get started clearing some space in this room while I decide what few things I want to keep." Mrs. Lumley made her way to the next door down. "That will keep you from having to stand around watching an old lady cry."

Chrissy reached out and put her hand on Mrs. Lumley's shoulder, giving it a very light squeeze. "Mrs. Lumley, I'm so sorry. Maybe there's somewhere we can just move your stuff to so you don't have to get rid of it. Maybe we can store it in the basement?"

The old woman reached back and tapped Chrissy's hand with her own. She leaned against the closed door and turned to face Chrissy. "No, dear, I'm afraid the basement is already full. Besides, it's time I let go of some things. Ginny deserves to come into a comforting environment. She's been through so much." She leaned on the doorknob, turning it. "All that clutter would just keep me from taking good care of her. I've looked out for her since we were young. We lost our parents at an early age, you know."

A lump formed in Chrissy's throat. "You're such a good person, Mrs. Lumley. Such a good *sister*."

Mrs. Lumley's smile turned wistful. "Well, like I said. She's been through a lot." She pushed open the door and, with Chrissy close behind, stepped into the room.

Chrissy felt her jaw wanting to drop open and clamped it shut, working harder to control her expression this time. Her headache intensified and she felt a tremor of dizziness as she took in the strange scene before her.

The room itself was as large as the one next to it, maybe even slightly larger, with the same window looking out from the back wall. There was no furniture in this room, no chairs or tables or wardrobes or dressers. There were only masks—hundreds of them, maybe a thousand. Mrs. Lumley hadn't bothered with display racks or cases for her collection, it simply sprawled where it liked. The walls were hidden behind drifts and dunes of masks piled up against them. They spilled out into the center of the room. Empty eye-sockets beyond counting staring up at Chrissy from every corner with indifference.

"What do you think honey? Aren't they nice?" Mrs. Lumley slipped her arm around Chrissy.

Chrissy just nodded politely, pretending to like what she saw. There were masks of all kinds. She saw beautiful masquerade-style masks, bedazzled with sequins and feathers, mounted on sticks.

She saw the huge furry face of some nameless creature hanging from the wall, its mouth agape, its round, black eyeholes wide as if with shock. There were eye-masks, like the Lone Ranger's, scattered around the edge of the collection, their elastic strings tangled and bunched. In a pile near the door were some cheap plastic masks; pigs, cows, cats, babies, clowns, painted in grotesque pastels with rosy cheeks and red, red mouths. Rubber monster-masks glared and bared their molded fangs from spots around the heap. All these masks and many more besides filled the room as if a dump-truck had come in, dropped them, and left.

Mrs. Lumley walked into the center of the room, smiling at the masks that gazed up at her from the floor. "I've been collecting these since I was a little girl. Halloween was always my favorite holiday. Ginny's too. I liked pretending to be someone else." She looked over at Chrissy. "You do things differently when you pretend you're someone else. You feel free to be whoever you are on the *inside* when you're wearing a mask on the *outside*."

The old woman leaned forward and picked up a paper-mâché' mask from the pile. It was gray with tiny, plastic leaves glued to the cheeks and brow. A long, beaklike nose protruded from between two gaping eyeholes and black feathers sprouted from across the forehead. "This one belonged to my friend Evelyn." She turned it this way and that, gazing at it fondly. "She would wear this with these long, pink rubber gloves that went all the way up to her elbow. She always looked marvelous." She set it back down and picked up another one, a grotesque, white furry bunny mask with a pink nose and huge buck teeth. It was meant to be pulled down completely over the wearer's head. "Gordon—Mr. Lumley— used to wear this one," Mrs. Lumley's eyes narrowed mischievous-ly, "for all kinds of different occasions." She held it up to her face and rubbed its rubber nose against her own, giggling. "I always liked how the fur tickled." She tossed it back with the others and continued picking up masks at random, giving bits of their history to Chrissy.

Chrissy felt the mute scrutiny of all the eyeless faces surrounding her and felt cold. She didn't really want to be left alone in this room to clear out space. It was creepy. She was also not feeling very well. Her roommate had the flu and Chrissy was afraid she'd caught it, despite all of her efforts to wash her hands and keep her distance. She wished there was at least a chair in the room where she could sit and rest. She began wondering how silly it would look if she were to just plop down, cross-legged, on the floor.

No matter how much worse she felt, though, Chrissy was going to have to stick this out and finish assisting Mrs. Lumley.

Above and beyond her wish to be helpful, Chrissy wanted the extra credit that this volunteer assignment would earn for her psych class. It would bump her grade up from a high *C* to a low *B*. If she maintained high grades this semester her parents would pay for her to go to London in the spring.

Awash in her own thoughts, Chrissy lost the thread of Mrs. Lumley's conversation. Realizing that the old woman had paused, Chrissy nodded her head vigorously, hoping that it was appropriate to what was being said.

"You see," Mrs. Lumley returned Chrissy's nod. "You know *exactly* what I'm talking about."

"Oh yeah. Of course." Chrissy had no idea what she was agreeing with, but it hardly seemed to matter. Her nausea was getting worse.

"That's why you have to value your friends." Mrs. Lumley went on. "Mr. Lumley and I had such a wonderful group of friends. We would throw these little dinner parties, and everyone would come over and play games. Oh, how we loved games. Even though Ginny was ten years younger we would let her play with us. It made her feel very grown-up. We'd play Charades, Password, Grease and Lasso, and Darn the Dunce. And of course, everyone would put on masks. A lot of these," she swept her arm around the room, "belonged to our friends. I kept them as the years went on. You're never too old to have a good time."

"That's a good attitude." Chrissy blinked her eyes rapidly. They'd gone blurry for a moment. Mrs. Lumley seemed to suddenly notice the young woman's discomfort.

"Sweetheart, you're looking kind of green around the gills." Her face scrunched with concern. "Are you feeling alright?"

Chrissy waved her hand dismissively. "Eh, I'm fine. I've just got a little cold or something. Don't worry about me."

"Nonsense." Mrs. Lumley patted the girl on her arm and shuffled past her. "I'm going to go down to the kitchen and get you a Tylenol and a glass of water. You wait here."

Chrissy shook her head. "No, Mrs. Lumley, you don't have to do that. I can go get it myself if you tell me where—"

Mrs. Lumley held up a stern finger. "Shush now. You wait here. You're the sick one. You're the one here to help us. The least I can do is get you a pill and a drink of water." And with that, she was out the door and headed down the stairs.

The moment the old woman was out of sight Chrissy crumpled to the floor, stretching her legs out in front of her. She leaned back on her hands and looked around at the masks. They seemed to be crowding past each other, eager to look at the girl who had stupidly allowed herself to be left alone with them. She was suddenly afraid of being buried beneath an avalanche of painted latex, plastic, plaster, and fur. Grinning mouths and empty eyes leered at her with predatory contempt.

"Fuck you." Chrissy did not hear the slur in her voice. "I'm not afraid of you guys."

They mocked her with their silence. *We think you are.* She could almost hear them whisper.

Chrissy rolled over onto her knees crawled to the corner of the room and grabbed up a cheap plastic Frankenstein mask. "Look, I'll put one on. How scared am I now?" She sat up and crossed her legs like a preschooler getting ready for story-time. She slipped the mask over her head, pulling the elastic band around and under her ponytail. The molded interior pressed uncomfortably against her cheeks, lips, and eyes. Her breath was loud inside the mask and blew back at her. It smelled musty. The eyeholes didn't line up with her eyes very well and she had to adjust it to see properly.

Now Chrissy was Frankenstein's monster. She looked around the room at the other masks. *No reason to be afraid now. What did Frankenstein's monster have to fear?* She grinned widely, the plastic scraping against her face. She giggled, the sound of it rattling behind the mask. She was too dizzy to stand up, too tired. Instead, she leaned her head over to examine the corner from where she'd pulled the Frankenstein mask. It seemed to have already been cleared out somewhat. Pressed back against the wall, hidden in the shadows of the mask mountain, Chrissy saw a wooden box with a hinged lid. It was the size of a backgammon case. She crawled in a little closer and reached back with one hand, leaning on the other. She slid the box over to herself, sat up, and hoisted the box onto her lap. From somewhere below, out in the house, she thought she heard Mrs. Lumley talking to someone but she didn't care. She was overcome with curiosity about what might be inside the wooden case. There was no lock, so Chrissy gently lifted the lid.

The first thing Chrissy found was what looked like a folded paper cone. She pulled it out and held it up, opening up the round bottom. It had the word "DUNCE" stenciled on it. She looked at it for a minute and then tossed it to the floor. It was becoming hard to think. She was getting sleepy. Her mouth stretched behind the mask as she yawned.

Beneath the paper cone (*dunce cap—it's called a dunce cap.*) was a thin, leather wallet. Chrissy opened it and found that it held several long, pins topped with shiny, round heads. They looked very sharp. She set the wallet next to the dunce cap.

Under the wallet Chrissy found a collection of old, Polaroid photos. Her eyes got very big as she flipped through them. Some of the pictures were of people in masks. Many of them showed a young girl, younger even than Chrissy. In all of them, the girl was tied to a familiar straight-backed chair set on top of a scarred but beautiful oak table. The girl was wearing the dunce cap. In some of them, that's all she was wearing. Chrissy's heart began to beat very fast. The people in masks were doing things to the girl. She shoved the photos back in the box and closed it. She looked up and around the room. The masks no longer seemed to be watching her. It was as if they were looking away, giving her privacy.

Chrissy opened the case back up and started looking at pictures again. The first few photos were close-ups of the young girl's face showing how her lips had been pinned shut. Lines of blood, black in the harsh glare of the flash, spilled down over her chin. Her eyes were haunted, but not surprised. *It's just fake.* Chrissy thought wildly. *These people like costumes. It's fake blood. The pins are a make-up trick.* She looked down at the wallet full of pins on the floor next to her.

She flipped over some of the pictures to look at the backs.

there were dates on them: *5/5/65, 7/4/65, 7/19/65, 8/11/65, 10/31/65*—that last one was very bad. Chrissy almost didn't understand what the man in the smiling fox-mask was doing to the girl. Then she held it to the side and realized what he had in his hand and what he was using it for—Chrissy gasped, and her eyes welled with tears at the dead expression on the girl's face. It was an expression that said, *I've been through this before and I will go through this again.* They had taken the pins out of her mouth in that picture. In the next picture, dated that same Halloween night, Chrissy saw why and gagged behind her Frankenstein mask.

The photos went on and on. The dates on the back kept spinning out. People in masks capered in the background. When the lower halves of their faces were visible Chrissy could see that they were laughing—laughing at the girl tied to the chair, propped up on the dining room table from downstairs.

Chrissy shoved the photos back in the box. She was disgusted and frightened, but she was also very sleepy now. She wanted to just push the box back into its corner and lie down. Somewhere, far back in her addled mind, a voice cried out against this. *You need to get up*, this voice insisted, *you need to get out of this house.*

Chrissy slumped forward instead, resting her chin in her cupped palms. Her eyes drooped. She was not going to be able to stay awake much longer. She wondered what had become of the masked people and the girl in the photos. *Dead probably.* She thought. *All dead.* Her eyelids dipped shut.

"I like your mask." At the sound of Mrs. Lumley's voice in the doorway Chrissy's head snapped up and her eyes flew open. For a moment, she was completely awake. She looked at the old woman and a scream caught in her throat. Mrs. Lumley's head had somehow grown larger and fatter. Her flesh hung from her cheeks and neck in smooth, pale dewlaps and her hair had turned brown. It was shiny, like newly burnt skin. It took Chrissy a few moments to realize that Mrs. Lumley was wearing a mask. A grotesquely exaggerated rubber Ronald Reagan mask. The old woman kicked up her feet in a merry little jig, her Reagan-face jostling on her neck. "It's fun to play pretend. Isn't it?"

Chrissy felt more tears spill sluggishly from her eyes, but her terror was already being numbed again by exhaustion. It occurred to her that the coffee she'd had earlier must have been drugged. Her last thought before falling into darkness was of the girl in the photographs.

***

Chrissy awoke very suddenly. One moment she was lost in oblivion, drifting through an oily scum of nightmares. The next moment she was awake, her dreams unremembered. She lifted her head and looked out into the front hallway of the first floor. It was very dark out there. Night had fallen. The lights in the dining room were glowing above her. Mrs. Lumley finally decided to turn them on, it seemed.

She tried to stand and realized she couldn't. She looked down at herself and found that she'd been tied to the straight-backed chair from the first room upstairs. An object had toppled from her head during her struggles and landed on the ground. It was the dunce cap. She tried to suck in a deep breath with which to scream and discovered her mouth had been sealed shut with duct tape. Her breath began whistling in and out of her flared nostrils. Someone had dragged her downstairs, brought the chair down after, and tied her to it, leaving her in front of the dining room table. Mrs. Lumley couldn't have done any of that. *Who else was here?*

As if she'd heard Chrissy's thought, Mrs. Lumley materialized out of the shadows of the hallway like a ghost. She still had on her Ronald Reagan mask.

"You're heavier than you look." Mrs. Lumley's voice held the same friendly lilt that it had all through their visit.

For a moment Chrissy grasped at the idea that she'd passed out from the flu, and this was all a horrible dream. But the stiffness in her bound arms and legs (especially in her ankles, pulled back and lashed to the chair) was too convincing. She gave up on the dream idea immediately.

"Good thing I'm stronger than *I* look. You might have some bumps and bruises though. Sorry about that. I had to drag you." Mrs. Lumley picked up the dunce cap and reset it on Chrissy's head. She walked back to the doorway between the dining room and kitchen and turned the corner. Chrissy heard a chain being unlatched and a heavy door being pulled open. She began struggling furiously.

"It's time sweetie. Come on up." Mrs. Lumley called down the stairway on the other side of the wall. A moment later Chrissy heard an odd mechanical buzzing sound. It went on for a good thirty seconds and then stopped with a loud *click*. Mrs. Lumley whispered something to someone and then two sets of footsteps made their way into the dining room. One set was Mrs. Lumley's careful but energetic. The other a slow shuffling that filled Chrissy with dread.

"I'm sorry I couldn't put her up on the table like the old days. It was tough enough getting her down here and besides, we wouldn't be able to get to her up there now anyway." The old woman chirped laughter and was answered by a low, reedy moan.

Mrs. Lumley was standing in front of Chrissy again, her eyes glittering behind her hideous mask. She held something in her hand that was too small for Chrissy to see. The old woman beckoned to the person standing just behind the chair and Chrissy's eyes rolled wildly. She screamed against the tape over her mouth, knowing it was useless but unable to stop. Slowly, Mrs. Lumley's companion straggled around the dining room table and into view.

It was another woman. She somehow looked both older and younger than Mrs. Lumley. She had long, stringy hair, iron gray with streaks of white. The skin on her face was lined and loose. A ring of ugly scars puckered her mouth around the lips. She leaned in close to get a good look at Chrissy. Her eyes were dull but hiding within was a hollow glint of recognition and dark amusement. Suddenly Chrissy realized she knew those haunted eyes. from the Polaroids she'd seen earlier that day. The girl was forty-six years older but still recognizable as the only one in the pictures without a mask.

Mrs. Lumley passed the small item she was holding into the twisted hand of the other woman. "You remember how this goes? Remember last time? Won't it be nice to do this up here now thanks to your chairlift?" The other woman didn't answer. She just stared into Chrissy's terrified face. "It'll be almost like old times except now it's *your* turn." Mrs. Lumley stepped behind Chrissy and laid her hands on the younger woman's shoulders. The other old woman stepped closer and held the item up to her face. It was the wallet full of pins. She opened it and drew one out.

Mrs. Lumley leaned down and spoke into Chrissy's ear. "I'm going to take the tape off of your mouth now. If you start screaming or squirming she's going to drive those pins straight through into your gums and you won't like that a *bit*. Do you understand?" Chrissy nodded her head and Mrs. Lumley pulled a corner of the tape away. "If you stay very, *very* still, I think it won't hurt so badly." The old woman chuckled. "Of course, I don't really know. I've never been the dunce." She pulled the tape the rest of the way off and Chrissy drew in a deep, shuddering breath. She didn't scream.

"Okay Ginny, time to start. I've got all the other things back here on the table. We'll have to cut her pants away. We won't be able to untie her like we did with you." Mrs. Lumley patted Chrissy on the arm.

Ginny reached out her hand, the pin poised between her first and second fingers like a pen and grasped Chrissy's chin. Her ruined mouth began to twitch. She was trying to smile.

Suddenly Mrs. Lumley's hands came away from Chrissy's shoulders and she hurried around to Ginny's side. "Mustn't forget this. You can't play without this." She pulled a shiny plastic mask down over Ginny's face. It was a pink, smiling baby mask. "*There.* Now you're ready." Mrs. Lumley backed away and Ginny took Chrissy's chin again in her rough, gnarled fingers. She took the pin in her other hand and pressed it against Chrissy's upper lip.

"Just like you wanted Virginia," Mrs. Lumley said soothingly from over her sister's shoulder, "After all these years *you* get to darn the dunce."

THE OTHER HOUSE

They sat beneath a Japanese Cherry Tree near the walking path that circled the Institute. Rod puffed on a cigarette, and Laura stared out at the parking lot. Rod fidgeted with his shirtsleeves, rolling them up, adjusting them. The dream from the night before was still fresh in his mind, making him feel shaky and sick on the inside. The nightmare about his father. Except nightmare was too polite, too innocent a word for it. He hadn't been sure that his dad wasn't standing over him, watching him with that horrible smirk on his face until the sky began to lighten outside his window. A part of him still wasn't sure. He had something to say, though and so finally broke the silence.

"You kept saying, 'was.'"

"What?"

"In the meeting, you said Dr. Lillen, 'was,' a good leader and that he 'was,' dedicated to getting Tacesom approved." Rod's voice was flat.

Laura sighed. "So?"

"So, I know what you're thinking."

"Which is what?"

He stared hard at the ground and tapped ash from his cigarette. "I don't want to say it out loud. He's been depressed lately. Disappointed. Not himself at all."

She shook her head. "I don't know about all that. He's been distracted, that's for sure. Misplacing charts, forgetting things. He double-ordered Lecithin the other day. He hasn't been in as much." She shrugged. "I mean, he's been jumping through hoops trying to get these trials approved and they just keep pushing back. It's bound to take a toll. But I don't think he'd do anything … you know …"

Rod cleared his throat. "Maybe not, but he hasn't been in all week. I haven't spoken to him since Tuesday. Have you?"

Laura's uncertain eyes were answer enough.

Rod continued. "I called over to his place yesterday, just to check on him. He never answered, so I went over there and went in."

"Rod…"

"What? He's not young anymore. Things happen. You don't hear from a friend in a few days, you check on them. Don't you?"

She sighed. "I guess. Was he there?"

"No, and neither was his car." He pulled a few small slips of paper from his jacket and handed them to Laura. "Look at this."

She flipped through them. "Old bills?"

"They're for household maintenance stuff. A locksmith, a tree-surgeon. Deliveries. Look, that's his signature on that one, and that one. I found these in his desk drawer." He tapped his finger against the pile of bills in Laura's hand. "Look at the address. I looked it up on the County Auditor's site. It's a house in Bright. The owner is listed as Brenda Lillen."

"Who's Brenda Lillen? Was that his mother?"

"His wife."

"I don't think I ever knew he was married. Is she dead?"

Rod shrugged. "I have no idea. He doesn't really talk about her. Mentioned her once or twice in passing. I never felt like he wanted me asking about it. I'd kind of forgotten about her till I dug this stuff up."

Laura frowned. "You're spying on him."

"Spying's a strong word."

"What word would you use?"

He considered for a moment. "Scared. About what these FDA setbacks might have pushed him into."

"And you think he—what?"

He shrugged. It was a defeated gesture. "I want to go to this address. Right now. We need to find him if we can. Help him."

Laura looked at him closely. "Jesus Rod, you're not kidding around, are you?"

The image of his father leaning over him with the pliers in his hand, smiling and humming continued to haunt him. The man was out there somewhere. What if this time the dream meant something more? Rod stood up and dropped his cigarette, grinding it into a drift of pink cherry blossoms with his shoe. "Not at all."

***

The neighborhood sprawled, like any other. A little more run down maybe. A little less hopeful. The car wound through the twisting streets and daylight faded fast around them.

"Did you see the card from Molly and her parents?"

Rod watched the street signs as they passed. "No. What'd it say?"

"Just how much he meant to them. What we all meant to them, and how Molly's life wouldn't be the same if not for the Institute. How he gave her peace of mind and every night without bad dreams, they would thank God for Dr. Lillen and the Institute."

"They're nice people." They passed a plump little girl who sat pulling grass from the ground beside the street. She waved as they drove by, and Rod waved back absently. "And that's one of the things that worries me. He cares so damn much about the patients. He was so worked up. He really believed the big companies were keeping us from getting Tacecom off the ground. I remember a couple of weeks ago, we were in his office, and he slammed his fist against his desk. I'd never seen him so upset. He said, 'no one else has come close to suppressing chronic night terrors. Not like us. And they don't want us to. They don't care who suffers. It doesn't matter who we can help. Until they figure out how to steal it out from under us they'll get their insiders to deny us FDA approval and just keep pushing anti-depressants as a band-aid. Business as usual.' He was speaking quietly but he was furious."

Laura nodded. "Well, he's right. Big pharma will let people go on suffering before some dipshit little clinic in Indiana can step all over their toes and do it better. He should be furious."

"Believe me, I understand." Rod flipped on the heater. "I've tried everything available out there. The heavy hitters just force me to stay asleep and I can't escape the nightmares. It's why I came to the institute in the first place. Dr. Lillen's therapies definitely help but, Tacecom could make them go away altogether. I get it."

Laura touched Rod's arm gently. "I never realized it was that bad. You never talk about your parasomnia."

He glanced over at her. "Yeah. It's that bad. I need Tacecom. I also know how hard you've worked on it. This would be huge for you. Dr. Lillen doesn't want to let you down either."

After a few twists and turns, they pulled onto a small cul-de-sac. There were eleven, similarly unkempt houses on either side of the street and one that faced out from the curve at the far end. This one was set further back from the road. A gravel driveway stretched back through a gate in the fence, ending in front of a gray garage. The house itself was a squat, one-story tract house that looked unlived in. Many seasons worth of leaves had fallen from the oak out front and covered the roof, choking the gutters. Strips of vinyl siding peeled away from the outer walls, revealing plywood beneath, and the lawn was a tangled, brown mess. It wasn't what either had imagined. Dr. Lillen's house in Evansville was the exact opposite of this one, immaculate and well-maintained. But it was his Chrysler sitting mute in the driveway. They pulled in behind it and Rod shut off the car. They both got out, and Laura looked across the ugly little yard with disquiet.

"This can't be right."

Rod gestured silently to the car parked in front of them, raising his eyebrows at her. He set off across the scrubby yard and Laura reluctantly followed. They reached the front stoop and Rod opened the tin storm-door, the springs screaming. He knocked on the inner door and waited. When there was no sound from inside, he knocked again. There was still no answer, so he tried the knob. It was locked. He grunted in frustration and pushed past Laura.

She turned to him. "So, what now?"

"Let's try the back door." He waited while Laura looked over her shoulder at the neighborhood. The street was quiet. Deserted. After a moment, she nodded, and they hurried along the walk around the side of the house. As they passed the garage Rod stopped and tried the knob. Just like the front door, it was locked. "We're probably going to have to try and see if he's got a key to the house hidden somewhere."

But when he turned the knob and pushed the back door opened. Rod and Laura exchanged apprehensive glances. He wasn't sure about what Laura was thinking but Rod wondered what they would find on the other side of the door. Or who. His father's dark, gleeful eyes swam into his mind again, but he pushed the thought away and pushed onward.

They stepped into a cramped kitchen. There were dishes floating in the sink. Gnats hovered over the basin, lighting on the cabinets and buzzing in the stale air. Laura moved up to stand beside Rod, her nose wrinkling at the smell.

He reached out and took her hand. "Ready?"

"Nope, but let's do it anyway." She squeezed his hand and together they moved cautiously out into the dark room beyond the kitchen.

The blinds were down, and the curtains drawn. Rod strode across the room to the front door, stumbling over what felt like a pile of magazines. He ran his hand over the wall next to the door till his fingers found a light switch. He flipped it and the room brightened.

Laura took a deep breath and called out. "Dr. Lillen? Ambrose?" Her eyelids fluttered. "Anybody? Is anyone here?" They waited for a response and, when none came, they moved further into the house.

Directly off the living room was a hallway with three rooms. The first one on the left was quickly dismissed. It contained a rumpled, unmade bed, a nightstand, and little else. They moved on to the middle room, its walls lined with tall shelves filled to bursting with dusty reference books. Stacks of magazines and digests rose from the floor, casting long shadows beneath the single, yellow bulb that burned above. Rod spared a moment to peruse some of the titles, stepping carefully amongst the periodicals on the floor. Laura remained in the doorway, casting worried glances back over her shoulder.

"What are you looking at?" Rod's gaze flicked over to her nervous face.

"I keep thinking I hear things." She peeked over her shoulder again. "The floors creaking behind me."

"Yeah, old houses settle. That's all it is." Rod hoped this was true. He came back out into the hall. There was only one room left to explore. "Come on, let's get this over with."

Unlike the first two rooms, the one at the end of the hall was closed. Rod stopped, his face drawn and uncomfortable. He knocked softly at the door. There was no sound from the other side, so he opened it.

In the center of the room was a huge metal desk covered with folders, notebooks, and loose papers. Shoved beneath it was an old-fashioned swivel-chair with a lidless, nearly empty bottle of vodka laying on its side near one of the rollers. A greasy drift of crumpled potato chip bags littered the floor. Three filing cabinets huddled against one another in the corner beneath a window, the top one yanked out over the lip, folders peeking out of it and more stacked, willy-nilly, on top. Across from these was a bookcase, similar to the one in the middle room, but instead of books, it held framed photos, plaques, drifts of cards, and other mementos. From one of the pictures, Rod could see the smiling, twenty-two-year-old version of himself, standing with Laura and two other grad students, from the day they'd started at the Institute.

He walked over to the shelf and picked the photo up. They looked young. Fresh-faced and ready to change the world. The other two students had left after just a few months, and he couldn't recall their names easily. So many had come and gone, but he and Laura had stayed with Dr. Lillen for eleven years. He set the picture back on the shelf.

Behind him, Laura pushed her way through the detritus around the desk, moving papers off of the swivel chair. She sat down. "What a mess."

"Yeah." Rod looked from one item to the next. Here was Dr. Lillen's FDA certificate of approval for Lucinol, the predecessor to Tacecom also framed. That had been a major victory for the Institute. Laura had spearheaded the final testing phases, and the day it came she'd thrown her arms around Rod and kissed him, right on the mouth. The ghost of a smile danced on his lips as he remembered that day. Then his eyes darkened, and the smile disappeared. "I know I should be happy that we haven't found … anything, but I don't know. This feels bad."

Laura was going through the papers on the desk, flipping open notebooks at random, scanning their contents. Her mouth was a hard, straight line, and her eyes glistened. "No. I know." She shoved a stack of file folders aside and sighed, heavily. "What if he didn't do anything crazy? What if somebody else did something?"

Rod felt a chill tickle the back of his neck. It seemed unlikely; the idea he couldn't let go of. That the face haunting his night-terrors was somehow behind Dr. Lillen's disappearance. Unlikely but not impossible. Instead of telling Laura any of this, he picked up an envelope that was under an old pocket calendar and opened it. Inside was a letter from a man named Danny Wunderlich. He remembered Mr. Wunderlich well. The man had come to the Institute with very little hope they'd be able to help him. He'd been to two other sleep clinics and half a dozen doctors and psychiatrists. He'd tried sleep aids, heavy-duty anti-depressants, and tranquilizers. He'd even given meditation and acupuncture their due. None of it worked. He'd seen an ad for the Sleep Institute online and read about Lucinol and Dr. Lillen's success. The letter, which had been sent two years after Danny's therapy, said that Dr. Lillen had saved his marriage, his job, and probably his life. Since starting Lucinol, he'd been nearly free of episodes. For the first time since he was fourteen years old, Danny Wunderlich wasn't constantly afraid to go to sleep.

Lucinol was good but Tacecom could get rid of the nearly. The constantly. It could give him peace.

Rod set the letter back on the bookcase and picked up something that had been laying beneath it. He looked at it for a moment then turned and showed it to Laura. "Hey, look at this." He handed it to Laura. It was an old photograph of an attractive young woman. She had long blonde hair and a pert little grin. Laura flipped the picture over and read aloud:

"I know you always liked my hair this way, but I don't know why. Maybe one day I will. Love you always.—B." She looked back up at him. "His wife?"

Rod stepped out into the hallway. "Yeah, must be. B for Brenda." He peeked into the small bathroom across the hall. A fat black cricket sat in the washbasin. When he turned on the light it chirped once and slowly crawled down the drain. He went back into the living room and sat in an easy chair by the window. He rubbed his hands across his face.

Laura stood in the middle of the room and watched him. "What now?"

He stared down at the floor. "Christ, I don't know. I mean, I definitely didn't want to find anything but now that we haven't it's almost worse. Do we call the cops?" He laughed.

"What about the garage?"

His eyes widened.

Laura went back into the hallway, speaking over her shoulder. "I saw some keys on the desk in here. Maybe one of them goes to the garage door." She came back out a moment later dangling a keyring between her fingers.

Rod stood up and took the keys from her. He put his hand on her shoulder and squeezed gently. "Listen. We might find ..." He swallowed hard. "We don't know if he's hurt himself, but it could be bad. I just want you to be ready for any possibility, okay? If you want to wait in here for me, or go out and wait in the car, I completely understand."

Laura smiled. "He's my friend. I'll be fine. I'm going with you."

He nodded. "Good. I'm glad because, honestly, I'm scared to death of what we might find out there."

They went back through the sour-smelling kitchen, walking slowly. As Rod was reaching out for the knob Laura touched his shoulder.

"Can I ask you a question? About your night-terrors?"

He turned to look at her and nodded.

"What's the content focus?"

Rod chuckled at her use of Institute jargon. "Well, Dr. Blaisel, why do you ask?"

Her cheeks burned red and she looked at the ground. "I just—I guess I just was curious. You were one of the first to use Lucinol but Dr. Lillen obviously never discussed your case with me. I'm sorry, I shouldn't have asked."

"It's okay." Rod leaned back against the stove, glad for an excuse not to head out to the garage just yet. He pulled his cigarettes from his jacket pocket and lit one. "The focus is my father. He wasn't a nice guy. He ..." His gaze flicked to the ceiling as he searched for the right words. "...He hurt me. In a lot of different ways. He enjoyed it. I went to the emergency room more than once thanks to him, though never the same one. He wasn't dumb. And there were other things. Things I never told but that I knew my mom suspected. She was afraid of him too." He dragged on his cigarette and inhaled blue smoke in a shaky breath.

"He went to prison when I was nine. Beat a woman into a coma. Some girl he was cheating on my mom with. Her family wasn't afraid of him, and they got him into court. He went away and that was it. We were free. My mom divorced him, we moved, and never really talked about him much after that. Then, when I was fifteen, he got out."

"Oh God."

"He never showed up to bother us, but that night I dreamed he was in my room. Watching me. Smiling. He always smiled at me when he ...Anyway, I woke up, and he was still there. Sitting on my bed, his hand on my bare foot. Under the covers." Rod's hand shook as he tapped ash from his cigarette onto the floor. "Of course, it was still just the dream. You know how night terrors work. I'd had them as a kid a few times. Worms. Always thought I was covered in worms, and I couldn't wake up. I'd fall out of bed wrapped up in my blankets, and crawl through the house screaming. But that only happened a few times. When he got out, it started happening almost every night. I'd close my eyes and at some point, I'd wake up and he'd be there. Sometimes just watching me. Other times …doing things."

"You don't have to say any more."

Rod held out his hand. "No, it's okay. Really that's the long and short of it. I was afraid to go to bed. My grades took a hit, I turned into kind of an asshole. I was just always exhausted. My mom didn't know what to do. She sent me to a couple of shrinks. They put me on Zoloft and that helped a little but not much. Sleeping pills worked sometimes, other times, they made it worse. They kept me from waking up. It's what drove me into sleep research and how I ended up at the Institute. Dr. Lillen is the only one who really helped me. Now, I only have my night terrors once or twice a month instead of every night." He crossed the small kitchen and tossed his cigarette butt into the sink and washed it down the drain. "I was looking forward to Tacecom almost as much as you were. I would have volunteered for the human trials myself."

"Really?"

"Absolutely." He turned and grasped the doorknob. "It would be nice to get rid of the dreams altogether." He opened the back door.

They stepped out onto the driveway. Night had fallen. Something stirred in one of the trees behind the fence and startled them as they approached the garage door. They both jumped and shared a moment of nervous laughter.

They stepped under the overhang and Rod tried the door. It was locked. He selected a key from the ring. It wouldn't fit. He cursed and tried another that didn't fit either. He fumbled in the dark with the third key. It took a few seconds but when he finally found the keyhole it slid in easily.

"There it is." He looked over his shoulder at Laura. Her face was hidden in shadow. "You ready?"

He turned the key, then the knob. He took a breath and pushed the door open, stepping into musty darkness. He felt along the wall beside him for a switch and when he found it, he flipped it. Light filled the room.

"Dr. Lillen?"

There was a tiny sting in his neck, right where it met the shoulder. He flicked at it reflexively and knocked something to the floor. He looked down and saw it was a hypodermic needle. He spun around, his vision going blurry. The last thing he saw before he lost consciousness was Laura standing over him, her face still filled with shadows.

***

Laura's voice came to Rod as the darkness began to recede. "I don't know if that was really enough. I had to guess at his weight. He might wake up so be careful.

"That's alright. I've got plenty more. I really didn't expect you for another couple of days though."

"Yeah, I had a whole thing planned out but when he dug up all that stuff at your house and told me he wanted to come find you I just rolled with it. Serendipity, I guess."

"He dug stuff up at my house?" Dr. Lillen's voice moved from one side of the room to the other.

"He was worried about you. He found some bills with this address on it. Like he was solving a mystery. It was sweet really."

"He's a nice boy."

Rod tried to ask what was happening, but his mouth wouldn't work. It felt thick and slow, as if it was being held shut with rubber bands. He moaned, and Laura spoke again.

"Oh damn. See?"

Footsteps came near and he felt fingers grasp his jaw gently. His head was moved slowly from right to left and he realized he could see the rafters in the ceiling above. His eyes were open. Dr. Lillen's square, pink face swam into view, his eyes peering over his spectacles at Rod.

"Roderick? You awake?" He shook Rod's face lightly. Rod tried to speak again but all that came out was a burble and a sigh. Dr. Lillen let go and disappeared again. "Ugh. He smells like smoke."

Rod's head was grasped by small, dry hands. Laura's face appeared, her hair hanging down, tickling his nose. Her eyes were sad but cold. She didn't say anything. She just looked at him. Then she was gone. His head sank to the side, and he could see them, walking back and forth under bright, fluorescent lights.

The garage had been converted into a makeshift lab. Rod's thoughts were fuzzy but that much was clear. There were two tables with vials and containers. A centrifuge sat dormant, waiting to spin into life next to a desktop computer and printer. Two rows of plastic drawers acted as a wall between the tables and there were notebooks everywhere. There was also a gurney. Someone was laying on it. Two feet hung at the end of stick-thin, shriveled legs. They were purple and full of twisting veins. Dr. Lillen's body was blocking the person's head, but Rod saw one of the bony feet twitch and knew the person was alive. He tried to sit up and couldn't understand why his arms and legs wouldn't work. With great effort, he managed to bend his head forward on his neck and look down at himself. He was on a gurney of his own, his wrists and legs clutched in heavy, vinyl restraints.

"How long can we maintain induced coma?" Laura's voice was curious.

"Well, let's see. She's been under for seventeen years. I've only had to use the ventilator twice. Once the body adjusts to the liquid nutrition it's amazing how well it handles permanent unconsciousness." He chuckled. "We can keep him that way as long as we want."

Rod tried to speak again. Tried to shout. His mouth opened wider, and he managed a loud buzzing sound. Laura turned her head and looked at him.

"Dr. Lillen?"

Dr. Lillen pointed to a cluster of bottles and vials on the table. "Saline, TPN, Lecithin, Propofol and Lethe, it's already mixed in 100ml vials. Push 30 units to start. That ought to quiet him down."

Rod watched Laura tear open a package and remove a syringe. She picked up one of the small vials and drew liquid in through the needle. She flicked the tip to clear it and walked towards him, growing larger with each step. Rod could feel his heart pounding in his chest. He strained and flexed, trying to free himself. He felt her grasp his arm and flip it over. Felt the needle penetrate his skin, and the cold burn of the mixture entering his bloodstream. A moment later his thoughts began to cloud again. Dr. Lillen's voice from across the room seemed to echo and swirl.

"We'll get him on the IV drip in a few hours. The Lucinol will work itself out of his system and the night terrors should begin recurring quickly. Once he hits 3 on the Glasgow scale we'll hook up the EEG. Hopefully we can get a baseline reading before the dreams set in. Once that happens, until we get Tacecom up to version 4, he's going to be in a perpetual state of nightmare."

"He said he would've volunteered for human trials."

Dr. Lillen clicked his tongue. "He doesn't understand what we really need of him. This is really the best way. The only way. It will be thanks to him that we can even get to human trials."

Laura was quiet for a moment and then spoke the last words Rod would hear from her. "We won't be able to let him leave afterwards, will we?"

"After six months of living in darkness and horror, there won't be much of him left to leave." Dr. Lillen moved across the room and Rod saw the face of the person on the other gurney. Most of her hair had fallen out and what was left was frizzy and gray. Her skin was thin and tight against her skull, but Brenda Lillen was somehow still very pretty.

Rod's mind filled with black nothing, and he felt relief. His eyes closed, and his heartbeat slowed. Then he felt a hand on his bare foot. He turned to look before the nothing dragged him down and saw his father sitting at the end of the gurney, wearing a wide, predatory smile. As a scream tried to fight its way from Rod's mouth, his father's hand slid up his leg.

"It's good to see you, Roddy. Let's have some fun."

FISHING HOLE

The little blue car buzzed west along Highway 52 under a sky still heavy with pre-dawn darkness. Every so often other cars would dump onto the road from on-ramps along the way but, for the most part, they had the road to themselves.

A steady stream of hillbilly bluegrass jingled and jangled out of the tiny dashboard speakers and Chris tapped his fingers enthusiastically against the steering wheel in time to the raucous banjo plucking, humming along with cheerful abandon. His friend Tony, yawning in the passenger seat, pulled his knit cap down over his ears. He knew it wouldn't muffle anything, but the gesture seemed necessary to him. He was not yet having as much fun as Chris, and he didn't expect to be anytime soon.

"Man, you are gonna *shit* when you see this spot." Chris's voice was bristling with excited energy. "There's only a few people that even know it's there. It's like a legend among these back-country fishermen."

"Sweet." Tony's tone was as flat as Chris's was light. He was not a morning person. He enjoyed fishing and being outdoors, but he enjoyed them best in the warmth of a late afternoon sun. He'd said many times that as far as he was concerned, heading out at the crack of dawn was for fanatics only. He glanced over at Chris who was bobbing his head from left to right, a goofy grin plastered across his face, as he yodeled along with the music.

Tony shook his head and yawned again, leaning forward to grab the steel thermos of coffee from the floor between his ankles. He unscrewed the cap and took a swig, grimacing as the hot liquid burned his tongue and throat. He looked out his window at the rocky hill that sloped up and away to the scraggy pine trees fifty feet above the road.

"So where is this place?"

Chris nodded and his grin widened as if he'd been waiting the whole ride for Tony to ask. "It's up near Brookville Lake. We're gonna have to do some hiking before we get there but from what Chorbley says it's gonna be well worth it buddy." Chorbley was Chris's older brother whose real name was Wesley. Chris and Tony had spent many beer-soaked days pulling crappie out of numerous unnamed creeks and ponds with him. If anyone would know the location of a legendary, remote fishing hole, Chorbley was that person.

Chris reached out and turned off the music. "We're gonna drive into Whitewater, near the lake, and head inwards a ways. There's a few twists and turns and then we park at the second lot after mile marker 13."

"That doesn't seem very hidden to me." Tony felt bad as soon as he said it. He knew Chris was excited and he was acting like a killjoy. The problem was that Chris's brother often exaggerated or outright invented things that had ended up getting them in trouble. The idea that he'd woken up at four in the morning for one of Chorbley's tall tales kept his mood sour.

Chris didn't seem bothered at all. "Well, after we park then we get out and head straight into the woods. We gotta be careful we go in a straight line from where we parked or else we'll end up missing it on one side or the other." He reached over to grab the thermos from Tony and took two big gulps. "Chorbs says we're supposed to walk through the woods for about a half hour or so and then we'll come across a rough trail that cuts through to the left. We follow that for awhile and then there's gonna be a fork. There's supposedly a little tree trunk with these fish shapes carved into it leading off to the right. That's the trail that leads to the fishing hole. They call it the Trapper's Trail."

Tony sighed. "That's gonna be a lot with all our gear on our backs."

Chris cut his eyes at Tony for a moment. "Simmer down Gramma. From what I've heard this fishing hole is full of some of the biggest catfish you ever saw. A little walking ain't gonna kill you." He chuckled and looked back out at the road.

"Has Chorbley ever been there himself?" Tony took the thermos back and had another drink. Dawn began to seep into the sky like blue-gray paint spilled over a black canvas. In the wooded thickets that filled the ravines and valleys along the highway birds began singing hesitantly. It was only a few at first, early risers reluctant to disturb the silence but soon a chorus of chirping and whistling would fill the crisp morning air.

Chris shook his head. "No. He said he's always wanted to check it out but, every time he was out here, he always forgot about it till it was almost time to pack up and leave."

"Of course. So how does he even know about it then?"

Chris shrugged. "His friend Link told him about it. Link says his cousin's friend has been out there four or five times and always comes back with an amazing catch." He flipped on the right blinker as they passed under a road sign proclaiming *Highway 101 North Next Right*. "Plus, maybe we'll see the Brookville Space-man."

Tony snorted. "*The what?*"

Chris's eyes went wide. "Aw, man! You've never heard of the Brookville Spaceman?" He shook his head. "That's why you should spend less time in Cincinnati and more time over here."

"For the Brookville Spaceman?"

Chris laughed at Tony's dubious tone. "Yeah, man. See this whole area up here—Connersville, Hagerstown, Brookville—the whole Whitewater Valley—is a hot spot for all kinds of weird UFO sightings. People see lights in the sky all the time. Sometimes they take pictures of what look like flying saucers. Crazy stuff."

"Yeah, that's like Gallia County. That's where they saw the Mothman." Tony felt a small bubble of interest beginning to form in his belly. He'd always enjoyed tales of the strange and this was a new one for him.

Chris nodded. "Yeah, I guess. But check this—the government dammed up the east fork of the Whitewater back in the sixties or seventies and that reservoir is what became Brookville Lake. Some people say that the whole reason they built it is because a UFO crashed up there. Supposedly there had been all this activity during this one week. People were calling the sheriff and the news reporting sightings left and right. Families were camping out in their backyards with old home movie cameras. There were UFO barbecues, UFO slumber parties, UFO *swinger* parties. It was nuts."

So far, Tony was not impressed with this story. "Sounds like a boring town filled with bored people looking for an excuse to get crazy."

Chris shrugged. "Maybe. Maybe not. Either way, the story goes that one night, after this had been going on for a while, there was a bright light that lit up the whole sky, and then an explosion out at the park. People panicked. Thought it was the Russians or whatever coming to get 'em. The next day there were government agents and Air Force guys swarming over the park. Very X-Files."

Tony took another swig from the coffee thermos and then poked Chris in the arm with it. "Well, if they thought the Russians were invading, I imagine government agents and Air Force guys would probably make sense."

Chris rolled his eyes, exasperated. "Yeah, except no Russians ever showed up. The sightings started to taper off and then a few weeks later they started damming up the river to make the lake. Some people—a *lot* of people—say it was to cover up an alien crash-landing."

"So, sort of like Indiana's version of—what's that town in New Mexico where the spaceship landed?"

Chris nodded. "Roswell. Yeah, kind of like that."

"So, what you're saying," Tony paused to take yet another sip of coffee, "is that the real reason they built Brookville Lake was to hide a UFO crash?"

Chris laughed. "Sure. It's as good a reason as any. The government doesn't want people poking around someplace where they might actually find evidence of aliens right?" He held his hand out for the thermos. "What better way to keep that from happening than to fill the place up with water? It's genius really."

"So, where does the 'Spaceman' come in?"

Chris finished chugging coffee and handed the thermos back. "Well, while they were building the dam, the workers started seeing this weird little hairy man around the work site. He'd show up, somebody'd see him and then he'd disappear but right after they saw him, stuff would go wrong. There were a bunch of accidents during the construction. I think a couple of people died. And it was always after they saw this little creature. A lot of people think that it was the pilot of the spaceship that crashed. Hence the name—"

"—Brookville Spaceman. Got it." Tony yawned. "Where did you hear all of this?"

Chris shrugged. "I don't know. I guess there's some articles and stuff on the internet about it. Some Native American groups got all bent out of shape and did a bunch of protests because the construction workers accidentally wrecked a bunch of old burial mounds. The local tribe said that the spaceman was really a vengeful spirit. Nobody else really thinks that though. Everybody basically thinks it's an alien. "

"You've read articles about this?"

Chris shook his head. "No. People just talk about it. Gina swears she knows a guy who says he saw the Spaceman when they were camping out by the lake. He said it was the middle of the night and their fire'd gone out. They got woken up by these splashing sounds and that something weird came out of the lake—something on two legs and hairy but short—and that it chased them through the woods all the way back to their jeep. She says they never did get their camping gear back. They went back the next afternoon and it was all gone."

Tony made a dismissive, *pssh*, sound. "Yeah. Stolen."

Chris shrugged again. "Maybe. I'm just saying, there's a lot of weird stories about those woods up around Brookville. Wouldn't it be awesome to catch a monster catfish *and* get a glimpse of an alien?"

The turn-off for their exit appeared and Chris maneuvered them onto it, heading north. State Road 101 stretched out before them, long flat fields replacing the rocky hills on either side, rolling off into the distance for miles. It was September, and the sweet corn would be harvested soon. The sky was much lighter now and rosy sunlight peeked over the horizon.

"It wouldn't *not* be awesome, I guess." Tony was finally starting to pep up, mostly he suspected, because of all the coffee. "Still, that gear's gonna get heavy. Those fish better be *huge* or I'm making you carry everything back out by yourself."

"You're an asshole dude." Chris laughed, reached out, and turned the stereo back on spilling the frenzied sounds of bluegrass music into the car.

***

The walk through the woods took longer than Chris had expected. By the time the boys found the first trail the sun was shining, high and bright. Choirs of crickets hummed and sang, hidden in the underbrush. They walked single file, enjoying a warm breeze that swept along the path carrying away the last lingering breath of summer. Their fishing rods and tackle boxes bounced and clacked amiably against their hips as they tromped through the knee-high grass talking about trivial things like jobs, school, and their frustrating lack of girlfriends. Leafy green bushes pressed in close on either side and pawed at their shirtsleeves as they passed.

Time became hazy. They could have been on the path for ten minutes or fifty. Tony was finishing a dirty joke *("—sure you can buy me a drink, just let me just put my glass eye back in—")* when they rounded a bend and came upon the fork in the path that marked the entrance to the Trapper's Trail.

Where the trail diverged, trees had pushed their way up to meet the path. They were shedding their dense gown of leaves, all shades of red, yellow, and orange in defiance of the coming winter. Long, twisting limbs hovered and grasped over the trail creating a shady tunnel out of each path that branched from the fork. A gray, gnarled stump rose up in front of the right-hand path from roots that sunk into the earth-like veins. It was nearly five feet tall and trimmed with furry brown ruffles of fungus. In the center of it, a few inches from the top, was a rough circle where the rippling bark had long ago been scraped away. In this circle was carved an image of two fish facing in different directions. They were simple in design, crude outlines of bodies with mouths open, and huge, staring circles to represent their unblinking eyes.

"There it is. The Trapper's Trail." Chris stepped over to the tree trunk and ran his hand over the carving. "Damn. D'you know how *old* this is?"

Tony shook his head. "No. Do you?"

"No man but it looks pretty fuckin' old." Chris turned to his friend. "Let's get in there and see if the fish are biting."

The boys followed the right-hand path under the canopy of limbs and were swallowed up by the gloom. The air was cooler, and sounds gave back a dry, brittle echo. There was no birdsong because it seemed like there were no birds flitting to and fro in the branches above. The droning of insects had also been left behind in the sunshine but there *were* bugs here. Large black moths fluttered slowly and silently back and forth across the path above the carpet of fallen leaves.

Tony eyed them with distaste. Their movements were jerky and sluggish, like little flying zombies. One buffeted his wrist with its powdery wings, and he yanked his arm with a gasp.

Chris looked over his shoulder at his friend. "You alright there Cap'n?"

Tony rubbed his hand against his jacket. His eyes ticked back and forth across the path tracking the movements of the moths as they whirled and swooped ahead of him. "Yeah, man. I just don't like these bugs."

Chris laughed. "Aw, come on man. They're just like butterflies. You're not scared of butterflies, are you?"

"Butterflies are pretty. These things are gross."

"Alwight baby Tony. I'll keep the bad butterfwies away so they won't huht you, otay?" Chris' words devolved into a chuckling series of gurgling coos.

The trail ahead swung sharply to the right and the brambles and trees huddled thickly in the crook of the bend. Tony found himself looking off into the woods beyond the turn. Suddenly a dark flicker of movement caught his eye. He stopped walking and scanned the spaces between the tree trunks.

"Hey man, did you see that?"

Chris stopped and turned around. "What? Was there a ladybug or something given you shit?"

Tony waved a dismissive hand at his friend. "No dumbass. Something was running through the woods over there." All of a sudden, he realized how close the forest was pressing in against them and how far from other people they really were. There was no one around to help them if they ran into trouble. "Hey there aren't any coyotes out here are there?"

Chris shrugged. "Do I live out here? I don't know." He turned around and started walking again. "Come on Gramma, the big bad wolf's with the pigs today." He walked on around the bend and disappeared from Tony's view.

Tony lingered a moment longer. His eyes darted from trunk to trunk trying to catch another glimpse of whatever it was that was moving around. It had seemed large but not tall. *Probably a deer.* Tony was sure there were deer back here. He wasn't afraid of deer. *Or it was a coyote.* Tony wasn't sure how he felt about coyotes exactly. He knew they usually were afraid of people, but the idea of them out here in the woods made him uneasy.

As he searched the woods for wild animals something brushed Tony's hand softly. He jumped and wheeled around. There was nothing there. Then he felt it again. A fluttery, fuzzy tickle against the palm of his hand. He looked down and uncurled his fingers.

One of the black moths had blundered into him and was now clinging to his hand with its thick, sticky legs. Tony cried out in disgust and began flinging his hand trying to dislodge it. The moth seemed to decide it didn't care for this sort of treatment and disengaged itself, wobbling drunkenly away through the air.

"Another ladybug?" Chris's voice lilted back to Tony from somewhere further up the path.

"Fuck you!" Tony shouted. "It was a moth." He yanked on the shoulder straps of his backpack and walked on around the bend nearly running into a stout gray creature standing at the edge of the path. It twitched but didn't run away. For the second time in less than a minute, Tony screamed. He jumped backward, his gear swaying heavily, pulling him off balance and into a tree. Tony forced his eyes open and tried to get a good look at whatever it was.

The thing was still. It was squat, much shorter than Tony but taller than a deer or a coyote, and broad around the middle. It held its spindly, stubby arms out at odd angles. It looked ancient and hunched like an old man with very thick, dry skin.

It was a tree stump, similar to the one that marked the entrance to the trail. Tony stared hard at it for several seconds. He was sure he saw it move, just a little bit, when he came around the corner.

Chris came hurrying back down the trail, his face full of concern. "Y'alright man? What the hell is going on back here?" Tony gestured with his hand at the tree stump with a heavy sigh.

"The Brookville Spaceman there jumped out at me and said *boo*."

Chris blinked at his friend, nonplussed. "*What*?"

Tony rolled his eyes. "Jesus. I came around the corner and the tree trunk here," he pointed emphatically at the stump, "startled me. Scared the shit out of me."

Chris studied the tree stump and then his friend's pinched expression. "See. This is why I brought you on this trip. You need to relax. You see what stress is doing to you? You're seeing things now."

Tony nodded. "Yes. You're obviously right." He started up the trail giving the stump one last glare as he passed. "Let's get this relaxing *over with*."

"After you, my good man." Chris let Tony slink by him and then followed along behind.\

A few moments later they stepped out of the shadows of the Trapper's Trail and into a wide clearing ringed with tall trees. Leaves floated to earth with casual grace. The ground was thick with tall, yellow grass, weeds, and scrawny shrubs that crouched at the edge of the woods. In the center of the clearing sprawled the fishing hole. A wide, shallow pond, stagnant and green with algae. A fishy, briny odor hung in the air all around. Reeds stood up from the water near the edge and made an eerie whistling sound as a breeze blew across them.

The two boys stood still at the mouth of the trail and looked out across the clearing. He didn't know how Chris felt about this place, but Tony was filled with a deep, unsettling loneliness. He could easily believe that only a few people ever made their way back to this spot. It felt like it was its own world, lying in wait beneath its own blue sky within its own strange universe. The air was warm and motile, brushing against their faces and chests in a secretive caress of pond stink.

"Yowza." Chris tapped Tony lightly on the arm. "This is just how Chorbley said it would be. Better, actually."

Tony nodded. "Yeah?"

"*Shit* yeah. Come on Tone, let's check out the pond." Chris strode forward through the clinging grass and underbrush and up to the edge of the water. He un-shouldered his pack, letting it drop to the ground, and set the rest of his gear next to it. With his hands planted on his knees, he leaned forward and peered into the murky depths.

Tony stood where he was and regarded the clearing and woods beyond with vague disquiet. After a few moments, he joined Chris at the water's edge.

"Look at 'em, man." A huge smile played on Chris's face. Sliding shiny and black along the surface of the shallow pool were the long bodies of fish, dozens of them, their oily backs rolling and flexing.

Tony's lip curled with annoyance. "Those aren't catfish they're carp." He dropped his things beside Chris's gear with a loud, heavy *chonk!* Rather than being startled by the noise, the slimy creatures continued their slow patrol with hardly a stutter. This close to the water the odor was overpowering, and Tony's sneer became a grimace. "Ugh and they *reek*."

Chris looked over at his friend, his expression finally sinking into a scowl. "Seriously, dude? Is this what you're gonna do all day? Complain?" He stood up and straightened his jacket. "Because if it's gonna be like that then we can just leave right now."

Leaving was exactly what Tony wanted to do. This weird little clearing and the trail that had led them here gave him bad vibes. He didn't believe in a Spaceman running around the woods, but the deep quiet and swaying trees made him uncomfortable. Not knowing *why* it made him uncomfortable deepened the feeling. He'd been ready to turn around and leave the moment they'd arrived, but he didn't want to disappoint Chris.

He knew that Chris had brought him out here in an attempt to stave off the drifting-away that had begun with the burgeoning of true adulthood. With Chris going to school in Bloomington and Tony working with his brother in Cincinnati there was not a lot of time for the kind of aimless hanging-around that had been the glue of their teenage friendship.

Now, to rationalize spending time together and traveling the distance between them, there had to be a plan—some kind of organized activity that would make the trip worth it. Tony knew (and guessed that Chris did as well) that this gulf between them would only grow wider and deeper. Eventually, it would become a chasm that they would have to work hard to bridge.

Tony decided he could bear the anxiety to give his best friend the afternoon he wanted. "Nah, man. I'm just sayin that they smell like fish, that's all." He forced a grin.

"Think it might be 'cause they *are* fish?" Chris laughed and cuffed Tony on the shoulder.

Tony chuckled and pointed fat finger at Chris. "*Your face.*"

The two boys fell into the old rituals of boyhood and unpacked their gear, finding a good, flat spot from which to cast. They pulled jars filled with dirt and blind, burrowing nightcrawlers from their packs. Tackle boxes were opened, and an array of small items were removed; and placed on the ground. Soon, both of them were grasping a fully armed rod and reel and with a flick of their wrists sent their baited hooks into the water.

Even though the fish were obviously plentiful and active, none of them were biting. The bobbers floated atop the rippling water, jostled by the bodies of greasy carp but otherwise remained still. Tony imagined his nightcrawler impaled on its hook watching the carp as they snaked past it, mouths shut. So far, the worm god was coming through for its tiny follower.

The day wore on. Chris and Tony had seated themselves several feet apart and facing opposite directions so that their lines did not become entangled. For a while, they kept up a constant patter of conversation but as the minutes turned into an hour and an hour worked on becoming two, the words dried up and silence filled the clearing.

Tony yawned and began reeling in his line. He decided to try a spot a few yards further around the pond.

"Hey man, I'm goin' over there to see if it's any better alright?" As Tony turned to Chris his words caught in his throat.

Chris was sitting there glumly staring out across the gritty water, pulling at his line. His face showed boredom and nothing more. He seemed completely unaware of the thing that was standing right next to him.

It was short—maybe four and a half feet tall—its head, such as it was—didn't come much above the line of Chris's shoulder. Its body was a mottled gray-black and covered with what appeared to be ribbons of peeling skin. Its arms were thin but wiry with muscle and its hands were large and flat. The creature's legs were mostly hidden by Chris's body, but Tony could see a long sliver of shin, jet black and smooth, ending in a mound of cracked flesh. It had no face, just a thick fall of long, stringy hair that hung forward from the crown of its head like a wig that had been dragged through a sooty fireplace and then put on backward. There was no hint of a mouth, no indentations to suggest eyes, just the tangle of its scraggly mane.

Time stood still and the whole world went quiet. Tony tried to blink but his eyelids wouldn't close. He shook his head violently trying to knock the vision loose. In slow motion Chris turned and looked back at him, concern spreading across his face.

Tony looked up at the sky for what felt like a long time. He was very confident that when he looked back, he would see only Chris eyeing him with confusion. Finally, he let his head swing forward on his neck.

There was Chris, setting his fishing rod on the ground, looking at Tony as if he'd gone crazy, and there was the thing standing just behind him. It was actually leaning forward, its grubby little hand resting on Chris's shoulder, its—*face?*—straining forward as if gauging his reaction to its presence.

Time began to catch back up to itself, and sounds came whooshing back with shocking speed. Tony began screaming.

"Gah! Behind you!" He pointed at Chris who whirled around violently and ducked as if to evade an oncoming blow. The thing took its hand away from his shoulder but otherwise held its position. Tony kept giving voice to hoarse cries, as Chris turned to him with agitated eyes.

"What man? What is it? A bee or something? A wasp?" Before Tony could answer, Chris hopped to his feet and whipped his head all around searching for the stinging insect that could be the only thing Tony was yelling about.

The faceless creature, small, silent, and very much still there, cocked its head. It didn't reach for him or approach. Its blind scrutiny fell upon him with a thick sense of malice and rage.

You are in a bad place. The thought wormed its way into his brain as if it had been whispered into his ear. *You are in* my *place.*

Chris, meanwhile, realized that there was no bee or wasp. He didn't see the thing, didn't sense it even though he was standing less than a yard away from it. It had been *touching* him, but he had no idea it was there. The thing seemed to ignore Chris completely. All of its malignant intent seemed focused on Tony.

"*What the fuck man?*" Chris looked down at Tony, his hands held out, exasperated. "What is your *deal?*"

Tony's eyes flicked away from the creature (*the Spaceman— holy goddam shit it's the Brookville Spaceman)* and up into Chris's accusatory, gape-mouthed stare. When he looked back the Spaceman was no longer there.

Had it ever been?

Tony looked down at himself, discovering the cringing position he'd worked his body into. Suddenly his cheeks and ears were burning with embarrassment. Chris stood a few feet away, awaiting an explanation.

Tony looked around the little glade, his eyes panning the trees and bushes, the reeds growing up from the water. He saw whispering grass, and the pond itself, rippling with a slowly drifting scum of algae. It was gorgeous. Everything was tinted with the strong light of early afternoon. No creature besides the fish and the two boys disturbed the placidity.

What just happened? He climbed slowly to his feet, brushing invisible dust from his pants and jacket. He glanced at Chris, abashed. "Sorry, dude. I just got a little freaked out."

Chris's eyebrows went up. "You think?" He made an exaggerated show of looking around the clearing, his hands planted on his hips. "You wanna tell me what it was you thought was happening? Did a tree trunk try to sneak up on me?"

A great wave of exhaustion drained through Tony. All his breath seemed to have been sucked out and he felt his legs weaken. He crumpled to the grass; his legs crossed in front of him. He dragged the knit cap from his head and shrugged, forcing a small, cracked smile. "I don't know. I guess—I guess I thought I saw the Brookville Spaceman or something." He watched, eyes cast sidelong, for Chris's reaction.

"What?" Chris had a confused and somewhat nervous look on his face. "Again? Are you serious?"

"No. I don't know." Tony sighed, looking at the ground, wanting to lie down in the scraggly grass. "I think I fell asleep for a minute and dreamt it. I'm really tired." He actually thought that this was probably true. Looking back now at the past minute or so, it seemed highly unlikely that he'd seen anything at all. Fatigue was dragging him downward, pulling his eyes shut. He yawned. It had been an early (*very* early) start for him and he'd been tired all day. He'd pounded coffee the whole drive and then carried his pack and gear a few miles through the woods. It made sense that after all that, as he relaxed in the warm sun, he might crash with fatigue.

Chris grinned and shook his head. "Oh man, you are one fucked up little monkey. You know that?" He laughed.

Tony laughed along with his friend. "Yeah, man. That was really weird." He yawned again, covering his mouth with the back of his hand. "I think this week's just catching up with me. I might just, you know, lay back and shut my eyes for a few minutes."

Chris hunkered down and settled himself back in his spot at the edge of the pond. He picked up his rod and began reeling in line. "Do whatever. I just wanted to get us out here to relax. A nap's as good as fishing as far as I'm concerned." His hook came up from the water, dripping and wormless. He sighed and turned to find his jar of bait.

"Meanwhile I'm gonna keep trying to pull one of these monsters out of there."

Tony nodded wordlessly and curled up on his side, pressing his face into the crook of his curled arm. Clover tickled his cheek and nose. He was already sinking rapidly into sleep and barely heard Chris speak.

"All that screaming you did you'd think all the fish would've gotten scared away, but they didn't even flinch. It's weird."

Yeah. Weird. Tony thought and then sleep overtook him.

***

Tony awoke, pushing himself up to a sitting position and wiping drool from his cheek and chin. Afternoon had slipped into dusk. It was cooler in the clearing and the shadows had deepened into a gray gloom. Above him, the undersides of the clouds had turned a rusty red-orange, and the trees were featureless black cutouts grasping at the sky.

"Shit, Chris, why didn't you wake me up? We're gonna have to go soon." Tony's head felt heavy, his brain sloshing around inside his skull.

His eyes were still fighting to stay open. When he got no response, he looked over to Chris's spot on the bank. "Did you hear me?"

Chris wasn't there. His rod and reel were there, lying on the ground, the line stretched out into the pool which had turned black in the early evening darkness. His tackle-box and backpack were still there. His jar of night-crawlers sat lidless. plump, pink bodies writhing through the loosened soil at the top, smearing the glass with slime.

"Chris?" Tony gazed out across the water to the trees that crowded together on the other side. There was no answer. "Fuck." He twisted around and looked behind him. Chris was standing across the clearing at the mouth of the Trapper's Trail, facing him. *At least, I think that's Chris.* It was hard to tell. He was standing beneath the overhanging arms of a spindly pine tree, bathed in shadow. *Who else would it be?* Tony scrambled to his feet. "You alright man?"

Chris didn't answer. He just stood there facing Tony.

Nervousness fluttered in Tony's belly. He took a few reluctant steps toward the figure that was *obviously* Chris. *There's nobody else back here. Nobody really knows about this place.*

Suddenly, Tony's dream from earlier tried to push its way into his mind. The thing (*Spaceman*) crouching behind Chris, watching him with expressionless hatred, dissecting him with its faceless gaze. A chill snaked down the nape of his neck. He shoved back at the unwelcome thought by pretending to be irritable and hungry.

"Dude." He called out to Chris, forcing his feet to carry him forward. "We ever gonna get some food or what man?" *Of course that's Chris, duh. That's his stupid army jacket.* Still, there was no reply. Three more steps and Tony became genuinely irritable. "Dude?" Another four steps, still no answer. *"Dude?"* Two more steps. Silence. "Chris—*asshole*—answer me."

When Chris shambled out from beneath the shadows of the pine Tony didn't quite grasp what he was seeing. There was something wrong with Chris's face. *Was he hurt? Had something happened to him while I was sleeping?* That might explain Chris's odd behavior. Maybe he was dazed or even in shock.

Chris was getting closer, not hurrying but closing the short distance rapidly. Tony could see him clearly but still couldn't understand what was wrong. Dimly, in the back of his mind, the creeping terror of what his eyes were communicating began to thaw his paralysis. All at once he understood the problem with Chris's face and he staggered back a few steps with the shock of it.

Chris *had* no face.

There was only a thick mop of ashy hair swinging to and fro as the Spaceman staggered and hunched towards Tony, a little unstable in its new Chris-body. It held out its arms—Chris-arms that ended in Chris-hands—and reached for Tony.

Tony's fight-or-flight response took command of his body and ordered *flight*. He began backpedaling, his arms pinwheeling madly as he stumbled away from the apparition that had nearly reached him. It made no noise. This was in sharp contrast to the howling cries that had begun tearing from Tony's lungs and out his tortured throat.

As he retreated into the clearing Tony lost his balance and nearly tumbled to the ground. As it was, he managed to halt and bend backward further than he would've dreamed possible, one leg dangling in space. He teetered on the edge of declivity for a second or two and then righted himself, planting his wayward foot back on the ground. He spun around, ready to launch into a sprint when his feet tangled in Chris's abandoned fishing gear. The toe of his boot slipped under the lid of the tackle-box, yanking it from the bank and sending it hurtling into the pond where it splashed loudly. Tony could not recover this time and went sprawling to the ground. He put his hands out to catch the worst of the impact and rolled away from the pond. He was moving on pure instinct now.

As he rolled, he saw the Spaceman-thing lunge with Chris's body at the spot he had vacated a millisecond earlier. It had somehow closed the distance in the blink of an eye. With a yelp Tony heaved himself up and barreled forward. His heavy, frenzied steps hammering the grass and leaving deep ruts. He didn't look back to see if the thing was able to stop its dive and recover itself.

He pounded towards the opening of the Trapper's Trail. In the few seconds between falling and regaining his footing, Tony had gotten the idea that if he could outrun the Spaceman and get beyond the other end of the trail maybe he would be safe. Like Ichabod Crane riding across that covered bridge before the Headless Horseman could catch him. Tony seized on this idea, grasping it in his mind with desperate, crazy hope. This was his mission—his salvation—to get to the other end of the trail. He never bothered to consider what would happen if the plan should fail. It didn't matter. He ran.

It only took a few seconds for Tony to reach the mouth of the trail. He smashed through the underbrush, heedless of brambles and thorns, and plunged into the thick gloom. He ran headlong at the same breakneck pace till he reached the spot where the tree-stump had startled him earlier that day. Somehow, he wasn't surprised to find that it was no longer there. A thicket of twisted briar bushes stood there instead. Some part of Tony's mind knew he wasn't mistaken about its location. It had been there beside the path just after he and Chris had come around the bend. He slowed to a jog and then to a standstill. There was the bend just a few yards ahead but there was no sign of the gnarled tree stump. His breath tore in and out of his lungs. His chest, shoulders, and thighs all burned. He allowed himself a few painful gasps before shooting a terrified glance back over his shoulder. He expected to see the Spaceman-thing standing a few yards down the path, studying him with that unnerving stillness that somehow conveyed such poisonous fury. For the moment, the trail was clear. He was alone.

Standing still in the growing darkness, Tony allowed the last few minutes to catch up to him. He covered his face with his hands and emitted a shaky sigh that turned into a squeal of fear. *Where was Chris? What happened to him?* Tony began pacing in a tight little circle there on the path. *How come this didn't happen to everybody that saw the Spaceman?* He suddenly recalled Chris mentioning someone being chased by something while they'd been camping out here. Maybe this *did* happen to everyone who saw it, or at least everyone who invaded its territory. Tony abruptly shoved these thoughts away. All that mattered was getting out to where he could find other people. He briefly considered going back to the clearing to hunt for Chris but dismissed the idea almost immediately. He told himself that it probably wouldn't help. The truth was that even thinking about going back there filled him with such a sickening dread that his breath caught in his chest. There would be plenty of time for rationalizing later. He could always return with a heavily manned search party. For now, he and Chris would have to tend to their own situations.

Tony strained and listened for any noises that would indicate something moving around out there in the dark. It was hard for him to hear over the din of his heartbeat slamming in his ears, but so far, no obvious sounds revealed themselves.

Slowly he began creeping along the path towards the bend. His head bobbed and jerked like a bird's as he tried to see in every direction at once. The gathering darkness pressed down around him creating an ever-shrinking box of visibility.

Tony knew he needed to get off this trail as quickly as possible. All of his muscles tightened as he approached the bend. Like a person who can't swim jumps into water to escape a fire, Tony forced himself to turn the corner, throwing his arms up in front of his face to ward off whatever might be waiting.

Nothing was waiting. He could see through to the other end. Pale blue twilight, shockingly brilliant against the funereal gloom of the Trapper's Trail, waited fifty yards away, beckoning to him, wanting to congratulate him on his narrow escape. Fifty running steps. His painful scowl began to melt into something that was almost a smile.

He turned to take one last look behind him before racing towards the waning but welcome light. If anyone or anything was on the trail behind him, they were far back, wrapped in a cocoon of shadows. Tony turned back and the path was still clear.

He began jogging towards the end of the Trapper's Trail. In just a few more seconds he'd be out there on the path back to the woods and then the parking lot beyond. He wasn't looking forward to making the trip back by himself with night stealing over the park, but he would hurry, and he would only look straight ahead. He would just focus on getting to the car quickly and safely.

Thinking about the car made him think about Chris. Poor, lost Chris. *Should I have gone back?* No. He nodded to himself firmly.

Chris wouldn't have wanted him to risk going back into the heart of the Spaceman's lair. Not if he had a clear escape route. If Chris was still out there and still himself, he would understand Tony's actions. Tony was sure that Chris would've done the same thing in his place and Tony would have *wanted* him too.

I'm sorry Chris. He blinked back sudden, uncertain tears. *I'll come back for you.*

Only a few more yards to go. Tony could see the edge of the tree stump with the fish carved into it. When he returned (with many, *many* more people in tow) he would bring an ax to cut that fucking thing down. Nobody else would be able to use it as a landmark to find their way back to that nightmare pond.

Suddenly up ahead, something stepped out from behind a tree just outside the mouth of the trail, blocking it and shutting out most of the light. Most, but not enough to hide the shaggy drift of hair that topped the shoulders of Chris's old army jacket. Tony was moving too fast to stop before the thing strode forward.

Without time even to scream Tony's body collided with the completely solid, completely real body that had been appropriated by the thing that had fallen from the sky and now haunted these woods. When they ran into each other it didn't so much as stagger back a step. It wrapped his friend's arms—arms Tony had punched jovially thousands of times—around his body and hugged him to itself.

Tony shrieked. His breath stirred the dank hair that hung just inches from his face. The creature's head cocked to the side curiously and finally, it began to speak. Stilted, garbled gibberish uttered in a deep, black tone. Tony couldn't understand what it was saying but somehow pictures began to form in his mind. Awful pictures. They began crowding out the thoughts and memories and dreams and emotions that made up who Tony was. His last thought before sliding into the darkness forever was to wonder how it could without a mouth.

MR. FLYSPECK

Celia stood in the foyer, looking up the staircase. Her grandfather's house was quiet. Empty. Sunlight spilled through tall windows and shadows couldn't find a foothold. It was bright and familiar, but she didn't want to be there. Not alone.

"Hello?" She felt stupid calling out. Grandpa's nursing home needed his insurance papers. It would only take a few minutes to find them. They were in his room somewhere, in a box. There was no reason to think about anything unpleasant. But she did. She thought of the attic. The creaky wooden stairs that led up to the ceiling. The huge, wooden wraparound desk against the wall. The bitter taste of pills on her tongue. The ambulance ride.

She thought of Mr. Flyspeck.

She'd been six years old, exploring the attic, looking for old toys. She'd heard a voice and looked up. She hadn't been afraid, only curious and surprised. Something was sitting on the desk. It looked like a rat or mouse. Three feet tall with orange fur and wild eyes. She remembered how it smiled at her. How it spoke.

He called himself Mr. Flyspeck. They talked about her mommy and her brothers, her grandma and grandpa. He said he lived inside the walls and could walk through closed doors. He liked to watch her sleep and take her baths. Then he told her about the pills on Grandma's nightstand downstairs. If she ate them all, she'd be able to walk through walls and doors, like him. She thanked him for such a wonderful idea and headed to her grandparents' room. She'd gobbled half the bottle before her brother walked in and caught her. She didn't remember the emergency room or having her stomach pumped, but she did remember her mother's tears shining red and blue in the spinning ambulance lights.

Grownup Celia pushed away the murky images. She stepped into Grandpa's room and opened his closet. There were boxes sitting in the shadows. She sifted through them, not finding the papers she needed. She looked up, frustrated, and saw a large, fireproof case huddled in the back corner. She crawled in and pulled it towards her. She lifted the lid and screamed, jumping backward, colliding with the wall. Lying in the case, smiling up at her, was Mr. Flyspeck.

When she'd caught her breath, Celia leaned forward and gingerly lifted the lid again. There he was, not moving or speaking. With a sudden bloom of understanding, she could see what her younger self had not. Mr. Flyspeck was a puppet. Her mind reeled. Why was this in her grandfather's closet? She studied its rodent face. It reminded her of Grandpa. A thought blossomed within her. An awful thought. She stared down at its familiar smile and started shaking it violently, hoping it might suddenly come to life and speak to her.

But Mr. Flyspeck said nothing and after a while, Celia began to cry.

GIANT

While he waited for Kevin, Ricky read the poster tacked to the telephone pole across the street. Under the words, "Missing Dog" was a black and white photo of a fuzzy mutt wearing a Santa hat and the name. The name, "Skipper," was printed below the photo along with a phone number and address. Ricky disregarded it almost immediately. He hadn't seen the thing and, besides, it wasn't his dog. He turned and called to his brother. "You're such a baby!" He leaned against the guardrail and spat a foamy wad of saliva over the curb and down into the creek below. On the sidewalk, his younger brother Kevin chewed his lip hesitantly and glanced along either side of the street to see if anyone heard. No one was out except one old lady watering her lawn four houses up.

"Am not! You're the baby. A big, fat baby *girl!*"

Ricky smiled sweetly back and shrugged. In the fall he'd be in the sixth grade and sixth graders couldn't be harmed by the feeble insults of scaredy-cat little kids. He began singing in a high-pitched, whiny voice. "Rock-a-bye Keeevin in the tree-top, when the wind bloooows the cradle will rock…"

Kevin made his way over to the guardrail and peered nervously into the shady throat of the creek. Lush, overhanging trees and bushes clung to its sloping banks. Up on the sidewalk, out amongst the well-kept yards and newly built houses, it was high Summer, hot and humid. But down there, down where the dark water whispered around large flat rocks, it would be cool and gloomy. There might be snakes. There might be all *kinds* of things. It was a wild and secret place. A dark green gash in the lacquered facade of suburban sprawl. The creek itself spilled out from a concrete culvert that ran beneath Cedar Drive. It cut a trickling, crooked course through a line of trees that rambled behind the development for miles.

Ricky saw the reluctance on his younger brother's face and sighed. "Come on man, don't you want to see an entire abandoned neighborhood? Jamie Lynch says its badass." He pulled a small flashlight from his back pocket. "We'll have this for inside the houses."

Kevin tried not to look worried. "So, we're actually going in somebody's house?"

"They're empty houses stupid. And yes. What did you think we were doing?"

Kevin shook his head. "Ricky, I don't wanna do this. Maybe Mom'll take us to the pool? We could go ask her. Let's go ask her right now."

Ricky glowered down at his little brother, exasperated. "Jesus Christ Kev, you're such a little pussy." He felt a little bad seeing how Kevin recoiled at the harshness of the word and tried to soften his tone a little. "We can go to the pool later. I want to go and see the abandoned houses." He gestured with the small flashlight, waving it vaguely at the woods. "Don't you wanna see that? It'll be like the ruins on *Johnny Quest*. We'll be like Johnny and Hadji."

Kevin squinted up at Ricky. "Well…who's gonna be Johnny and who's gonna be Hadji?"

Ricky rolled his eyes and grunted. "Oh God, *you* can be Johnny. Okay? And I'll be Hadji. You can lead the expedition and pick the first treasure to bring home." He held the flashlight out to Kevin, butt-end first. "I'll even let you carry the flashlight."

Kevin reached out reluctantly, his fingers grazing the plastic hilt of the flashlight. "What if Mom calls for us? What if we get in trouble?"

Ricky flapped his hand, dismissing this concern. "Don't be such a goody-goody. Nobody's gonna get in trouble. When was the last time Mom called for us in the middle of the day?"

"What about that time Dad came early to get us for the weekend?" The younger boy's eyes were filled with doubt.

Ricky threw his hands up in frustration and shouted. "That was a *Friday!* Today is *Wednesday.* Nobody's coming to get us. Mom's asleep on the couch. *Please* act like you've got some balls and come exploring with me. I swear to God if you just do this I'll go to school and tell everybody how cool you are."

Kevin smiled despite his apprehension. "For real?"

"Yes." Ricky hiked one leg over the guardrail and stepped onto the concrete lip of the culvert. "For real. Now come on." He climbed the rest of the way over and Kevin, with a final, longing glance back at the sunlit street, followed along.

The boys hung from the culvert and dropped, their sneakers plunging into the ankle-deep water. It was shockingly cold on such a hot day. They turned and headed up the center of the stream. Ricky made no effort to stay dry, kicking and splashing, soaking his shorts and shirt thoroughly. Kevin, by contrast, stepped cautiously from rock to rock, keeping his feet out of the water as much as possible.

They tromped along the creek for a good half hour before encountering a sharp bend to the right. The boys followed this and soon the stream narrowed to a bare trickle just a few inches in width. Thick, dark mud clung to their shoes and sticker-bushes scratched at their clothes. They hadn't seen any snakes or frogs, but bugs were plentiful. Spindly-legged mosquitoes buzzed from all around, lighting on the boys' arms, necks, and knees, drawing blood before flitting off again. There were moths, fluttering sluggishly through the shadows and a choir of crickets, cicadas, and katydids singing from the bushes and trees.

Ricky stopped, bent down, and flipped over a huge, flat stone riddled with fossilized shells, holding it up on its side.

"Want some lunch Kev?" He smiled wickedly as dozens of gigantic black water bugs trundled busily through the dripping along the rock's underside.

Kevin yelped and nearly tripped over his own feet as he back-pedaled. Ricky laughed at his brother until one of the bugs crawled over the edge of the stone and onto his hand. Ricky let out a startled scream and dropped the rock, shaking his arm wildly to dislodge the intruder. Kevin exploded into a hysterical fit of giggles as his brother hopped and jittered, howling with revulsion.

When Ricky realized the bug was gone, he became still and favored his brother with a steely glare that dried up all the younger boy's laughter. He jabbed a ferocious finger in the air to punctuate his words.

"I hope to *God* something big and nasty crawls on you like that. I can't wait to laugh my *ass* off and just watch you scream."

Kevin's expression drooped miserably. "I'm sorry Ricky, I didn't mean it."

Ricky scowled at his brother for another few icy seconds before turning and resuming the path. "Come on." Kevin followed behind silently at a distance, his shoes churning mud as he shuffled with downcast eyes.

Midday had come and gone by the time the boys stumbled out of the thinning screen of trees into a horseshoe-shaped clearing. The clearing sloped forward and then dropped twenty feet into a wide, bowl-shaped gully. At the far end of the bowl, the ground climbed back up a grassy incline, becoming the highway. The boys could see tractor-trailers, tiny in the distance, silhouetted against the summer sky. Up on the rise, the trees continued along the left-hand side of the horseshoe and became thick again beyond the gully. Ricky walked over to where the ground dropped off and peered over the edge.

"Kev," Ricky motioned his brother over with a flick of his hand, "Come here." The younger boy joined his brother at the edge of the drop-off and looked to where Ricky was pointing.

Down below, on the floor of the gully, were three derelict houses languishing in varying degrees of disrepair. All of them were tall, wooden affairs with steeply pitched roofs and gabled porches. The one closest to the highway was in the best shape of the three. It still stood, tall and proud despite its mottled, peeling clapboards and shattered windows. The posts supporting the porch-roof leaned a little to the right giving the house a disapproving sneer, but it seemed solid enough.

The house in the middle was also still standing and there were even some faded scrapes of paint left to show that it had once been yellow. However, the porch had, at some point, collapsed and now the pointed gable lay in the lap of the front yard in a pile of wood-chunks and rubble. Planking had been stripped from the outer sidewall letting sunlight in to show a decayed piano tipped over on its back.

The house closest to the drop-off—the one that Ricky planned to enter—was in the worst shape of all. No one could say what caused it to collapse in on itself. It looked as if an earthquake had shaken it to its foundation or a huge, unseen boot had come down from the sky and stomped it flat. Whatever it was had left the attic window sitting where the front door once was. Sunlight glinted off aluminum beer cans atop the roof which now hovered only a few feet off the ground. The walls had bowed outward, planks and plaster littering the overgrown yard. From the rise above, Ricky pointed down at the clapboard ruin.

"Alright Johnny," his attempt at an Indian accent was very bad. "Let us explore the ancient Mayan temple."

Kevin looked from the house in the gully to his brother's excited face. His eyes were more doubtful than ever, but he managed a shaky smile. "Y-yeah, okay Hadji. Let's take Bandit and see what's down there. Prob'ly nothing, but we need to be really careful anyway. Okay?"

Ricky clapped Kevin on the shoulder and kept speaking in his Hadji voice. "Yes, very good Johnny. Here we go!" He began making his way down the sloping brown side of the drop-off. Clods of dirt and small rocks came loose and tumbled to the gully floor as the boys half-walked, half-slid to the bottom.

The ground at the foot of the slope was hectic with scraggly weeds. The yard was an ocean of hip-high, bronze-tinted grass, waving in a late afternoon breeze. Small, nameless flying things like living dust-motes flitted gracefully above the boys' heads and soft shadows slunk forward as the day grew long.

Ricky and Kevin pushed through the grass and crept toward the house, studying the grounds with curiosity. While he was looking up into the trees beyond the gully, Kevin tripped over something hidden in the grass at his feet. "Crap." The younger boy turned and looked at the ground. "What's that?"

Ricky leaned down and felt for whatever it was his brother had stumbled over. After a moment he held up a very old, very rusty length of chain. The links were as thick as his fingers. Dangling from the chain was a dented, aluminum sign that read, *No Trespassing*. He examined the sign for a moment and then held it up to show his brother. "Just an old sign. Come on, keep going, we're almost there."

Soon the grass gave way to a pile of smashed paving and gravel and the wreck of the house loomed before them. It was like a shipwreck resting at the bottom of a trench. Ricky though about hobos and geezers—crazy old homeless men who crawled into abandoned houses or squatted under playground slides. They wore filthy coats and had ratty beards and would sometimes do stuff to little kids who invaded their hiding places. Sex stuff. And then they usually murdered those kids.

He was brave, though. Reckless and brave and excited. He wanted to explore the house very badly. He wasn't even sure *why* he felt this need. It was just something that burned through his veins like fire. He picked up a good-sized hunk of concrete and stepped toward the house. With a grunt, he launched it through the attic window and a moment later hit the floor inside with a *crash!* When there were no angry running footsteps or howls of rage to answer the thrown rock, Ricky walked right up to the crooked window-frame and peeked inside.

"Hey! Anybody in here? Heeey! We're the cops! We're comin' in!" He was greeted with silence. He turned and gave Kevin a thumbs-up. Kevin, looking very dubious, joined him by the window. Ricky smiled and patted him on the arm. "You ready for this, buddy?"

Kevin managed an unconvincing smile and lied. "Yep. Sure am."

"Alright then, here we go." Ricky reached in and grasped the sides of the old window frame, heedless of errant nails or bits of glass. He dragged himself upward and disappeared into the dark. A moment later he leaned out the window and reached down to help his little brother up. Kevin took Ricky's hands and was dragged over the sill into the musty shadows of the house.

The boys stood and looked around the room. Splintered furniture, filthy blankets, and old magazines lay scattered about the room, covered with a thick fall of dust and cobwebs. At the far end was a trapdoor that led from the attic to the 2nd floor, which now lay toppled into the basement somewhere below. That's where Ricky wanted to go poking around.

Kevin pulled the flashlight from his pocket and turned it on. Its beam looked very small and weak. "Ricky, what if there's…things…down there? You know? Bugs. Spiders. Snakes. That kind of stuff."

Ricky turned to his brother, the flashlight throwing his face into ghoulish relief. "Kev, don't worry. There's nothing in here. We would've scared it out when I threw that rock in and yelled. Don't worry. There's nothing in here but us." He strode over to the trapdoor, kicking detritus out of his way.

"Be careful, don't fall." Kevin aimed the beam of the flashlight down the trapdoor.

The collapsed second floor was little more than a narrow crawlspace. Ricky climbed down through the hole, debris falling all around him. He dropped, landing on his hands and knees, and the house groaned like an old pirate-ship rolling on the tide.

Somewhere beneath him, something snapped. Ricky froze, waiting to see if the ground was going to disappear under his feet. When ten seconds went by without that happening, he began to inch forward along the dark passage.

Shafts of sunlight cut through the gloom here and there, from holes in the ceiling and walls. What they revealed, mostly, was dust, floating in the air like a dry, scratchy mist. It got into the back of Ricky's throat making him hitch and cough. He crawled a few inches and stopped. Kevin was calling from above and behind him.

"Ricky? I don't like it up here. It's dark."

Kneeling in powdered plaster and demolished wood, Ricky rolled his eyes and shook his head. "Well, it's *really* dark down here." His shout was loud in the tight space and sent little quakes and vibrations down into the walls. It made him a little uneasy and he tried to call back with less force. "Besides, you've got the flashlight."

"I know." Kevin sounded close to tears. "But it's barely doing *anything*. Are we done exploring yet?"

For God's sake. Ricky was close to the end of his patience. *What did I bring him along for?* "Not yet. If you're not gonna come help me then shut your goddam—"

Suddenly there was a high-pitched shriek from above. "*Rick-eeeeeeeeeeeeee!*" Kevin came crashing through the attic door, slamming into the floor behind Ricky. The whole house shook as dust and debris rained down with a gritty patter.

Ricky spun around in the tight space, the floorboards groaning in protest. "Kev?" He was scared. "Kev, you okay?"

Whooping coughs answered him, followed by a tearful wailing. Ricky's heart began to hammer inside his chest. "Kevin, say something. Are you hurt?" In a panic, the older boy crept hurriedly towards his brother.

Kevin sniffled, wiping his nose with the back of his hand. "I'm okay." He was lying on his back with his knees drawn up to his thin chest. He pushed himself up on his hands, letting his feet smack against the floor. Immediately there was a sick, wooden ripping sound and a hollow *crack*. The younger boy dipped an inch or two and his face went slack with terror. "Ricky?"

Ricky felt a horrible chill spread through his body. *Oh no*. He thought. *Oh please no. Oh SHIT no*. "Kevin, I'm being deadly serious now, do—not—move."

Kevin began to whine and tremble. His voice was choked with mounting alarm. "Why? Am I gonna fall? *Am I gonna fall?*" He started squirming and the cracking in the floor became louder.

Ricky tried to calm his voice to keep from scaring his brother. "You're not going to fall buddy but you've gotta sit still." Instead of calm, the words came out clipped, as if Ricky were angry.

Kevin began to cry harder."I'm sorry! I'm trying not to move!"

"It's okay buddy, it's okay, it's okay." Ricky kept repeating the phrase as he scooted forward, hoping the words would swallow up Kevin's hysteria. The wood beneath them creaked and shifted and there was a loud *pop* like an air-rifle being fired. The brothers both froze, their wide eyes locked.

"Ricky…?" Before anything more could be said the floor beneath Kevin gave way with a mighty scream and the boy disappeared into the darkness below.

Ricky slid forward and howled, a mixture of fear and grief exploding inside him. "Kevin! No!"

He peered over the lip of the hole despite the way the floor beneath him sagged. A moment later he heard the clatter of wood hitting somewhere far below. It was oddly muffled, as if the ground below was carpeted. He waited to hear the sickening thud of Kevin's body hitting but it never came. A moment later the younger boy's voice, hollow in the huge space and full of dismay, came floating up through the gloom.

"Ricky?"

Ricky's pulse quickened. "Kevin?" He strained to pick out his brother's shape in the shadows. He squinted and there, about seven or eight feet below the hole were two white spots with another sliver of white between them—Kevin's hands and forehead. He'd managed to catch on to the edge of an old floorboard that hung out above the basement and was now dangling there. "Holy shit! You didn't fall!"

Kevin grunted. "Yes, I did."

"I know dummy, I mean you didn't fall *all the way*." Immediately, he wished he hadn't called Kevin a dummy. "Are you okay?"

"I'm scared. My arms are hurting, and this board keeps moving. I don't know how long I can hold on."

Ricky sat back and gritted his teeth, trying to think of a way to help his brother. He was sweating heavily and trying not to give in to panic. He wiped his arm across his face, streaking his forehead with grime.

His first thought was that he'd have to find a way to get down there and hoist his brother up. This plan seemed fraught with disaster, and he dismissed it almost immediately. He couldn't see the surface he'd be dropping to or how far down it was. There was no way of telling how much floor was available for walking and standing on. What if only a few scattered boards were clinging to a couple of rotting supports? What if Ricky's dropping down caused Kevin's board to move or break? What if the vibration of Ricky's landing jostled Kevin's hands free? It was unbearably risky. Without more light to help appraise the landscape of the lower floor there was no way he could safely get down to his brother.

"Ricky?" Kevin's voice was cold with terror. "There's something moving around down here, down underneath me. In the basement."

"Don't worry about it buddy, it's nothing. Probably just a cat or something." Ricky scooted a few inches back from the hole and began feeling randomly around on the floor for anything that might spark an idea. This was a waste of time, he knew, but his brain seemed stuck.

"I don't think so. It sounds *big*." Kevin let out a desperate sob. "Please hurry. It sounds big and weird. I don't think it's a cat. It sounds like it's getting closer to me."

"It's not getting closer Kev. You're up in the air."

"I think it's coming up the wall." The little boy began crying helplessly. "Please, please *please* hurry!"

Suddenly, Ricky's hand bumped something heavy. It rolled a few inches away from him. He reached out and after a moment of groping his fingers closed over the flashlight. A burst of excitement and triumph bloomed in his chest, and he smiled. "Hold on buddy, I'm gonna check your situation. I found the flashlight."

Kevin's voice was a shaky whisper. "Okay."

Ricky thumbed the flashlight on. It was surprisingly bright in the cloistered crawlspace. He lay on his stomach and shined the light down the hole where his brother was hanging. His smile vanished instantly.

Kevin's head came up and he squinted into the flashlight's beam. Ricky had guessed correctly that his brother was holding on to an old plank of flooring that jutted out over a massive stone basement. Most of the rest of the first and second floors had crumbled down into the bowels of the house. All that remained were a few splintered floorboards clinging to four or five cross-beams at either end of the room. They gave the impression of a mouth full of crooked teeth, open wide and hungry.

It was immediately clear that Ricky was not going to be able to get down to his brother. The plank Kevin hung from was wobbling like a diving board and could go at any minute. Ricky shined the light around the cavernous basement, looking for anything that might give him an idea. He swung the beam up the back wall and his eyes suddenly went wide.

Something *was* moving down there.

Far up on the wall, something seemed to flinch when the flashlight beam struck it. Ricky shined the light back down. There, again. A large (*very large*) dark, oval smudge seemed to drop a few inches below the flashlight's glow. A lump formed in Ricky's throat. Whatever that was could certainly not be what it *appeared* to be. Not the thing that Ricky's eyes were trying to convince his brain it was.

That's not possible. Sweat dripped from his hairline into his eyes. *Not in real life.* He moved the light down and the thing moved again, this time to the side but Ricky tracked it with the flashlight beam. It was too big to be spot-lit entirely by the tiny pinprick of light. It seemed to be the size of a truck tire, but it was hard to tell from that distance in the dark.

"It's moving again!" Kevin squealed. "I can't hold on!"

"Hold on Kevin, just don't move or talk or anything, I'm fig-uring this out." An overwhelming fear settled into Ricky's arms and legs and numbed his brain. He leaned forward and stared down at the floor of the basement. As the flashlight beam played across the nameless debris at the bottom of the chasm Ricky began to realize that some of what he'd thought was plaster-dust actually seemed to be thick garlands of dusty cobwebs. He scanned the floor with the light and yelped suddenly at something that had been revealed. In the corner, near a pile of flooring was a horribly familiar shape that seemed to be wrapped up in tattered bandages like a mummy.

"What is it? Why'd you scream like that?" Kevin sounded breathless.

"Nothing buddy, don't worry about it." Tears squeezed from the corners of Ricky's eyes. *What am I gonna do* What had begun as a pleasant afternoon lark had turned into a horror movie.

Kevin called out again. "Can you find some rope or something? I'm starting to slip."

Rope. He didn't know where there was rope but Ricky *did* know where there was something similar. He sprung to his feet and reached into the attic door to pull himself up. "Kevin, hold on a little longer! I'm going to get that chain from outside."

Kevin's cry was fierce. "NO!" Please don't leave me alone in here! I think that thing is a rat!"

Ricky didn't think it was a rat—not a normal one anyway but kept that thought to himself. "I have to go outside to get that chain. I'll be right back in, now quit screaming or you're gonna fall down there."

Kevin's voice trembled. "Okay but hurry up."

Ricky had hauled himself into the attic before his brother said, "okay." He sprinted across the floor to the window and quickly squirmed out, dropping to the ground. The sun, which had been shining brightly when the boys went into the house, was now hidden behind a screen of long, colorless clouds. The little gully was filled with shadows and the air had cooled. Ricky thought there was probably going to be a thunderstorm before too long.

He shot across the yard and into the long grass, kicking his feet, trying to find the chain. Now that he was outside it felt like time had sped up drastically. Every moment, he was sure, was the moment that his brother's fingers were slipping off the end of the plank, dropping him into the basement with…well, Ricky didn't want to think about *that*.

His breath was coming fast, and he began whipping grass aside, bent at the waist trying to find the chain. He found it less than a minute after bursting through the window, but to Ricky it felt closer to ten. He grabbed the chain and began reeling in the rusty links, wrapping them around his forearm. He had no idea how long it was and hadn't even considered that it might not be enough to reach Kevin. It felt like minutes were flying by, spinning out riotously and escaping with all hope of saving his little brother.

That's when Ricky heard a sound from within the house. It was very faint but unmistakable. His brother was screaming and if Ricky could hear it out here then it meant Kevin was really giving his little lungs a workout.

He turned and ran for the house, letting the unwrapped part of the chain trail behind him like a long, gray ribbon. When he reached the window, he tossed in the section he'd managed to gather up, hearing it clink to the floor as it unwound inside the attic. He leapt up at the sill, nearly banging his head on the topmost part of the frame. As he sailed back into the murky attic his brother's screams came at him in waves of increasing volume. Ricky rolled on his side and realized that Kevin was screaming words. After a moment he understood what Kevin was saying and his blood ran cold.

"*...get away, get away! Ricky, hurry up it's HUGE!*"

"I'm coming buddy, hang on!" Ricky snatched up the pile of chain that had settled in the dust on the floor beneath the window, laying it over his shoulder, and ran for the attic door. He was a step away from dropping down through the hole in the floor when the length of chain that still hung outside the window caught and jerked him right off his feet. He landed, hard, on his butt and the air whooshed out of him. The house shivered and creaked. Ricky sat there, dazed, and shook his head. Down below, Kevin's screaming rose an octave and splintered.

"*Ricky! Rickeeeeeeeey!*"

Ricky climbed to his feet, a little unsteady but unharmed, and looked back to where the chain had snagged over the windowsill. He ran over and lifted the rusted links and began hauling in the rest. It was the *No Trespassing* sign. It had bound up on the outside and gotten stuck under a piece of clapboard. Ricky shook it violently, suddenly furious at its audacity, and hissed at it through clenched teeth.

"*Ooooooh!* You piece of *shit!*" He yanked more chain, pulling it through the gravel at the base of the house, and finally, after a few moments, managed to get the rest of it through the window. All the while Kevin's impossibly high-pitched shrieks sailed up from the darkness, rattling in Ricky's ears and heart.

The older boy, now free of snags, rushed back to the attic door and slid to a sitting position. He was in a hurry but would not make the mistake of dropping full tilt down the hole. If the floor collapsed it would mean the end for both of them. He scooted to the edge of the opening and forced himself to climb carefully down. The seconds ticked by maddeningly and it felt like a long time before his feet touched wood. Once he was down in the truncated hallway, he tugged the chain in after him.

Ricky picked up the flashlight from the floor where he'd left it and shined it through the broken floor into the basement. He aimed the light at the back wall where the large, moving shape had been and the wall was bare. He shined the light all along the basement floor. No sign of anything moving. His brother continued to scream, and his cries had melted into one long, squealing wail.

"Kevin?" Ricky shouted down, trying to cut through the caterwauling. "Kev!" Kevin either didn't hear or was too scared to pay attention. Time was fleeting. It already felt like an entire day had passed since the younger boy went through the floor. Ricky couldn't waste another moment. He opened his mouth and shouted as loudly as he could.

"*Kevin shut your fucking mouth and listen!*" Almost immediately the screaming dried up to a trickle of tearful whimpering. Ricky very rarely used the "F word in front of Kevin because the younger boy always tattled. Hearing it now had shocked him quiet. A lunatic giggle tried to worm its way up Ricky's throat and he swallowed it down with a grimace. If they got out of this alive, he was going to use the "F" word *every day* from here on out. He continued in a much less aggressive tone. "Kevin, can you hear me?"

"Yes." There was a lot of panic in that quivering word.

"Where is it?" Ricky did not need to explain what he meant.

A horrible keening sound came from his brother. "Oooooh, it's up under the floor where I'm at. It's right in front of me. Ricky, it's huge." His voice was beginning to rise again in volume and pitch. "It's upside down and looking at me. Ricky, *God*!" He broke into a sob and then, somehow, managed to get a hold of himself. "It's a few feet away. I've never seen one this big."

Ricky's heart was thudding, and adrenaline shot through his veins like rocket fuel. He lay on his stomach, his arms and head positioned over the hole. He began threading the chain down to Kevin. "Is it moving?"

Ricky saw Kevin duck his head below the level of the floorboard and quickly looked back up. "No. It's just looking at me."

Ricky nodded to himself. "Alright. Look, I'm lowering this chain down to you. When it gets down in front of your face, you're gonna have to let go of the board with one hand and grab onto it, *quick*, and hold tight. Okay?"

"But I'll fall!"

Ricky continued to lower the chain. It was swinging and bumping against the planking now. "You're gonna fall if you *don't* do this. Plus, how long do you think that thing is going to just sit there and watch?"

Kevin sounded doubtful but resigned. "Okay. You're right."

"I know." Ricky took the pile of chain that was next to him and shoved it under his body, hoping his weight would help keep it from unspooling when Kevin grabbed on. He wasn't entirely sure this would work but there was no other option. "You see it?"

"Yep."

"Okay. Wanna do the count of three?"

Kevin's voice was choked with fresh tears. "Yeah, that sounds good."

"Okay." Ricky could feel his heart pounding against the floor. "Here we go. When you grab it, try to stick your fingers through the links to hold on better." His throat worked and slow tears spilled down his dirty cheeks. "One."

"I love you Ricky, I'm sorry."

Ricky sniffed and his chest hitched. "Two. I love you too buddy, don't worry about it." He took a deep breath and tightened his grip on the chain. He closed his eyes and said a very quick prayer in his head. *God? Please don't let this go wrong.* He took one more deep breath and shouted. "Three!"

Several things happened at once. Kevin let forth a hoarse shout like some ancient barbarian charging into battle. At nearly the same instant the chain pulled taut in Ricky's hands and slipped forward alarmingly and began swinging. Kevin's full weight, slight though it was, dragged Ricky and the chain further over the hole in the floor as he let go of the plank. There was a vertiginous moment when Ricky thought Kevin wasn't going to be able to hold on. He could see him down there hanging on with one hand while the other one groped at the jutting floorboard. Then he had both tiny, white hands and both legs wrapped around the chain. The strain on Ricky's arms was intense but it wasn't as bad as he'd expected. He felt like a super-hero, as if he could pull a full-grown-man up to his level. He let out a triumphant laugh.

"I got you! Kev, we did it! I got you, man!" A beautiful smile spread across his face.

Then Kevin screamed.

Something long and black and tapered had snaked around the lip of the floor down there and was pawing at Kevin's legs. Another appeared, and another, and yet a fourth, all poking and prodding at the younger boy with fluid, yet somehow mechanical, movements from beneath the floorboards. Ricky watched helplessly, horrified but fascinated. He couldn't believe what he was seeing.

Kevin's eyes shined in the gloom, wide and scared. "Pull me up! It's coming Ricky, it's coming!"

The chain began to bounce and swing, making it hard for Ricky to keep the slack beneath his body. He slipped one forearm under the chain and began scooting backward on his stomach. The flaking, rusty links pressed painfully into his skin, making him wince. He gave another mighty heave and was rewarded with a few more inches ratcheting over the lip of the hole. He knew that if he didn't sit up to gain some leverage he was never going to get his brother out.

He focused his strength on his tormented arms and began rising, first to his elbows and then, slowly, to his knees till he was on all fours. The pressure from the chain had grown immense as if there were a two-ton boulder at the end of it instead of a fifty-pound child. Ricky's elbows dug into the rough wood. As he worked his way to a sitting position his brother's frightened shrieks continued to reverberate through the ruined house.

"It's coming up Ricky! Hurry! Oh God, it's climbing up after me!"

Ricky didn't waste any energy trying to respond. He just kept tugging at the chain, straining and sweating, as he finally managed to sit up and plant his rear on the dusty floor.

He took two or three gasping breaths and then really settled into dragging Kevin up. Now, instead of only a couple of inches at a time, Ricky was able to gain five or six with every pull. He leaned back against the weight of his brother on the chain and braced himself against the floor with his feet splayed. The muscles in his arms felt like they were going to pop free right off his bones. Despite this, he began to pull faster, knowing that each link that snapped back up into the crawlspace brought him closer to getting Kevin back.

Ricky had tuned out his younger brother's squalling and concentrated all his energy on the physical act of pulling. He'd retreated into a silent chamber of focus where all he could hear were his own grunts and the clinking of the chain against wood. With reserves of strength he didn't know he possessed, Ricky began hauling up longer segments, hand over hand. He'd found a rhythm and was rocking back and forth, the burning at his elbows and shoulders far from his mind. I

t was almost anticlimactic when Kevin's hand, waving madly at the end of his skinny wrist, popped up through the hole in the floor grasping madly for the sides. The younger boy found the floor and grabbed it, helping Ricky in the final massive tug that brought Kevin up from the depths of the house. His top half burst through like a fish breaching the water, and he flopped down into the dust between Ricky's feet, sobbing.

With a startling crash, the world and all its cacophonous racket slammed back into Ricky's head, shoving him out of his reverie. He let the chain fall from his raw, bleeding hands and grimaced as his arms began cramping up. He wanted to lay back and close his eyes for a while but the floor was bending and creaking beneath their combined weight. He knew they needed to get back up to the attic.

"Kevin. Hey, I got you man!"

Kevin had his face buried in his arms, crying and moaning. He didn't answer.

"Kev, come on. You gotta get up so we can get out of here. You wanna get out of here, don't you?" When his brother still didn't respond Ricky's frayed nerves snapped and he hissed with fury. "You get your *ass* up off of that floor. *You hear me?*"

Kevin finally choked back his tears and raised his head. His face was streaked and filthy, his hair matted with sweat. He looked small and frail, like a cat rescued from a well. "I'm sorry, I'm just scared—I'm sorry. Please don't be mad."

Ricky cut off Kevin's apology with a wave of his hand. "Shut up. Don't worry about it. Let's just get out of here before this floor drops us both down there."

"What about the giant…"

"I said *shut up*. We're getting out." Ricky had decided that probably, in their panic, he and Kevin had imagined something climbing around on the wall down there. He doubted they'd seen anything at all. The silk-enshrouded mummy and other odd shapes were just old garbage covered in dust. It didn't matter anyway, they were leaving.

Ricky helped Kevin carefully to his feet and hefted the smaller boy up through the attic door by his underarms. As Kevin's feet left the ground the floor beneath them bowed ominously downward. "Hurry up." Ricky stood on tiptoe, waiting for his brother to finish pulling himself up into the attic. A moment later Kevin clambered the rest of the way through the door and Ricky followed, wincing at the pain in his shoulders and arms.

Once they were on the much more solid floor of the attic, they both collapsed onto their backs, breathing heavily. Kevin's skinny sides heaved in and out under his ribcage and Ricky's arms, hands, and legs shook and spasmed.

A few seconds passed. Ricky sat up, leaning on his hands, and coughed. He looked over at Kevin, the smaller boy wheezing in the dust, and called out to him. "Hey. You okay over there?"

Kevin lifted one arm into the air and gave a thumbs-up. "I'm alright. Thanks for saving me."

Ricky sighed. "Yeah, no problem." He cocked his head and frowned. "Hey, you hear that?"

Kevin lifted his head off the floor and listened. After a moment he nodded. "Yeah. What is that?"

Before Ricky had a chance to wager a guess, four long, probing legs, as thick around as Kevin's shin, rose up through the attic doorway, clicking and clattering against the floor. Kevin screamed and was on his feet in an instant, backing away towards the window.

"Holy shit." Ricky's eyes popped wide as he watched the thing crawl up into the attic only a few feet away from them. There was no denying it now.

A massive spider, gray-black and hairy, yanked its fat abdomen up over the edge of the trap door, its legs spread around it in a seven-foot span. Two smaller appendages pawed the air above its head and Ricky could see its slavering mouth parts working furiously beneath a constellation of eight shiny, black eyes. It made a strange hissing sound, like air escaping from a basketball and it bounced lightly on the sharp tips of its feet as it faced the boys.

Ricky began backing away, not hurrying but not moving slowly either. He heard Kevin scrambling up onto the windowsill and out of the house behind him and was glad. If anything happened in here, Ricky wouldn't want him to see it. Hopefully he'd be climbing up the rise and out of the gully in a minute or so.

The spider scuttled forward a few inches for every couple of steps Ricky took backward. It was surely capable of great speed, but it seemed hesitant. *Maybe it's not used to being out of the basement, away from its web.* Ricky could feel his pulse in his throat. The spider's questing footsteps reminded him of pencils being tapped against desks and Ricky absurdly wished that he would survive to return to school in the fall. Suddenly, he felt his lower back collide with the windowsill. There was nowhere else to go.

Ricky didn't know whether to turn his back on the huge, palpitating creature and hurry out head-first or try and climb out backward and drop. If he dropped, he risked hitting his head on one of the large chunks of concrete that lay beneath the window.

The spider was not pausing in its approach now. It continued towards Ricky with a hypnotizing slowness. It had closed most of the distance and was almost withing grabbing distance. *Screw it*, he decided, *I'm going out backward.*

He placed his palms against the sill and hoisted himself up and out the window in one fluid movement. There was a nauseating drop and then he hit the ground, gravel digging painfully into his back. Almost immediately the spider was climbing out the window, its drowsy scrabbling replaced with wicked speed. It raced down the front of the collapsed gable, its long legs pistoning wildly. As Ricky dragged himself off the ground, he heard a voice calling from the field behind him.

"Ricky! It's coming!" Kevin was standing in the tall grass watching the scene unfold, mouth agape.

Ricky sprinted through the broken terrain of the yard, listening to the typewriter sounds of the spider's legs as it gave chase. He knew that he could never hope to outrun it. He imagined how it would feel to have it sink its enormous fangs into the back of his neck, paralyzing him so that it could spin a gauzy suit of silk for him. Ricky closed his eyes and tried to put a little extra steam in his stride.

"Stay away from my brother!" Kevin's voice rang out clear beneath the cloudy sky and echoed around the gully. Ricky opened his eyes in time to see a small piece of concrete leave his brother's hand. It sailed past Ricky and crashed into the ground behind him. It had missed its intended mark but suddenly the furious scurrying sounds stopped.

Ricky risked a glance over his shoulder and saw the spider had stopped and risen up on its four back legs, its front legs undulating hideously in the air. He stopped and faced it, realizing the ground at his feet was littered with chunks of rock and concrete of all sizes. He picked up a large piece of flagging and whizzed it at the spider. *His* throw did not miss. It struck the creature hard between its third and fourth legs on the left side. It made an awful squealing sound and scrambled backward towards the house.

Ricky picked up another piece of rock and threw it, catching the spider on top of its head near its crown of eyes. It flattened to the ground for a moment, its legs jerking with confusion. Ricky backed up till he was standing next to Kevin in the field. From this distance, somehow the spider's size was even more impressive. It was as if their father's easy chair had grown legs and started walking around. It looked dizzy and stunned as it reversed across the yard.

Kevin whispered beside him. "I've got two more rocks if it looks like it's gonna chase us again."

Ricky nodded, his gaze utterly possessed by the gray-black monstrosity that was, even now, squeezing itself into a space beneath what used to be the porch. He could see it hunched in there, watching them.

Where had it come from? He wondered. *How did it get so big?* And on the heels of that, *Was that mummy-thing in the basement really a dead person?* He found himself remembering the missing dog poster back in the neighborhood. He wondered how many posters this thing was responsible for.

As the questions rolled around inside his head, thunder rumbled from somewhere beyond the rise. Ricky felt a drop of rain on his nose. It was going to storm soon.

"Come on Kevin, we need to get home."

Kevin took Ricky's hand and the older boy, usually disgusted at such gestures, let his hand be held. They backed away from the ruined house never taking their eyes off the twitching black shape beneath the porch until they were halfway up the rise.

As the brothers climbed out of the gully, it occurred to Ricky to wonder what sort of nightmares might be hiding in the other two houses down there. Strangely, he felt a wild urge, far back and deep down, where his brain met up with his heart, to go back and explore them. *Not today though.* He smiled to himself, putting his arm around Kevin's thin shoulders as the rain began to fall. He looked over his shoulder, taking one last look at the forlorn houses. The giant was nowhere to be seen.

Not today...But maybe someday.

THE 16TH FLOOR

"Scott, can you come back here a second?"

Scott looked up. He'd been reading movie reviews and was afraid that maybe his manager Dean had somehow caught him doing it from the computer in his office. He walked down the aisle slipping between gray-walled cubicles, bumping his elbow against the massive printer at the end of the row.

"Oh, sorry," Scott said to no one as he rubbed his arm where it struck the copier. No one noticed his collision or heard his apology.

Scott stepped into Dean's office which was really just two and a half plexiglass walls screwed into the floor. Inside was a desk on rollers covered with photographs of Dean and his friends engaging in various forms of outdoor activities. There were no pictures of a wife or children because he had neither. Dean was a believer in the joys of bachelorhood or so he'd said during Scott's job interview. Scott wouldn't have said that he disliked Dean—he seemed to be a decent enough guy and he'd been friendly so far—but there was something about him that made Scott wary. Dean reminded him of an excitable dog who might suddenly bite during a game of fetch.

"What's up, Dean?" Scott started to lean against the doorway of Dean's office and then, realizing how flimsy the "walls" were, stood up quickly, shoving his hands into his pockets.

"Not much buddy. Not much." Dean swiveled around in his office chair and looked up at Scott. "Need you to do me a favor."

"Alright."

"No hesitation. Good man." Dean leaned back in his chair. "The uppers have decided they want to go paperless, which we've mostly already done, but there's a whole shitload of what we like to call, 'the Ancient Files' upstairs." Dean made air quotes with his fingers. "Some of these files probably go back thirty years or more. There's not much reason for us to still have them but every now and again a few of the more senior clients need a record or somebody dies and the lawyer in charge of the estate requests one. So, we want to audit them to kind of sift through and figure out which ones we really need to hold on to and which ones we can chuck." Dean picked up a coffee mug with the words, "Da Bomb" written on the side from his desk and took a quick sip. "What I need you to do is to take a list of files, go up to 16, hunt them up, and then bring them back down here and box them up for the Accounts manager."

Scott hoped the boredom in his voice wasn't obvious. "Yeah, okay. Sounds good. You want me to head on up there now?"

"Not yet. It'll take me a while to get you a list together." Dean's friendly grin froze up a little bit. He turned toward his desk and flipped through some scattered papers. "Oh yeah, and I guess I should tell you. The 16th floor—its, well—abandoned I guess you'd say. There's nobody working up there and hasn't been for years."

Scott nodded again. He didn't know why Dean thought it mattered to him whether or not there was anyone working on the 16th floor, but Dean went on.

"I guess it can be kind of creepy up there." He chuckled, clearly embarrassed. "I know that sounds stupid. I'm just saying it's a mess. I'm not sure the custodians ever actually go up there. If they do it's not often and some of the lights might be out. That wasn't even our office originally. It was some import business or something. We just kind of shoved the Ancient Files up there after they moved out. There's still a bunch of their crap laying around. Some of it's pretty weird. I've only been up there once or twice." Here he paused and took a long sip from his coffee. "You should just be careful not to trip over anything or hurt yourself. I would just go get the files as quick as possible and then come on back down. We don't want this project to take more than a couple of days. Okay?" Dean shot him another mealy grin.

"Yeah, I got it." Scott was intrigued. Now he couldn't wait to get up there and start poking around. He liked old things, and he liked weird things.

As a kid, he'd been an avid junk collector. He'd scrounge through thrift stores with his mom on Saturday afternoons where he'd grab up anything he could convince her to buy for him. He'd once gotten an old Underwood typewriter for four dollars. It still had a ribbon in it and had worked for years after. He also had a set of wooden warriors (complete with a dead, speared lion) and a set of dinosaur cookie cutters. Even as an adult he'd collected a few quirky odds and ends sand the prospect of going up to an abandoned office floor and hunting through a bunch of old stuff was very appealing to him. They couldn't even call it stealing if he took anything because it hadn't belonged to his company in the first place.

Scott took a step back into the main aisleway. "Just let me know when you've got the list together and I'll get started."

Dean gave Scott a thumbs-up and went back to flipping through the papers on his desk.

***

When Scott returned from his lunch break that afternoon there was a thin sheaf of papers, held together with a clip, waiting on his desk. It was the list of files he was supposed to bring back from upstairs. He took his jacket off and draped it over the back of his chair and then, with list in hand, walked over to Dean's little office.

"Hey Dean, I'm going on up to 16 now."

Dean was at his desk with an oily Italian sub in front of him. He half turned and held up his hand for Scott to wait. "Alright man," he said around a mouthful of half-chewed sandwich. "When you get up there get off the elevator and go to the hallway on the right. The first doorway you see is the one you want. It used to be suite 350 or something but there's no actual door there anymore." Dean hefted his sub and took another chunk out of it.

"Gotcha." Scott gave a little half-wave. "See you in a little bit." He turned and started to walk away. He had only taken three steps when Dean called his name.

"Hey Scott, listen..." Dean regarded Scott solemnly. "While you're up there..."

"Yeah?"

Dean paused a moment, his eyes troubled, and then breathed a tiny sigh. "While you're up there try not to goof off too much. Okay?"

Scott chuckled. "Oh yeah, of course. I'll just get the files and get back down here."

Dean shot him another thumbs-up. "Excellent. See you soon my man. Good luck." Dean turned back to his sandwich.

In the lobby, Scott's footfalls clacked and echoed off the granite floor tiles. He walked up to the elevator, pressed the button, and waited. A few moments later there was a *ding* and the door opened. A young man with glasses and lanky brown hair stepped out. He had a McDonald's cup in his hand and was sucking noisily on the straw, trying to get the very last drops of soda from the bottom of the cup.

Scott nodded to the soda drinker, whose name was Matt. "What's goin' on man?"

Matt disengaged his mouth from the straw. "Not much. Where're you headed?" They passed each other as Scott stepped forward and stuck his hand in the elevator to keep the doors from closing.

"I'm going up to 16 to pull some old files."

Matt's eyebrows went up. "16? Good luck." He shook his head as he walked into the hallway sucking away at his drink.

What the hell? Scott stepped into the elevator, and let the doors close him in. He didn't really know anyone at Jarvis and Lloyd very well yet. Matt had trained him on the office computer system and was probably the person that Scott had interacted with the most except for Dean. He made a mental note to ask Matt later what the deal was with people wishing him good luck. He reached out his hand and pushed the button marked *16*. The elevator jerked upward three floors and stopped. The dinger went off and the doors opened.

Scott stepped off the elevator and into the lobby. Several of the fluorescent lights were out. Many were flickering and weak. Across the lobby against the wall was a small table that held an incredibly dusty vase. The last remnants of the plants that had withered and died there hung sadly over its lip. Scott shook his head and looked to his left. A dark hallway ran perpendicular to the lobby. The electric lights along that side had gone completely dark. One small triangle of sunshine spilled out of one of the abandoned offices to cut through the gloom. A galaxy of dust motes floated gracefully in that scant burst of light. The air had a musty, forgotten smell, and silence filled all the empty spaces.

Scott thought that there was no way the custodians had been up here recently. It looked to him like no one had been up here for months.

Scott turned and walked into the other hallway. There were at least a couple of lights still on, but they only accentuated the neglect. There was a doorless doorway that opened into a larger, mostly unlit space. That was where Dean had said the Ancient Files were.

On the floor along the wall sat the remains of a business hastily abandoned. There were cardboard boxes lined up outside the doorway in both directions. Scott leaned over and examined them. Most were filled with stacks of old papers; forms, invoices, requisitions, and the like all with the name "Midwest Imports and Artifacts" printed across their tops. One of the boxes held what seemed to be random office supplies and Scott hunkered down for a closer look.

Crouching within the box were a stapler, a cup full of various pens and pencils, a couple of pocket-sized calendars, some other odds and ends, and something Scott couldn't identify. He reached in and pulled the object out. It was a small statuette about six inches tall. It looked like a naked man with the head of an owl. It had a square base and was carved from some kind of dark, gray stone. It was quite heavy. He grinned. This was just the kind of thing he liked. He set it back in its box. He thought maybe he would retrieve it when he left. He stood back up and glanced down the hallway. It went on for a little way beyond the office where it hooked left to meet up with the dark passage on the other side of the lobby. Halfway down, on the left-hand side was an alcove which, based on the layouts of the other floors, Scott guessed was a restroom. There were no lights on back there. It was cavernous and forbidding somehow. He didn't think he'd be using it, no matter how badly he had to go. Sitting just outside the alcove, alone and out of place was an old office chair. Looking at it, Scott wondered who had left it there. *How long ago had* that *been?*

"Hey! Anybody up here?" Scott wasn't expecting a response, and none was forthcoming. He stepped through the doorless entrance and into the gloom of the large suite. Weak sunlight fought its way through the grime-covered windows at the back of the office. Against the wall, as promised, were five massive filing cabinets. They were all taller than Scott and together spanned half of the length of the office. *Jesus Christ*, Scott thought, his gaze sweeping from one end to the other, *there must be a thousand files in there.*

With a sigh, he consulted the list he'd been given. The first file he needed was for **Worghum, Alan A**. There were a few squat desks scattered throughout the space and he turned to the nearest one and set his list down on it. There was an old calendar-blotter on the desk that caught his eye. It was dated from four years before. The letterhead read, "Midwest Imports and Artifacts" *("bringing the outside world in")* just like the papers in the boxes outside. There was also a Midwest Imports stick-it note resting on the blotter, its stickiness long since departed, the corners curled up like the legs of a dead bug.

He looked around at the lonely outcroppings of desks and chairs and tried to imagine people working here. He could almost see them, on their phones, setting appointments and trying to placate clients; walking up to the desk by the doorway to maybe pass a few flirtatious words with the pretty (or so Scott imagined her) receptionist. He walked over there, his files forgotten for the moment. The reception desk sat behind a low, "J" shaped barrier. A few yellowed gum wrappers littered the floor beneath the desk. *How appropriate*, Scott thought, *they had a gum-chewing receptionist. Maybe they had a wise-cracking mail—carrier too. Could've made a sitcom.*

Suddenly, he realized that he had to pee. He temporarily put his make-believe show on hold and made his way out into the hallway. The moment he stepped out of the office Scott felt something was wrong. He looked down the hall towards the dark and cavernous restroom. *Not going in there, that's for sure,* and scanned the boxes along the wall. He peered out into the elevator lobby, but he couldn't quite put his finger on what it was that was bothering him. It was a disquieting feeling like he'd discovered someone was going to play a prank on him.

"Hello?" The word slipped hesitantly out of his mouth. No one answered back and his bladder reminded him that he had places to go. He walked into the lobby and pushed the *down* button for the elevator. He intended to head down to the first floor, hit the restroom, and then go out to have a cigarette. After that, he'd come back up and get started on pulling those files.

It was just as the elevator's bell went off that Scott realized what was different in the hallway. The chair that had been sitting by the bathroom, adrift like an empty life-boat, was no longer there. He spun around and walked quickly back into the hall, leaving the elevator to open onto an empty lobby. He looked to where the chair had been and found only bare carpet. He peeked around the corner of the doorway into the office and didn't see it anywhere in there either. *Am I sure there was a chair there in the first place?* It had only been a few minutes ago that he'd been out there examining the contents of the former Midwest Import and Artifacts Company. He remembered thinking the chair was creepy just sitting out there as if an invisible someone had been sitting in it, watching him. The answer was yes, he was sure.

"Alright then." Scott backed out of the hallway and into the lobby feeling slightly uneasy. He stepped up to the elevator and pressed the button again, casting a look over his shoulder as he waited for it to arrive. When the bell dinged, and the doors opened Scott stepped in as quickly as he could. He pushed the first-floor button repeatedly until the doors slid slowly shut. Once the elevator began its descent he leaned against the back wall and laughed inwardly at himself. His anxiety drained away almost immediately. He was still sure there had been a chair in the hallway the first time he'd been out there but as he sunk into the well-lit world of the lower floors, it didn't seem to matter so much. Sure, it was weird but weird things happened all the time. *No big deal.* The elevator arrived at the first floor and the doors opened letting in a flood of comforting noise.

Scott stepped out and joined the mass of people coming and going. He waved to the security guard, Ray, as he passed on his way to the restroom. After relieving himself he walked past Ray once more as he headed for the revolving door at the front of the vast foyer. The first-floor lobby was the complete opposite of the one on 16. It had been re—modeled a few years earlier and gleamed with shining glass and marble.

"Hey Ray, how's it going?" Scott called as he strode past, pulling a pack of cigarettes from his shirt pocket.

"Can't complain, Scotty, can't complain. How 'bout yourself?" Scott turned and walked backward for a moment. "Not a lot. Just goofing around up on 16." He turned back around and kept walking. He did not see the expression on Ray's face as it soured at the mention of the 16th floor.

***

Twenty-five minutes and two cigarettes later, Scott found himself back upstairs in the funereal lobby on 16. He crossed the hallway and stepped into the office. The chair he'd seen outside the restrooms was still missing and he was still puzzled by this, but pushed it from his mind. He walked over to the desk where he'd left his list and grabbed up the cluster of papers. He examined it for a moment, noted the first few file names, and then set off to find them.

He walked up to the cabinet furthest to the right, muttering to himself. "Worghum. Worghum." He leaned in close to the drawers searching the labels for the right set. "Where are you buddy?" He went back to his list and checked Worghum's file number. **1139**. He jogged back over to the cabinets and found the drawer marked 950-1150. He knelt and pulled it open, gritting his teeth at the loud metal scream. In just a few seconds he had the thick green folder in his hands. It had the same smell as the old paperbacks that Scott would get at the thrift stores with his mother, the moist, forgotten smell. He took it over to the desk with the old calendar-blotter, which he was now thinking of as his desk, and dropped it next to the list which he picked up and consulted again.

Scott gathered nine more files, trotting back and forth between the cabinets and his desk. Outside the filmy windows the sunlight began to weaken as afternoon slid casually towards dusk. A single fly buzzed, unenthusiastically around the office, lighting occasionally on the relics left behind by the departed Midwest Import company.

Scott crouched in front of the second cabinet from the right. He'd just pulled **Lucas & Sons Funeral LLC** (*file#1506-a*). He shut the rattling drawer and stood up, his knees popping. He turned around to take the file to his desk and nearly tripped over the young woman who had been standing there directly behind him.

"Whoa, shit!" He cried, startled, taking two fumbling steps backward and nearly falling. The woman, who didn't seem startled at all, watched Scott with her hands clasped behind her back, smiling like a sleepy cat.

"Hey," Scott said, regaining his composure. "Didn't see you there. Sorry about that." He took a deep breath and smiled down at the woman. She was shorter than he was with frosted brown hair that fell, thick and curly to just above her shoulders. She had a smattering of freckles across her nose and cheeks, and wore very red lipstick. She stood there, still not speaking or moving, petite in a white blouse and tight gray slacks. Her eyes were big and brown and they sparkled with amusement. Scott thought she was cute, and he was sure he'd seen her around the building before, though he wasn't sure when or where. He reached out to shake her hand.

"I'm Scott, by the way. I work down on 13." His hand remained un-taken extended in space and hovering for a few long seconds while the woman smiled up at him wordlessly. Her eyes were fixed on his and Scott's face suddenly flushed as the awkward moments ticked by.

What's the deal here? He wondered. *Does she not speak English?* He was just about to pull his hand away when the woman reached out and grasped it, shaking it delicately.

"I'm Angela."

"Hey. Yeah, nice to meet you, Angela." Scott grinned as the tension broke and melted away. "What floor do you work on?"

"Downstairs." Angela dropped his hand and crossed her arms under her bosom. "I like to hang out up here sometimes though. It's quiet. And weird."

Scott chuckled. "Yeah, that's for sure." He glanced around the office as if to verify this statement. "How long has it been empty like this?"

Angela moved, sidling over to Scott's desk, and brushing her hand against the calendar blotter. "Four years or so I guess. Maybe five." She rose up on tiptoes and slid her butt onto the desktop. Once she was comfortably seated Angela swung her feet slowly to and fro.

"Really?" Scott eyed her with doubt. "You think that long?"

"Well, I mean—that's what this calendar says." She pinned him with her wide, dark eyes as if she were trying to see through his skull and into his brain. The little scarlet smile remained pert and amused on her lips.

"Yeah but, that can't be right. Can it? Maybe that was an old calendar when these guys moved out."

Angela shrugged her tiny shoulders, the gesture oddly birdlike. "I guess maybe. I don't really know." She gazed down at the calendar and was quiet.

"I can't imagine that they'd let a whole floor just stay vacant for four years. They would try to lease it to *somebody*. Wouldn't they?" Scott chided himself inwardly. *You sound so goddamn boring right now.*

Angela shrugged again without looking up from the calendar. She was gently rubbing the palm of her hand over its yellowed, wrinkled surface, caressing it. "Maybe they've tried."

This girl, Scott thought, much like the floor they now occupied, was a bit on the eccentric side. The way she stared and the way she smiled—there was a quiet aggression about it that made him a little nervous but also a little excited. He wasn't sure yet that he liked her, but neither could he say that he didn't.

"So what department are you in again?"

Instead of answering, Angela looked up at him suddenly and asked a question of her own. "Have you been to the office on the other side yet?"

"Um," Scott faltered for a moment at the sudden change of subject. "No. No I haven't. Is it cool?"

"*Is it cool?*" She rolled her eyes as if Scott had just asked if money was a good thing to have. "It's the *coolest.*" She giggled and hopped up from the desk taking Scott by the hand. "Come on. You'll really like it over there." She turned and began dragging him along as if they'd known each other for two years rather than two minutes.

Scott allowed Angela to pull him out the door and across the lobby to the dark corridor on the other side. He was struck again by the fact that no one had been up here to fix the lights. He couldn't believe, however, that this floor had been without occupancy for half a decade. That just didn't seem possible.

They stepped through the open door of the second office. As they crossed the threshold Angela let go of Scott's hand and took off on her own across the room. He watched her go, enjoying the way her backside moved beneath the tight fabric of her pants, and then took a moment to survey the vast asteroid belt of objects that lay spread out before him.

The office with the Ancient Files in it had a few bits of detritus left behind by Midwest Import. Mostly these were just items that attested to the fact that someone once had a business there, little more than empty desks and derelict chairs. In this second office, however, items of genuine fascination had been left behind. It was as if, on their last day, the Midwest Importers had simply stood up, taken their phones, and exited the building leaving everything else behind.

Scott walked over to a table to his left. Stacked upon it was an iron and glass treasure trove trimmed in brass. Old nautical devices, barometers, sextants, compasses, and other things Scott couldn't identify had sat gathering dust here for God knew how long. He knew almost nothing about antiques and had no idea if these were authentic, but they certainly looked and felt old. He picked up a heavy, brass-encased compass, wiping away a layer of thick grime from around the face. Scott flipped it over and looked on the back for a label. Stamped into the casing was the name "E. Ritchie-1866-pat."

"Holy shit." Scott turned the compass over and gently set it back on the table with the other mariner's items. He walked around the table and looked for something else to examine. His heart was pounding in his chest. *This is amazing.* Dean had told him there was "weird stuff" up here. *Was he kidding? Did he even know what this stuff was?* Scott had trouble believing that anyone who'd been up here hadn't looted the place entirely. It was a junker's gold mine, a hoarder's wet dream. On the far wall was a low shelf and spread across it were small knick-knacks, books, wooden toys, statuettes, candelabra, and paraphernalia of all kinds.

Scott strolled over to a large bookshelf near one of the windows. It was probably a highly valuable item in its own right. It was made from a dark, rich wood, mahogany maybe, with elegant spirals carved from top to bottom on either side. There were only a few old books still leaning drunkenly against each other here and there within the bookshelf's shadowed frame. Scott glanced at the aged spines reading the titles that were printed in English. On the bottom shelf, shoved as far back as it would go, he discovered a small, ornate wooden box. He hunkered down and dragged it out from its resting place and into the wan light of the office. The box had a small plaque attached to its lid which was covered with words in a language that Scott wasn't familiar with. There was a lock on the front of the box but when Scott tried the lid it opened easily on silent hinges.

Inside was a book that looked much older than all the others on the bookshelf. Its binding was a thick and weathered vellum, stained yellow-brown and blind-stamped with a strange, looping design on the front and back. Scott had never held anything that felt so full of history. Something about the weight of it in his hands and the texture of its cover was unsettling. It felt *dangerous*; like a hoary old crocodile pretending to sleep until some foolish creature ventured close enough for it to snap its jaws around. With wonder, he opened the book to the title page. Imposed over a depiction of many figures writhing in agony in a myriad of poses and positions (*Hell*, Scott assumed) was a marquee that declared the book's title as the *Alphabetum Diaboli*. There was more writing underneath, but time and moisture had distorted the letters and it seemed to be in another language anyway. Scott opened to a page in the middle. It showed a diagram of several pointed stars nested within one another and covered with strange symbols and numbers. Only one word on the sheet was remotely recognizable to him.

Exorcismus.

He felt goosebumps rise along his arms as a chill slithered through him and he shut the ancient text.

"Scott?" Angela's unexpected voice came from directly behind him, just like before, and startled him into dropping the book gracelessly into its box. She had once again managed to sneak up on him without a sound.

He stood up quickly and faced her, smiling but red-faced. "Jeez Louise, you're good at sneaking up on people, aren't you?"

She was standing very close to him, the buttons of her blouse a mere breath away from the ones on his shirt. She didn't answer but just stood and looked up at him with that wide-eyed, probing stare. After a few silent seconds, Scott made a nervous sound that was something between a clearing of the throat and a long sigh. He took a step back and broke the moment by looking up and out, across the office.

"Man, have you seen some of this stuff?" He inwardly cringed at the adolescent fluster in his voice.

Without saying a word or changing her expression Angela stepped forward and pressed her body against Scott's, wrapping her arms around his waist, her hands coming to rest lightly on his hips. The moment he felt Angela's hands on him Scott lost his breath. It wasn't that women made him particularly nervous but something about her predatory stare made him feel small, young, and weak. It was a look that seemed to say "I wonder how you taste?" Like an owl regarding a rabbit.

"Did you find anything interesting?" Her strange, searching eyes would not let him look away again.

Scott started babbling about the book he'd found. "Yeah," he said, looking down into the vacuum of her gaze, "I found this crazy old book. You want to see it?"

Angela pushed in closer, her pelvis grinding softly against him, her little smile widening into a shark's grin. She shook her head, her curls bobbing softly against her cheeks.

"Nope. Want to see what *I* found?" She licked her moist, red lips slowly and salaciously.

A blissful heat settled over Scott, flushing out the awkwardness. "Yeah, I'd love to see what you found." His voice came out smooth and assured, much to his surprise and relief. He leaned in towards Angela tilting his head, his mouth parting slightly as he anticipated the soft press of her lips on his.

At that moment his cell phone began to go off in his pocket, buzzing and vibrating from around his crotch. The unfortunate timing of the call shot an arrow right through the moment, deflating it. Angela cocked her head to the side, her eyebrows going up quizzically.

Scott straightened up and took a step away from her, his face pinched into an expression of disappointed apology. "Sorry." He reached into his pocket, dragged the squalling device out, and glanced at the screen. "It's my boss." Angela watched him, saying nothing. He accepted the call and held the phone up to his ear. "Hey, Dean, what's up?"

"How's it going up there?" Dean's voice had a hurried, distracted quality to it and the reception seemed remarkably bad.

"Good, I guess." Scott's eyes flicked over to Angela and smiled. "These file cabinets are kind of tough to navigate though. I haven't actually been able to pull that many files."

"Yeah, I gotcha man, they're a royal bitch to deal with." Dean made a tired sighing sound into Scott's ear. "Well, it's almost five. Why don't you just bring the ones you've got on down and tomorrow you can get started bright and early."

"Okay, I'll get them and be down in a few."

"What was that?" Dean's voice was fuzzed with a snatch of interference. "Didn't hear you there Chief."

Scott turned away from Angela and walked a few feet towards the office door, trying to improve his signal. "Dean? You there?"

"Yep. That's better."

"I said I'll be down in a few."

"Sounds good partner. See ya in a sec." Dean hung up before Scott could say anything else and Scott closed his phone, shaking his head.

"Hey, sorry about that. That was my…" He turned to where Angela had been standing and found the spot was empty. He looked around the office, his eyes skipping from pile to pile of Midwest Imports' exquisite remains. She wasn't in the room anymore.

"Angela?" Scott called out. "Where'd you go?" He walked into the elevator lobby crossing the semi-lit passage into the other office. "Angela?" It only took a glance around to see she wasn't in there. He came back out into the hallway and looked towards the black cave of the restroom. *Could she be in there?* He wondered.

Suddenly a disconcerting thought occurred to him. When had Angela actually come up to the 16th floor? He realized that, even if she'd been quiet enough to sneak up behind him while he was pulling files, he would certainly have heard the elevator bell ding if she'd come up from another floor. She must have been hiding out in the restroom (or around the bend where the two hallways connected—he hadn't explored down there yet) since before he'd come up. *Why would she do that?* He couldn't really guess why but considering her strange behavior it didn't seem too far-fetched. She wouldn't even tell Scott what floor she worked on. *Does she even work here?* That was a disturbing idea, but Scott knew he'd seen her around the building before, though he still couldn't place exactly when or where that had been.

It was with a dizzying sense of discomfiture that Scott packed up his files, grabbed his list, and left the 16th floor. He did not call out for Angela again as he stepped out into the hallway, and he did not look over his shoulder to see if she was standing silently behind him as he waited for the elevator to arrive.

He stepped out into the comforting artificial light of the 13th floor and strode into his office with the files from upstairs tucked under his arm. It was almost five o'clock and there were very few people left working. Scott passed through the aisle of mostly empty cubicles, deposited his things on his desk, and went to Dean's office where Dean was locking his desk drawers.

"Hey Scott," He said looking up, "just getting ready to head out. There's about a half-dozen beers with my name on them waiting at WingsWorld."

"Cool. Hey, I left those files over on my desk." Scott hooked his thumb back toward the corner. "Did you want to look at them before I left or anything?"

"Nah. We'll wait till the end of the day tomorrow to see what'cha got there Chief." Dean stood up and clapped an amiable hand against Scott's shoulder. He walked around and said goodbye to the designer who sat across from his office, and then suddenly stopped, turning back to face Scott.

"Hey, man. Was there, ah, anybody up there? I mean, did anybody pop up there to…see what you were doing? Harass you? Anything like that?"

Scott wondered if Dean knew about Angela. He wanted to ask, just to satisfy his curiosity about the strange woman he'd met up there, but decided against it He didn't want it to sound like he was up there fooling around while he was supposed to be working and he didn't want to get her in any trouble either. He had no idea if she and Dean knew each other or if Dean might know her supervisor. It wasn't just work reasons, though, that kept Scott from mentioning her. Now that he was back down here the whole scene up on 16 seemed to take on a dreamy haze. It felt like something that had happened to him while being intoxicated and he couldn't quite remember the details properly. It just seemed like too much to try and explain. "Nope," Scott said, shaking his head. "Just a couple of sleepy flies."

Dean shot Scott a thumbs-up. "Alrighty then pal, see you tomorrow." He turned and walked out the door.

Scott put his hands in his pockets and took a deep breath. He walked slowly over to his desk (bumping his elbow against the copy machine again), put on his jacket, and went home for the night.

***

The next morning arrived gray and drizzling. Thunder rumbled irritably across the horizon and the occasional flash of lightning lit up the sky to startle the slow wakers who were still waiting for their coffee to brew.

Scott rolled into the lobby a few minutes before seven, shaking rain from his dripping umbrella. At that time of morning, only a few bleary-eyed stragglers were moping their way to the elevators or waiting in line at the commissary. There was also Ray the security guard standing with his hands in his pockets in front of his desk, his guard's hat cocked back on his head.

Scott had not slept well the night before. He remembered slipping through a jostling tumble of vague and uncomfortable dreams, tossing and turning, and sweating his way towards dawn. He'd woken up with a headache thudding at the back of his skull and his first thought after, *ugh, my head hurts,* was of the girl he'd met the day before. He was determined to find out who she was and where she worked. He wanted to ask about her bizarre behavior from the day before. He also just wanted to see her again. Something about her made him want to get close to her.

Scott nodded to Ray as he walked past and received a "G'morning," in return. He'd nearly turned the corner to the elevators when it occurred to him that Ray saw everyone who passed through this lobby day in and day out. Surely he'd seen Angela before. He probably knew her well.

Scott turned around, nearly running into a somnolent woman in a long, wet coat ("*Jesus. Fuck.*" had been her half-hearted response as she dodged around him) and hurried over to the security desk.

"Help you with something Scotty?" Ray asked curiously.

"Hey, Ray. Yeah, maybe." Scott fidgeted a moment, trying to think of the best way to ask about Angela. "I've got kind of a weird question."

"Well, I can't say I'm surprised. Everybody goes up there has some kind of question about it."

Scott blinked, nonplussed. "What?"

Ray blinked back at Scott awkwardly. "Wait. What are you asking about?"

"I was going to ask you about a girl that works here. What did you think I was asking about?"

Ray's eyes did a strange little back-and-forth dance in his wrinkled face. "Oh, hell, I don't know. It's early. I think I'm still half asleep." Ray fiddled nervously with his hat. "You go ahead and ask what you wanted to."

Scott felt a low weariness drain through him. He suddenly wasn't sure he still wanted to know anything about the dark-eyed girl who'd grabbed his hand so confidently the day before. He thought it might just be better for him to go upstairs, get this project over with, and get on with his life. He'd already pestered Ray though and decided to go ahead and ask. "Eh, it's no big deal. I just wanted to ask about this girl I met yesterday. Angela. She works here in the building somewhere."

Ray seemed to recover himself. "Oh. Sure. Was it Angela Duncan or Angela Haverkast?"

"See, that's just it. I don't know. We met and just kind of hit it off while I was pulling files, but I never got her last name or which department she was in."

"What does she look like?"

"Well," Scott ran his hand over his wet head, "She's cute. Short and skinny. Curly brown hair."

Ray considered for a moment. "Well, that sounds like Angela Duncan, I guess. You got yourself a new work buddy"?

Scott shrugged. "I don't know. We were just kind of goofing around up on 16. I was getting the feeling that—" He was going to tell Ray that he was getting the feeling that she kind of liked him and then realized how childish that would sound, at least to his ears. "Ah, never mind. It's no big deal. I was just curious."

Ray favored Scott with an odd expression. "You say you guys were messin' around up on 16?"

"Well, not really, *messing around,* so much as just looking at all the crap that's up there. You ever checked that stuff out?"

Ray leaned against the security desk, wincing. "Ugh, these rainy days are hell on my knees." He straightened up and regarded Scott solemnly. "Yeah, I've been up there plenty of times. Not for a while though."

"There's a lot of crazy shit up there."

Ray nodded. "I know. Listen, did she go up there with you yesterday?"

"Scott shook his head. "Nah. She just sort of showed up while I was getting files. To be honest it was kind of weird. I didn't hear her at all till she said my name. Didn't hear the elevator go off or anything. It was like she just appeared out of nowhere."

"Mmm, hmmm." Ray looked up at the ceiling. "Well, listen Scotty, better that you don't go poking around too much up there. A lot of that stuff is old, and it's been up there a long time. Better to just not go up there at all."

"Well, I can't *not* go up there today. I have to keep getting these stupid files." Suddenly he remembered he had another question for the old security guard. "Oh yeah, and is it true that nobody's had a business up there for almost five years?"

Ray didn't say anything for a few moments. He and Scott just looked at one another letting the space between them thicken. Finally, Ray spoke.

"It's been a long time. I don't remember how long. Just be careful up there around all that old junk Scotty."

Scott rolled his eyes. "Why do people keep saying that? Is it haunted or something?" He suddenly realized that he was talking loudly. He lowered his voice. "I mean, I could just about believe it."

Ray stepped behind the security desk and sat down on his chair. He looked down into the little closed-circuit video monitor that showed him views from various cameras around the building. "You ought to get up to work Scotty. You're gonna be late."

Scott looked up at the wall clock above the commissary door. "Dammit. I'm already late." He turned and headed towards the elevators. "Later Ray."

Ray waved to Scott's departing back and went on looking at the security monitor.

Scott stopped on 13 long enough to stow his jacket and umbrella at his desk. He grabbed a donut from a box that someone had left in the break room and then headed straight upstairs. Heavy, ashen clouds clung to the sky outside and the 16th floor was even darker and more dismal than it had been the day before. The rain slopping against the building sounded like low, chattering voices and Scott kept turning to glance behind him as he worked, trying not to be caught unawares again by Angela (or anyone else).

All morning long he roved back and forth from the filing cabinets in the abandoned office to the small desk where he set the files he pulled. Names and numbers slid across his mind like lines of marching ants (**Williamson, Axel T.** (*file#1201*), **Bellamy Financial Services Inc.** (*file#240-a, 240-b*), **Southern Ohio Builders** (*file#766*), **Lance, Friedrich and Friedrich Wealth Management** (*file#418*)—it all became a litany of meaningless gibberish in Scott's mind. If anything, or anyone watched him from anywhere in the office, he didn't notice it. Scott had found a groove and lost himself in his task. By the end of the morning, he had pulled more than half of his list. Another couple of hours and he'd be completely finished.

At noon Scott decided to stop for lunch. He thought a sub sandwich from the commissary sounded delicious, so he left his files and the dank office behind and took the elevator downstairs. The doors opened onto the first floor, and he stepped out thinking that a little carton of chocolate milk might be nice too. He planned to take his lunch and eat outside under the overhang and watch the rain come down. Despite how unsettling the day had started, Scott thought was beginning to go rather well.

As he was passing through the lobby Scott noticed a small, feminine figure standing at the security desk chatting with Ray. She was wearing a cream-colored cardigan and a brown skirt today but there was no mistaking those springy curls.

He veered over towards the security desk and slipped up next to the woman, leaning in close. She looked up and regarded him curiously. Ray stood back and watched, his eyes flat, his mouth tense.

"Hey, what's up?" Scott smiled broadly down at the woman. "What happened to you yesterday?"

The woman's dark eyes reflected confusion and nothing more. "I'm sorry?" She took a step back, putting some space between herself and Scott.

"You know. You disappeared after my boss called." He noticed she wasn't wearing the distinctive red lipstick she'd had on.

"W*hat?*" The woman pulled her cardigan close around her. Compared to the birdlike grace she'd displayed the day before her movements were jerky and awkward. "I'm sorry, you're thinking of someone else." A harsh, nervous little laugh fell out of her mouth in a breathy rush. "We've never met."

His smile faltered. *What kind of game was she playing?* Somehow Scott wasn't entirely surprised. She had been a whirlwind of crazy behavior the day before; sneaking around, spying on him, staring at him, grabbing onto him. *She likes to freak people out, make them uncomfortable. It's how she gets off.*

"So, you don't remember me *at all*? You don't remember meeting me yesterday up on the 16th floor? Hanging around with me? Nothing?"

The woman goggled at him, unbelieving. "What are you talking about?" She sounded outraged "I'm sorry but you've obviously got me confused with somebody else, guy. I told you, I've never seen you before in my life."

Scott nodded and let a sarcastic smile spread across his face. "Okay, you're right, I must be crazy. We've never met, *Angela*. You didn't sneak up behind me—twice—yesterday up on 16 and you didn't...well, you know what else you *didn't* do."

Her mouth dropped open and her eyes flicked from Scott to Ray. She looked genuinely scared. "Ray? Who is this guy?" She took another step back. "How does he know my name?"

"It's okay hon," Ray said as he came around the desk and gestured reassuringly at Scott. "Scotty's new here. He don't know a lot of people. He just got you mixed up with somebody else. Angela Haverkast probably."

"But she's fat." Angela protested. Her voice held none of the sultry lilt that it had the previous afternoon.

Scott looked at Angela while Ray tried to allay her fear. She really did seem to not know who he was or what he was talking about. There was no mischievous glint at the corner of her eye and no hint that she was putting on some kind of an act. Her disavowal was very convincing. *Does she really not remember me??*

He suddenly felt his anger at Angela's supposed mind-game disappear, replaced by a deep, chilling embarrassment. A mortified knot grew in his gut, twisting and bulging. His gaze dropped to the floor.

"I'm sorry." Scott's voice was very quiet, very low. "You reminded me of someone I met up on 16 yesterday."

"See?" Ray's mouth stretched into a strained smile. "It was just a misunderstanding."

Angela stepped away from Ray's security desk and fixed Scott with a suspicious glare. "I've never been to the 16th floor. I didn't even know there *was* a 16th floor here." She gave Scott one last disapproving look and then turned and walked away. Before she was out of his earshot, Scott was able to catch only one word amongst her angry muttering: *Psycho.*

Scott stood rooted in front of the security desk, stunned and embarrassed. He watched Angela walk away and felt doubt, like a physical ache, roiling through his body. He knew, absolutely *knew* that he hadn't been mistaken about her identity. The woman who'd just rebuked him there on the first-floor lobby was the same woman who'd flirted with him (in the strangest way possible) the day before in the deserted offices upstairs.

In another way, however, she was not *at all* the same woman. The 16th floor version of Angela had been confident and lithe, her movements deliberate and poised and silent as star-shine, her voice a dark, velvet purr. First-floor Angela, by contrast, struck Scott as being nervous and angry. *To be fair,* he chided himself, *this impression of her is based solely on how she reacts when a strange man walks up to her and accuses her of trying to bang him in an abandoned office.* He acknowledged this point in his mind, but the concession didn't change the fact that this person seemed to be just another harried worker flitting through the building like a distracted ghost.

Ray walked over to Scott and touched his arm. "You okay Scotty?"

Scott looked at Ray with naked confusion. He wiped the tips of his fingers across his dry lips and shrugged loosely. "I don't know man." He gestured to where Angela had just been standing. "I swear I met that chick yesterday. I really did, but she was completely different from that lady. Same lady, but different lady." He uttered a crazy little laugh. "Sorry, I know I sound like a nut."

Ray patted Scott lightly on the back. "No need to be sorry, I believe you. Well, I believe you met *someone* anyway. Someone that looked just like her."

Scott shook his head. "She told me her name. Told me her name was Angela."

"I know," Ray favored him with solemn eyes. "Listen, since you're working up there I should tell you a few things about that office, but I can't do it right now. I can sneak away for a few in," Ray glanced at his wristwatch, "about twenty-five minutes."

"What do you mean? What kinds of things?"

Ray shook his head. "Not out here. We'll go sit outside where we can smoke." Ray circled back around behind the security desk and sat down, checking the monitor. "You probably won't believe what I have to tell you but considering the couple of days you've had, you might after all."

Scott felt a gauzy film of unreality drift down upon him.

"Alright." He looked around the lobby as if he'd just woken to discover himself in an unexpected place. "I have to go back up there and get my files. I'll drop them off in my office and then I'll come back down here."

"Ah," Ray's bushy, gray eyebrows drew together with disapproval. "That's not a great idea." He pointed to the line of people standing outside the commissary waiting to place an order. "Why don't you go over and get yourself something to eat—they've got clam chowder in the deli today—and go wait for me out at the tables."

"I have to get those files to Dean. I'd really like to have this shit done by the end of the day today. I don't really want to be up there any more than I have to."

"I know Scotty, but trust me, Dean would understand—"

"It's okay." Scott seemed to have come back to himself somewhat. "It'll only take a few minutes. Then you can tell me whatever it is you want to tell me." Scott rapped his knuckles on the security desk and then, without another word, turned and hurried back to the elevators. Ray watched him go and when Scott turned the corner, he looked down at the three security screens, glancing up from time to time to utter a greeting or a reply to the rain-soaked figures who walked past.

***

The elevator doors opened onto the familiar dusk of the 16th floor lobby and Scott stepped out as a roll of thunder rattled the windows and walls. He had intended to do exactly what he'd told Ray, which was to go in, grab the files he'd gathered, and head back down to 13. Now that he was up there, however, a strange impulse drove him to the opposite side back into the treasure den left behind by Midwest Imports and Artifacts. He had an urge to take a very quick look at some of the items he hadn't had a chance to peruse the day before.

The storm light from outside the windows painted the suite in blue-gray shadows and Scott felt like he was walking into an aquarium. He let his gaze meander across the silent and dusty huddles of objects that waited around the room. He passed a table with the old nautical items on it. and walked over to a shelf along the back wall. This was where he'd noticed all of the jumbled knick-knacks the day before. There were a number of dead things mounted on white backing and framed behind glass. Butterflies, rhinoceros beetles, a huge millipede curled up in a spiral, several large scorpions, a tarantula that was bigger than Scott's open hand, and an emaciated, mummified bat. There was a stack of small rugs next to a glass case that held a delicate-looking pair of spectacles. Further down the shelf past some mismatched marble chess pieces Scott found a collection of jewelry. Elaborate beaded bracelets and gaudy necklaces all lay tangled together like a nest of shiny, chunky snakes next to a silver display case full of rings sheathed in red velvet.

None of the jewelry held much interest for Scott and he was about to walk away when his eyes happened upon a small, oval brooch. It was made of opal, inlaid with ivory. The ivory was carved, very intricately, into the shape of a tiny carousel horse. It was a lovely little piece, strung on a simple, silver chain. Scott picked it up and looked at it closely. The carousel horse was incredibly detailed with minuscule ribbons threaded through its mane and tail and wound in a coil down its carven pole. He thought his mother would love it. She had a decent collection of carousel items—snow globes, collector's plates, things like that— but no carousel jewelry. Scott imagined her face lighting up as he handed it to her. He imagined her surprised gasp and her grateful smile. There was no way he could leave this piece here knowing how happy it would make her, so he slipped the brooch into his pants pocket. *Nobody's gonna miss this...*

He took one last look around the office, still amazed at the fact that all of this stuff was just sitting around up here undisturbed, and then turned and walked out into the elevator lobby. He crossed to the other side and was about to step through the doorless doorway to get his stack of files when he heard a sound from halfway down the hall. He jerked to a stop and turned around, his pulse thumping in his ears.

He wasn't sure because the sounds of the rain, the muttering thunder, and his own footsteps had melted together into a cluttered, distracting wash, but Scott thought it had sounded like a word.

In fact, it sounded to Scott like it might have been his name.

He stood motionless, trying to filter out the background noises and straining to catch any other sound that might explain what he thought he'd heard. A moment later, it happened again, and this time there was no doubt about it. A fuzzy, echoing voice called out.

"Scott. Sco-ott."

The hair on his arms and neck stood up and a chill slid down his spine like a drop of ice water. The call had come from the inky depths of the restroom. He waited to see if it would come again.

"Scott. I'm in the bathroom. Come find me."

"Oh, Jesus." Scott took a breath. "Angela?" He hadn't meant to call back. He had, in fact, meant to turn around and quickly walk to the elevators. This seemed like the perfect time to get downstairs and meet with Ray to hear whatever it was he wanted to talk about (although now Scott thought he had a pretty good guess what that might be). Instead of moving out of the corridor, his feet actually carried him *forward* a step towards the restroom. "Angela? Is that you?"

"*Scotty.*" The distorted voice was low and jagged. It bounced merrily around the tiled bathroom walls sounding horribly present and horribly *real*. Whoever it was, it was definitely not Angela (Duncan *or* Haverkast, Scott was very sure of that). His eyes widened and his heart began to pound in his chest.

He started backing away towards the elevator getting ready to turn and run when he caught another sound from within the lightless restroom—a deliberate echoing shuffle. He realized, with terror, that it was the sound of feet scraping slowly (*but not too slowly, not slowly enough*) across the tile floor towards the entrance. Towards *him*.

Whether it was someone playing a prank on him or whether it was something else entirely, Scott had finally had enough. With arms and legs flailing he fled into the lobby. He slid to a stop in front of the elevators and began slamming his open palm repeatedly against the button.

There was a clap of thunder and suddenly the already weak lights of the 16th floor flickered. "Come on. Shit, come on." Scott resisted the urge to turn and look behind him. He pressed himself against the wall and continued to pound the elevator button.

"Comeoncomeoncomeoncomeoncomeon."

The bell dinged as the elevator arrived, to Scott's enormous relief.

That's when he heard the voice call from just behind him in the lobby. "*Scotty it's me.*" There was a tone of oily glee in that cracked voice. It was a voice that reminded him of black water sluicing through gutters choked with decaying leaves and clumps of garbage.

He didn't want to turn around and see. The doors to the elevator were opening. He could jump on and wait for them to close behind him without facing whoever, or whatever it was, that was calling his name in that low, craggy voice. He didn't want to, but he did anyway. Scott spun around with a panicky jerk and looked.

He let loose a sharp, hoarse cry of horror when he saw who it was. He knew that it couldn't be her but there she was, grinning at him viciously through violently red lips, holding her arms out to embrace him.

It was his grandmother, whose funeral was the only one he had ever attended.

"*Scotty.*" His name dripped from her dead mouth. It looked like she'd pressed her lips into the open guts of a fresh road-kill.

Lipstick was smeared all over her cheeks and chin. She looked up and out at him from beneath her brows like a coyote as she shambled forward. A string of saliva hung from her lower lip. She was wearing a blouse that Scott remembered well from his childhood, a polyester nightmare from the seventies covered with large blocks of vibrant colors. She had worn it all the time and when she was alive Scott had found it whimsical. Now that she was ten years in her grave (or rather out of it at the moment) it looked more like Grammy was wrapped in a cocoon of vomit.

"Grammy please." Scott began to cry, his back to the wall now as he tried to shrink into himself. He didn't notice that the elevator doors had closed and that it was on its way back down. "Grammy please don't." Tears spilled from the corners of his eyes as he shook his head back and forth trying to disbelieve this apparition into nothingness.

Instead of going away Scott's dead grandmother lurched ever closer. She seemed very solid, not at all how he would imagine a ghost to be. She cast a shadow on the floor that undulated in the watery light from the windows. He could hear her tiny, grunting breaths as she scuttled towards him. She didn't move very fast, but she was only a few feet away now. Her eyes were horribly bright and shone with hideous delight. Her long, bony fingers grasped and twitched like spider's legs as she reached out to take him into her arms. Her feet shushed across the smooth tiles, the black orthopedic shoes she'd always worn scraping and clacking. Her tongue wormed out from between her square, yellow teeth and licked across her lips leaving a ropy scum of spit.

Suddenly there was a bright flash of lightning. A moment later an ear-shattering crash of thunder rattled the building, and the lights went completely out. Scott was plunged into almost total darkness. He sank to the floor, weeping.

In his worst, deepest, unremembered dreams he had never come across a vision so repulsive and now he was alone in the dark with it. He wasn't sure if it was worse to have to face its bright, greedy eyes and its drooling red mouth, or if it was worse not to see it but wonder where it might be. Pitched into blackness he realized the sound of it scuttling through the echoing gloom of the foyer was worse than either one.

He covered his face with his hands and screamed, waiting for the moment when she would hug him, just as she had when he was a boy. Would she be cold? Would she smell? Scott continued to shake his head in negation, unable to conceive of what would happen once she reached him. Through his fingers he could just make out her bobbing shadow as she crept forward.

She was almost upon him when the elevator bell dinged, and the doors opened. Ray sprung out into the lobby with a lit flashlight in his hand. He swung it around and the light strobed across the shape of Scott's revenant grandmother like a noxious kaleidoscope. She had been crouched down right in front of Scott's face reaching her long, branchlike arms around him.

When the light struck her, she looked up in shock. Ray waved the flashlight, shouting. "Back! Get back you old bitch!"

The storm continued outside, the rain pounding hard against the windows. Thunder rumbled like a giant's footsteps and Scott's paralysis shattered. He sprung to his feet on shaky legs. "What's going on?" He screamed at Ray as the security guard brandished his light like a gun at the hissing thing before them. *What is it, Ray?*"

Ray waved his free hand fiercely towards the elevator. "Hurry up, push the button. She ain't gonna sit still for long." The grandmother-thing was crouching there in the yellow beam of light like a huge, pale scorpion. Its mouth was still stretched into a hungry sneer, but its eyes were filled with murky confusion. It looked from Ray to Scott and back again, seeming unsure as to whom it should approach.

Scott, heeding Ray's instruction, pressed the elevator button and waited. Ray was shining the beam of the flashlight on the apparition which seemed to have lost some of its boldness. It stood before them, no longer grinning, its arms lowered. It scowled at them looking like a spoiled child being denied candy. It was slowly starting to lose its resemblance to Scott's grandmother. Its skin had begun to yellow, and the arrangement of its face began to change. The features were spreading and widening, and the corners of its mouth now stretched nearly to its ears. Its eyes had grown into large, unblinking circles and while Scott couldn't see it happening in real time, it seemed to him that the thing's nose was thinning and elongating.

The elevator bell dinged behind the two men, startling them and the doors slid apart. Scott dashed behind Ray into the chamber, having never been so happy to see the bank of buttons that marked the floors below. He put his hand out to hold the doors open for Ray who stepped quickly back from the lobby floor and over the threshold. Scott wondered if the thing would try to charge in as they waited for the doors to close. He pressed the button for the 1st floor and took a deep breath. He removed his hand from the opening and the doors began to shut.

The thing in the lobby did not try to advance on them but simply stood there, watching as they fled. Illuminated by the narrowing light of the elevator's interior, it no longer really resembled a human being at all. The elevator doors clicked shut in front of Scott and Ray's faces and the sight of it, standing, alone and disappointed on the 16th floor was cut off. The elevator began to descend taking them back to the world of sanity and light. Neither man spoke on the trip down and Scott leaned against the wall, breathing deeply, wiping tears from his face.

***

They were in Ray's tiny office. It was little more than a large closet that held a metal desk and a three-drawer file cabinet with a very old television sitting on top of it. There was also a coat rack and a couple of mismatched swivel chairs and that was all there was room for. There was no smoking permitted inside the building but both Scott and Ray were puffing on cigarettes anyway. Smoke filled the little box of a room and floated lazily towards the ceiling fan that spun above them. They sat that way for some time. Finally, Ray broke the silence.

"So, I guess you figured out the 16th floor's not a great place to be." Ray dropped the butt of his cigarette into a styrofoam cup that still held a couple sips worth of coffee in it. There was a hissing sound as the stub hit the cold liquid.

Scott nodded his head slowly, looking down at the floor between his feet. "Yeah. Yeah, you could say that." He took a long drag on his cigarette, looked up at Ray, and exhaled. "So could you tell me a little bit more about that please?"

Ray sat back in his chair and gazed up into the gently spinning blades of the ceiling fan, crossing his arms. He sat that way for a moment, taking time to consider how to begin and then he looked back over at Scott.

"Well." He frowned and cleared his throat.

"Look." Scott flashed a rueful grin. "I'm obviously going to believe whatever it is you say. After what we saw up there, I'll believe anything anybody ever tells me for the rest of my life."

"Okay," Ray began. "The thing is, I don't have any for sure facts. I just know what I've seen and what other people have told me they've seen." Ray lit another cigarette, his third since they'd gotten to his office. He took a puff on it and went on. "I guess it started when that company up there, Midwest Importers, left. Well, for all I know it started even before they left. Maybe that's what made them leave. Who knows? Anyhow, one day they just sort of up and moved out. Had to be five years ago or more. I know I've been here goin' on ten myself and I'd been here awhile when it happened. Can't remember if I'd gotten my five-year set of wine glasses yet but it was damn close to that."

"Four years. That's what the calendar up there said." Scott tried to rub the chill from his arms. "Now I guess I know why nobody ever moved back in."

Ray nodded. "Only four? Seems longer than that, but time starts to get fuzzy at my age." He shook his head with a contemplative sigh and went on. "But yeah, I think that is exactly why nobody else ever took over those offices. Oh, people would come and look the place over. Your company thought about takin' over that floor not long after they vacated. That was probably the worst it ever was before today. Your boss Dean had himself a nasty scare up there."

Scott gaped with surprise. "Dean? Are you serious?"

"Yep. He's one of the ones that helped put those those big old file cabinets up there in the first place. He's the reason there's no door on that office."

"Shit, I knew he was being weird." Scott shook his head. "Why would he send me up there if he knew? What happened to him?"

"Well, Scotty, they still got a business to run you know? Can't stop makin' money on account of your building is haunted. If it makes you feel any better, he probably didn't like making you go up there. He seems like a nice enough kid." Ray blew smoke out from the corner of his mouth, so it didn't go into Scott's face. "Back when he first started they got him and another guy—Pete? Tommy?—I can't remember, to heft those file cabinets up to the 16th floor. It was a Saturday. They didn't want 'em disturbing the office during the work week.

The import people'd been gone about a year or so I guess and nobody'd really done anything with it yet. The custodians had started to talk amongst themselves. I hadn't seen anything—yet—

but I heard somebody say once that they wouldn't go in the bathroom up there anymore 'cause they saw a ghost in there. I laughed about it then."

Ray picked up the cup they'd been using as an ashtray, swirling the contents, and went on. "Well, so Dean and this other guy start luggin' those cabinets up there on dollies. There's a freight elevator in the back up there around the corner from the offices. They rode up and down for a good couple of hours getting those big-ass things set up.

Round about that time, so far as I know, the guy helpin' Dean went out to use the bathroom and left Dean in the office by himself. When he came back out the door to the office was shut tight and Dean was on the other side screamin' his fuckin' head off. That guy, Pete-or-Tommy or whatever, tries and tries to open the door but it won't budge. Meanwhile, he hears Dean in there screamin' at somebody and he hears somebody else's voice in there with him screaming back, laughin'. Pete-or-Tommy didn't have a cell phone so he ran down the stairs to 13 and called down to the security desk. He was damn lucky I was there. I don't always work weekends and when I don't there ain't nobody down here at the desk."

Scott wasn't sure what he was feeling about this whole experience but he suddenly felt bad for thinking such un-generous thoughts about Dean. "Jesus Christ, what happened to him?"

Ray set the cup back down and shrugged. "Well, I picked up the phone and that guy told me somebody's locked in the office with Dean up on 16 and

that they're fighting or something. I told him I'd meet him up there and I grabbed my keys and my flashlight, which is the only goddamn weapon I'm allowed to carry, and I hurried on up the elevator.

"I was some concerned because I knew that nobody else should've been up there. On weekends, everybody that comes in the building has to sign in at my desk and there were only four or five other people besides Dean and what's-his-face working. I doubted very much it was any of those folks and wondered who the hell could be up there causing trouble." He paused a moment to take a breath before continuing.

"When I stepped off the elevator what's-his-name—wait, *Dave*! Shit, I remember now, his name was Dave—well, he was pounding on that office door hollerin' and I can hear Dean on the other side just pounding back, screamin' and crying and I could hear that other voice too, laughing like I don't know what. It shook me up some bad. Whoever the guy was in there with Dean sounded *big*.

"Well, we pulled at that knob and yanked and pried and couldn't open that door for shit. I mean, the knob turned in our hands, it wasn't locked, but the door just wouldn't come open. I realized we were gonna have to take the door off so I tell Dave to wait there and keep trying the door and I headed back down here to grab my toolbox. I got back upstairs and now Dean's just whimperin' like a beat puppy on the other side of that door and the voice on the other side has *changed*. Now it was a high-pitched voice, like a woman's or a little kid's and it was singing to him. Loud. Oh god, but it was an awful sound. Made my balls crawl up into my belly like a turtle into his shell.

"How many fuckin people are in there with him?' I asked Dave and he said he didn't know. He said the singin' started just a couple of minutes after I left to get my tools."

Ray's cigarette had burned down to the filter, unsmoked between his fingers as he told his story. He dropped it absently into the cup and sighed. "Well, I got out my electric screwdriver and started undoing the door hinges. It took a few minutes and I was sweatin', wonderin' what we're gonna find when we got in there. The door started leanin' as I got each hinge off and finally the last one popped off. The door falls out into our hands and me and Dave tossed it aside and busted in there like SWAT.

"Dean was crumpled up against the wall next to the door just sobbin' and hitchin'. His eyes were screwed shut tight and his arms were up over his head. All the singin' and shoutin' had stopped but both of us—I swear this is true—we both heard this giggling coming from the *other* office across't the lobby. I told Dave to get Dean outta there and get him downstairs so I could go over to see what was what. I was some younger then and braver. I was ready to bust some ass." He chuckled softly, his eyes looking haunted.

"So, I got over into that other office. You've been in there so you know how crazy it is—all that shit layin' around everywhere. Plenty of things for at least one person to hide behind but not really anywhere for a big fella to go. The laughing had stopped by this point. Dave and Dean had gone on downstairs and it was dead quiet. All's I had was my flashlight and all of a sudden I got a real bad feeling. I called out, 'Whoever's in here better come out right fuckin now!' I tried to sound real hard, but I was nervous as hell.

Then I heard a voice from right behind me say my name. I turned around and that was the first and the *worst* time I ever saw something up there."

Scott had been waiting for this with dread and fascination. "Holy shit, what was it?"

Ray was quiet for several long seconds, just breathing loudly through his nose. Finally, he spoke. "It was my wife. Naked. Covered in blood and holdin' this big ol' hatchet down at her side. There was more blood and other gooey shit drippin' off the head of it. She just smiled up at me and licked her lips. I'll never forget that look on her face. Like she'd just baked a pie and wanted me to try it and tell her how good it was."

"Damn Ray." Scott's eyes flicked to Ray's desk. There was a graduation picture of a young woman Scott assumed was Ray's daughter or niece (or even granddaughter) but it was the only one he had. "Is she…I mean, was she?"

"What? Dead?" Ray shook his head, "Nah, she's alive. Alive and kickin'. Hopefully she's makin' me chili tonight, I feel like I could eat a whole pot of it right now." He stopped and had a coughing fit into his fist for a moment, a dry, rattling sound deep in his chest. When it passed he went on. "I knew right away that wasn't really her. There was no way in hell she was standing there in that office with her tits hangin' out covered in blood and God knows where she would've gotten an ax from. I screamed like a little girl and took off runnin'. I turned to see if she was following me but there was nobody there. I was all by myself. I took the elevator down to check on Dave and Dean. Dave quit not long after but somehow Dean managed to stick it out, but I guarantee he's never gone back up there again. In fact, I have only been back up there a handful of times since then. I hate it up there." He started to pull yet another smoke from his pack and then decided against it, putting the pack back on the desk.

"Well, we never could get Dean to tell us what it was he saw. He got calmed down some and said he didn't want to talk about it. We told him we'd believe whatever he said. I didn't tell him then about what *I'd* seen. I have since, but at that moment I was too shook up to think about it much less talk about it. I did tell him, though, that we heard other voices in there with him and knew something had been in there. He wouldn't budge though. Never has neither. He went so far as to say he saw some folks that couldn't have been there but he wouldn't say who or what they were doing to him. All he'd say is that they showed him things. Awful things. After awhile we just left it go and decided not to talk about it no more.

"The files got put up there and so nobody needed to tell anybody else anything. One of the custodians found the door and called me about it a few days later. I told him we'd taken it off and forgotten to move it. He went and put it in a storage closet and s'far's I know it's still in there somewhere. He never did ask why we took it off."

Scott was astounded. "Wow. Dean." He leaned back in the rickety chair and ran his hands through his hair. "How does he still work here after that?"

Ray shrugged. "Eh, you get past it, Scotty. Sometimes you can't let something like this chase you off of a good job. I bet Dean's makin' good money up there. He's got that nice little car and he's always travelin' around. He does well for himself. Worked his way up. If he'd left over that who knows where he might've ended up. You'll see for yourself." Ray grabbed a half-finished bottle of water from the desk and took a swig from it.

"I mean, hell. I've seen shit off and on for years ever since that day. After that, it's mostly been on the security monitor but it's still kind of upsetting. Speakin' of which, that's how I knew you were in trouble. After you had your little moment with Miss Angela—sorry you had to go through that by the way. That was tough to watch. I figured I should keep an eye on you and there's a few camera's on every floor. I was watchin' you on the one above the elevators up there. Soon's I saw you start runnin' for the lobby I knew I needed to get my ass upstairs. Let me tell you, son, your *incident* might not have lasted as long as Dean's but it was every bit as bad. I hate to ask but, who was the…you know. Who was it pretending to be?"

Scott looked down at his feet again and answered in a meek whisper. "It was my Gram—my grandmother. She's been dead a long time."

Ray sucked air through his teeth with a hiss. "Yikes, that's bad Scott. I'm sorry." He looked down at the floor, not wanting to see Scott's wounded expression any longer.

"Anyhow, the custodians kept getting spooked. I watched it happen sometimes. I'd see 'em up there working and suddenly they'd jump and spin around like something was behind 'em. I got no sound on the monitors so I never know what they're hearin' but it sure keeps 'em from going up there. They've actually gone through two clean-up companies since this shit started. Sent in a nice crew of Spanish ladies. I felt real bad for 'em but what could I say? You can't really tell people about that so much.

"That first agency had a few people up and quit before they terminated their contract. After that, they went back to hirin' their own people. I don't know if the building owners tell them they don't have to go up on 16 or if they just look the other way but they've had the same couple of guys now for a few years. They don't really go up there too much unless a pipe bursts or something. That's happened before and I was asked to accompany them while they fixed that. Didn't see nothing at all those times.

"Nobody has much reason to go up there anymore so I don't know how it's gotten around so much but everybody kinda knows that there's something wrong with that floor. I know a few people have gone poking around up there. Maybe a few just went up out of curiosity or *because* of the stories they'd heard.

"However it happens, word's gotten around and now the whole building has a reputation. People say they've heard and seen stuff all over the place, but I've never had anything happen anywhere but up there. I check every floor a couple times a day except for 16.

"Sometimes I start feeling guilty about not doing my job completely and so I sort of poke my head in each office up there. Couple of times I've heard my name. Once I looked in the hallway and saw a young woman I didn't recognize just standing there by the bathroom, lookin' at me. Smiling. She didn't say nothing and so I just backed away and pretended I didn't see her. If I came across an actual person up there, I'd never even know it. I always just assume it's that whatever-it-is."

"What is it, do you think?" Scott asked. "A ghost or something?"

Ray sat and thought for a minute. He shook his head. "No. I guess if you consider a ghost a person who's died and is just hangin' around then I don't think it's a ghost. I don't know if there even is a name for whatever that thing is but I don't believe in my heart that it was ever a human person. I do believe that it is very, *very* bad."

"Has it ever physically hurt anybody?" Scott leaned forward. He was thinking about what might have happened if Ray hadn't shown up before the thing had been able to get him in its grasp. He couldn't imagine the outcome, but the idea gave him a shudder.

"No, so far as I know it's never actually hurt anybody in a literal sense but I'm not sure that it *couldn't* hurt somebody. I don't know what might've happened to you if I hadn't gotten up there in time."

They both sat back in their chairs, not speaking for a while. Scott was thinking that, while Dean and Ray might have been able to get past their experiences on the 16th floor, he wasn't sure that he would be able to keep working in that building. Ray looked at him from beneath his wily brows and seemed to read his mind.

"Listen. Scott. If you need to figure out what you wanna do that's perfectly understandable. Your reality took a real hard kick to the behind today and you probably need to sort of, *digest* that." Ray picked up the nearly empty water bottle and drained it. "I can go up and talk to Dean about it for you. Believe me, he's going to understand. He'll understand better than anybody else ever could. Whatever you decide to do he's gonna be okay with it."

Scott looked at Ray for a moment and then stood and stretched. He walked over and patted the older man on the arm gratefully. "Thanks, Ray. I really appreciate that. I think I'm probably going to go home for the day. I honestly don't think I can face going upstairs, even to get my jacket right now."

"Sure Scotty, sure." Ray stood up and opened the door to his office. A cloud of smoke billowed out into the corridor and faded away into the air above them. Both men stepped out and headed into the lobby, stopping at the security desk. "Don't worry about your jacket. It'll be fine till you decide what you wanna do." Ray's voice and the look in his eyes told Scott that Ray understood he probably wouldn't be coming back.

The two men faced each other there on the first floor of the building. The rain still fell from a battered sky and the thunder continued to grumble and grouse. There were still people coming and going, walking into the commissary and passing by the security desk on their way to the elevators, swinging purses and briefcases and umbrellas. The two men did not notice any of them as they regarded each other from opposite sides of the desk. The older man smiled at the younger man and the two shook hands. They exchanged farewells and the younger man turned and walked away from the security desk, turning once to wave one final time.

After that Scott didn't look back. He walked out into the wet, gray afternoon and never returned again.

***

Scott entered the house he shared with his parents and called out to see if anyone was home. His mother was in the family room watching a movie on TV. She asked why he was home so early. Was everything okay? He said he wasn't sure and then went to his room.

He sat on his bed leaning forward with his face in his hands for a very long time. After a while, his mother came once and knocked on his door.

"Scotty? You okay?"

Scott sat up and looked at the door. "Yeah, Mom, I'm fine. Just tired. I think I'm going to take a nap."

"Okay." Scott's mother sounded unconvinced, but she didn't try to draw him out any further.

He did, indeed, plan on taking a nap and he sincerely hoped that his mind took pity on him and kept the nightmares at bay. He reached into his pants pockets to remove his keys and wallet and pulled out the small opal brooch that he'd taken from the 16th floor. He held it cupped in his palm and appraised its lovely details. He ran his thumb over the raised edges of the little carousel horse at its center. His mother was going to love it. He hoped giving it to her in the morning might help to offset the news that he'd quit his job. He laid the brooch on the table beside his bed, a pretty souvenir of a very bad day. He undid his pants, stripped them off, and lay down on top of his covers. He was asleep in minutes.

Sometime later in the night, long after darkness had fallen, Scott awoke to the sensation of someone climbing into his bed with him. His eyes snapped wide open, and he saw a dark, hunched shape rising above him. He felt it pressing down against the bed and then his body as it clambered up onto his belly. It didn't feel like arms and legs against him; more like a cold, jelly slipping around him, sticky and slick. The thing made clicking and clacking sounds as it squirmed up towards his face. He opened his mouth to scream but even as he sucked in a gasp of air he felt something long and wet slide between his lips, twining around his tongue like a lover's kiss. It filled his mouth with an unspeakable taste and then withdrew from him. As he lay frozen in an ecstasy of error, he heard a sound coming from it. It was a low chittering buzz that sounded like laughter. It spoke his name in a voice that was not remotely human, but was somehow, very familiar.

UNREMEMBERED

"You like girls?"

The question surprised a laugh out of Thomas. "Yeah, of course."

"Alright, just checkin'." Dennison grinned. "These days you don't wanna assume nothin'." He swept his stubby arm at an array of porno magazines stacked on wire racks along the counter beneath the drive-thru window. Several had been removed from their plastic covers. "Feel free to peruse the materials when it gets slow but make sure you listen for that drive-thru bell. I don't want some old lady to drive up and get an eyeful of snatch. Ya' know?"

Thomas nodded, wishing a little that his new boss wasn't standing quite so close to him. "I've got it. Shouldn't be too big of an issue."

Dennison had already shown him how to ring up sales and when to re-stock the beer coolers and count inventory. Told him to give cops that came through free coffee, soda, and small snacks ("but don't let 'em take advantage of ya'."), to ID anybody who looked too young to buy alcohol ("If they look young enough to be hangin' out with you…card 'em.") and to empty the trash sometime during his shift.

"Don comes in around 6:30 or so. Till then, this ship is all yours." Dennison squeezed past and stepped into the annex which contained the restroom and the small business office.

Thomas took his place on a wooden stool behind the register and looked around the little convenience store. *Here we go.* He wondered what his mother would think if she knew he was working the graveyard shift at a *Hoosier Daddy* drive-thru. Of course, since her "troubles" (he still refused to even *think* the word,

Alzheimer's, despite what her doctor said) she had no real idea what Thomas did these days. At some point, fairly recently, she'd come under the impression that he was back playing little league ball for Neal & Son's Hardware. He didn't try to argue the point but simply told her he was heading to practice whenever he went out and this seemed to satisfy her.

Dennison walked back into the room, slipping into an over-sized flannel coat that, large as it was, still didn't fit comfortably around his gut. "Alright Tommy, I'm takin' off. If somethin' happens—you know, some kind of emergency, like a fire or whatever—my number's next to the register." He regarded Thomas from atop his glasses, "But don't call unless all hell is breaking loose. Got it?"

"Yep, I've got it." Thomas fidgeted with a pen on the counter. "And thanks Mr. Dennison—for the job. I really appreciate it."

Dennison's expression softened and he flipped a little salute. "Call me Denny." He turned and walked down the center aisle to the front door, a huge ring of keys jangling in his hand. He swung the door open and stepped out, turning the key to shut Thomas in for the night. Before closing it, though, he stuck his head back in.

"Hey, remember—keep this door locked till Don shows up in the morning. Hear me? Don't open up for nobody but Don."

Thomas nodded for the hundredth time that night. "Absolutely. It will stay shut."

Dennison pointed across the store. "And when you take the trash out the back, don't forget to put the brick in the door 'cause that one locks automatically. You'll get stuck outside in the dark otherwise. You don't want that."

"Right, the brick. I will, don't worry. I can totally handle this."

The fat man lingered a moment longer, looking around the cinderblock walls of the store as if he might never see it again. Then, without another word, he shut the front door and disappeared into the darkness.

Thomas sat and felt the silence of the empty store close around him. This was going to be a lonely job. He didn't imagine too many people drove through after midnight. Denny told him he could turn on the little radio in the office if he wanted and Thomas had just gotten up off his stool to go do that when the drive-thru bell clanged to let him know someone was pulling up to the window.

He turned and slid the window open, leaning out into the chilly night to face his first customer. It was Denny in his massive, black Continental.

Thomas smiled down into his boss's thick face. "Good evening sir, what can I get for you?"

Dennison grunted. "First off, cut that 'good evening' crap out. Don't sound so happy. People will think you're bein' a smartass."

Thomas flushed. "Oh sorry."

Dennison waved his hand. "It's okay. Grab me a pack of Parliaments and one of them girlie books."

Thomas surveyed the array of magazines. "Which one?"

"It don't matter, ass is ass." Dennison waited while Thomas grabbed one and pulled down a pack of smokes from the shelf. He put them in a bag and turned to the register. Before he could punch in the prices Dennison stopped him.

"I don't need rung up, kid, I'll put some cash in tomorrow. I'll remember."

Thomas handed the bag through the window to Denny. "Anything else?" The younger man tried not to sound too happy or interested.

"Just mind the doors." And with that the ancient car pulled away, engine rumbling.

Jesus, I get it. Thomas slid the window shut and went to turn on the radio in the office. It was nearly two hours before he saw another customer, a car full of giggling, drunk girls stopping to buy three bags of little powdered donuts. After that, time spun out with glacial slowness.

Thomas got up from his stool and straightened the bubblegum jars on the counter. He popped $0.75 into the register and helped himself to a chocolate bar. He went into the beer cooler and stared at the neatly stacked cases for a few empty minutes. He counted them. Then he counted them again.

He left the cooler and looked at the clock on his phone. It had only been thirteen minutes since the donut girls had driven through, but it felt as if hours had come and gone. He was standing in the center aisle of the store just staring around at the racks of chips and crackers, when the radio in the office suddenly went silent.

Thomas walked back to the annex and stepped into the office. He picked the radio up and shook it but no sound came out of it. He flipped it over and examined the back. A cord ran from the bottom corner to a plug behind the desk. Next to the cord was the on/off switch which had somehow been set to the "off" position.

He looked up from the radio and over his shoulder. He peered out the office door into the store and a sudden little chill rushed down his back. "Hello?" He spared one more glance out into the store and then set the radio back on the table. "Fuck it."

He decided it was a good time to take out the trash. He gathered up the bag from the office and carried it into the hallway, setting it on the floor. He pushed into the tiny restroom across from the office and yanked the bag, overflowing with paper towels, out of the bin beneath the sink. The last trash can was under the register. He jogged over and pulled it from the can. He tied it and made his way back to the annex.

Grabbing up the bags, Thomas walked down the short corridor to the back door. He turned the knob and opened it, stepping out into the darkness behind the drive-thru. He'd taken two steps forward when he suddenly remembered what Denny said about the door and the brick.

He spun around, the bags swinging wildly in his hands and just managed to wedge a foot in the door before it snicked shut. On the floor, against the wall was a chipped and battered piece of flagging. Denny had called it a brick, but it looked more like a broken chunk of masonry with a couple of deep grooves cut into it. Thomas used his toe to shove the hunk into the doorway and let the door shut against it.

The dumpster abutted a hill behind the drive-thru lane. The hill rose steeply from the lot about twenty-five feet and then flattened out into woods and fields that wound off down the road to either side of the building. A stern, gray, crowd of buckeyes marched across the rise, hoarding shadows beneath their crooked branches while the slope was a tangled mess of overgrown shrubs and grass. A breeze whispered through the unruly growth and ruffled Thomas's hair as he strode across the parking lot.

He slung the bags into the dumpster and almost didn't see the little girl staring at him from a few feet away on the hill. She sat so quietly and with such unnatural stillness that if a car hadn't driven past, spotlighting the hill with its headlights, Thomas would have missed her entirely. The car's lights tossed his shadow out in front of him and he caught sight of the tiny figure watching him with her wide, dark eyes. He shouted with surprise and jumped.

"Whoa!" The car passed, dropping both Thomas and the little girl back into darkness. When he'd caught his breath, he laughed at himself for being startled. "You scared me there." His smile faded as the little girl continued to stare at him.

What the hell is she doing out here by herself at this time of night? Thomas glanced over his shoulder at the store and realized, from that spot a person could look right in through the drive-thru window. It was disconcerting, wondering how long she'd been sitting there, maybe watching him. He wondered if maybe she'd run away from someone. He scanned the dark parking lot for movement but saw nothing. He looked back at the strange little girl.

"Hey, are you okay? Do you need me to call somebody for you?" He took a reluctant step forward, not wanting to frighten her.

The little girl stood up slowly. She was dressed in a tattered sweater that was too large for her and a long skirt. The clothes were plain and seemed grimy and she wore no shoes.

As he looked at her, Thomas realized she was standing on a set of stairs. They were rough stone, set into the hill and hidden by the dense underbrush. Sweeping his gaze along the slope he could make out where they peeked out of the grass here and there until they reached the trees at the top.

Suddenly and wordlessly, the girl turned and started climbing, her long dark curls bouncing as she went. Her bare feet made no sound against the rocky steps. Thomas didn't try to stop her, he just watched as she headed up towards the dark trees at the top. Just before she disappeared into the black beneath their branches, she turned and called down to him in a thin, high voice.

"Don't let him in."

Thomas felt cold. He stood a moment longer, looking up at the dark trees the girl had disappeared into. They seemed to have swallowed her completely.

He wondered if he should've gone after her, followed her up the steps and into the shadows but the thought made him nervous. He was uneasy about the idea of such a young girl running around alone at 2:30 in the morning but she hadn't asked for help, and he thought it might scare her to have a grown man, a *stranger,* chasing after her through the night. How would that look to anyone else?

He decided to just go back inside and finish out his shift. As he scootched the triangular hunk of stone out of the doorway, letting the back door swing shut, he thought about what she'd said. *"Don't let him in."* It was spooky. It had been an interesting, if unsettling, first day at Hoosier Daddy's. He almost mentioned it to Don, the guy who relieved him for the morning shift, but Don was bleary-eyed and grumpy, and Thomas decided against it. They passed minimal greetings and parted ways.

For the next three nights at the drive-thru, Thomas saw the little girl on the hill when he took out the trash. He never saw her from the window, even though he watched for her. It was only when he made his way to the dumpster that he noticed her sitting there quietly on the hill, watching him. Each night he would ask if she was okay, if she needed him to call someone, if her parents knew where she was, and if she wanted to come inside and have a soda. She remained silent except for that one, disquieting phrase she repeated before retreating up the steps each night.

"Don't let him in."

He asked Don about it one morning as the man came shuffling in, smelling of sour breath and cigarette smoke. "Who's that little girl that hangs out by the dumpster?"

Don raised his eyebrows, the barest hint of curiosity peeking out through half-lidded eyes. "What little girl?"

Thomas shrugged. "That's what I'm asking you. I've run into her every night when I take the garbage out, sitting on those old steps on the hill. A little girl with long brown hair and ratty clothes. She might be homeless or something."

Don looked thoughtfully out the drive-thru window to the scraggly hill beyond. He seemed like he had something to say and then, with a scratchy sigh, decided not to. "Don't know, Chief. Wouldn't think little kids oughta be out here that time of night." He turned back to the counter and said no more about it.

The fourth night was a Friday. Car after car rolled through, the bell dinging incessantly, keeping Thomas busy selling cigarettes, beer, wine, and snacks. On top of all that he couldn't stop thinking about how, when he'd taken his mother her medicine that night, she'd mistaken him for his father and tried to kiss him on the mouth as he sat on the bed holding out her glass of water. Her memory had been declining for weeks but this was the first time she hadn't known who he was.

Customer traffic died off and loneliness began to creep in. Thomas turned on the little office radio and set about finding small, menial tasks that would help distract him from thoughts of his mother. He'd been organizing credit card receipts under the register drawer, singing along with the radio when he turned around and yelped, startled by a stern face peering in at him from the darkness outside the window.

The face belonged to a tall, thin man. His eyes glared with intensity, and his lips pressed tightly together with disapproval. His face was long and haggard, and his skin had an unhealthy, yellowish tint. He was wearing an old work coverall that had seen better days and was coated in a fine layer of dust.

Thomas pressed his hand against his forehead and took a deep breath. "You're the second person to sneak up on me this week man, Jeez." He shook his head and sighed. "What can I get for you?"

The man just stood there, not answering. His expression was cold and hard, almost accusatory. It made Thomas a little uneasy.

"So, you need something?" Sweat began to gather at his hairline as the man continued to regard him silently. *Who is this freak?*

Then Thomas thought of the little girl. He wondered if this guy was connected to her somehow. Maybe her father or uncle. The thought chilled him as he faced the flinty-eyed stranger. *Could be he didn't like that I offered to bring her in here. Or maybe she was hiding from him.*

Thomas crossed his arms and tried his best to look unintimidated. "Look dude, we don't really do walk-ups here. You wanna come through the drive-thru you've gotta be driving something. You wanna walk, you can come inside the store between the hours of seven am and ten pm."

The man's hard expression didn't change, and his mouth stayed shut. Thomas suddenly wondered what he'd do if the guy tried to climb in through the open drive-thru window to get at him. Maybe it had nothing to do with the little girl at all. Maybe this guy was working himself up to try and rob the place.

Thomas swallowed hard and tried to keep his voice as level and confident as possible. "Seriously, if you're not going to buy anything you need to move on." He paused and considered his next words carefully before deciding to go for it. "Or else I'm calling the cops."

He stood there and waited to see what kind of reaction his threat would elicit. He wasn't sure if it was more or less unsettling when the man didn't react at all. His heart was pounding, and he remembered what the little girl had said to him before running back up the stairs into the woods each and every night.

"Don't let him in."

He was screwing up his nerves to leap forward and slam the window shut, buying himself a few seconds to spin around and call the cops when the drive-thru bell went off and yellow headlights flooded the dark lane where the man stood. After the thick silence of the past few minutes, the sudden "ding ding" of the bell caused Thomas to let out a startled, "hwugh" sound as he faced the grill of the oncoming car. When he looked back the man's face had disappeared from the window.

The car pulled up and a skinny man in a corduroy jacket smiled up at Thomas. "Hey, how you doin'? Can I get a pack of rolling papers and a Lucky Lady scratch-off?"

Thomas leaned out the window, looking left and right for the man who'd just been staring him down. He scanned the hill where the steps marched upwards to the woods, following the slope to the mute, dark, trees at the top. There was no sign of anyone. It was as if the man had just vanished into thin air.

The customer in the car turned to see what Thomas was looking at. He glanced back with a cocked eyebrow. "Somebody pull a drive up and dash, man?"

Thomas looked down, his eyes wild. "Did you see him?" His voice was high-pitched and breathless.

"Nah, I didn't see anybody." The man waited a few moments while Thomas continued to stare, dumbfounded, out into the night and then gently prodded him. "So, uh, can I get them papers and that lottery ticket man?"

Thomas wiped his hand across his face and nodded. "Yeah. Sorry 'bout that, absolutely." He rang the order up and handed it out the window to the patiently waiting customer. The man paid for his items and drove off leaving Thomas no company other than the tinny songs that squawked from the office radio.

He slid the drive-thru window shut and latched it, then strode across the store to the front entrance and checked that the doors were locked, yanking hard on them. He walked back to the space behind the register and leaned against the counter for the rest of his shift, gazing out the window, watching for movement. Two more customers came through, but the intensely silent man did not make another appearance.

When Don came in that morning something about the way Thomas looked roused more than his usual, grumbled hello.

"Ya alright there, Chief?"

Thomas said he was fine, just tired, and scurried out the door. As he climbed into his car, he stared up the shaggy hill. In the soft, pink light of sunrise, he noticed the silhouette of a post or a sign peeking out from the top of the stairs. It stood just inside the ring of trees and in the darkness he hadn't been able to see it. A few steps beyond the sign, shadows spread and deepened, keeping their secrets hidden from the morning light. Thomas pulled out of the parking lot, wondering what was really up there, and drove home.

The next night went by uneventfully, but Thomas still prowled the store restlessly. He stopped every hour or so to check the doors, continually watching out the windows for any sign of the man in the old coverall, or the little girl. When morning came, Don stopped him on his way out.

"Hey, Chief?"

Thomas waited, rubbing his red-rimmed eyes with his fists. "Yeah?"

Don pointed at the annex. "You ain't taken the trash out last couple'a nights." He regarded Thomas evenly from under his bushy brows. "I went ahead and done it for you but you gotta do it tonight. Okay?"

Thomas nodded. "Oh man, I'm sorry, it totally slipped my mind. No worries, I've got it tonight."

Don waved him off and Thomas made his way out the door. He did not look forward to the coming shift.

After dinner that night, Thomas stood at the sink, washing the dishes. His mother sat at the small table behind him, talking about the court shows she'd watched on television that day and how Sandra Siskind next door had a man at her house for several hours that day that wasn't her husband. Thomas didn't bother reminding her that they hadn't lived next door to the Siskinds since he was in high school. He just nodded and said, "mmm-hmmm," in the appropriate places. He was drying the last few bits of silverware when she said something that caught his attention. He looked over his shoulder, holding his dripping hands over the sink.

"Wait, Mom, what'd you just say?"

His mother pointed up to the ceiling. "I said I think I'll clean out the attic tomorrow."

Thomas shook his head. "No, before that."

She sat for a moment, her brows knitted together in concentration as she tried to recall what she'd been talking about a few moments before. "Er, well, I was saying that I couldn't find your grandma's snickerdoodle recipe in the drawer, and I'd pulled the whole thing apart looking for it because I really wanted snickerdoodles and I felt so silly because whatever you do don't let him in I already had it out on the table. I've been very absent-minded lately." She took a sip of coffee from her mug and smiled up at him sweetly. "Was that it? You wanted to hear me say I'm going to make snickerdoodles?"

Thomas's heart thumped with nervous speed, but he kept his voice steady. "Yeah, I just wanted to make sure you were on record saying you'd make them. I didn't want you to forget." His head buzzed with confusion. *Did she say what I think she just said? Is it just the dementia? Am I going crazy?* His thoughts bounced and fluttered like uneasy birds, and he had a nervous hollow in his chest as he drove off.

The first thing Thomas did that night upon arriving at the drive-thru was to take the trash out while Denny was still poking around in the office. When he came back in, brushing his hands off on his jeans, the large man was pulling on his too-small coat. He turned and winked at Thomas,

"Don't like goin' out there, do you?"

Thomas grinned with embarrassment and shook his head. "Nah, not when it gets late and I'm here by myself. Go ahead, call me a pussy."

Denny held out a conciliatory hand. "Nope. I don't blame you one bit. Don't like it myself. That hill and them woods is friggin' creepy."

He turned and yanked on the door, about to leave when Thomas called out to him. "Hey, Denny," he swallowed as Dennison turned, a trifle impatiently.

"Yeah?"

"What's up there on top of the hill—in the woods? Does somebody live up there?"

Denny made a sound that was half cough, half chuckle. "Just the opposite. It's a memorial for a little girl that got killed up there. Murdered."

An icy finger traced its way down Thomas's spine, sinking into his shoulder blades and ribs. He thought of the girl on the steps, watching him with her sad, ancient eyes and of the man with the stern face.

Don't let him in.

Thomas, with some effort, managed to keep his voice neutral. "How long ago was that?"

Denny shrugged. "I don't know, I ain't the story keeper. Twenties, thirties maybe. Sometime 'round there. There's a sign up at the top of the steps says the spot's a historic landmark so they couldn't bulldoze or blast it when they built this place. Needless to say, it happened a long time ago."

Thomas nodded, feigning only mild interest. "Do they know who killed her?"

The fat man rolled his eyes behind his little round glasses and looked at his watch, sighing. "Christ kid, I don't know. Some guy. Some crazy pervert, like it always is. You can look this shit up online if you want details. He squinted in thought for a moment. "I think her name was Abigail or Alice or something. I actually went up there once when I first started workin' here. Sad little spot." Denny leaned on the door. "Anything else?"

Thomas shook his head and fabricated a smile, waving as Denny heaved his bulk out the door, locking it behind him. Silence crept into the room. Thomas took a few deep breaths and looked out the drive-thru window to where the dumpster sat at the foot of the stone stairs. If anything was looking back, he couldn't see it.

***

Thomas double checked that the front doors were shut up good and tight before turning the office radio up loud. He went about the usual tasks of restocking the candy racks and shifting the milk with the oldest expiration date to the front of the cooler. He glanced out the drive-thru window from time to time, wondering who might be wandering around out there, but for the first couple of hours he was alone.

It was a little after two when the radio shut itself off. It hadn't done that since Thomas's first night at Hoosier Daddy's. He stood up from the counter and went into the office. The radio lay on its face, its cord yanked free of the wall. Thomas looked from the empty socket to the dangling plug that hung over the edge of the desk. His pulse quickened and the hairs on his arms stood up.

He backed out of the office, peeking around the corner before entering the store area, his eyes straining to see the whole room at once. He stood in the center, turning slowly, trying to pick a rational thought out of all the crazy ones flying through his mind.

You are acting like a child, He scolded himself, *an idiot child. What you are thinking is silly and impossible.* Another voice spoke up in his head, cooler and calmer than the first. *Don't let him in...That's what the girl kept saying and then Mom said it in the kitchen. You heard her. Twice.*

Thomas would have gone on arguing with himself for a while if the dinging of the drive-thru bell hadn't yanked him out of his thoughts. He turned and saw the tall cab of a shiny pickup roll up to the window.

He jogged around the counter, unlatched the window and slid it open. A young man with shaggy blonde hair and a matching mustache grimaced uncomfortably at Thomas, his face red.

"What can I get for you?" Thomas asked.

The blonde man squirmed in his seat. "Hey man, I know the answer's probably gonna be "no," but can I use your bathroom? I've been holdin' one in since midnight and it's turned critical. If I don't go here I'm gonna shit my pants. I promise I'll buy something from you but—" the man squeezed his eyes shut and gritted his teeth, and Thomas knew he was clenching. "—but please I *gotta* go."

Thomas thought about the radio unplugging itself. He thought about the memorial at the top of the hill, the little girl, and the angry-faced man. Having someone else with him in the store, even if only for time it took the man to move his bowels, would be a huge comfort. "Yeah of course, pull around to the front, I'll go let you in."

The man's face crumpled into a strained but grateful smile. "Oh God, thanks buddy." He dropped the lever into drive and shot around the corner of the building.

Thomas slid the window shut, grabbed the keys from the counter and jogged over to the front doors. He unlocked them and pushed one open, leaning out into the cool darkness. The big black truck was parked across two spaces and the blonde man was scrambling out the driver's side door. Thomas stepped aside as the man hurried through the door, hitching at his pants.

"Where's the John?" His voice was a breathless squeak.

"Back there." Thomas pointed to the annex hallway. "First door on the left."

"Thanks, man!" The blonde man ran across the room in a comical, tight-legged shuffle and smashed through the bathroom door.

Thomas watched him, amused by the mad bathroom dash, and sauntered back to his spot behind the register. He was starting to feel foolish about letting his imagination run away with him. He thought the stress of his mother's worsening condition was insidious in the way it worked on his nerves. He wasn't sure how to manage it, but he knew he needed to figure something out.

It had only been a couple minutes when the blonde man came out of the bathroom. He strode across the concrete floor with a decidedly un-silly swagger, his mouth set in a hard, straight line. Thomas hadn't heard the flush go off and frowned at the idea of what would be waiting in there for him to deal with later.

"You all set then?" Thomas wasn't going to ask the man to buy anything if he didn't bring it up himself.

"Almost but not quite." The man's eyes were wide, his pupils dilated. His mouth had turned up at the corners in a grin, the tips of his mustache quivering in and out with each heavy breath. His right hand disappeared around his back and returned gripping a pistol. He pointed it right into Thomas's stunned face. "I'm also gonna need you to give me all the money in the register." He paused thoughtfully. "And one of them nudie magazines."

Thomas's eyes crossed as he looked into the barrel, an endless black tunnel that blotted everything else out. He'd never had a gun pointed at him before. It felt like he'd had the wind knocked out of him. Time stretched out and even the man holding the gun seemed to recede into a blurry haze. For the moment, all Thomas knew was the gun.

After what seemed like a very long time, he heard himself say, "Yeah, of course. Hold on a sec." With an enormous effort he managed to pull his gaze from the gun barrel and when he did the rest of the world snapped back into place. The man was right there, grinning at him with wild-eyed glee, his yellow teeth bared.

Thomas bent to the register and did a false ring-up to get the drawer open. He reached into the till and grabbed up all the cash. He set the thin sheaf of bills on the counter and turned to grab a magazine as the man had requested.

The man's smile vanished instantly at the sight of the money. He gestured to it with his empty hand. "What's that? What the fuck is that?"

Thomas looked at the cash, confused. Everything was happening very quickly, and his brain was still trying to catch up. Was this the same guy who'd stumbled across the room, ass-cheeks clenched together because he had to take a shit?

"It's all the money there is." Thomas looked back down into the empty till. There was a quarter, two dimes, a penny and a soda—bottle cap left in the tray. He fished out the change and tossed it onto the counter. "Sorry, forgot that."

The blonde man cocked the pistol. The click was very loud, and Thomas's hands immediately went up. The man was blinking his eyes rapidly, squeezing them tightly shut and opening them wide.

"That's it? Are you fucking *joking*? This is a liquor store. You should be rolling in money, *swimming* in it."

Thomas wanted to explain that when Denny left in the evening, he took most of the cash with him to deposit at the bank, leaving only enough to make change. Very few people came in during the overnight shifts most of the time and there just wasn't ever that much cash. He wanted to say this but couldn't seem to get those words out of his mouth. The gun pointed at his head made this impossible. Instead, he just shrugged and made a sympathetic face.

"Sorry, man. All's there is."

The blonde man pressed both hands to his temples and shrieked at the ceiling. Again, the moment the gun was turned away from Thomas he felt everything come back into sharp focus. He was able to think more clearly and with that came the knowledge that this crazy person was very close to killing him. His breath came in hitches, and he watched as the blonde man spun in a circle, waving the pistol wildly.

"What'm I supposed to fuckin' do? I don't know, I don't know. WHAT DO I DO?". He was rubbing his hand harshly over his face, his eyes closed tightly. "It's not gonna be enough, I know it's not. Don't you think I *know* that? You think I'm *stupid*?"

When he said the word, *stupid*, he turned and looked directly at Thomas again, bringing the gun back up. It seemed like the last question was directed at him and the man repeated it, his eyes blazing. This time it was a statement. "You think I'm stupid."

Thomas opened his mouth and was trying to think of a satisfactory reply, when a small, sad voice came from behind the blonde man.

"You're a very bad man."

The man whipped around, and Thomas saw the little girl from the hill, standing there, pale and disheveled, her eyes solemn and wide.

Without hesitation, the blonde man swung the gun around firing three shots into her chest. Thomas's hands flew to his head, fingers twining in his hair, pulling and tugging. He screamed. A loud, high-pitched wail that was cut short as the bullet ricocheted with a *ping* off the floor behind the girl who stood unharmed, rooted to her spot. The blonde man took a startled step back, the gun still raised.

"Whatinthehell?"

He fired again with the same results. The bullet screamed off the concrete, knocking over a cardboard display. The girl just kept staring at him, her eyes fixed on his, filled with accusation.

"You shouldn't have done that. My Daddy's on his way." The girl's mouth parted in a terrifying smile that stretched further across her face than was possible. Her tiny square teeth shined out from between shiny black lips and her eyes gleamed with malice. "He's mad at you."

The blonde man turned back to Thomas, confusion splashed across his face. He made little whimpering noises, unable to form real words. Sweat sprung out from beneath his hair, making his forehead shiny.

Thomas was backed up against the drive-thru window. He was trying to decide whether he was dreaming or awake when he felt the glass ripple beneath his back. He looked over his shoulder and cried out in terror.

The stern man in the coverall was pushing his way through the closed windowpane as if it were made of soap instead of glass. His facial features distorted and stretched as he forced his way into the store. His hands came through, grasping and twitching like white spiders. Thomas jerked to the side and tripped over the stool, slamming to the ground. He gulped for air, feeling as if his lungs were collapsing under the weight of fear. The apparition heaved and shoved its way through the wall and in a moment was standing above Thomas, looking as solid and real as anything else in the store. It spared a glance down, holding one bony finger up to its lips in a secretive gesture before climbing over the counter towards the blonde man.

Thomas had nearly forgotten about the blonde man. The last twenty seconds or so had somehow flattened out and expanded into a silent film where Thomas, the girl and her father were the only players. Now, the screams of the man with the gun sliced through this illusion and Thomas pulled himself up off the floor, clinging to the counter as he climbed to his feet.

It was like peeking into someone else's nightmare as they slept. The blonde man had fallen to his knees, the gun clasped loosely at the trigger, forgotten. Tears shined on his cheeks and his lips were peeled back in a pleading grimace as he sobbed incoherently.

The little girl was no longer in her threadbare sweater and heavy woolen skirt but wore a tattered church dress. It may have been pink at one time but now it was ashen gray and covered with mold and filth. Her arms and legs had thinned down to waxy sticks and her face was little more than a skull, all cheekbones, teeth, and deep black eye sockets from which twin pinpricks of frosty blue, glowed merrily. She capered around and around the blonde man, skipping and laughing, reciting a rhyme in a singsong, helium-high voice.

"Hing-hang-hung see what the hangman done? Hung-hang-hing see the robber swing..."

But it was the father's face that held the simpering man's attention. Thomas was thankful that the specter's back was to him because whatever it was showing the blonde man seemed to be peeling away the man's sanity in sheets. As Thomas watched, the father ghost's arms stretched and elongated, the skin roughening to the harsh gray texture of old tree bark. A sound began to build, very low at first like the whispering of many voices but soon grew to a rumbling chorus. It seemed to come from everywhere and nowhere at once, bleeding from the walls and churning from beneath the floor. Words that dripped with fury and loss, grief and outrage funneled from somewhere beyond the walls that kept the living and the dead apart from one another.

"I can't find Abby... Lucas, I can't find her!"

"Come on! The woods! Oh dear sweet Jesus in heaven, he took her in the woods!"

The sounds of dogs barking—the shouting voices of men in the distance—a woman's voice screaming in pain and disbelief...

"Nell, you stay where you're at. I said STAY PUT! Don't come over here!"

The mourning choir reached a crescendo, the walls of the store trembling, racks of snacks and cooler cases rattling. The voices echoed and the ghostly father wrapped his hideously stretched arms around the blonde robber, the little girl clapping and laughing with Christmas morning excitement. The blonde man's eyes were so wide it looked like they would tumble right out of their sockets and his mouth yawned in terror. The father spared one quick glance over his shoulder at Thomas who was too dazed and terrified to shut his eyes.

It turned back to the robber whose screams had reached a pitch Thomas didn't realize a human voice could find. The thing that had started as a little girl crept up behind the kneeling man and wrapped her own arms around him in a terrible embrace. There was a flash of light and Thomas finally covered his eyes and wished he had another two hands to jam against his ears. There was a thick, sloppy ripping sound and the blonde man's screams were cut off abruptly. A noise swept through the store like the wind sighing through willows and then it was over.

Silence.

Thomas waited with his hands pressed to his face. It felt like a long time, but he had no way of knowing how long it really was. He drew his shaking hands away and looked to the center of the room.

The little girl and her father were still there, restored to their original appearances. The blonde man, however, was nowhere to be found. No scrap of clothing, no splotch of blood, no gun, no mark of any kind to be seen anywhere. He was simply gone.

The two apparitions and Thomas regarded one another from across the room. His heart was still beating hard but, in spite of everything that had happened, was slowing down. His breath was returning to normal, and he was surprised to find himself unafraid of the spirits sharing his space. He wasn't sure how this night would be digested in the coming days and weeks but for now, he felt calm. Grateful.

The father still said nothing and approached the counter fading a little bit with every step until there was nothing left.

The little girl came forward, seeming to glide more than walk. She stopped when she reached the annex. Something down the hallway had caught her attention near the back door. She stared down that way for several moments before turning back to Thomas, her dark eyes solemn as ever. "I told you not to let him in." And then she was gone. No fading, no smoke or pop of sound, she just was no longer there.

Thomas stood leaning against the counter, waiting for the shakes to hit or to faint or start laughing or screaming or crying or gibbering, but none of that happened. He just felt odd warmth creeping into his body.

He was wondering whether or not the blonde robber's bullet casings had disappeared with him, when the drive-thru bell dinged. He turned and slid the window open as a youngish woman pulled up in a Buick.

Thomas leaned out the window, feeling a soft, sweet breeze kiss his brow. He looked out at the hill behind the dumpster for a moment and saw the little girl sitting on the steps halfway up. Her eyes shone in the dark, two melancholy stars. His heart ached for her and suddenly he thought of her looking down the hallway of the annex. He thought of the brick they used to hold the back door open. The brick that wasn't really a brick but a piece of chipped granite that looked like a broken-off corner from a tombstone or memorial.

Thomas thought it wouldn't hurt to run it up the steps to the woods, in the daylight of course, to see the spot for himself. He owed Abigail and her father that much at least for saving his life. Even if the stone didn't belong up there, he could sit and spend some of his memory on her. He understood the importance of remembering and the terror of being unremembered. He understood how precious it was to know that someone knew who you were. Perhaps he'd take flowers too.

He waved to the small dark figure, and a moment later she stood and went up the steps into the woods. Thomas wasn't at all surprised to see that her feet did not quite touch the ground. At the top she turned to look at him one last time, returned his wave, and then faded into the gloom beneath the trees. Thomas watched for another moment or two and then, swallowing the lump in his throat, looked down at his customer.

"How's it going? What can I get for you tonight?"

TRAILER TRASH

"I'm not one hundred percent convinced of this Alex. I need you to know that right now." Sergeant Howard glanced back and forth between the two file folders open on the desk in front of him.

"I know, Don, I know. But look, these two are desperate to stay on the street. They'll do anything we want." Alex tapped the photo paper clipped to the folder on the left. "This guy, especially. He'd suck his own dad's dick to stay out of jail just so he could get his medicine."

"Yeah. And you're not gonna be armed. You're gonna be in a car with this guy—this *desperate* guy, as you call him—and his trick girlfriend, driving out into the middle of East Buttfuck, Nowhere, with a bug in your ear and no gun. Even if they don't decide to kill you and leave your body in the woods—even if they actually take you to see this Grayson guy—now you're in the lion's den and I can't back you up." Howard shook his head, doubt written across every crag and crevice of his weathered face. "I don't feel good about this."

Alex smiled. The sergeant was fiercely protective of his team. He worried over them like a mama bear over her cubs. He even looked a bit like a bear with his fuzzy chestnut hair, bristling beard, and beer-barrel frame. He would bluster and grouse about this surveillance operation and try, through disapproving scowls and gloomy pronouncements, to discourage Alex from going out on it. Alex knew, though, that ultimately, he would have his way and Howard would let him go.

The Meth Suppression Task Force had been chasing rumors of Isaiah Grayson all over Indiana for months. Lately it hadn't even been rumors, but more like the ghosts of rumors. Then Alex had stumbled on two brain-fried tweakers trying to score behind a dipshit little bar in a dipshit little town called West Harrison, right on the Ohio border. It was these two dead-eyed, slack-jawed freaks that were going to serve him Grayson on a silver platter.

The ISP wanted this bust. Alex *really* wanted this bust, and his division needed it. Taxpayers wanted to see that all the high-tech gadgets and helicopters and guns they were paying for got put to good use now and again. Howard would not say no whether he could provide backup or not.

"I know but look, that's the beauty of this plan. Monty and Tonya don't know shit from Shakespeare. They don't know that there isn't any backup following along behind us and I'm damn sure going to tell them that there is." Alex tapped at his temple emphatically. "They're too dumb not to believe whatever I tell them. There's no way they're going to throw me over. Then at Grayson's, when they pat me down and don't find a gun, they're not gonna worry." He leaned back in his chair with a confident chuckle. "I'm not even the one doing the buying, it's still Monty and Tonya making the deal, I'm just along for the ride."

The sergeant looked doubtful. "Yeah, but what if they find your bug?"

"They're gonna be looking for a wire strapped to my chest, not a tiny mic in an earring. This isn't a cartel we're dealing with here, just some crispy-chicken rednecks in a trailer. They don't even know this shit exists." Alex grinned broadly. The fish was almost in the net.

Sergeant Howard sighed. "And you aren't worried that your, *informants*, might accidentally fuck up, get twitchy, and end up getting all of you killed? That ever occur to you?"

"Yeah, it's occurred to me." Alex shrugged. "What can you do? It's the job, right?"

"The job is not running willy-nilly into harm's way without weapons or backup."

"But sometimes it is. Sometimes it's gotta be." Alex stood from the hard plastic chair and paced around Howard's office, agitated. "Look, this guy moves around. We never know where he's gonna be and we don't know where he's been till two weeks after he's left. We have one, *one*, blurry photo and a few shaky eyewitness accounts. The guy's harder to find than goddam Bigfoot but now we've got a chance to get what we need." He pointed to the door behind him that led out into the communications center. "You guys'll be listening. You'll be able to get the warrant and I can take you right back there within the fucking hour."

He stopped and locked eyes with Howard, no longer grinning but deadly serious. "We need this, Don. You know we do. We get Grayson, shut down his meals-on-wheels operation, grab his money, maybe bust a few other incidentals, and who knows? Maybe we get two or three more guys in the budget for next year to back me up next time I've gotta do some shit like this." Alex crossed his arms. He had nothing else to say.

Sergeant Howard looked up at him for a long time. Alex knew he saw the truth in his plea and the futility of trying to stop him. He needed to get out there and hunt down the vermin that spread their disease so gleefully among the people that his team was sworn to protect. That's why Alex had been chosen in the first place. He needed to drag these dealers kicking and screaming to the ground as badly as their buyers needed their poisons.

With one final, deep, heavy sigh, the sergeant flipped the folders closed and stacked them on top of one another. He shoved them forward on his desk and nodded. "Alright. Do it. Make sure you remember to turn your mic on. Me and Lucky'll be listening back at dispatch. As soon as we get the deal recorded, we'll send it to Judge Marksberry for the warrant and then we can call in the locals."

"Perfect. Thank you, sir. We're gonna skewer this son-of-a-bitch." Alex rubbed his hands together. "I can't wait to see his face when I come walking up to cuff him. He's gonna shit his pants." He grabbed Monty and Tonya's files, ready to leave, but before he could get out the door, Howard gave him one last stern warning.

"First whiff of trouble…any little twitch or quiver in your gut…any hinky little instinct that says something ain't right…anything at all and you bail. You hear me trooper? You bail and get your ass outta there." The sergeant regarded Alex from behind his desk with a mixture of apprehension and pride. "Got it?"

Alex shot him a tight salute. "Got it." But he knew that no quiver or twitch was going to get in the way of this score.

****

"Want me to roll the window up, bro?" Monty looked at Alex in the rearview mirror with merry, bloodshot eyes. "You gettin' cold back there?" He giggled wildly.

Squeezed into the back seat with his legs folded up like a collapsible card table, Alex shook his head. "No man, I'm good."

Monty laughed again, a high-pitched, gobbling sound. "Yeah you are. You're soooo good." He slapped his palm against the steering wheel, hooting and snorting.

In the passenger seat next to him, Tonya, with her long hair, long legs, and short skirt, took a cigarette from the pack in her purse and lit up. She had been quiet the entire ride except for humming something under her breath off and on. It had been a few minutes after she'd trailed off into silence that Alex placed it as The Zombies' "Time of the Season." It got stuck in his head where it played, over and over again as they sailed through the dark, Indiana night down a narrow, blacktop road.

Alex leaned forward as far as he could and tapped Tonya's arm. Her skin was cold. She was wearing a tank top and he could see the jumble of amateurish, badly done tattoos that ran from her bicep to just above her elbow, the most prominent one being a confederate flag. She turned her head and looked over her shoulder at him.

"'Sup, Punkin?'"

"Can I get one of those?" Alex pointed to the cigarette between her fingers.

She smiled a sad, tight-lipped grin that hid the gaps where some of her teeth had fallen out. "'Course you can."

She pulled the pack out of her purse, offering it back to Alex, along with a small green lighter. He lit a cigarette and returned the pack and the lighter. Still smiling, she took them back, turned around, and started humming again.

Alex sat back, and looked out the window, puffing on his smoke. Tall, straight trees hemmed them in on either side of the road, high skeletal branches held aloft. Every so often there would be a telephone pole with a light attached to it that would dazzle his eyes for a moment as they rocketed beneath it. Mostly, though, the darkness swelled, unchallenged except for the headlights of Monty's Regal.

They were deep in the boonies and getting deeper. Every so often they passed houses, squat, ramshackle places set far back amongst the trees, but those became fewer and further between.

Alex was unfamiliar with this area and felt a tingle of disquiet at the base of his spine. Even though Sergeant Howard and Lucky could hear everything that was happening, they had no way of knowing where he was. The microphone was not a homing device and was too small to be equipped with GPS. If anything were to happen, they might never find him.

Squash that shit right now, Alex chided himself as he smoked his cigarette. *Everything's going to be fine. Just remember everything you told Howard and keep your eyes on the goddam prize.*

Instead, he thought about how easy it had been to flip Monty and Tonya over on Grayson. He'd been visiting the County Sheriff's department, providing some training for low-level undercover work, and had advised them to keep him updated on any meth-related cases that came up. The day before he was to head back to HQ a young officer named Flynn called him down to the interrogation room. He had two suspects in custody who'd been picked up trying to get meth money by prostituting the woman behind a broken-down local dive bar.

Alex had walked into the room and sat down across from them. Monty was a giggling, grizzled Clyde, beating out a hectic rhythm against his thigh with his left hand, scratching madly at his dirty mane of yellow-blonde hair with the right. Tonya was his fever-glow Bonnie, her jaws locked in that tight-lipped grin as she surveyed the room with impossibly wide eyes.

One of them, or both, gave off a strong odor—not exactly the usual stink of junkies who'd gone a few days without a shower. This was a dirtier smell. A deep smell, wet and fungal. It reminded Alex of earthworms squirming blindly on the sidewalk after a long, hard rain.

He pushed back a few inches from the desk and addressed his detainees. "So. Names. LeGault, Montgomery Marcus and Beechwood, Tonya Lynn—correct?"

Monty chuckled and glanced sidelong at Tonya. "Yep. That's right. Ain't it baby?"

Tonya nodded. "Yes sir, that's correct." Her voice was soft and flat, barely more than a whisper. She began to hum.

"And you guys wanted to buy some meth—is that correct?"

Tonya looked down at the corner of the desk and said nothing but Monty fixed Alex with a huge, broken-toothed smile. "Yes sir, officer, I'm not gonna try and lie to the law 'bout it no more." His smile disappeared and his face became solemn. "Yes, we was tryin' to buy some crank. We was out behind Preacher's and we thought that asshole might give Tonya a few bucks for a handy but instead he goes back in and calls your boy who come along and grabs us. We didn't try no resistin'. We come peaceful. We ain't a danger to nobody but us selves."

Alex regarded Tonya with sympathetic eyes. "Ms. Beechwood, is this true?"

Without pulling her gaze from the desk she gave a quick shake of her head in the affirmative. "It is."

"And who were you going to buy from? Who's your dealer?"

Monty flapped his hands desperately, appealing to Alex. "That's just it! That's just it officer. We was only so desperate 'cause there's a guy in town right now sells shit that is ab-so-lutely off the fuckin meters. He travels around and only stops for a week or two. Only comes round every couple of months. He's here now but we'd already spent my disability check so we did what we had to do. That shit is A+ believe me. Well worth a handful of jizz. Ain't that right Sugar?" He elbowed Tonya beside him and she nodded again.

"Not your hand though, right Monty?" Alex favored the stringy tweaker with a withering, sarcastic grin. There were two files on the desk—the same two files Alex would later show Sergeant Howard. They contained Monty and Tonya's priors. He flipped both folders open. "Well, never mind. Listen you two, we've got us a problem." He held up the folder that held Monty's file. "See, you guys have quite extensive records. Both of you. Add on solicitation and attempted possession of an illegal substance and you guys could be looking at some serious jail time here."

Monty's jaw had gone slack. His eyes darkened and he began to sputter and chuff. "But-but-hold on now, just hold the fuck on officer. We's sick people, man, disabled. Both of us. We can't be in no jail. They's gotta be somethin' we can do." He looked over at Tonya. "Maybe she can throw a little, somethin-somethin, your way right now and we call it evens?"

Alex couldn't believe what he was hearing. "Are you seriously trying to fuck yourself over worse here? Bribing an officer with sexual favors?" He shook his head. "Monty, come on, be smart for once. Work with me here and maybe quit trying to put dicks in your lady's mouth. What is it with you?"

"I don't know," Monty was blubbering now while Tonya continued to hum quietly under her breath. "I don't know officer it's all we got to give."

"Try to think along different, *legal* lines. Will you?"

"Yes sir, yes I will." Monty swiped at his running nose with his already crusted sleeve and snorted back up snot. "What else can we do? Help us."

Alex was quiet for a few moments, pretending to think. He knew the question he wanted to ask as soon as Monty had mentioned that their dealer was a guy who traveled around. It was probably a long shot but maybe this was the guy they'd been looking for.

Finally, he spoke. "Well. What's the name of this dealer? The one who travels around?"

Monty looked up at the ceiling, trying to remember, snapping his finger in the air. "Shit, yeah it's—ah—Graverton—no, no! Grayson, it's Grayson! He rides around in a trailer, parks it out near the campgrounds a few miles outside of Bright."

Alex's heart began to beat very fast. With deliberate casualness, he shrugged his shoulders. "Okay, well, that's a start." He pulled his notepad and a pen from his shirt pocket and flipped it open. "You said his name was…?

"Grayson. Don't know his first name."

Alex knew it. Isaiah. The Meth Suppression Task Force of the Indiana State Police knew it too. He was wanted across fourteen counties. If Alex could pin him down—catch his ass—it would be huge for the Southeast division.

He told Monty and Tonya to sit tight and then tried hard not to run down to the office he was using at the Sheriff's department. He made a few phone calls and spoke with Sergeant Howard, and Sergeant Brixley, from Northeast Division. A tentative plan came together to get a warrant. A plan that would require someone who knew where Grayson was going to be. That someone would be escorted by an undercover officer who could then record a drug deal going down.

Monty and Tonya were their someone's and Alex had worked undercover many, many times. The snag was that there were no surveillance vans currently available that could be planted nearby to house any backup, and no seasoned troopers available to provide support, even if there *was* a van. Alex would be out there, floating in deep, black waters with only the most tenuous and flimsy of lifelines.

"Talk to your perps first before we get rolling on this." Howard had said. "They might not even be okay with this. We don't really have much on them that a half-bright public defender couldn't get them out of easily enough."

"Yeah," Alex had replied with a smile in his voice. "But they didn't ask for a lawyer. We read them their rights and then they just started talking. It's almost too easy."

Calls were made to the DA. A plea deal didn't even need to be cut. If Monty and Tonya agreed to participate in the sting then they'd be released, all charges dropped. Of course, Alex wouldn't present it to them exactly that way.

"If you do this for us, I think I can get the DA to reduce your charges and maybe get you by with just probation—no jail time. Maybe." This was how Alex had spun it. All Monty and Tonya had to do was drive Alex out to Grayson's and pretend he was their cousin. Then they'd buy meth within earshot of Alex, using Grayson's name at least once. Then they'd leave and the sergeant would send the surveillance audio to a judge who'd sign a warrant. Monty and Tonya could go free to try and sell themselves for drugs again and the law could swoop down on Isaiah Grayson, guns blazing. Alex could see commendations in his future. His very near future.

Of course, Monty and Tonya agreed—what choice did they really have? They were fed the fiction that there was going to be backup, tons of it, following behind at a safe and invisible distance. This backup, they were told, would be heavily armed and monitoring their every move should they develop a case of second thoughts out there in the woods.

Now here they were, cruising through the damp, midnight chill of late September, the leaves whispering and sighing in the breeze above them. Tonya had gone back to humming, "Time of the Season," but Monty had fallen into a morose silence. He twiddled his thumbs restlessly against the steering wheel and glanced at Alex in the rearview mirror every few seconds.

After twenty minutes or so he jagged the car left onto a dirt road that cut suddenly into the woods. Thick darkness swallowed them up as they bounced and humped along the rough lane between the trees. A minute later, Monty finally spoke.

"Spooky back here."

"What?" Alex had been mentally prepping for the meetup as the cool air from the window washed across his face.

"I said it's spooky back here. Gives me the creeps." Monty had reduced their speed considerably. Night sounds began to filter in from the shadowy depths beyond the reach of their headlights. Somewhere an owl screeched, and the crickets sang in mournful chorus as the car rolled through.

"Remember those two guys who disappeared a couple'a years back out at Brookville Lake?"

"Yeah." Alex met Monty's hectic gaze in the mirror. "Some people said the Brookville Troll killed 'em."

"It's not a troll, it's the Spaceman." Tonya drawled from the passenger seat.

"Alright, whatever. Spaceman." Monty shook his head. "Either way that shit is creepy. This place makes me think of that. Ya know?"

Alex sighed. "Monty, shit, I don't know. I don't believe in that kind of stuff. Only what's real."

Monty tittered, a high-pitched, breathless sound. An unpleasant sound. "You're probably right. Stuff like that probably ain't real." He giggled again. "By the way. We here."

The dirt road abruptly widened into a broad, gravel expanse, ringed with trees. Alex could see discarded cinderblocks, an old battered microwave, and other, detritus, yellow in the Regal's headlights. They crunched along for another thirty feet or so and a dirty gray trailer appeared, nestled against the woods at the far end of the gravel. A man was sitting on the ground, leaning against the back tire of the trailer, his legs stuck out in front of him.

As Monty stopped the car, Alex sat up straight. "Alright you guys, let's do this just how we rehearsed and you'll be back out on the street in twenty-four hours." He thought for a second before adding, "And don't forget, there is backup waiting out there in the woods. So nothing funny."

Monty turned and looked Alex in the face. He was very close, and his grimy smell wafted into the back like a fog. "Don't you worry 'bout nothin' boss. We got ya." He smiled, a far less crazy smile than Alex had seen from him, opened his door, and climbed out of the car.

For the first time since this plan was hatched, Alex felt a tickle of doubt. It flitted and bounced around his gut like bats. He lamented his lack of a gun, but it was too late for that now. He flipped the lever on the side of the driver's seat and pushed it forward, climbing out the open door as Tonya got out on her side. The doors were slammed, and they walked through the gravel to the trailer.

The man sitting on the ground popped to his feet the moment they were all out of the car. As they approached, he pounded on the dented side of the trailer and shouted. "'Saiah? Hey man, we got customers." To Alex, Monty, and Tonya he held out his hand. "Hey. Y'all just stay put and hold on a sec. 'Kay?"

Monty held his own hands up, arms bent at the elbows, to show he wasn't holding anything. "Hey man, it's all good. We're cool. Just here to do a little bidness."

The other man did not lower his arm or change his posture. His brows were drawn together with concern. He was short with a thick black beard and close-set eyes. "That's fine, but I said wait so y'all gonna have to wait."

The three of them stopped and stood where they were. There was no light on in the trailer and with the headlights of the Regal turned off, it was nearly black there in the clearing.

As Alex looked around the yard his eyes played tricks on him. It seemed like shadows moved and danced against the deeper black of the woods, mocking him. His body hummed with electricity and a bell started clanging over and over in his mind tolling, *bad idea, bad idea*. Sergeant Howard had been right. This was foolish.

Don't be such a bitch. His inner voice was harsh, commanding. *You're an Indiana State Trooper and these are just a bunch of brain-dead, shit—kicking, sister-fucking, inbred meth-heads. You are equipped to handle this situation. You've trained for it. You don't need a gun. You will see this operation carried through, you will walk out of here alive, and you will get your man.* His nerves seemed to sing a little bit more quietly after his internal scolding and he tried to get into character as they waited for something to happen.

A moment later the trailer door banged open beneath its cheap, tin awning and a flashlight clicked on, its beam trained on Alex's group. At the other end of the light was the vague impression of a tall, skinny person. A voice called out.

"Hey there. Who we got out here Ezzard?" The flashlight's beam swept the gravel clearing, shining in Alex's eyes and blinding him. "Who the fuck is that out there?"

The bearded man called back from somewhere ahead of them and to the right. "Bunch 'a tweakers. Say they here to do business with you."

Monty lifted his hands all the way in the air. "Hey! Hey, Grayson, it's me. Monty LeGault. You 'member?"

The flashlight-holder's voice came back doubtful. "Gotta be honest with you Monty, I'm afraid you ain't ringin' too much of a bell for me."

"You called me Squirrely Sam."

"Ohhhh, yeah." The flashlight beam was quickly aimed down at the ground and Alex watched its bobbing progress while its owner strode towards them. "Squirrely Sam and Long, Tall Sally. You got ol' Sally with ya?"

"Yep, she's here."

The man with the flashlight whistled appreciatively. "Man, she had a mouth on her. I remember *that*." The bobbing circle of light reached their feet and the person controlling it stood before them.

He was still bathed in shadow but was illuminated enough for Alex to see that he was a long, skinny scarecrow of a man in a filthy tank top. He had long sideburns that stopped just short of being mutton-chops and a rockabilly pompadour swept back across the top of his head. In the dark, his eyes were just two black pools, his mouth a bottomless ravine. He brought the flashlight back up and shined it in Alex's face again.

"Who's this Jethro-lookin motherfucker? I don't remember him."

"Oh," Monty sputtered, "That's my neph—er, cousin. Denny. He's ridin' out to the campground with us tonight. "

"That so?" The man seemed to be staring at Alex but it was hard to tell.

"Yep." Alex did a very passable imitation of Monty and To-nya's white-trash twang. "We gettin' fuuucked up tonight boy."

The man just stood there, the silence gaining weight with each passing second. Alex began to sweat. *Shit, he knows*. He began thinking about the likelihood of survival if he just cut and ran for the woods when the man dropped the flashlight to his side and stuck out his hand to be shaken.

"Isaiah Grayson. Goddam nice to meet ya." Alex took the meth dealer's hand and gave it a shake. Grayson turned and started back towards the trailer. "Y'all come on in and we'll get you good and set and you can get on with your partyin'."

They followed him up to the trailer. Ezzard had gone in ahead of them and switched on a light and now stood leaning in the doorway. Alex could see one arm of a ratty brown couch and a long out-of-season Christmas tree beyond a plywood partition. A shadow moved, just on the other side of the couch, just out of Alex's field of vision.

Someone else was in there. Alex's heart began to beat faster and every instinct that he'd developed over thirteen years in law enforcement cried out against going through that door, but it was too late to back out now.

Monty and Tonya had caught up to Grayson a few yards ahead of him and the three of them were muttering and chuckling. Tonya climbed the steps to the door and patted Ezzard's sweat-stained paunch. He smiled, moving aside for her and she climbed past him and out of sight.

Monty followed close behind and bumped fists with Ezzard. Grayson stopped at the door and waited. The drug dealer's mouth stretched into a toothy grin as Alex climbed past him up the steps.

"Come on in Alex. We gonna get you set up real nice."

Alex cleared his throat. The nagging fear that this had all somehow gone terribly awry made it hard for him to reproduce his earlier twang. "Uh, yeah. Thanks." He passed through into the doorway and then stopped cold.

Alex. He'd called him *Alex.*

The panic that had been brewing over the last few minutes finally broke and Alex spun around to leap from the trailer. Grayson was already there filling the doorway and smiling.

"What's wrong Alex, I mean, Denny? Where ya goin' little guy?"

"Fuck you! You're under arrest!" Alex took a swing at Grayson, his fist careening at the other man's face. Instead of striking hard flesh, however, when his fist connected with Grayson's jaw it was like punching into a moldy, long-forgotten cake. Grayson's face caved in with a sickening give. Spongy dumplings of flesh, bone, and teeth flew like brown and red confetti, and more dripped from Alex's curled fingers and wrist.

He yanked his arm back with a disgusting, squelch as the lower half of Grayson's face collapsed in on itself. Alex's mouth dropped open and his eyes went wide. Grayson tried to smile with what was left of his mouth, a twitching, cavernous ruin, and dropped Alex an obscene wink.

Alex jerked his head away, turning to look into the tiny hallway to his left, and saw Monty and Tonya. Before entering the trailer, they had been dirty and disheveled with soiled clothes and sallow skin, but they had also clearly been living, breathing human beings.

Now, standing hunched in the shadows, two corpses wearing Tonya and Monty's clothes stared back at him from eye sockets picked clean by grave scavengers. Grayish green flesh, mottled with tiny bits of clinging fungus hung in thick ribbons from their skulls, their lips rotted away to reveal denuded jaws. Blowflies circled their heads like black, buzzing haloes, occasionally landing to crawl through the dry straw of their hair. They were still lively enough, though, that Alex could hear Monty's finger-bones clattering together as he continued to jitter and jive, and Tonya's endless humming vibrating through her exposed trachea.

As he tried to make sense of the nightmares surrounding him, Alex heard a shuffling sound from the living room area behind him and he turned. When he saw what was standing there he began to scream. He couldn't understand exactly what his eyes were trying to tell him. His head began to ache with the effort of assigning a shape to the tall, dark being that shambled across the filthy floor toward him. Human, it wasn't. That one was easy to toss out. Other things suggested themselves though in a gauzy, shifting way where, for a second it was almost an insect but not an insect at all. Points of light would blossom in colors never seen by any sane person, like eyes opening within what was maybe its head and then they would close, and mouths would appear with moving, slathering tongues and dripping teeth. Was it a dog with an ape's body? Was it an inside-out octopus? Did it have feathers or was it made of fecal matter? Yes. And no. All of this and none of it.

Alex could no longer hear the blistering screams that tore from his own throat, but it seemed that there was no bottom to the well from which they were drawn. He wished for the mercy of death or madness but his mind clung to rationality with a heartbreaking tenacity.

It came closer, reaching for him. Some part of it, a darkly glowing tendril, touched him with a loathsome, groping sensation that was nearly a caress, and Alex could sense its hunger. It's eagerness to have him, to consume him.

With a miserable understanding, Alex collapsed to the floor, his body unable to stand any longer beneath the weight of his terror. Behind him, the Grayson-thing dripped laughter from the depths of its cavernous face and shut the trailer door.

***

Back at the dispatch room of the Dearborn County Sheriff's Department, officer Chris "Lucky" Ferguson and Sergeant Donald Howard listened to Alex's terror-soaked shrieks. They heard the sounds of his struggle. Heard the dark laughter of his captors. Whatever was happening had to be very bad to reduce a man like Alex to such shrill frenzy.

"No!" They heard him cry. "Undo these straps, undo them RIGHT NOW goddammit! Oh God, do you see that? What IS it? What the fuck IS IT?" He moaned, his voice small and tinny in the headphones. Howard dropped his and ran from the office shouting for someone to get the fucking helicopter up. Lucky kept listening, not wanting to hear any more but unable to put his headset aside.

"Keep that away, please! I'll do anything. You can kill me please I'll—what are you doing with that? OH MY FUCKING GOD THAT HUUUURTS!" There was the sound of garbled laughter and someone singing. A woman. The song seemed vaguely familiar to Lucky. Some song from the sixties—something spooky.

There was more laughter and then Alex's voice again. "Get it out of me!" Then a long, tremulous howl of absolute soul-shattering pain and despair. The sound of sanity breaking free and fleeing in horror. Alex seemed to be crying and laughing all at the same time and then came the last words anyone would ever hear him speak. "No, no! I don't want it, I DO NOT WANT THAT! Wait, what? Oh dear Jesus…how…how many fucking legs does she have?" Then there was a horrible buzzing feedback, and the connection went dead. Ice-cold tears spilled down Lucky's cheeks as he threw his headphones down onto the table and vomited into the waste basket beside his chair.

***

Six weeks later.

Two men and a woman are brought into the Bloomington PD on suspicion of trying to sell meth on the Indiana University campus. They're kept in separate holding cells but are brought together into an interrogation room by a vice detective named Scott.

He's heard whispers of a traveling meth operation selling out of a beat-up trailer and, for some reason, he's got a feeling about these three. One of the men has dry, dirty, shaggy blonde hair. He twitches and giggles. The second man is clean-shaven with short sandy hair. He has a large earring in one ear. Scott's not sure, but he feels like he's seen the man before. Probably picked up dozens of times for drug charges but that doesn't seem to be where he's familiar from. No matter. The woman is skinny, all legs and long bleached hair. Her mouth is closed, and she doesn't speak as Scott begins to ask them questions about a man named Grayson, but she does keep humming something under her breath. The tune is as vaguely familiar as the face of the second man. It finally comes to him, as they're promising to take him to the man he's looking for, the man who killed a decorated state cop before disappearing into the night, and who is wanted by every law enforcement division in the country. The song is "Time of the Season" by The Zombies. He loves that song. He has a good feeling about this bust. A very good feeling indeed.

LATE NIGHT LAUNDRY

Ellen lay in bed in her new apartment unable to sleep. Bad dreams had plagued her since she'd moved in, and she tossed in her sheets until the clock radio showed 2:45 a.m. She sat up and swung her legs over the edge of the bed, planting her feet in a pile of socks and underwear on the floor.

That's what I'll do. She thought. *Laundry. Maybe I can bore myself to sleep folding it.*

She put her glasses on and gathered up a hamper-full of clothes from around her bedroom. She pulled on a pair of gym-shorts and carried her hamper out the front door and into the hallway. The building was quiet. Ellen made her way down to the first floor and descended a set of rickety stairs into the basement.

The basement laundry room was empty except for 2 coin-operated washer/dryer combos. A battered door at the back of the room led outside to where the dumpster crouched against the stone wall that surrounded the building.

Ellen dumped her clothes into the washer along with a cupful of detergent. She was getting ready to head back upstairs when she heard a tapping at one of the grimy windows behind her. She turned and saw a face peering in at her. It was a little girl. Ellen walked over to the window for a closer look.

"Hello?" Ellen whispered. "Are you okay?"

The little girl didn't seem to hear her. She had long blonde hair and very white skin. She wore no shoes. The little girl stared in at Ellen with frightened eyes. She tapped the glass again and then hurried off towards the dumpster.

Ellen thought the little girl might need help, so she went out the basement door and into the chilly night. The darkness outside was thick. She looked for the little girl and found her peeking out from behind the dumpster. The girl waved and Ellen went to where the girl was standing.

She crept around the corner and found the girl on the ground, motionless. She bent over the little body and put her hand against the girl's chest. She wasn't breathing.

Ellen was about to call out for help when she heard a deep chuckle from the shadows by the wall. She looked up and saw a huge, dark shape rising up before her. Great, black arms reached out to grasp her.

"Join us."

She stood frozen in terror and never had a chance to scream.

In the morning James, from apartment 1, decided to take the garbage out on his way to work. He strode through the basement and out the back door. He was startled by the sight of his neighbor standing near the dumpster. She didn't speak but she waved him over as if she wanted to show him something.

James walked behind the dumpster to find out what was wrong.

ON POWDERED WINGS

Glenn felt an unpleasant tickle at the nape of his neck. He reached back and swatted at the spot, too late to catch whatever had lit there. He looked around the room, checking to make sure the window was shut.

"Goddam bugs." He turned back to his monitor and frowned at the rows and columns of numbers that spread across it. His eyes were burning and watery from going over the sums and balances again and again. Child support, two high-interest loans, his car payment, his ex-wife's car payment, the mortgage payment (on a house he no longer lived in), and the rent on his shitty apartment.

Glenn heaved a growling sigh and pushed away from the desk, rubbing his eyes. He started for the kitchen to get some more coffee, when something small and dark flew at his face and batted against his cheek. Startled, he threw his arm up defensively and let out a yelp. He staggered back a step, jamming painfully against the edge of the open closet door.

"Ow, *Christ*!" Stumbling away from the closet, he plopped down onto his bed and tried to rub his back where he'd collided with the door. He looked around the room again and this time spotted the culprit clinging silently to the curtain across from him. It was a big, black moth. Its wings flexed insolently, taunting him.

Glenn glared at it. His jaw clenched and his eyebrows drew together. In that moment all his problems, small and large, somehow became the fault of the calmly quavering insect on the curtain. He searched the floor for something to kill it with and found a wrinkled apartment guide peeking out from beneath the bed. He leaned forward and grabbed it, rolling it up as he stood. He moved towards it, pushing through the dirty clothes on his bedroom floor.

He stood, transfixed for a moment, watching its black wings and its barely visible, twitching antennae. It seemed entirely indifferent to his presence. It mocked him with its nonchalance. Fury bloomed in his cheeks and forehead.

He shouted and swung the magazine with hysterical force at the curtain, pounding at the spot the moth clung too. It was too fast for him and anticipated his strike. It took off from the curtain with a casual flutter of its wings and floated gracefully to the ceiling. Meanwhile, in his violent zeal, Glenn had managed to step on the curtain, where it pooled on the floor, tearing it from the rod. He let out a strangled cry and spun around. His heart was pounding, he was dizzy, and his head ached. The moth was now nestled comfortably against the screen of Glenn's computer monitor.

You weren't even close.

Glenn pulled his arm back, ready to pulverize the dusty intruder against the screen when a moment of clarity crowded its way past the rage.

All you're going to do is wreck your computer and then what? Then when it lands on your TV are you going to smash that in too? How about your mirror? Let it go.

Glenn let the apartment guide slip from his fingers. His head was throbbing. He winced, kneading his temples, and lurched out of the bedroom, flipping off the light as he passed.

In his small kitchenette Glenn poured himself a lukewarm mug of coffee. He took a swig, and grimaced. He refilled his cup and made his way into the front room of the apartment. With a groan he settled gingerly into a ratty, thrift-store easy-chair. For a twenty-dollar piece of trash it was surprisingly comfortable. He leaned his head back, closed his eyes and took another drink. He thought about the business with Alvita Criado. It had been very unpleasant, and the memory dragged the corners of his mouth down into a scowl.

It had started a few weeks earlier when a man named Efrain Criado, a man Glenn had never met, seen or heard of, died of a sudden heart attack. After submitting a claim for his $250,000 life insurance policy, his widow Alvita received a letter, drafted by Glenn from within his small, gray cubicle, stating that her husband's policy had unfortunately been rescinded. The heart attack had been caused by a congenital defect which hadn't been disclosed on the original application. According to the letter, they regretted to inform her of this unfortunate miscommunication and would refund the $7000.00 that had been paid into the policy. The letter wished her all the best and was signed, *"Sincerely, Glenn R. Michels, Claims Representative."*

A few days after sending the letter, Glenn received a call from the distraught widow.

"Mr. Michels, how will we make this right? How will we fix this so I'm not left out in the cold?" She had a very thick accent. It wasn't exactly Spanish, and it wasn't quite Caribbean. Glenn idly wondered where she was from.

"Look, Mrs. Criado, I wish there was something I could do to help you." Glenn's tone had been low and miserable. These conversations made him feel dirty. "I really do. The problem is that your husband's condition wasn't disclosed on his application and therefore wasn't considered when assessing his risk. If they can't properly assess the risk then, unfortunately, the policy is considered falsified. I'm sure it wasn't intentional but that's the way they view it. I'm very sorry."

Her voice had come back louder and shakier. "He did not even know he *had* this heart disease. How can you tell something if you don't know about it?" She'd begun choking back sobs. "How can you punish us for things we couldn't control?"

"Mrs. Criado, I'm really very sorry." He had started to sweat. And guilt churned like acid in his stomach. "What you don't understand is that this is something *I* can't control either. If I could, I would love nothing more than to approve your claim, but those issues are decided by someone else in a different department and, unfortunately, they have the legal right to do so."

Her sobs had been replaced by a derisive laugh then. "Ha! Legal right? We'll see who has the legal rights here, Mr. Glenn Michels. We'll just see." Then there had been a loud click in Glenn's ear and Mrs. Criado was suddenly gone. Glenn sighed as he hung up his receiver. He had a feeling he'd be hearing from her again and three days later he did.

"Mrs. Criado—Alvita—" Glenn's tone had gone from professionally cool to defensive as soon as he realized who was on the phone with him.

"I'll thank you to call me Mrs. Criado or nothing at all Mr. Michels." The widow's emotions were in tighter control that day, but Glenn sensed the roiling chaos that surged beneath the surface. It was a slight, wavering tremor in her voice that betrayed her calm façade.

"Okay then. *Mrs. Criado*, I'm not sure what else there is for us to talk about. I told you when we spoke the other day—"

"You told me nothing. I'm only calling today to ask you for your supervisor's name and extension please."

Glenn gave Mrs. Criado the information and was promptly hung up on. He'd felt better. She was in someone else's hands. She would almost certainly threaten a lawsuit and she would be calmly invited to go ahead and do so. Any half-competent lawyer would explain that she had no case and that, presumably, would be the end of that. Glenn had gone back to his paperwork after that, a tiny grin surfacing as he imagined the tongue lashing that Steve, his supervisor, was going to receive. Several more days went by quietly with no word from the widow and Glenn figured the situation had been put to rest.

Then she showed up at Glenn's office, appearing right outside his cubicle like a sudden storm.

Glenn had been sitting at his desk, writing an email to his ex-wife's attorney (Lisa was petitioning to raise the amount of his child-support payment) when a voice called from behind his back—a familiar voice with an unmistakable accent.

"Mr. Michels turn around please. I want to see the face of the man who would steal from me."

Glenn couldn't believe it. *How did she get in here?* A person had to have a security badge to get into the office unless they had an appointment, and she most certainly did *not* have an appointment. Not with him. Reluctantly, Glenn spun around on his swivel chair. He was very nervous, scared really.

Alvita Criado did not look at all the way Glenn had imagined her. He had pictured a hunched-over old lady in a shawl, with gray hair, maybe pulled into a bun. The woman who stood before him that day was none of that. For one thing, she was young—younger than Glenn anyway—in her late thirties or very early forties. She was short and curvy. with huge, smoky eyes. Long black hair fell in messy tangles past her shoulders, and she was dressed i simply but stylish. In spite of everything, Glenn thought she was very attractive.

"Mrs. Criado? You shouldn't be here." Glenn saw heads popping up over cubicle walls and chairs sliding out into the aisle as people responded to the sounds of raised voices. He and Mrs. Criado were center stage. "How did you get in here?"

The small woman's eyes flashed with fury. She waved her hand with a dismissive gesture and chuffed like an agitated horse. "Are you worried? Are you feeling like someone just pulled a rug out from under you Mr. Michels? Thinking about how embarrassing this is going to be for you? Yes? You aren't thinking of anything else. *Are you?*" Her voice had gotten very loud. "You care nothing for my suffering. You don't care about anyone but Glenn R. Michaels." H knew the eyes of the entire office were devouring the exchange.

"Please lower your voice. We can talk about this rationally. I'll call my supervisor down and we can figure this out together but—"

Mrs. Criado cut him off. "Stop whining, pig. You can do nothing. You can say *nothing* that will make me feel better. I am here to share a little of my," she spun her hand in the air as she searched for the right word, "my misery, with you and *you will listen to me.*"

Glenn thought about how he'd looked around at his co-workers. They hadn't had a day this good since the time Lionel Pragar had come into the office stinking drunk and tried to fondle a young intern while singing Billy Joel's "My Life" at the top of his lungs. Glenn's ears and neck burned with embarrassment at the knowledge that he was the new Lionel Pragar.

"Mrs. Criado, I'm not kidding. Unless you calm down, I'm not going to discuss anything with you."

The small woman laughed, an ugly, jagged sound, and clapped her hands in mock applause. "Oh, it's starting to find its balls now, huh? Good for you, but it don't matter a damn to me. I'll yell and scream and holler as much as I want. Till my lungs shatter and my throat shreds. I'll stomp my feet and curse your name and you're going to hear every word of it because *you owe me this.* Me and Efrain."

It was like his ex-wife all over again. Lisa, berating him for his inability to provide a more comfortable existence, saying he wasn't a real provider, tearing him down in front of the family-court mediator, and worse, in front of their daughters. Anger, like hot venom, spread through his body. His hands balled into fists at his sides as he stood from his chair. He could feel his left eye twitching.

Glenn pointed a shaky finger at Mrs. Criado. "I—am—sorry—for your loss, Mrs. Criado. *Sorry.* I truly am. But I am *not* the one who denied your claim. You want to explode on somebody? Rain down hell? Find the asshole that sent the email telling *me* to inform *you* that your policy was denied." Glenn was breathing hard. His hands were shaking.

Mrs. Criado strode forward until her upturned face was only inches from Glenn's. "Shift the blame you snake, just go ahead and shift it." She was shouting now. "The letter had *your* name on it. You're the one and only asshole I want to rain hell down on. My husband put his faith and his hard-earned money into your worthless company thinking that, if anything should happen to him, I would be cared for.

Your letter—*yours*—shit and pissed all over him."

"We gave you your goddam money back." Glenn's voice had matched Mrs. Criado's in volume. "You can't say we cheated you. We gave you back every penny you paid us."

"You mean you flung it back in my face as if we weren't good enough for you to keep your promises to. That's barely enough to cover his burial. How'm I supposed to live now? What am I supposed to do?" Mrs. Criado reached forward and grabbed double handfuls of Glenn's shirt and tugged violently at him, her knuckles pressing into his soft belly.

"Get a fucking job I guess!" Without thinking, Glenn shoved Mrs. Criado, hard. She stumbled backward a few steps, losing her grip on his shirt, and tripped as her feet tangled together. She went to the ground, landing on her ample behind with a soft, thud and a collective gasp swept through the crowd of gawkers.

Mrs. Criado's dark eyes went wide with shock for a moment before narrowing to furious, black slits. Somewhere, across the office, a door opened, and the crackle of hurried, heavy footsteps approached.

Someone had called security. Mrs. Criado stood and swept her gaze across the room, meeting the hungry eyes of each curious face that regarded her. She straightened her shirt, tugging it out from beneath her bosom and dusted off the back of her pants. Then she turned back to Glenn.

"You will not hear from me again Mr. Glenn Michels. I will not call you or write or visit your office anymore."

"Mrs. Criado, please...I'm so sorry." Glenn was suddenly filled with dark, heavy shame. He couldn't believe that he'd put his hands on a woman—*a widow*—grieving the loss of her husband. A widow who was angry over what could rightfully be seen as an underhanded trick by the insurance company to screw her. If Lisa were here she would sneer and say she wasn't surprised at all but Glenn was. He would never have thought in a million years he was capable of such a thing. "I didn't mean to push you like that. I'm really so very sorry. About all of this." His cheeks were burning but the rest of him was ice cold.

The apology hung in the air between them as a tall, skinny security guard burst into the aisle. "Is there a problem here?" All eyes now turned to him and somewhere, behind a cubicle wall, someone snickered.

Mrs. Criado spat a frothy glob of saliva to the floor. Her eyes, filled with contempt, locked on Glenn who stood looking at the ground, unable to meet her gaze. "There isn't anymore. Not for me."

"Okay but I'm going to have to escort you out now ma'am." The security guard stood, watching her nervously. "Follow me this way please."

Mrs. Criado turned a vicious eye on the young guard, as if noticing him for the first time. He chewed his lips, uncomfortable in the heat of her scrutiny, but did not look away. After a moment, the petite, angry woman nodded her head and sauntered down the aisle. Past Glenn and the guard, blind to the eyes that avidly drank in every detail of her departure. The young security guard turned and followed her and soon they were at the other end of the office and out the door.

Sprawled in his second-hand easy chair with kettle drums pounding behind his eyelids, Glenn was helpless against the memory. Thinking about it made him nauseous. He sat that way, sipping his cold, bitter coffee for a long time, trying to blot out the ugly scene with any other thought, even thoughts of Lisa and the divorce. But Glenn couldn't erase the image of Mrs. Criado's eyes blazing with malice, staring him down as she spat on the floor before walking away. It just kept playing over and over in his mind like some nightmare video on a loop. Eventually he slipped into an uneasy sleep dreaming of beautiful but angry women who shrieked at him from above on brightly colored wings.

The next day crawled by slowly but uneventfully. When his work was finally over, Glenn stepped into his apartment, tired but glad to be home. He microwaved a burrito for dinner and washed it down with three bottles of very cheap beer, watching an endless parade of reality TV. When he realized it was midnight, he dragged himself out of his chair and down the hall to take a piss and then tumbled into bed. His eyes slipped shut almost immediately and he fell into a fuzzy sleep.

An hour later, he snapped suddenly and completely awake, blinking in the darkness. "Hello? Lisa?" As soon as the words were out of his mouth, he remembered that he was alone, or at least he was supposed to be. Some sound had broken through his thin shell of sleep. He lay there, propped up on one elbow, trying to filter out all the usual night-sounds to catch whatever had startled him into consciousness.

A thump. At the window above his bed. A soft *tap* that finished with a fluttery burst against the screen. It came again. Then a third time. Glenn climbed to his knees on his mattress and scooted to the window. He pulled the curtain aside and was greeted with the sight of dozens of gray, undulating moths, pressed against the window. The thumping was their fuzzy little bodies hitting the screen as more and more came to light there. They squirmed against each other, the buzz of their wings like whispering voices as they tried to find purchase with their sticky feet. *Thump*, there was another—*thump*—and another.

Glenn uttered a disgusted grunt and slammed his open palm against the window. A few disengaged, hanging in the air, ghost-like, before resettling somewhere else. Most of them didn't seem to notice at all. He tapped the window in different places, hard, with his fingers, trying to startle them off. They were indifferent. Not only were they not leaving but more continued to drop out of the night sky, thudding onto the moving gray mass.

Glenn swallowed hard and let the curtain back down. He didn't like looking at them clinging that way. *Why are they doing that?* There were no lights on in the apartment. It made no sense. There wasn't anything there to attract them. Glenn lay back down on top of his covers and gathered his pillow in his arms. *What is going on?* He decided to put a call in to the front office first thing in the morning to find out if anyone else was having problems.

He closed his eyes and tried to get comfortable, but sleep evaded him. The sound of the moths plunking against the outer screen continued through the night. For a good, long time Glenn pretended to ignore it, hovering i between fully alert and fitful dozing. Every time he started to slip into any real kind of sleep the image of them all, fluttering and thumping on the other side of the wall, would drag him back to waking.

Finally, when the red numbers on his clock showed 5:27, Glenn got up, grabbed his blanket and stomped out to his easy chair where he couldn't hear the moths anymore. He wrapped the blanket around himself and fell almost instantly into a deep, peaceful slumber. At 6:30 his alarm began blaring. Glenn's eyes, bleary and sore, snapped open and he sighed heavily. It was time to get up for work.

The only good thing about that day was that it was Friday. Glenn drifted through it in a gray haze. He felt like a miserable phantom trapped in a box, pushing papers listlessly around, pretending to read them. Nothing that crossed his desk got done and the hours dragged on with endless monotony. Finally, at quarter of five, Glenn shoved everything into his desk with a disgusted sigh, stood, and shuffled out of the office.

After walking into his apartment, he locked the front door and went straight to his bedroom, dropping, fully dressed, onto the disheveled covers. He was asleep in minutes. It was just after nine o'clock when he was startled awake by the thudding at his window.

With a yelp of frustration, Glenn rose to his knees on the mattress and tore the curtain aside revealing a mottled-gray blanket of furry bodies, writhing against the screen. There were more than the night before—many, many more. Glenn couldn't see any patch of sky through the tightly packed mass. With soft thumps, more kept adding themselves to the orgy of wings and grasping legs.

Glenn pounded the window, rattling it in the frame. "Get out of here! Go! Shoo!" He hammered his fist against the glass as hard as he dared, over and over again until his neighbor whacked their own fist against the wall that separated the apartments.

Glenn pulled back, letting the curtain fall and fished his phone out of his pocket. After a few moments of searching, he found the number to the apartment complex office on his contacts list. In his exhaustion he'd forgotten all about calling to complain about the moths, but he'd be damned if he was going to let this go on any longer. He pressed *send* and held the phone up to his ear. After five long, patience-testing rings a refreshing, if distant, female voice came on the line.

"Thank you for calling M & R Properties LLC. The office is now closed." Glenn gritted his teeth, his forehead getting hot. "Our business hours are Monday through Friday, 9am to 9pm, Saturday 10-8 and Sunday noon to 6pm." He glanced at the clock on his phone. 9:09. "If you have questions about availability in any of our communities or would like to schedule a walk-through please leave your name, number and a good time to reach you. If you are a tenant with an emergency maintenance issue, please call our on-call service at…"

With enormous effort, Glenn managed to keep from dashing his phone to pieces against the wall. He thumbed the *end* button and tossed it on the nightstand. For the second night in a row, he found himself gathering up his blanket and going out to the living room to sleep in his easy chair. *At least I don't have to get up for work, thank Christ.* He curled up like, blanket clutched tightly to his chin, and tried to find his way back to sleep. He spent some time, seething there in the cool dark of his living room, before it finally came, bearing bad dreams.

The next afternoon, after waking up groggy and out of sorts, Glenn called the management office back. This time the pleasantly cool feminine voice was alive. "It's a great day at M & R Properties. This is Whitney, how can I help you?"

Suddenly, with the silky voice of the receptionist in his ear, Glenn felt embarrassed about his problem. What was he supposed to say? *Hi, I'm calling because a bunch of moths, really nothing more than ugly butterflies, are keeping me up at night. Can you help me with this?* In the light of day, after a couple of cups of coffee and a shower, it sounded absurd. His ex-wife had humiliated him enough over the course of their marriage and divorce, he didn't need to do it to himself.

"Sorry," he mumbled, "Wrong number."

Glenn slipped his phone into his pocket and went into the bedroom. He crouched on his bed and shoved the single panel curtain as far to the left as it would go on its rod. He examined the window, trying to understand what was drawing the moths which were, at the moment, completely absent. He ran his fingers along the edges, looking for gaps through which his air-conditioning could slip. He didn't know if cool air would attract them or not, but it didn't matter because his window was well sealed.

He wondered if there was a strange smell that was getting their attention. He leaned his forehead against the glass and sniffed. Just the usual musty mildew smell. Nothing out of the ordinary. He let the curtain fall back and climbed off the bed. As he headed out into the hallway he glanced back over his shoulder at the window. *This has been the weirdest week.*

With the moths stealing his sleep and the Criado woman terrorizing him with her grief, Glenn hadn't felt so drained since his wife asked for the divorce. He thought maybe he'd go call the kids. That would lift his spirits. Either that or it would make him feel worse.

He settled back into his chair and dialed his eldest daughter's number. When her voicemail picked up, Glenn clicked the phone shut and sighed heavily, a lump in his throat. He turned on the TV, letting its vacuous nonsense anesthetize him. This went on all through Glenn's dinner of bologna and cheese on bread (with a side of four beers) and continued afterwards until he fell asleep in front of the nattering television.

Glenn woke on Sunday with a slime of drool dribbling from the corner of his open mouth and a crick in his neck. He'd slept the whole night through, free from moths or dreams. Just this slight change made the day feel like a fresh start. He decided to go out and take a drive. He showered, dressed, and stepped outside his apartment for the first time since coming home Friday night. It was a beautiful day. The sun was high, and the humidity was low. A sweet breeze blew across the front step and Glenn smiled for the first time in weeks.

After a day spent cruising around town with the windows down, running errands and enjoying the weather, Glenn returned home with Chinese food from the place up the street. He ate with the radio on instead of the TV and only had one beer.

He didn't feel any anxiety until it was time to go to bed. Glenn was afraid of lying down in his room and having his first good day in ages ruined by an army of tiny, flying intruders knocking at his window. He thought about it for a while and then decided to make his chair comfortable with a sheet, his pillow and blanket. He set about creating his makeshift bed and once it was properly fluffed, he climbed in and curled up with a small, sigh. The sheet was cool against his bare back and the blanket settled around him. Glenn closed his eyes and soon drifted into a peaceful sleep.

He woke up some time later, panting. Something was wrong. After a few seconds he realized he was hot, coated with a sheen of sweat, his blanket twisted around his body. He sat up in the dark, the sheet sticking to his back, and looked around, confused. *Why is it so goddam HOT in here?* He tried to disentangle himself from his damp cover, struggling to yank it out from beneath him. He swept his phone up from the table beside him and stood with a grunt, looking at the screen. It was 2:33 am.

"What now?" He asked the empty room with an angry sob. "What is it *now*?" The boxy little apartment had become an oven, roasting Glenn like a chicken. *The air conditioner.* Glenn realized it was making an unpleasant buzzing sound. He blundered across the room to where it stuck out from the wall. There was no cool air blowing from it, just the stuttering, mechanical rattle of something breaking down.

Glenn smacked it on the side with his palm. The sound hiccupped for a moment but didn't stop. He wiped his forehead with the back of his hand and went back to his chair, falling into it gracelessly. There was no sleep for him the rest of the night.

He did not go to work the next morning. He called the emergency maintenance line and was told by an annoyed voice on the other end that someone would be dispatched as soon as possible.

"Don't go anywhere, though," the voice drawled, "It could be as late as eight or nine in the mornin'."

Glenn was outraged. but somehow managed to keep his tone even and patient. He said he'd be there and then hung up. He went outside and sat on the front step. It was much cooler out there. While he waited, he called and left a message at work that he was sick and wouldn't be in. He ended up dozing there on the stoop like a homeless person.

The sun was shining brightly when a voice startled him from his fractured nap.

"You Glenn Michels?" It was the voice from the phone, and it still sounded annoyed. Glenn looked up at a tall, thin man with white hair and a white bushy moustache. He wore a work-shirt and held a battered toolbox at his side.

Glenn wiped the corners of his mouth and stood. "Yeah, that's me."

"Say you're havin' some trouble with your air conditioning?" The man gazed over Glenn's shoulder, appraising the building. Glenn nodded and led the maintenance-man into his apartment, a blast of hot air rushing out at them.

Within seconds the man had his tool-box opened and was working to get the face off of the AC unit. Glenn walked back to the tiny kitchen and got a glass of water.

"So, when'd you notice the problem here?" The man made little grunting sounds as he spun the screwdriver at each corner of the air—conditioner.

Glenn finished a huge gulp of his water. "Right before I called you."

The maintenance-man nodded. "That's a helluva time to find yourself without air conditioning." He pulled the last screw out and took the face off the AC unit. He turned it back on and immediately the strange, grinding buzz started up. The man cocked his head and frowned. "Sounds like you got something stuck in the intake. Could be you just need to change your filter." The man switched it off and stood, his old knees popping. "Gonna have to check the front of the unit." Glenn waved his hand in acknowledgment and the man went out the front door, leaving it wide open.

Glenn drank more water. He was running with sweat, shiny with it. He couldn't stand heat like this indoors. Outside was one thing, usually you were only outside long enough to get from your car to whatever air-conditioned building you were heading for. Inside, though, the heat just grew fat, even with all of the windows open. Just sitting around doing nothing felt like work and sleep would be impossible until this could be fixed. He could hear the maintenance man out there, tinkering around and grunting. A couple of minutes had gone by when the old man called out with surprise.

"Whoa! Holy *shit*."

Glenn rubbed his hand across his slick, glistening face. *That doesn't sound good.*

"Mr. Michels, you wanna come out here and see this?" The man uttered a short, barking chuckle. Glenn walked across the room, his waterglass still clutched in his hand, and stepped out the front door.

When he saw what was scattered on the ground beneath the opened-up casing of the air conditioner unit, his breath caught in his throat and his eyes went wide. The glass slipped from his hand and shattered on the stoop sending water and glass in all directions. The old maintenance man hopped back with a shout, but Glenn didn't notice him at all. His eyes were glued to the brownish-gray cascade of delicately folded moth bodies that had spilled from his air conditioner out onto the pavement.

Hundreds of them.

Most of them were dead, dry little husks lying still and silent, but Glenn could see some weak twitching and squirming in the pile. He felt his stomach lurch and his temples began to pound.

The maintenance man stuck the end of his screwdriver into the unit's cavity and scraped out another sheaf of bugs. "That's the damndest thing I ever saw. I can tell you that right now."

Glenn looked up at the man dumbly and then back down at the pile. His heart was pounding. "How—how did they—how did this happen?"

The maintenance man shrugged and scratched at his mustache. "Well, thing is, it's *not* uncommon that you get a few bugs in an air conditioner. They fly too close or crawl on it and, *whoosh!* Sucked right in. But I ain't never seen anything like this before. Never. They all must've just kept followin' each other in. You know, maybe to mate. Pher-o-monies they call it."

Glenn raised his eyebrows. "Pheromones?"

"I b'lieve its pronounced, 'monies', but yeah. Then they all just clogged the intake, and it started workin' overtime till the fan motor burnt out." He nudged the drift of moth-bodies with the toe of his boot. "We'll have to replace the motor or else get you a new unit. Either way, it's gonna be a couple days." The man looked out into the parking lot and spat on the ground. "Weirdest thing I've seen in fifteen years."

Glenn leaned against the iron rail that ran alongside the stoop. "I've been having trouble with moths for the last few nights. Hitting my window."

"Well, I mean, *that's* normal enough. Ain't much you can do about that. 'Specially in the summertime." The old man stuck his hand into the unit and dusted the last few moths out onto the ground. He leaned over, groaning and grabbed the front panel of the air conditioner and spoke over his shoulder as he began replacing the screws. "I'll go right over and see whether it's easier, quicker and cheaper to replace the motor or the unit, and then I'll place an order for you." He finished working and dropped the screwdriver back into the toolbox, closing it with his foot.

"Has anybody else said anything about moths—ah—bothering them lately?" Glenn felt like a fool asking but he had to know.

The old man picked up his toolbox and shook his head. "Nawp. Just you." He glanced at the open door. "Need me to re-attach the inside face?"

Glenn started to say no and then was assaulted with a horrifying vision—the pile of dead moths outside returning to hideous, whirring life like tiny, winged zombies, squirming their way into his apartment through the gaping cavity of the air conditioner. "Yes please, I'd appreciate it."

The maintenance man heaved a heavy sigh and twitched his mustache. He slipped into Glenn's front room to re-affix the face of the air conditioner.

Glenn watched pensively from the doorway, mopping sweat from his face with the back of his hand. The maintenance man finished and shoved past Glenn's hovering form, ignoring his mumbled words of thanks, saying only, "Get that glass swept up," as he made his way down the stoop.

That night Glenn took three cold showers, drank glass after glass of water, and lay naked in his chair. He'd gone out and purchased a box fan after cleaning up the glass on the porch (the dead moths he'd simply swept into the bushes at the side of the stoop with a scowl of repulsion) and even with that blowing on his damp body no sleep would come. He squirmed in a swoon of misery wondering how people had ever existed before indoor climate control, having forgotten that his own family had not gotten air conditioning until he was sixteen.

Then there were the moths. Even from the living room, Glenn could hear them plunking against the screens of both bedroom windows and the large one in the front. He kept the blinds closed, not wanting to see such a big area covered with wriggling, agitated little bodies. *This was all their fault.?* Glenn knew it was crazy but sensed they were doing this on purpose. Those filthy, scrabbling little insects were trying to drive him crazy with sleep deprivation. Back in his chair, the cool water from his showers had been sucked into the stifling air. He closed his eyes and tried to relax but sleep was beyond reach and the heat held him tightly in its dry embrace.

When morning came, exhausted and sore though he might be, Glenn was relieved to be heading to work. He couldn't wait to feel the blast of cool air from the vents in his car and to luxuriate in the sweet chill of his little gray cubicle.

He left an hour and a half earlier than usual and when he arrived, he had the place mostly to himself. He settled into his chair with a tired groan and leaned forward, resting his head against the edge of the desk. *Maybe I can sleep for a few minutes before anybody really gets here.* The idea was irresistible. He closed his eyes and cradled his arms around his face. Sleep was just beginning to overtake him when a strident voice cajoled from behind him.

"Hey there, Lazy-bones, you need to start getting to bed earlier, huh?"

Within the cavern of his arms Glenn's lips pulled back from his teeth in a grimace. A sudden, black hate blossomed in the center of his chest and spread ice through his veins. He sat up and turned slowly in his chair to face the man standing at his cubicle wall. The man's goofy grin retreated when he saw the look in Glenn's eyes.

"Need something, Ernest?" Glenn's voice was all gravel and broken glass.

"Um. No, not really." Ernest rubbed his nose. "Just, you know, saying good morning." The space between them filled up with seconds, ticking by silently. When it was clear that Glenn was not going to say anything else, Ernest backed away with a half-hearted wave. "Well, have a good one buddy."

Ernest turned and scuttled away down the aisle. Glenn watched him go and felt a pang of guilt. *Man, you were such an asshole to him.* These sleepless nights were wearing him down, exposing the frayed wires beneath the surface. He would have to be more careful how he reacted to people. He made a mental note to stop by Ernest's desk later to throw a couple minutes' worth of small talk his way just to show that everything was okay.

With his shot at dozing gone, Glenn decided he might as well start working. He slid the center drawer of his desk open, looked into it, and screamed. There was a huge black butterfly, dead, lying on top of his legal pad, its delicate wings were spread open, at least seven inches from tip to tip.

Glenn stared down at the bug, vaguely curious as to whether anyone would come over to find out why he'd cried out, but it didn't really matter. All that concerned him at that moment was the butterfly.

He looked at it for a long time, his stomach churning as he tried to understand its meaning. He marveled at the creature's beauty. It had two sets of wings, an upper and a lower, velvety black with charcoal-gray striations spreading across them like veins. Instead of reflecting the fluorescent office lights the wings seemed to swallow it up greedily. The body itself, furry and thick, was also black except for the head, which was a vibrant, violent red. Long white antennae hung limply to either side. For a relatively small thing, it cut an imposing figure.

Glenn's heart pounded. It felt like someone was knocking on the inside of his chest, desperate to get out. How was this happening? Where did the butterfly come from?

A prank. It had to be a prank. Someone who knew about his moth problem thought it would be *hilarious* to give old Glenn a little shock. Just a harmless prank. *When I find the shithead that did this I'm going to*—but who knew about the moths? Glenn hadn't told anyone. Only the old maintenance man from the apartment complex knew, and it would be quite a stretch to think he could have somehow done this.

Glenn's head hurt, and he couldn't look at the dead butterfly any longer. He didn't want to touch it, but he certainly couldn't leave it in his desk all day. He reached into the drawer and gingerly grasped the barest edge of one wing between his thumb and forefinger, repulsed by the gritty texture. He lifted the thing, tiny flecks of powder drifting from the paper-thin wings, and dropped it into the garbage can. It landed with a heavy, unpleasant *thud.* Glenn was glad he couldn't see it anymore but felt a peculiar sense of unease at having thrown it away. It felt disrespectful somehow, almost sacrilegious.

He turned back toward his desk and was startled again, silently this time, by something else in his drawer. Something that had been hidden beneath the butterfly's body. It was a small newspaper clipping.

He picked it up and read it, his mouth dropping open slowly as he realized what it was. He stood up, the paper dangling between his fingers, and looked out across the office. It was still early and only a couple more of his co-workers had shown up. The place was still mostly deserted. Glenn sank back into his chair and looked again at the clipping.

It was a copy of Efrain Criado's obituary.

How did she get in here?

A chill raced down Glenn's arms, making the hairs stand on end. He looked back down at the obituary in his hand. There was no picture of the deceased and precious little text. It gave his name, age, date of his death, that he was a resident of Shaker Heights, and that he left behind a devoted wife.

How devoted?

Glenn thought about the butterfly that had been lying on top of the obituary in his desk. Thought about the moths in his air conditioner. That happened after he'd left the bedroom to escape their incessant tapping at the window and discovered he could sleep, more or less soundly in his chair. He'd made a move and they countered with an escalation.

As he stared down at the limp newspaper clipping, an impossible idea began to form, ridiculous but obvious. His chill deepened and he turned to scan the office, suddenly feeling watched, as if by dark, accusing eyes.

Then logic snapped back like a rubber band in his mind, and he strained away from such a ludicrous premise. He looked up and around his cubicle to verify he was still awake, still in the real world.

Looking at the solid, mundane artifacts of his ordinary, sadsack life, Glenn realized that the only obvious thing, the most obvious thing of all right now was that he felt very guilty about everything in his life. His marriage, his kids, his work, and the thing with Alvita Criado. It was clear that all that shame was taking deep bites out of him, every day, and he was letting it. He needed to do something to allay some of that shame, something to make him feel a little less like a piece of garbage.

Maybe I should just call her. The idea had a simple, childish appeal at first, but he realized quickly it was a bad one. *Call her? And say what? Hello Mrs. Criado, Glenn Michels here. I wanted to apologize about the way my company treated you and your late husband. See I'm going a little crazy over here since my wife kicked me out of my house for being a loser and it would make me feel a lot better if you could just forgive me. You cannot bother this widow and fling her husband's death back into her face to soothe some ridiculous delusion you're having, that's why. It would be cruel.*

He went back and forth on the idea for hours, feeling both selfish for wanting her forgiveness, but desperate to have it. Finally, at the end of that long, disorienting work day Glenn pulled up the Criados' information in the system.

He scanned the information—phone number, address, policy number, adjuster code and stopped on the last one—Who had been their adjuster? Who'd been the one to deny this? Beside the code were three initials—LMS—Linda Marie Schmidt.

Linda. She was the one who had found the loophole in the Criado's records that allowed the company to deny their claim. What a bitch. On a whim, Glenn scribbled her name onto a piece of paper with the Criado's information and folded it up, shoving it into his pocket. He didn't expect to use it, would in fact probably throw it away as soon as he walked in the front door, but for the moment it seemed to calm his paranoia and ease his breathing.

That night Glenn fell asleep comfortably in his chair. The maintenance people had found a working AC unit in storage and switched it out with Glenn's. It had been pumping out cold air full-blast when he walked in that evening and Glenn allowed himself a moment of satisfaction. He set his keys, his phone, and the paper with the Criados' information, on the kitchen counter and got himself a beer from the fridge. He spent a pleasant evening in front of the TV watching a documentary on the History Channel about the Crusades and at some point, drifted into a deep slumber, snoring contentedly.

In the dream he was getting a massage. Glenn couldn't see his masseuse, but somehow, he knew it was a woman. He was lying on his back, and she was dragging her fingers across his bare chest, shoulders, stomach, and legs. She softly grazed her nails across his groin. and he felt himself getting excited.

She let her fingers wander all over his face and it started to feel a bit odd. She probed gently into his nostrils, stuck her finger between his lips, and stroked his closed eyelids. Then she took a spray bottle out from behind her back and began spraying lines of lotion all over his body. She didn't rub it in but kept squirting it in loops and whorls. It tickled pleasantly. Then she began dripping it onto his face. Again, he wasn't sure that he liked that exactly, but he let her continue. Soon his whole face was buried in lotion.

Glenn was starting to feel uneasy. He definitely wanted the woman to stop now. He opened his mouth to tell her to ease up and she sprayed a continuous stream into his mouth. It just kept coming and coming, sliding down the back of his throat.

He began to thrash about on the table as the lotion choked him. He tried to hop up but was having trouble moving his arms and legs. It felt like he was drowning in the soft, white substance and the woman kept implacably adding more. He tried to scream and couldn't. He struggled and squirmed rocking back and forth on the table trying to sit up, trying to cry out. Darkness was beginning to draw a gauzy veil down over him, but Glenn resisted it.

"NO!" he thought, "No, no, no!" He tried with all his might to sit up, his muscles clenching, his mind fighting, and finally, with a mighty, straining heave Glenn lurched awake.

He was coughing. There really was something in his mouth. It was thick and felt somehow wet and dry all at the same time. Glenn began to wretch and tried to stand from his chair but found himself restrained. With great effort he yanked his arm free of whatever was holding him down and began clearing his mouth, spitting and sputtering. He wiped his face clear and examined the stuff in his hands. It looked like extremely thin, glossy cotton in a big, sticky ball. *What the FUCK?* Glenn pushed up against the arm of the chair and looked down at himself. He was crawling with caterpillars. Thick, black, squirming caterpillars. They were spinning a silk blanket over Glenn's entire body.

There were hundreds of them—hundreds and hundreds. He'd been completely webbed to the chair, his arms and legs wrapped up in a shimmery cocoon. That's what he'd been choking on— they'd been shooting it down his throat. They were on his face. *In his mouth.* A massive wave of disgust, hot and thick, swept through him from the center of his chest all the way out to the tips of his fingers.

With a shrill, sobbing cry he stood from his chair and began beating his hands against his body, trying to rid himself of the small, wriggling creatures. He hopped from foot to foot in a panic-stricken dance, yanking clumps of webbing and plump caterpillar bodies from his hair, his chest, his belly. He could hear them plopping to the floor like fat globs of dough and could see them scurrying off to spin more silk. He felt them writhing around in his boxers and thought of the way the masseuse tickled his lower body in the dream.

As he peeled off his underwear and tried desperately to dis-lodge the intruders from his nether regions, Glenn looked wildly around the room and saw that they were everywhere, trundling patiently over every surface, covering the walls and furniture with their silken discharge.

He felt his mind trying desperately to escape his body, this room, this whole life, as the larval moths skittered to and fro, up and down all around him. He felt it trying to fly away, out of his skull and up into the sky, where it could climb, higher and higher and further from the knowledge of this moment.

They're trying to kill me.

Glenn knew at that moment that it was all true no matter how crazy or impossible it was. Glenn was being punished with a plague of moths for his role in cheating Alvita Criado out of her dead husband's life insurance, and they were going to murder him. He had to get to her. Had to beg her, *plead* with her, apologize, grovel, whatever it took, to get her to forgive him. It was the only thing that made sense and, in that moment, it was all he could think of.

Glenn made his way to the kitchen counter, black bodies bursting under his bare feet squirting their vital fluids across the floor. He grabbed the sheet with the Criado's information on it. A phone call was not going to do. This would have to be in person. He snatched up his keys and then with a sudden, violent belch, vomited onto the floor, splattering bile and nameless, undigested chunks all over his feet. As he watched, the caterpillars plowed their way through it like tiny boats through a brownish-gray harbor. His gorge rose and he threw up again. When he was done, he forced himself to look away. He spun, keys and paper in hand, and ran to his bedroom to find pants.

Glenn sat on his bed and began rifling through the dirty laundry on the floor and as soon as he was in the door, he heard the *thup thup* of moths hitting windows. As he found pants and pulled them up the sound of tiny bodies slamming into the window became faster and more frenzied. It sounded like soft, muffled machine-gun fire. Glenn grabbed a dirty shirt from beneath his feet and tugged it down over his head and fled the room.

The sight of the living room assaulted Glenn as if for the first time as he came skidding through the hallway. Tears welled in his eyes. All of this because he'd sent a letter of bad news on behalf of someone else. Sudden hot rage sprung up alongside his helpless terror. *Linda fucking Schmidt. That cold bitch.* Thoughts of earning forgiveness were replaced by an urge to blame the *real* villain here. He was going to tell Alvita Criado that the person who'd betrayed her and her husband was Linda can't-pass-up-a-chance-to-screw-someone-over Goddamn *Schmidt*. This was all *her* fault. A bright spark of hatred flared up in Glenn's gut towards the woman who worked upstairs from him *Fuck you Linda, this curse belongs to YOU.*

Glenn grabbed his phone from the counter, shoving it into his pocket, and strode across the room, nearly slipping in the gooey remains of squashed caterpillars. He burst through his door out into the late July heat and ran, barefoot, to his car. Immediately a cloud of moths came flapping and fluttering, seemingly from out of nowhere, and surrounded him like a cyclone. He waved his hands frantically trying to clear them away as he yanked his car door open and slid in. He slammed the door shut, letting in a couple dozen of the flying bugs, and spent a few satisfying minutes clapping them between his hands and smashing their bodies against the dashboard. When Glenn felt like he'd rid the car of moths, he keyed the ignition and sped out of the parking lot.

He cruised through the shabby streets of his neighborhood. past laundromats, fast-food restaurants, check-cashing places, and tanning salons. None of it looked familiar anymore. Everything was strangely bright as if he was hung over and all the little shops and buildings blended together.

Glenn picked up the paper from the seat next to him and glanced at the address. He had a vague idea, by the zip code, what part of town Mrs. Criado lived in, though the actual street name was unfamiliar. He pulled his phone out at the next stoplight and dialed her number. He wanted to make sure she was home before he went goose-chasing all over Cleveland looking for her address. The phone rang once, twice, and was picked up on the third.

"Hello?" Her voice, which had been ringing in his head for days, was unmistakable.

"Mrs. Criado, please, listen to me. I'm coming to see you. We have to talk." He was out of breath and wheezing and knew he must sound crazy.

The voice on the other end laughed. She didn't ask who it was calling her and didn't sound surprised at all. "Ha! And what is it you want to say to me? Are you bringing me $250,000?"

"No. I'm sorry, no, I don't have any money but—"

"Then we have nothing to talk about. It was nice catching up with you Mr. Michels but I have to go now."

"I want to tell you the name of the person who denied your claim!"

There was a heavy pause on her end. When she finally spoke, it came out in a breathy whisper. "You are the one whose name was on that letter."

The frustration from their first meeting flared up and, for a moment, overcame Glenn's terror and desperation. "Goddamit, yes! Yes, okay? Yes, I sent the fucking letter, but Linda Schmidt was the one who told me to send it." He sped through a stop sign, nearly colliding with another car coming the other way. The other driver laid on their horn and waved their middle finger at him.

"Linda Schmidt?" Mrs. Criado sounded doubtful but there was a hint of interest in her tone.

"Yes. Linda Schmidt. She's an adjuster at the insurance company. It's her job to say what claims get accepted or denied. She could've said yes, she could've accepted your claim, and I would've sent you a check in place of a letter. Instead, she did a little research—because that's what *her* bosses tell her to do: find ways to screw people out of their money—and she found her loophole and denied your claim. Linda Marie Schmidt." Glenn realized he was out of breath. He felt like his heart was going to explode.

"But you are still wrapped up in this Mr. Michels. Don't think this gets you out of the cook-fire."

"I know. You're right, fine, and I've suffered. You have no idea how I've suffered."

There was a dark chuckle from her end. "I have an idea."

"I just—I just want to come see you. Talk this out, see if there's anything I can do to ease your grief. I'm so sorry about all of this Alvita, so sorry for the part I played." Glenn pulled on to the cross-town expressway. Rush hour was still a ways off and he had the road mostly to himself. "Isn't there anything I can do or say to make this better?" He sped along, the morning sun bathing the four lanes of highway in bright gold.

Mrs. Criado was quiet for a moment. Glenn thought he heard the sound of a pen or pencil scraping against paper. When she spoke again her voice held a note of sympathy. "Mr. Michels you don't need to come here.."

"Alvita?" Glenn didn't want her to hang up. Needed to know she forgave him. "Please—I'm so sorry."

"Thank you for saying that. We will not speak again." There was a click and she was gone.

Glenn's breathing began to slow. His mouth hung open as he pondered her words. Was it over? She'd thanked him, and had sounded like she understood. Maybe that was enough, maybe that was her forgiving him.

Something dark hit the windshield with a wet *thwack*. Glenn started with a shocked little yelp. *What the hell?* A smear of orange and black, about four inches wide, spread across the glass in front of him.

Oh Jesus no.

Glenn looked up into the sky ahead. The sunshine became dappled with flickering shadows that seemed to jitter out of the clouds and down the road. Suddenly another dark blotch smacked against the windshield sending little greenish-white tendrils of liquid guts across Glenn's field of vision. The cloud of shadows was coming at him fast now.

Monarch butterflies, thousands of them, descended upon Glenn's little car on powdered wings. Another, then another, and another began to splatter against the windshield. Glenn screamed and turned on the wipers trying to clear them. He swerved across the four lanes. A pickup truck trying to pass him blared its horn and was forced into the grassy median. Glenn's car was now engulfed by a fluttering, sunset-colored whirlwind. He could no longer see the road through the mosaic of butterflies. Their vibrancy and beauty, even in death, struck Glenn with wonder and he smiled as he took his hands from the steering wheel and pressed the gas pedal to the floor. He thought of his daughters as he sped, unseeing, towards the massive, concrete side of an oncoming overpass. They would be okay. *His* life insurance policy was up to date and airtight. They would be well cared for.

Everything was going to be okay.

***

Hey Linda, come here, you've gotta see this."

Linda Schmidt stood from her desk and smoothed down the hips of her pleated, khaki slacks. It was Dan Rimmert asking her to come over to the window. She made her way to the window where Dan stood, coffee cup in hand. A couple of other people had come over to gawk with them.

"What is it, Dan?" She looked out to see what was happening.

"I don't know. Don't look like birds does it? Locusts maybe? Man, looks like that scene from, "The Swarm." You remember that movie?"

Linda did not. The only movies Linda enjoyed were love stories with happy endings. Dan was right, though. A huge wave of *somethings* was streaming across the sky in their general direction. As she watched, a bubble of anxiety began to swell in her chest. There was something ominous about that dark gathering of bodies undulating towards them. It seemed like an endless battalion stretching back for, miles. They were starting to block out the sun as they got closer. She took a step back from the glass.

"Well, that's very interesting Dan, but I need to get back to…" Something thumped lightly against the window and stuck.

"Look!" Dan chuckled. "A butterfly. Ain't it pretty?"

Linda's mouth turned down in a grimace, and she looked nervously back at the approaching cloud. She did not think the butterfly was pretty.

Not at all.

FLOOD PHOTOS

For my father, Richard Kombrinck.

Two men sat quietly in an over-bright hospital room. One of them was in an uncomfortable chair, pulled up to the bedside of the other. In the bed was the father of the man in the chair. He was dying.

Blake held his father's hand lightly, his face twisting as he fought back tears. His father let his hand be held, lying awake but silent. He stared up at the ceiling, trying to ignore the tubes in his nose and the needles in his arms—trying to ignore the clock in his body that was winding rapidly down. Neither man had spoken for some time.

A nurse came in to take vital signs, leaving a small cup of pills. Blake pulled away from the bed to let her do this and his father, sitting up to receive his medicine, saw the anguish straining his son's face. He saw the storm getting ready to break. When the nurse left, Blake pulled the chair back up to his father's bed. His throat worked as he tried not to weep.

"Blake, did I ever tell you about the time the river flooded back in '59?" His father grimaced as he downed his pills with a small sip of water. Everything, including breathing and swallowing, seemed to hurt now.

Blake patted his father's arm. "Yeah. You've shown me your flood album with all the pictures you took. Remember?"

Blake's father cocked an annoyed eye at his son. "Of course I remember. I've got cancer, not Alzheimer's." He shook his head.

"What I mean is, did I ever tell you what happened in the woods when I went out to take those pictures?"

"I don't think so." Blake crossed his legs and thought for a moment. "You told me about how your basement filled up with water and how you lost Blinky when you went out to the woods with your camera. That's all I can think of."

"Well, I never told you how I lost Blinky." Blake's father smiled wistfully. "She was a really good dog. Loyal." He leaned forward and stuffed a rolled-up pillow between his lower back and the mattress, getting comfortable.

"It was late January. There'd been a lot of snow that winter and then we got hit with a warm patch. All the snow was melting and then it started raining. It just poured nonstop for a whole week. Your grampa started making jokes about building an ark and then the river flooded, and he stopped joking about it.

"The Scioto overflowed its banks. All that snow runoff mixed with the rain and built up this huge wall of water. It broke through the sandbags and the whole town was underwater in a matter of hours. All the streams and creeks turned into rushing, rapids. You should've seen it—like something out of a disaster movie. Filthy gray-black water swept sticks and leaves and debris all around the trunks of the trees. The clouds moved in and just sat there, dropping their load on us without mercy."

Blake's phone began going off in his pocket, interrupting his father's story. He dragged it out, checking the number on the screen, and held a finger up for his father to wait. "Hey. Yeah. Yeah, it's fine. We're just talking." His eyebrows drew together. "Christ, I don't know. Why would you ask me that?" He breathed a heavy sigh. "I know, I'm sorry. Yes. I'll tell him. I love you too." He ended the call and slid the phone back in his pocket, muting the ringer as he did.

Blake's father grinned at him. "Shelley?"

Blake nodded. "Sorry. Yeah, she told me to tell you hi and that she hopes you're feeling okay."

The older man nodded. "Well, you tell her I'm doing as good as I can and that I love her and Seth and Danny." He looked down and considered his hands solemnly for a moment. "Do you think she'd bring them up to see me?"

Blake stared down at his knees, picking nervously at a small hole in his jeans. "I mean, yeah, I'm sure they'll get up here. I'll make sure they come and see you."

Blake's father made a snuffling sound and looked at his son. "'Course you will. That'll be great." He knew Blake's wife would not be coming to his room with his grandkids. Blake heard the knowledge in his father's voice and grasped the older man's hand.

"Dad, look at me." His father's gaze slipped to meet his son's. "I promise that I will bring them up to see you before—" He paused to swallow the lump in his throat, "—to spend a little bit of time with you. Okay? I promise."

Blake's father felt a swell of pride and love billow within his chest, so strong it was almost painful. He squeezed his son's hand tightly. "Okay. Okay."

"So the river flooded. What happened then?"

Blake's father leaned back against his pillow. "Well, then Raccoon Creek, which ran across the back of our property, over-flowed its banks. It was wide and deep, almost as wide as the Scioto in some places. There were spots where you could actually take a small boat out on it and fish. It was full of rainbow trout, bluegills, and mollies. Full of snakes and snapping turtles too. Your gramma hated the idea of me and my friends playing down there. I was forbidden to, but I just couldn't help myself. I took a lot of whippings for the sake of hanging out at the creek.

"In the fall and winter, when the trees were all bare, you could look right down into the woods and see everything from my bedroom window. Before it got cold, usually a couple of weeks before Halloween, I'd be able to watch foxes hunting mice along the forest floor or deer wandering along, getting ready to hunker down till spring."

The older man stopped and coughed several times into his hand, wincing at the pain in his throat. When the fit and subsequent wheezing passed, he went on. "That's what I was doing the day I lost Blinky. Watching the flood. It was a Saturday and the worst of it had passed. There was still plenty of water everywhere. Our basement was a mess. Everything in my dad's rec room was either underwater or floating on top of it. The river was still pumping into the creek like a faucet, but it had already crested and was starting to come down some.

"Blinky was sitting at my feet, wagging her tail, licking my hand now and again. I was secretly watching for dead bodies. I saw a couple of dead cats and a few other things that I wasn't sure of but in my head, I just *knew* sooner or later one of my neighbors was gonna come floating along at some point. I wanted to be the one that let the police know."

"Dad," Blake chuckled darkly, "That's really morbid."

"I was a young boy. Boys are weird. They can be a little creepy. You were. Remember that dead mouse you used to keep in a box? What did you call him, Squeakerton?" Blake's father straightened up on his bed and regarded his son stiffly. "May I go on?"

"Yes, please do." Blake tried to suppress a smile and failed.

"Thank you. Anyway, there was probably eight feet of water sluicing along through the woods. I had just decided to go downstairs and get a glass of juice when I saw something big go splashing along, carried by the current. I thought it was a horse or something. It was just big and brown and moving fast. It wasn't a person though, I knew that.

"I kept my eyes on it till it drifted beyond where I could see. It suddenly occurred to me that if it was a horse or a cow or something that belonged to somebody, and I went down there and found it, maybe I'd get a reward.

"I grabbed my Ensign camera, tapped my leg for Blinky, and snuck downstairs. I thought maybe if I found whatever-it-was I could take a picture of it and then try to go find the owner. You know how half-assed kids' ideas are. Your grandparents were in the family-room, arguing about the basement, and never even noticed me grab my boots and slip out the back door with the dog.

"The yard was a marsh. I got my galoshes on and squelched through water that came up above my ankles. Blinky was wet up to her knees and her belly was soaked but she was ready to follow me anywhere. She hopped along through that waterlogged grass with her ears up and her tail wagging.

"We headed across the yard and crossed into the woods. There was a lot more floodwater down that way, pooling around our legs. Blinky was almost swimming. I knew we weren't going to be able to get too far in, but there was a spot where the ground sloped up and away from the creek. I hoped that maybe we could scout along the higher ground for a ways and at least see if we could spot anything.

"We splashed along until we got to the rise. We followed it for a quarter mile or so, the water racing along a few feet below us. I had my eyes peeled for anything big and I was snapping pictures left and right. The flash lit up the trees like tiny bursts of lightning.

"There was a spot where the high ground dipped deeper into the woods. I started to head that way when I noticed Blinky had stopped a few feet back. She was whining, her ears drooping, and her tail between her legs. She just looked up at me with these worried eyes. 'Come on girl,' I called out to her. 'We can still go a little further.' But she didn't budge. She just stood there, bobbing her head back and forth like she was saying 'no.' "

Blake's father reached over to the hospital tray and grabbed a cup, half-full of water. He took a sip and set the cup back down. For a few moments, he was lost in the memory, almost feeling the cold air of the woods on his face, and the even colder water at his feet. He thought he'd cried out all his own tears days before, but was surprised to suddenly feel them behind his eyes. He sat quietly that way, letting them fall for a while before finally speaking again.

"I went on without her. I didn't know why she was so spooked and, honestly, I didn't care. All I could think of was how many funny books I'd be able to buy if I got a reward for finding somebody's animal down there. It never even occurred to me I might not get a reward or that I might even get in trouble. It also never occurred to me that the thing I saw wasn't a horse or a cow, and I never once thought that it could be something dangerous.

"I came to a place where the ground went down into the water and then came up again on the other side and ended. It was like a little island. The creek came swirling across that low spot and I had no idea how deep it was. I decided I'd hop across to the other side of the rise and just take a good long look around.

"I made it over to the little island no problem. I was a little nervous. The creek was really pounding past me, moving fast. I thought if I fell in I'd be swept away. I got my feet planted so that I felt pretty steady and then squinted and strained to see through the trees, looking for anything moving.

"I was starting to feel foolish. I'd come running out into the cold and wet and I hadn't found anything. I was turning to head back when something found *me*.

"I heard a splash and looked over and watched as this, thing, came up out of the water. It sort of had a body like a snake. Long and coiling and scaly. It was brown with dark, round markings, like a boa constrictor. Thing was, its body was as big around as a rain-barrel. Huge and thick. I couldn't tell how long it was because most of it was still underwater."

Blake's eyes went wide and round. "Are you serious?"

His father nodded. "You bet your ass. Its head was decidedly less snake-like. I guess it was kind of horse-shaped but also sort of like an alligator with big, black, shiny eyes. It had a stubby snout and a long lower jaw that hung open, with a forked tongue between rows of sharp, white teeth.

"It just came surging up out of the flood with this awful growling sound and scrambled up the little hillock I was standing on. It had these weird flipper-feet. I watched one, then two then three sets of them pulling the thing up onto the land. God knows how many more it had.

"I was kind of stunned, but by the time I saw that third set of legs I snapped back to reality and pissed my pants, even as I was leaping across the water back to the rise. I was really scared and confused. I had no idea what I was even looking at, and in my panic my jump was bad.

"I landed, smack at the edge of the bank with most of my body in the water. It was freezing. I started screaming and got a great big mouthful of filthy creek-water. Behind me, I heard the-the thing make this awful choking roar and then there was a loud, heavy splash.

"I started flailing my arms and legs trying to get a hold of a root or a branch or something that I could pull myself up with. My camera was pounding against my chest on its strap, and I just kept tearing big clumps of cold mud and clay away from the bank. My hands were slippery with it.

"I felt the water churn around me, and I knew that it was coming up under me. I finally managed to hunch my way up onto the bank, but my feet were still scrabbling under the water." He paused for a moment, staring down at his hands, lost in the memory. He realized that his son was watching him, a concerned look on his face, like his old dad might be drifting into delusion. The dying man came back to himself, cleared his throat (even though it was painful to do so) and went on.

"Suddenly I felt something slimy nudge up against my ass. It shoved me against the bank, and I knew that the creature was right there with me. I heard its head come up out of the water and I knew, just *knew*, that this was going to kill me.

"I shoved my face into the mud, crying, wanting it to be over quickly. My little heart was pounding, and I just couldn't get away.

"That's when I heard Blinky barking frantically from somewhere above me. I looked up. I could see the thing's shadow wavering on the bank in front of me and then Blinky was sailing through the air from on top of the rise.

"She leaped over my head and landed on the thing's face. I felt it pull back away from me and with a crazy spurt of adrenaline I clambered up onto the ground. I spun around and saw my dog clinging to a head as big as she was. She was holding on with her back legs, tearing at its snout with her front claws, biting at it mercilessly.

"The thing was twisting and looping its body in the water, not sure what to do. It had forgotten all about me and seemed to just want to be rid of the barking, biting dog on its face.

"I grabbed my camera, getting ready to throw it at the creature and the flash went off. Blinky looked back at me then as if to say, 'Run! Get the hell out of here dummy!' In that instant, the thing grabbed Blinky's leg in its jaws and bit down. She let out this long, painful howl and then was dragged underwater as the thing submerged.

"I started screaming for her. 'Blinky! Come on girl, where are you?' But she was gone. They were both gone. I don't know if it was cowardly or not, but after a few seconds of waiting I ran on back towards home. I didn't try to poke around the woods or the water to find my dog. Under the circumstances I guess most ten-year-old boys would've probably done the same thing." He fought back sudden, bitter tears. "Never have quite forgiven myself for it, though. I guess now's the time, if I'm gonna."

"Dad, it's okay, you don't have to..." Blake struggled to find something to say, the words hanging incomplete in the air.

The older man held his hand up, shaking his head. He was getting tired and didn't know how much longer he could keep talking. His voice was very gentle as he patted his son's arm. "Don't worry about it, just let me finish this last bit, okay?" His son, who looked so much like his mother and was fighting back tears of his own nodded and the old man attempted to bring his tale to a close.

"I got home and busted into the house, crying. Told my parents the whole crazy story. They were angry that I'd gone out but were relieved I hadn't gotten myself drowned.

"They didn't believe me about the monster, but my dad did go down there and try to find Blinky. He came back an hour and a half later without her. I went upstairs, got out of my wet clothes, took a bath, and cried myself to sleep for the next week. There were nightmares too. Sometimes there still are, but over time it started to fade a little bit in my mind.

"I could almost believe that I just fell in the water and imagined the monster part. I could tell myself that Blinky had drowned just trying to pull me out of the water, and that might have worked except for two things.

"A week or so after that, as the floodwaters kept receding, a couple of fishermen reported seeing something unusual in the river down near Pilotsville. Something they said was like a giant snake with a crocodile's head. The newspapers got a hold of the story and called it the Flood-Dragon. For a month or so people called in to the sheriff to say that they'd seen it splashing through their backyard or at the side of the road or down in a canal somewhere. I don't know that too many actually did, but I believe those first two fellows really caught a glimpse of it.

"Eventually the excitement kind of died down and now, nobody even remembers that part." Blake's father smiled wistfully. "It's funny. When my parents read about the dragon in the papers, they gave me some very odd looks. They never said anything, but I like to think they wondered if maybe I'd been telling the truth about what I'd seen." He paused and took another drink of his water. "And that's how I lost Blinky in the flood of '59." He set his cup down and regarded his son with raised eyebrows. "So. Think I'm crazy?"

Blake shook his head. "No, I don't think you're crazy. I'm also not sure that you were almost eaten by a monster in Raccoon Creek fifty years ago, but I think you must've seen something weird. I'm sorry about your dog though."

Blake's father nodded his head and tugged at his covers. He sighed. "Yeah, well. Me too."

"One thing though, Dad—how did you develop the pictures you have in that flood album? If your camera got all wet in the creek, how did you manage to save them?"

"Honestly, it was just a sturdy camera. I was like you, I thought it was done-for and I just put it away in the back of my closet. Didn't think about it for years. Then, in my teens, I found it while I was cleaning my room. I was shooting for the school paper and they had their own darkroom. On a whim I took the film in and processed it. A few pictures didn't come out but, for the most part, everything I took that day was intact. They don't make them like that anymore. The camera itself never did work again but that roll of film was just fine."

Blake smiled and looked up at the clock on the wall. "That was a great story, Dad." He leaned over and kissed his father on the cheek, something he hadn't done since the sixth grade. "Even if it didn't happen exactly that way. it was one hell of a fish tale." He stood up, smoothing his hands down over his jeans.

Blake's father laughed. "I assure you that it did happen exactly that way." He pulled the pillow out from behind him and lay back on the bed., feeling fragile and thin, like a tree at the end of Autumn with only one or two leaves left to fall. Then he looked up at his son with that same old mischievous smile. "If you get a chance though, you should go over to the house and grab that photo album. It's in the hall closet under the shoe-polishing kit. I'd love to see it again."

Blake stepped around the bed and made his way to the door. "I will Dad. It was nice visiting. I'll see you in a day or so, okay?"

Blake's father held a hand up to wave. "Can't wait son. Bring the kids if you can."

Blake returned the wave as he walked past. "Will do." He stopped in the doorway and looked back one more time. "I love you, Dad."

"I love you too. I'll see you later." He closed his eyes as his son left the room and in moments Blake's father was fast asleep.

***

A month after the funeral, Blake found himself sitting on the floor in front of the hall closet in the condo where his parents had lived. It belonged to him now.

He left Shelley and the boys at home so they wouldn't see him weep as he sorted through his father's things, deciding what to keep and what to get rid of. He'd managed to get most of the old man's suits, shoes and shirts pulled out and packed up before the first tears really began falling but it was the camera equipment, the detritus of his father's professional life, that broke Blake's heart. He sat on a little round stool in his father's studio. His face was buried in his hands as he sobbed, surrounded by white umbrellas, lights, and oversize prints of his father's work.

This went on for what seemed like hours before his cries trickled down to coughs and wet sniffles. Slowly he regained control of himself and sat up. He looked at a pile of high-powered lenses on a table across from him when he remembered the flood photos and the story his father told him that day in the hospital. It was the last time they'd ever spoken.

Blake found the album just where he was told it would be, slid underneath an old shoe-polishing kit at the back of the hall closet. He dragged it out and began flipping through the pages. He smiled through his tears as he looked at pictures his father had taken as a boy and thought of the wild tale the old man had spun.

The first few photos had been carefully set. The dog (*Blinky. Her name had been Blinky.*) sitting at attention in the sodden backyard. The woods at the far end of the property. A closer shot of those woods. The sky. All in shades of dark and light gray.

The further into the album Blake got, the more evident it was that the pictures had been hastily snapped. Here was one of what seemed to be a tangled mess of twigs and leaves. Then there were the shots of the flood itself. It was impressive how high the water had gotten. Blake could see the rippling current that had sliced between the banks. It was a wonder his dad hadn't perished.

Blake spent the better part of an hour looking over the flood photos. He came to the end of the album and was getting ready to close it when he noticed a piece of paper sticking out from behind the last photo. He pulled it out and examined it.

It was another picture. The true last picture in the album. He looked at it for a very long time, his tears temporarily forgotten in his extraordinary wonder.

It was dark and the lens had mud or dirt streaked across it but the long, sharp white teeth and one giant, black eye were unmistakable. The edge of one massive, scaly coil and what might have been a stumpy flipper were also visible in one corner, partially obscured by a shaggy blur that Blake thought was probably Blinky's tail.

His heart was filled with a mixture of sadness and awe, and he stared at the photo until his eyes stung. After a while, he dried his tears, slipped the picture back into the album. He knew he would never show his wife, nor his children. It was a secret that he would keep forever, between his father and himself. He smiled, looking like a much younger version of himself as he closed the photo album and slipped it back into the closet.

I REMEMBER COFFEE

I remember coffee.

I used to need two cups every morning, just to wake up. Now, I hardly sleep. They're always banging on the walls, the doors, the boards nailed over the windows. If the noise doesn't keep you awake, the smell will. You'd think after a while you'd get used to it. You don't. It just gets worse. Stronger. You've smelled rotten meat before. Just imagine being buried under it 24 hours a day for seven months.

We used to leave sometimes, to scrounge for food and supplies. But it wasn't long before there were too many of them shambling around out there, grabbing at you. Biting. We lost nine people, including Carrie, before we realized it was too dangerous to leave.

God! I would give anything for a cup of that shitty instant coffee she used to make. I thought it tasted like garbage. Now that I've eaten actual garbage…and rat and…well, never mind. Let's just say I miss my morning coffee. I'd give about anything for one more cup. One more *sip*.

Sounds like Michael and Brad just took Lindsay in the other room. I won't tell you what goes on in there. After a month or two, boredom makes people dangerous and strange. She hasn't fought back or cried in a long time. Not since Del, Mike B. and Clutch died. And by, "died" I mean, were killed. By the rest of us. Now she only has to deal with two guys taking her in the room, and we have enough spoiling meat to last us a while longer.

Carrie thought this thing would blow over. She was an optimist. In the mornings, before this all started she'd say, "Wake up, it's gonna be a beautiful day," even when it wasn't. I was always such a grump before I'd had my coffee. She held on to her hope till the moment they tore her guts out in the alley behind the grocery store. I tried to go back and help her. Clutch dragged me back to our building. Saved my life. Just writing that sentence makes me want to laugh. When I think about the way things are out there and the way they are in here. Not much difference anymore, really. I guess I'm actually glad that Carrie isn't here to see this. I miss her though. I wish it would've been me. In this world that's a very selfish thought to have.

Well, if anyone finds this letter, I hope it means that the living survived the hungry dead. Maybe you're reading this over a cup of coffee. I doubt it. Carrie was the optimist, not me. I'm going to go downstairs, while the others are busy, and pry the boards and nails away from the door and open it. If somebody's going to eat me, I think I'd rather it be the monsters outside rather than the ones in here with me.

SIMULACRUM

It had taken nineteen days for Ian to finally find a book he could use. Nineteen long, weary days. It was not some old, forbidden grimoire, hand lettered by a twelfth-century sorcerer in human blood, bound in human skin. He hadn't pored over crumbling records in the dusty back room of an ancient library to find it. There were no cryptic puzzles that, once deciphered, would lead him to its location. He had spent hundreds of dollars on other publications; lexicons, pamphlets, manuals and monographs and a good many diabolical encyclopedia that all turned out to be useless. Countless hours had been wasted perusing the internet, always leading him on wild goose chases that only brought frustration. Ian had begun to lose hope that he was ever going to be able to fulfill his desire and was nearing despair when, quite by accident, he found what he'd been looking for.

He'd stumbled upon a website that did not seem to be what he considered *complete bullshit,* as so many of the others were. It was on the message board of this website that Ian discovered a thread (posted by a member called *bestservedcold74*) that mentioned the title and purpose of a book. Another round of searches led him to the online catalog from which he could order a brand new, paperback copy, and several clicks later, he had secured one for himself. He paid extra for rush delivery and two days later he was holding it in his hands.

Upon receiving the book Ian read several chapters and was relieved to find he would not have to kill anything for the ritual he'd be using. So far, he had performed four unsuccessful summonings and two of them had required him to make a blood sacrifice. Ian was not a violent person under ordinary circumstances, and it broke his heart when he'd had to use his ceremonial blade (purchased for $99.99 from another occult website) on innocent, trusting strays he'd found wandering the neighborhood. Especially considering that their spilt blood had been wasted, failing to call anything forward to answer Ian's summons.

The pain of those little murders, though, was nothing compared to the heartbreak that had driven him to this strange plan of vengeance in the first place. Every night he dreamed of Samantha screaming in terror and writhing in agony. Her absence dug a cavity into his heart and filled it with white-hot rage. It drove every molecule of remorse from his battered soul, and it was the image of her beautiful, smiling face (oh how they had loved each other once. Why had she *gone*?) that brought him to this nightmare purpose.

Now it was time for him to try again. His mother and father were going out for the evening, and he didn't know when he'd have another chance like this. He'd come back to stay with them after Samantha left. He knew they were worried about him. The house was full of concerned looks and pauses which might have become the beginnings of conversations *(Are you alright son? How are you holding up?* they seemed to want to ask him) but the words never came. They were a frozen lake that separated him from his parents. They could look at each other from across those unspoken words but they couldn't reach one another.

Ian watched from the window as his parents' car backed out of the driveway and buzzed off down the street. When he saw them turn the corner, he went down to the basement and prepared for the ceremony.

When he was a teenager, the basement was where Ian went to be by himself. He'd had an old RCA stereo with a turntable and a tape deck, and he would sit in front of it for hours listening to an endless loop of dark, moody, music. Posters for fantasy movies and strange, obscure comic books adorned the dark-paneled walls. It was a world arranged and created by him. When he'd finally moved out as an adult, his parents had left everything the way it was down there. His bookshelves, bursting with second-hand paperbacks, his drawing table and art supplies, his stereo and his box full of tapes. It all sat there waiting and when Ian moved back in after losing Samantha, descending those orange-carpeted steps was like crawling back through time.

Sadly, not even the solace of his beloved basement could damp the fury that raged within him when he thought of Samantha. *Why?* The question clanged on and on in his mind like a litany. *Why? Why? WHY?* No matter how he attacked the problem Ian could not understand why.

No answer made sense. The universe pushed us down like bullies and stole from us, laughing and then left us there on the ground bleeding and alone. It had come to a point where he could not stop thinking about her. He imagined all sorts of scenarios like, what if she had never left? What if they could still be together? Dark curiosities wormed and writhed within him that, try as he might, he could not force back down. Thoughts like where she might be and what she might be doing and who she might be doing it with. They filled him with so much dread and hurt and scalding hatred that he sometimes found himself gasping for breath.

That night, thoughts of Samantha swam freely in Ian's mind mingling with dreams of dripping, red revenge. They became inseparable. He decided that now was the moment to begin, while his intent burned hot upon his heart, close to the surface.

He walked into the back room of the basement where his parents stored years' worth of discarded clothes and unused appliances. He pushed past boxes full of junk and made his way to the back of the room where he'd hidden his small supply case.

Inside the case (which was just a cheap, plastic toolbox) were chalk and candles, matches and a small bottle of oil which had supposedly been infused with the sweat of a virgin. These were the implements Ian used when trying to call down into the dark, past the boundaries of our world and into the stinking shadows beyond. Into the place where he hoped to contact something that might be willing to make a deal with him. He wanted to find something that smoldered with the desire to commit horrible atrocities on behalf of his pain.

So far, he had been unable to raise anything to do his bidding (though once, at the end of a very long and arduous ritual, he did hear a mad, echoing laughter bubble forth from the center of his circle for just a few moments), but he hoped that this ceremony, which was different from the others, might yield success.

Ian took his toolbox out into the large furnace-room where he'd been attempting his conjury. He took the chalk out and squatted on the limestone floor. He consulted the book to be sure he was drawing the diagram correctly. The size of the circle generally didn't really matter because the things he was trying to call forth were not constrained by the physics of our world. This time it was slightly different, however. The circle had to be large enough to completely surround the item which was to be placed in its center. The item wasn't huge, but Ian wanted to be sure he had enough room.

He made the circle about ten feet in diameter. He then drew the markings that the book instructed which were supposed to help the thing find its way up from below and into the circle above.

Once the circle was laid out upon the floor Ian went into the back room and dragged the item out into his makeshift ritual-chamber. It was pieced together precariously on a folding chair that he'd found in the garage. Ian was careful not to jostle it too much. It was fragile and he didn't want to waste precious time reconstructing it. He managed to get the chair into the room without anything falling off or out of the object and he maneuvered it to the center of the circle. He sighed with relief to find that he'd drawn the circle big enough to fully encompass it. He stood back and smiled for a moment, admiring his work.

The item was a body that Ian had constructed for a being (as a person uncomfortable with religion, Ian tried not to think of them as *demons*) to inhabit once it slithered up from whatever lightless nest it called home. The core of the body was made from two large lawn bags filled with fallen leaves. It was October and they were abundant. His parents had been pleasantly surprised to come home and find the front and back yards neatly raked. He'd bought four brooms that he shoved through holes cut in the bags to suggest arms and legs and then he'd thrown a very large, very old brown and white afghan over the top of it. On the area that Ian thought of as the "face" he had sown two large silver buttons to serve as eyes. Just beneath the buttons he'd strung a piece of yarn threaded with needles to be its mouth.

Looking at it slumped on the chair made him think of a scare-crow that had gotten too tired to stand in its field anymore. It was ugly and it gave off a wet, fermenting odor thanks to the leaves and the moldering afghan. Ian couldn't conceive of what would happen if something did decide to take hold of his puppet. It made him nervous to imagine this thing suddenly filled with hideous life, standing and grinning through its sewing-kit mouth. He wasn't sure that was something he wanted to see but he knew time was fleeting so he began the ritual.

Ian reached into his case and took out three candles, placing them at points along the circle to form a triangle around it. He lit them and then stood carefully back so that he did not cross the boundary of the circle.

He sprinkled some of the consecrated oil into the flames—the books said this would tempt the being upward. Then he took a crumpled piece of paper from his pocket and gently unfolded it. It was a photograph of Samantha. She had been caught off guard when this picture was taken, and her startled laughter had been frozen there forever. Looking at it filled him with the same old sadness and impotent rage.

Taking the photo in one hand and the book in the other, Ian knelt on the floor in front of his scarecrow and said the words that would hopefully coax something to bring it to life.

It was not the longest ceremony he had ever performed. It lasted about an hour and a half, but it was an hour and a half of intense focus. Ian had to try and concentrate all the rotten hurt, and anger and sadness and loss into a single stream of will that could wrap around the words of the spell.

He spoke slowly not wanting to disturb the delicate atmosphere by stumbling over his words. Many minutes passed and the small furnace room began to hum with gathering static electricity. Ian felt the hair on his arms go rigid even as the temperature seemed to plummet. Everything in his field of vision faded away except for the circle, the candles, and the lifeless body of leaves. Ian's heart began to beat faster. Something was about to happen.

Then he fainted.

When Ian awoke, he sat up, rubbing the back of his head where it had struck the hard floor. He looked to the chair in the center of the chalk circle. In the gently flickering candlelight, he saw that his scarecrow was no longer sitting in it and the picture of Samantha was gone.

He quickly scrambled to his knees and stood up, turning to look behind him. There was nothing there. Ian blinked in confusion trying to understand what had happened. He didn't know how long he'd been lying on the floor unconscious. It could have been hours. Maybe his father had discovered him down here after arriving home and had disposed of the leaf-man. *No*, Ian thought. *He wouldn't leave me on the floor like that. He would've called an ambulance or something.* He was having trouble forming coherent thoughts. His brain felt like it had been pulled through a meat-grinder.

He had decided to head upstairs to see if anyone had come home when he heard a shuffling sound coming from the back room. Ian spun around and peered into the darkness behind him. Deep in the gloom a hulking, misshapen figure stood amongst the boxes. Two green sparks burned within its shadowy form seven feet above the ground. *Those are its eyes.* Ian's breath caught in his throat.

The spell had worked.

There, hunched amidst a jumble of moth-eaten old clothes and old school papers was an actual—*something*—from beyond the veil. Something that had animated the simulacrum Ian had constructed so it could wreak the bloody reprisal that he himself could not.

It waited, taking slow, ragged breaths as Ian stared wordlessly at it. He spent a few moments trying to remember what the book had told him to do if the summoning was successful. He took several steps back and turned to face the thing in the storage room.

"I—uh," Ian bent and retrieved the book. He wasn't sure about the wording. "I command you come." He looked up hesitantly from the page to where the thing stood. A second or two later it came shambling out of the darkness of the back room and into the slightly less dark hallway stopping a few feet from Ian.

The body was no longer what Ian had created. He had fashioned a mannequin out of unwanted objects and household items. What stood before him now, while still somewhat resembling the basic form of the construct, was something of flesh and bone and hair and teeth and claws. It was much bigger than what Ian had made; both wider and taller. In fact, it towered over him.

He looked up into its glowing green eyes with a mixture of wonder and terror. Its mottled brown (*hide? Skin? Pelt?* Ian didn't know what to call it) exterior was thick and wrinkled, like the flesh of a rhinoceros. Its underside, arms, and legs were all covered with long, dark hair. The arms hung to the ground, each of them ending in three long, curved talons that looked sharp enough to tear through steel. Its legs were short and thick and bent at the knees. The feet were long flat paddles tipped with uneven toes that twisted and forked like tree branches. There was no head or neck to speak of, only a flattened area near the top from which its eyes gleamed. Where Ian had strung its mouth was now a wide grinning maw filled with hundreds of crooked, overlapping needle teeth. Whatever it was that had left its underworld warren to answer Ian's summons had not just inhabited his simulacrum—it had formed a living, breathing body out of it. A body that looked perfectly

well-equipped to cause irreparable trauma to anyone who stood in the way of its dark pursuit.

Ian's shock began to dissolve and became excitement. He glanced at the book and then stood up straighter, meeting the emerald gaze of his otherworldly assassin.

"Creature. Do you accept the terms of our contract?" The terms Ian was referring to had been declared during the summoning spell. By answering the call, the thing had essentially already accepted the offered terms, but form and tradition were important parts of any ritual and Ian did not want to deviate from the book. "Will you stand as my emissary?"

The simulacrum bent forward in what Ian took to be a nod and uttered a hollow, rattling growl. It seemed satisfied with the terms it had been offered.

"And you know the one you seek?"

Again it nodded and growled.

"And you will return to me with the head as proof that you have carried out my vengeance?"

The creature dragged its claws across the floor and opened its mouth letting forth a rumbling groan. It seemed to be smiling. Ian took this as a yes. He pointed towards the stairs.

"Then go."

At once the simulacrum gathered itself together and with a hissing shriek began dragging its bulk across the floor. Ian watched it pass and was struck again with awe and wonder. He wanted to reach out and touch it as it hunched by but didn't dare.

For a moment the idea that he might either be dreaming, unconscious on the floor, or insane occurred to him. Any other person would have said that both possibilities were far more likely than what his senses told him was happening. He dismissed the thought quickly though. If he was dreaming, then he would wake up at some point and realize it. If he was insane, well, what did it matter? This was the world he lived in whether it was real or not. He still needed his closure. He needed revenge.

Ian watched the thing's wide back as it turned the corner and began clomping up the stairs. It was a narrow staircase and he hoped it would be able to get out without smashing through any walls. He walked out into the family room and saw that the simulacrum had the ability to narrow and elongate its body. *Why wouldn't it?* He surprised himself by letting out a high-pitched giggle. Even if he wasn't insane right now Ian thought he probably wasn't too far from it.

The creature topped the stairs and disappeared from sight. A moment later Ian heard the back door open and then slam shut. It was out in the world now. He went over to the stereo and put a Stranglers cassette in the player. The first song began to play, and Ian flopped down on the couch, waiting in the dark for his simulacrum to return with a head for him.

****

Samantha woke to the sound of someone pounding on the door. She wondered if Charles was going to answer it. *Probably not.* She had no idea what time it was, but it felt late. The sky outside the window was dark. Huge clouds drifted slowly across a sliver of moon like barges on an upside-down river. She turned her face into the pillow and sighed. She was lying on her stomach, naked. Her arms and legs were splayed across the dirty mattress bound at the wrists and ankles by heavy nylon straps that stretched under the bed. Charles had set the straps on the inside of the bedframe between the front and back legs so that Samantha couldn't slip them over the edges. She couldn't remember how long she'd been pinned that way, but it felt like a long time.

From across the room Samantha could hear Charles clacking away at the computer. He was watching porn or else uploading videos of the things he'd been doing with her. She knew he did the former because she could hear the tinny sex sounds blaring from his small computer speakers and she knew he did the latter because he told her so.

"You ought to be proud. All kinds of people are going to be watching you." That had been on day one. His Computer City work-shirt had been open, exposing his round, sweaty belly. He'd worn no pants, his boxers stretched between his ankles above his dark socks, and he fondled himself casually. "Does the idea of it turn you on?" The question had come out thick, his voice cracking. Samantha hadn't answered him. She didn't have to.

Charles seemed to think everything turned her on. He chattered away at her as if she enjoyed having his abundant bulk squashed down on top of her as he grunted and heaved. He'd convinced himself that she found pleasure in the way he left streaks of Dorito dust on the sides of her breasts and thighs when he groped and probed her with his filthy fingers. Somehow, in Charles' mind, all of this was fulfilling some kind of dark fantasy that was burning within her.

She doubted if he ever wondered whether she enjoyed being strapped to a mattress sodden with her own urine (it definitely didn't bother *him*). She was surprised that he even took the time and effort to clean her off when she had to do more than just pee (though since he only spoon-fed her one bowl full of soggy cereal a day those times had become much less frequent).

Across the room Samantha heard the chair squeak as Charles leaned back and swiveled around at the pounding on the door. She didn't bother turning her head to look at him, but heard him stand up, his underwear snapping as he pulled them over his jiggly hips. "Shhh, stay quiet now sweetie." *Sweetie.* The way he whispered tenderly to her, as if they were in this together made Samantha's skin crawl.

She didn't make a sound. Charles had a large hunting knife that he'd shown her several times to encourage her not to struggle so much during their "sessions." She thought that if she tried to call out now, he would surely use it on her. He hadn't bothered telling her to be quiet before because his apartment was on the sixth floor of an old, abandoned factory on a block lousy with old, abandoned factories.

He'd told her that his brother owned the building and had wanted to turn it into a nightclub someday. He let Charles live there rent-free in exchange for keeping an eye on the place and he almost never checked in on his strange, chubby brother.

On that first day, when she woke up, bound to the bed with him on her back, Charles told her that she could scream all she wanted. No one was going to hear her and even if someone did, in this neighborhood, nobody was going to stick their nose in anybody else's business.

She had stopped screaming for help on the fourth day. No one was coming to help her. Whoever it was outside was probably not there for her anyway. The police announced themselves when they went banging on doors. This person hadn't said a word. Samantha did not feel any hope at all. Anyone who was wandering these streets at this time of night and crawling into (supposedly) deserted buildings was almost certainly up to no good. They might even be worse than Charles.

The pounding continued. It sounded like whoever was out there was using some kind of hard object on the door like a baseball bat or a crowbar. It didn't have the muffled thud of a fist. It was a hard sound. It didn't matter what they had, though, they weren't getting in. Charles had made sure that his grubby little love-den was well sealed off from anyone who might pry from the outside. The door was a metal fire-door, its frame solidly set into brick. It would take a grenade to blow it off its hinges.

Even if they could pick the lock or use a gun on it, Charles had four crossbars, two at the top and two at the bottom that bolted from the inside. The only vulnerable place in the room was the window and that was six stories up from the ground on the face of the building. Nobody was getting into this apartment.

Samantha could hear Charles breathing behind her near the door. He didn't say anything to the intruder. He just stood and listened as the constant pounding went on and on. There was no break to its rhythm. If anything, it was getting louder and more insistent. It went on for what felt like forever before Charles finally spoke.

"Hey asshole, you're not coming in here." He meant to sound hard and menacing but his voice came out petulant and weak. In a fair fight where he wasn't hidden in someone's backseat with a syringe full of sedative, Charles would have been a threat to no one, including Samantha

The hammering on the door didn't pause or slow down at the sound of his voice. Whoever was out there kept up their monotonous tempo with an eerie persistence. Samantha, who was desperate to be discovered, felt a chill spring up beneath the slimy sweat covering her bare back.

She was afraid of Charles and what he might do the longer he had her in his apartment. She knew that as he got bored, their sessions might become even more horrifying. She also knew that eventually he would tire of dealing with her, or she would no longer be attractive to him, or he'd want someone else and when that happened that would certainly mean the end of her. Faced with those prospects Samantha was still afraid of the person at the door and what might happen to her if they got in.

Charles was becoming agitated. Samantha could hear the sound of his feet padding on the floor as he paced back and forth in front of the door. He was making whining sounds in his throat like a yappy little dog being teased.

"What do you *want*?" He beat his fist impotently against his side of the door. "Huh? *Who the fuck are you? I've got a gun!*" The pounding kept on as if they knew he was lying.

Samantha's heart was racing. Charles was panting behind her, mewling. He was melting down. She had no idea what he would do if he thought he might be caught with her. Probably he would kill her and then himself. That's how these stories always seemed to end.

Charles began to sob loudly as he battered at the door with both fists. The person on the other side kept up their own pounding and it soon formed a weird syncopated rhythm.

"You can't have her." Charles' voice was a wet, blubbering mess. "She belongs to *me!*" He let out a strangled cry. "*I love her!*" The noise on the other side of the door kept up, implacable.

As the person or people outside continued to bang on the door, Charles' weeping and hitching gradually dried up. He stood silently behind Samantha for some time, and this was even worse than his wheedling and crying. The air in the room suddenly felt thick and heavy, and she knew something was about to happen.

"*Fine then,*" Charles called out suddenly. "You can have her if you want her so bad. Hope you like dead pussy. I can always get another one." Samantha heard his footsteps as he came across the room towards her.

Her face twisted with sorrow, and tears streamed from her eyes. She couldn't believe that this was how she was going to meet her end.

Before Charles could reach her to do whatever it was he planned on doing there was a huge *boom* and a roaring metal shriek.

Charles stopped dead in his tracks. There was another boom and another deafening squeal. There was the dusty sound of crumbling brick and the *ting* of several small metal somethings hitting the floor. Suddenly Samantha knew that somehow the door had been torn from its hinges.

Whoever was out there had gotten in.

She couldn't see what was happening, but she heard everything.

When the door crashed to the floor Charles began to scream. From further back, near the empty doorway, came a low rumbling growl. Heavy scraping footsteps shuffled over the threshold and into the room. Charles seemed to be trying to form words, but it all came out in an ululating howl. Samantha heard his feet thudding against the floor as he backed towards her and then suddenly, he tripped and fell over on top of her.

She whipped her head to the side to try and see what was going on, but the intruder was well beyond her field of vision. The only thing she saw was a voluminous shadow falling across her as the person stepped forward and reached out for Charles.

Charles was kicking his legs and flailing his arms. His feet were drumming painfully into Samantha's exhausted calves. Then his weight was lifted off of her entirely. Whoever was back there was huge and incredibly strong. Samantha began to scream. She didn't know what else to do. She didn't understand what was happening and she didn't know how this would end. She only knew that if she didn't open her mouth and let out the terror it was going to split her open and spill her insides out. She and Charles made a nightmare duet as their soaring wails mingled in shrill harmony.

Then Charles' cries were cut short with a wet ripping sound like a very thick piece of cloth being torn along a seam. Something hot and wet rained down onto Samantha's body. It splashed against her face and rolled down her cheek like heavy tears. It pooled on the pillow and Samantha could see that it was blood. Her breath caught in her throat, and she strained helplessly against the straps that held her down.

Samantha heard something heavy fall to the floor behind her and knew that the intruder had just dropped Charles' body. She tried to plead for her life as they stomped towards the bed, but no sound came out. Suddenly, she couldn't remember how to speak. She felt the person's immense bulk lean over her and heard its wheezing breath. Since they had begun knocking on the door, they hadn't uttered a single word.

Something sharp pressed softly against Samantha's leg near her ankle. It felt like some kind of huge, curved knife. It slid down her leg and she squeezed her eyes shut waiting for it to cut into her flesh. Instead, it sliced through the strap holding her leg to the bed. It did the same thing on the other side. It leaned even farther over (*no person could possibly be tall enough to lean that far, could they?*) and cut the straps that held her wrists. She was free. Her rescuer stood up and waited, making no sound except to breathe.

After a few moments of silence, the tiniest glimmer of hope crept into Samantha's mind that she might actually escape this awful dream. She didn't want to let it. Hope was dangerous. Hope was the false friend who told you everything was going to be okay and then, when you realized that *nothing* was going to be okay, it pushed you off the ledge, laughing. Still, no matter what happened next, she'd at least be able to move her arms and legs. That evened the odds at least a little bit.

After lying on her stomach a few moments longer, Samantha finally rolled onto her back for the first time since she'd been brought to the apartment. Her muscles screamed, charley-horses twisting inside both calves, her shoulders pinched with a delirious ache. She opened her eyes wanting to see the person who had cut her free.

Whatever she had expected, this was not it. She didn't even understand what she was looking at. Suddenly her heart sank, and her hope slipped away like steam. She realized she must actually be dreaming because what stood before her was not human. She didn't know what it was. She had never seen anything like it before in any book or movie. She looked up, up and up until she found its glowing green eyes. There was a lot of hair and a mouth filled with what looked like hundreds of shiny sewing needles. She sighed.

"Dammit, I thought this was real." She pushed herself painfully up to a sitting position, wincing at the way her thighs stretched and burned. She took a closer look at the monster standing in front of her. She was amazed at how detailed her imagination could be. She would never have suspected such wells of fantastic invention were hidden within her.

Then she saw that it held Charles' dripping, severed head in its left claw, his mutilated body lying on the floor a few feet away. She was spattered with his drying blood. Dream or not the terror came flooding back in and Samantha began to scream again. At the sound of her voice, the thing stepped towards her reaching its arms out. Samantha's eyes widened and her throat was scoured with the force of her cry.

Finally, as her brother Ian had done earlier that same evening, miles away, Samantha fainted.

***

Ian's parents had called him at 11:30 and told him that they might not be home till very, very late. Ian had said that was fine and that they should try to have a good time. As he hung up the phone he wondered if, subconsciously, they knew to stay away that night. He sat down on the couch in the upstairs living room and fell asleep waiting.

Sometime later, he awoke to a sound at the back door. It was a furtive shuffling noise followed by a soft *tap tap tap* on the outer windowpane. Unreality washed over him as he stood up and walked through the dark kitchen and into the back dining room.

Outside the window he saw something large moving amongst the shadows. The tapping came again for a moment and stopped. Ian's heart was pounding. He tried to swallow but could only manage a dry click at the back of his throat. Summoning up as much courage as he could, he stepped to the back door, undid the latch, and opened it.

There on the steps, folded up in their grandmother's old brown and white afghan was Ian's younger sister Samantha. Her eyes were closed, and she wasn't moving.

She had been missing for three weeks. The police had come up with no solid leads. No trace of her could be found except for her empty car, discovered in the parking lot of an all-night diner. There had been a massive search party that turned up no further clue to her whereabouts. Ian and his parents had been frantic. All anyone knew was that she'd stormed off one night after arguing with their mother about where she was going to go to college, and she had never come back.

Ian stepped out the door and leaned over her. There were splotches of blood on her face and arms, but he could see that she was breathing. For a moment he didn't move. He was afraid if he did then this dream would simply break apart like clouds after a storm and she would be gone again.

When he could stand it no longer, Ian crouched down and slid his arm under his sister's neck. He could tell she was naked beneath the afghan and wondered what nightmares she had endured out there in the heartless world.

He cradled her to his chest and began rocking back and forth. Tears formed at the corners of his eyes and spilled down his cheeks. A moment later, with a fluttering of her eyelids, Samantha woke up. She looked into her brother's worried face and smiled.

"This has turned into a really great dream big brother." She whispered hoarsely.

"Shhh, it's not a dream. I sent somebody to come and find you." This reminded Ian of the simulacrum and he looked up and out into the night.

There was no sign of it. The afghan that Ian had used as part of its body was now swaddling his sister. A large pile of dead leaves swirled in a sudden breeze that swept through the yard but nothing else stirred in the darkness.

A severed, human head stared back at Ian from his parents' picnic table. Blood seeped out from the ragged stump of its neck. Its mouth hung open in a silent scream and its lifeless eyes bulged.

Ian smiled. He had been promised proof that his vengeance had been carried out on the man who had hurt his sister and there it was, bleeding on the patio. Ian had never expected that his creature would also return Samantha to their family alive. He hadn't even been sure she still *was* alive when he'd begun delving into his dark pursuit. He muttered a tearful *thank you* as he held Samantha close to him and from somewhere out in the night, something seemed to answer him with a low guttural growl.

THE BOY FROM DELEARY PARK

There's a church at the corner of Pin Oak and Farbach Ave that takes up most of the block. It's the Pierce Township Methodist Congregation and that's where my family went every Sunday morning when I was growing up. After services, my brother and I would go across the street to a scrubby little playground nestled against a wide strip of woods. Deleary Park. It's not there any-more. They took out all the equipment about seven years ago and built a nice new park three streets over. It's got safer, modern equipment with a walking track and a skate park. Much different than when I was a girl, when it was just a couple of wobbly see-saws, a rusty swing set, a square of blacktop for jump rope, tag, and whatever else we could think of.

We didn't need more than that. We just loved having a place get out from under our parents for a little while. There was a tiny dairy bar, not much more than a cart with a roof on it, where you could get chocolate or vanilla soft serve with rainbow sprinkles (if you wanted them) or an Icee. My mom would give my older brother, Will, three dollars to split with me and they'd leave us at the park for the afternoon. We'd stay till dark, me playing and running around all day and Will leaning against the fence trying to charm the high-school girls. When the streetlights came on, that was the signal to clear out and all of us kids would trickle through the gate onto the sidewalks and walk home under the stars.

Sometimes I babysit my nieces and nephew and watch them climbing the jungle gym or going down the slides at the new park. Honestly, I don't like going there. It reminds me of things I'd like to forget. Things that are always lurking in the corners of my mind—a memory of Deleary Park that keeps me up at night, or rather, a memory of a boy I met there. A pale, strange little boy named Oscar Lunnge.

The first time I saw him he was standing near a break in the hedges that ringed the park, back by the see-saws, where the woods started. He was watching us kids as we played. His mouth was a thin, straight line, and his eyes were like two little black raisins shoved into a big ball of dough. I don't remember what I was doing or who I was playing with, but I remember the way he stood there, one white hand resting on the seat of the see-saw, looking so alone and unhappy. Just a shy little fat boy, and I felt sad for him.

He caught me looking at him that day, saw that I'd stopped to watch him, and when I caught his eye, I waved to him. Motioned for him to come over. Instead, he turned and disappeared through the hedge into the trees.

I forgot all about him over the next week as I did chores and played badminton with Holly Remmert across the street and bugged Will to walk me to the dairy bar. I didn't think about him again till the next Sunday when he came out of the woods and spoke to me.

It was the first really hot day of the year and only the second week of May. I'd gone off by myself to stand in the shade by the hedge for a little while. I don't remember the game we'd been playing, but I was slick with sweat and out of breath. Despite the warmth my mother said it was too early in the year for shorts and had me wearing jeans and a cardigan over my tank top. I plopped down in the cool grass beneath the hedge, panting.

Buckeyes littered the ground, and I gathered them up, arranging them in loops and patterns. I'd managed most of a figure "8" when a shadow fell across me from behind. I looked over my shoulder and there he was, standing close enough to reach out and touch me. His cheeks were pasty and smooth, and his brown hair clung to the top of his skull like frosting. He had on, of all things, a faded *Wonder Woman* t-shirt and cutoffs. He looked at me with the cautious, painful hope of an outcast.

I knew about being an outsider. I was in first grade when we moved to Pierce. It was bad enough being the new girl in school but even worse, I wore metal braces on my legs to correct a defect that affected how I walked. They came off when I was nine but those first two years were rough. Kids called me Robocop or C-3P0. They said I didn't take baths because I'd rust. Other stuff.

Mean stuff. Even years after, all the way into high school, I still heard the occasional snicker behind my back, or the word "cripple" whispered as I passed by in the hallway. I was always picked last for gym, even though my legs had healed just fine, and I was always the last one to find a lab partner in science class. Because of this I gravitated to the outcasts, freaks and weirdos who shuffled around the edges of the playground like kicked dogs.

"Hey, what's up?" My smile was polite but not over-friendly. I'd found that if you came on too strong the weird kids thought you were setting them up to be the butt of a joke and they'd be scared back into the shadows.

"Hi." His voice was a thin, breathy whisper.

I stood up, brushing grass from my jeans and faced him. "I'm Leslie." I extended a hand to shake. He looked at it like no one had ever done that before but after a moment he took it and we shook. His grip was feather-light and very dry.

"I'm Oscar Lunnge."

"Nice to meet you Oscar Lunnge, did you just move here?" He gave his head a wordless little shake my and curiosity deepened. "Well, where do you go to school?"

"Where do you go to school?" He parroted my words back, surprising a giggle out of me.

"I go to McLellan but next year I'll be switching to Pierce Middle."

He looked off into the distance for a few silent moments as if suddenly the clouds had become very interesting to him. I was about to ask him if he went to church when he spoke again. "I don't go to any school."

"You don't go to school? Not at all?" I was fascinated by the idea of a kid who didn't have to go to school.

A strange, pained look crossed his face. "I mean, my father teaches me. At our house." He nodded at me, his lips parted in a terse, puckered grimace and I realized he was trying to smile. He seemed horribly unpracticed at it and the result was pitiful.

"So, you're home-schooled?"

"Yes. I'm home-schooled." He shoved his hands into his pockets and then immediately pulled them back out, crossing his arms over his plump chest and finally dropping them back to his sides. His level of discomfort seemed intense, but I prodded him further.

"Do you go to church? I go to the one across the street."

He stopped smiling and issued a stiff little wave, almost a salute, with his left hand. "I have to go now. See you later." He backed a few paces away from me till he'd reached the break in the hedge and then disappeared into the woods.

I walked over and peered down the shady trail. I could see the leaves and branches wavering in his wake but was too late to see which way he'd gone. Of all the awkward little boys I'd befriended, this one seemed like he might be the strangest of the bunch. The thought gave me a little thrill and I wondered what secret shames he'd suffered at the hands of other kids.

I wouldn't have admitted it then, but I enjoyed spending my time with the losers and cast-offs because I knew they would eventually reveal their worst humiliations to me. Stories of playground chants, stolen gym clothes and cruelly accurate caricatures passed from desk to desk. Next to these torments the minimal teasing I took seemed much more bearable. Hardly worth thinking about at all. Compared to them, I was popular. Superior. It was sick, I know, and mean, but that's the way it was. I got off on it.

Not only that, but I also became a hero to those poor, lost souls. I thought about what it would be like to bring Oscar out amongst the other kids. I lied to myself that it was because I wanted to help him make friends, but somewhere, deep down, I knew the truth. I knew that if I coaxed Oscar into joining the crowd in the park, they would eat him alive like hyenas. They would tear into him mercilessly making fun of his pudgy body, his hair, his clothes—it would be a frenzy. Afterwards, I would whisk him back to the hedges to try and make him feel better. I would speak softly to him and pretend to be his friend. I would fuss over him and say what assholes those kids all were, and he would be so grateful to have just one person on his side. He would be my pet then, devoted to me entirely.

Please understand, at the time I wasn't thinking of it in such cold, stark terms. I was a child and could easily delude myself that I was trying to help him. With half-formed plans of how best to gain the shy boy's trust I left the shade to rejoin the normal kids in the sun. The flowers to Oscar Lunnge's toadstool.

The following Sunday was a gray, dreary mess. The ground was soaked from the previous night's thunderstorm. Earthworms writhed on the sidewalk and the sound of cars splashing through puddles echoed all over town. Because of the wet weather, Deleary Park was mostly deserted. There was a trio of teenage girls in the sheltered bus-stop listening to a boom-box, a young woman pushing a baby carriage around the birdbath, and standing back by the see-saws, Oscar Lunnge.

I made my way over to him, the sodden ground squelching around my sneakers. He was wearing the same clothes I'd seen him in the week before, the Wonder Woman shirt and jean shorts. I realized that, not only was he awkward and unpopular, he was also probably poor. He held his arm out and moved his hand back and forth in a stiff little wave.

"Hey Oscar, how are you?" As I sidled up to him a breeze shushed through the branches above the hedge, sending raindrops down onto our heads. I squealed and jumped back, covering my head but Oscar just stood there ignoring the rainwater soaking him. When it passed, I shook my head at him. "You're crazy, you know that?" I smiled to show it was meant affectionately but it didn't seem to matter much to him one way or another.

"Yes. I'm crazy." He cocked his head and looked at me. For the first time, I saw genuine interest creep into his face. "You want to come to my house with me?" He paused and squinted his eyes for a moment, as if in concentration, and then opened them again. "And hang out?"

I knew this was a chance to show Oscar I was trustworthy, his friend. It would be a step in drawing him out into the harsh light of day where a circle of kids waited for him. My pulse quickened. "Maybe. Where do you live?"

He turned his whole body and pointed to the break in the hedge where the path wound into the woods. "In there." He turned back and favored me with a twitching, unpleasant grin.

Disquiet tickled at the back of my mind. "You and your parents…you live in the woods?"

"Just my father and me. And—" His face clouded for a moment, then he went on. "Our house is through the woods. Yes. I want to show you my room. My things."

I tried to imagine the kinds of treasures he might keep in his room and couldn't. What was important to Oscar Lunnge? What strange objects would he stash in boxes and hide under his bed? He didn't seem like a reader so I didn't expect he'd have any books, and he was poor so toys and games would probably be limited. Maybe it was stuff he'd scrounged from thrift-shops or even junkyards. The weirder, the better as far as I was concerned.

"How far is your house?" I looked out across the park for my brother. I spotted him sitting at the bus-stop talking with the girls who had the radio. I figured if Oscar's house wasn't too far away, I could go with him, hang out for a bit and be back well before dark to walk home with Will.

"Not far at all. Ten minutes through the woods maybe." He waddled over to the break in the hedge and beckoned to me, smiling in that peculiar, off-putting way. "Come on. I want to show you my stuff. And we have—" he paused, squinting again before going on. "Popsicles. You like popsicles?"

I did like popsicles. Also, my curiosity was running away with me. There was a darkly exciting freak show aspect to all of this. I just had to see the place he called home. I glanced over at Will one last time, wondering briefly if I should tell him where I was going when Oscar called to me in his hushed, raspy tone.

"Come on Leslie, I want you to meet my dad."

"Okay, here I come." I joined him at the entrance to the woods and we set off down the path.

The temperature felt ten degrees cooler under the dripping canopy of trees. All the sounds from the park, and the streets beyond were muffled. All I could really hear were our footsteps on the leaf-littered path, and the sighing leaves. Oscar made almost no noise as he trundled onward ahead of me, and I was surprised. A boy his size jogging such uneven ground should've been panting and wheezing but it seemed like he wasn't breathing at all.

We'd been walking for a few minutes when he ducked suddenly into the trees to the left of the path. "Hey!" I stopped and put my hands on my hips. "Where are you going?"

He turned and smiled at me with puckered lips. "This way. This way to get to my house."

A little splinter of doubt slid into me. Sometimes bad things happened to pretty, young girls when they ran off into the woods with strangers. In fact, ten or so years before that, a girl named Lisa Miles had disappeared after she'd come home from college. They found her purse, one of her shoes, and her broken glasses on the riverbank by the bridge which was just a mile or so away from where Oscar and I were standing. They never did find her body.

Now, here I was, following a boy I barely knew, willy-nilly down the trail like a fairytale naïf traipsing along behind a gnome who promised—what? What exactly was it I was out here for? A popsicle? A chance to see Oscar's rock collection or jar of dead bugs? No one knew where I was and all I really knew about Oscar was his name. I stopped, trying to decide if I was going to follow, or turn and go back to the park.

He saw my hesitation and tromped back to where I stood at the side of the path.

"Hey, it's okay. We can go back to the park if you want to. If you want to go back to the park it's okay, we can go."

I looked into his smooth, round face—into his tiny little black eyes and thought, *What am I worried about?* I thought that if I turned back it would be admitting I was scared and that was one thing I never wanted to admit. After the bullshit I put up with over my leg braces, I thought of myself as a tough, resourceful girl, unafraid of anyone or anything.

"No, it's okay, I was just trying to get the spot straight in my head in case I ever wanna come back by myself." I decided, though, to make one concession to ease my concern. "But I want to call my mom when we get there. To let her know where I am."

Oscar nodded enthusiastically and said he had a phone in his room. Then he was off plowing through the calf-high weeds, with me galloping behind. We walked for another six or seven minutes in a mostly straight line from where we'd left the path. I wondered how deep we'd have to go before we got to his house. I wasn't even sure how far the woods stretched. I'd never thought they were big enough to get lost in, but once I was wandering through their green guts, it seemed like a real possibility.

Oscar's ten-minute walk had spun out to nearly a half hour before we finally came to a place where the trees opened up and formed a ring around a wide, flat clearing. The bushes and trees stopping right at the edge in an almost perfect line all the way around. The earth was a sickly gray, more like ash than dirt, and salted with tiny, white stones. At the center of the clearing sat Oscar's house.

I'd never seen a house that looked so old. It was neither wood nor brick but two stories of cobbled stone that jutted up from the ground like an arrow pointing to the sky. Its roof was wooden and steeply pitched, a few thin slats missing here and there. The second-floor windows were boarded up and the large, first floor window was nearly opaque with grime. A rusty, red metal tube with a wheel attached to it was thrust into the dirt and it took me a minute to realize it was an old-fashioned water pump. It was like we'd come through the woods, not just in distance but in time. I wish it had occurred to me at the time that there were no power lines running to the house which meant there was no phone line and that Oscar had lied about me calling home. Maybe I would've realized that something was wrong and that I needed to turn around and get away as fast as I could. Instead, I was overcome with curiosity, burning to know what a house so strange and ancient must look like on the inside.

We walked up to the front of the house and found the heavy, wooden door hanging wide open. A smell drifted out. It was like a car radiator that had gone bad. A hot, chemical smell. Oscar made his way in, swallowed by the gloom and I followed. We were standing in what I guessed was the kitchen. There were old, shabby cabinets hung around the room. Under the cabinets was a long counter with a filthy double basin. sunk into the chipped, granite top. Strings and splatters of some dark, viscous matter clung to the sides of the basin. A huge table dominated the center of the room, overflowing with a manic array of oddments. Dirty dishes, metal rods, books, loose papers, stained rags, and other, less identifiable things, all threatening to slide to the floor at the slightest disturbance. I

didn't see a fridge anywhere, or a stove, and was going to ask Oscar about where they kept and cooked their food when a tall, lanky man in a strappy undershirt and black pants came around the corner from the hallway beyond the kitchen. He stopped and peered down at us from behind an enormous pair of square-framed glasses. He smiled, showing a lot of shiny, white teeth.

"Well, hey there!" He planted his hands on his hips. "You must be Leslie, yeah?" His voice was loud and strident in the small, cluttered room. "Oscar said you'd be coming by to see us."

The sudden appearance of the man and his booming, cheerful voice scared me. Something felt wrong. He said Oscar told him I'd be coming to see them, but we hadn't talked about it before that day. I looked at the pudgy boy standing next to me, my heart beginning to beat faster. His expression was blank, like the face of a statue. He pointed at the man.

"Dad."

I looked back to the man, my manners overriding my growing unease. "It's nice to meet you." I noticed, suddenly, that Oscar's father was holding a jar in his hand. The room was dark so I couldn't tell exactly what it was, but something twisted and writhed behind the glass.

"Awww, well it's nice to meet you too, sweetheart. Why don't you come on in here and we can all get to know each other. I've got some questions." He took a step back and gestured towards the hallway with his free hand.

"I need to call my mom and let her know I'm here if that's okay." As my pulse sped up my mind seemed to slow down. I felt sleepy, like I was caught between waking and dreaming. Mr. Lunnge's words seemed strange. Questions? What kind of questions could he have?

"Oh of course sweetheart. There's a phone right in here."

"My feet began carrying me forward even as I was thinking that I wanted to turn the other way and leave. Oscar stepped behind me, blocking the way back and, with his hand against my back, softly urged me on.

I walked past Mr. Lunnge into the almost total darkness of the hallway. I heard his feet shuffle behind me as he and Oscar ushered me through the open doorway of the room across from the kitchen. My eyes weren't ready for the sudden brightness of this new room. Golden sunlight streamed in through six tall windows that lined the walls, three on either side of the room. Somewhere deep within my mind, a voice seemed to whisper that this did not jibe with the design of the house. No such windows had been visible from the outside, besides which, a few minutes ago the sky had been gray and overcast, the sun lost behind a screen of clouds. That voice, so full of concern and alarm, was very faint, though, and the door was already shutting behind me, the lock turning loudly.

In the center of the room was a green dentist's chair bolted to the floor with an old-fashioned gooseneck lamp peering over the back. Small leather straps sat curled on each arm and another one lay unsnapped on the seat. Next to the chair was a rickety cart with two shelves. On the top shelf was a tray holding an array of ancient, tarnished instruments that looked made for probing, scraping, slicing, and snipping. There was a spool of thick, dark thread and I imagined that somewhere on the tray were the needles that went with it. The lower shelf was crowded with an assortment of objects that were somehow more ominous than the instruments above. I could see a tall jar, similar to the one Mr. Lunnge was holding, filled with a cloudy green liquid. There was a small, square pan or bin filled with dark soil from which sprouted strange white fungi. They looked like slimy fingers poking up from beneath the ground. I'd never seen anything like them. There were other things too, strange lumps and shapes that I couldn't quite make out but that filled me with dread, nonetheless.

In a strange, detached way, I could feel the fear creeping up my legs, churning in my guts and settling, in my chest. The voice in my head gibbered and sobbed that we had to get out at once, but with a sinking heart I knew it was much too late. A strange, doomed lethargy numbed me. I was more sad than scared, imagining how my mother would cry when I didn't come home. I barely flinched when Mr. Lunnge's hand came down on my shoulder.

"You want to help me with something sweetheart?" His tone was kind but there was a cold eagerness that frosted the edge. I turned to look up at his face and began to cry. His eyes—they gleamed, wide like someone pretending to be crazy except he wasn't pretending. His head tilted and he grinned madly down at me.

"I want to go h-home." The words came out in a stuttering sob, tears streaming down my face and still he grinned. "I want to go home! I want to go home!" I was trying to scream it but it came out in weird, breathy whistles.

"Oh honey, it's okay. It's gonna be okay." His voice held no hint of comfort or sympathy as he took his hand from my shoulder and unscrewed the lid of the jar he was holding. The dark, moving thing inside came flying out with a horrible, angry buzzing. It hovered in the air between us and I saw that it was some kind of wasp or hornet but unlike any I'd ever seen. It was huge, the size of a grown man's thumb, its black body ringed with velvety purple stripes, its stinger long and vicious. More disturbing though, was the fact that it seemed to have many more legs than it ought to. I could never have been accused of being a bug expert, but I knew I'd never seen a bee or wasp with dozens of legs hanging from its plump body, all of them pawing obscenely at the air.

I was staring, hypnotized when it darted forward with shocking speed and latched onto my face near the corner of my mouth. I screamed and staggered backward, reaching up to bat it away. Instead of knocking it free, I ended up smashing its hot, fleshy body into my cheek. I pulled my hand back to smack at it again when a flare of white agony surged down my neck, across my chest and up into my head, squeezing my ears and bulging behind my eyes. The thing had plunged its stinger into the soft skin underneath my chin. I could feel its venom sinking into my skull, my face stiffening in a painful rictus, my teeth clenching. It was excruciating. Scream after maddening scream jammed up behind my locked jaw, unable to fight their way out of me. My vision exploded into electric-blue auroras that blotted everything else out and all I could hear was my poisoned blood rushing in my ears.

I grasped my face in both hands and rubbed, scratched, tugged, and kneaded my swollen, feverish cheeks, hoping somehow to root out the pain. Within a few moments, the bright blue lights had faded to black, and my knees went weak. I was out before my body hit the floor.

At some point, I floated out of the darkness to an echoing place of gray haze within which were only the voice of a man asking me questions and my own as I answered.

"How old are you?"

eleven

"How much do you weigh?"

i don't know

"Do you love your family? Your mom and dad?"

yes

"Have you ever kissed a boy?"

yes. danny lanham. on the lips.

"Have you ever kissed another girl?"

ew, no.

"Are you a virgin?"

i think so. if that means I haven't done, IT, yet then yes i am.

"Have you ever seen a ghost or a spirit? Have you ever seen a monster?"

no, but will says he saw my gramma sitting in our kitchen the day after her funeral. i believe him, he sounded sad when he said it.

"Have you ever drank blood or urine?"

god no!

"Have you ever killed an animal? Something other than an insect. A mouse or a rat? A stray dog maybe?"

i could never. i love animals. i have a dog named peter brady and three goldfish named inky, blinky and clyde.

"This last one is important Leslie. Have you ever, accidentally, or deliberately, killed a human being?"

of course not. i'm just a little girl.

After that, there were no more questions, and everything went black again. I don't know how long it was before I finally crawled out of the darkness but eventually my eyes opened, and I realized I was awake.

I was in a different room than the one Mr. Lunnge and Oscar had led me to. This room had no windows and was lit by six naked, fluorescent bulbs in the ceiling. It was much smaller than the first, covered in a peeling, lavender wallpaper that wrinkled and bulged from years of moisture and rot. I tried to sit up but couldn't. I looked down and found myself strapped into the green dentist's chair, my wrists held tight by the leather restraints on the arms. My clothes had been completely removed, replaced by a short, thin cotton gown that smelled like sweat, piss, and misery, and was spotted with faded pink stains. A tube stuck out of my arm at the crook of my elbow, threaded into a vein with a thick needle. I could feel another one wrapped around my leg, the needle shoved in high on my inner thigh. I couldn't see what the tubes were connected to, only that they both drooped over the chair. I could see, however, that the tubes were clear. Nothing was currently being siphoned out of me or pumped in.

Panic set in quickly and my heart began pounding, a headache thumping in time with it. I squeezed my eyes shut and tried to think through the pain. I was in a lot of trouble here, the worst of my life. I couldn't believe I'd gotten myself into such a mess. Why did I follow a kid I knew nothing about back to his house? Why did I let him and his father bring me to that room with the chair—

Suddenly a realization bloomed in my mind.

"Does he have two dentist chairs?" I mumbled out loud, remembering that the one in the bright room had been bolted to the floor. I was startled when Oscar's monotone voice came from my right.

"After the stinging, you see how things really are. It's the same chair, the same room. The way it really looks. Now you'll see everything for what it is."

I turned my head to face him, and it took a moment for my brain to make sense of what it was seeing. I didn't gasp or scream because in that brief span of seconds I believed I must be in the grip of whatever drugs Mr. Lunnge had used to subdue me and that it was a hallucination.

Oscar no longer looked like himself or like a boy at all. He didn't look human. *Wasn't* human.

His head was a fat, bulbous mound of crudely molded wax or putty. It was pale gray in color and pocked with indentations and grooves left by the hands that shaped it. His eyes weren't raisins but two pennies, Lincoln side out *(In God we Trust…Ha!)* glinting in the flat light of the fluorescent bulbs. A plump, round nose had been formed in the center, and below that a thin trench had been dragged nearly all the way across the face. A line of what looked like brown lipstick was drawn in a circle around the trench to complete the illusion of a mouth. The whole thing seemed to be mounted to a thick wooden disk that poked up out of the neck of Oscar's t-shirt.

"Oscar?" It came out as little more than a horrified squeak, but he seemed to understand. The big, lumpy head nodded slowly and sadly and turned away from me.

Seeing him *(it)* move was like watching the most outstanding special effects in the most realistic fantasy movie ever made, except I knew it wasn't a movie. All I could do was sputter and hitch while taking in the complexity and grace of his arms. They were a sophisticated apparatus constructed from long, thin dowel rods, elastic bands, and cords attached to tiny pulley systems and springs for maximum articulation. His hands, especially, were a miracle of engineering. An intersecting web of tiny cogs, pins, bars, and strips of wood, thin as twigs, all working together to create the full mobility and grasp of a human hand. His fingers were nimble, but his movements were nonetheless stiff. I remembered how oddly he'd carried himself back at the park, back when I thought he was a real boy and now I understood why. This is what I'd been looking at. This grotesque puppet cloaked in a thin glamour to trick people into seeing what their eyes expected to see—an ordinary, if strange, human boy.

After a few moments, I managed to control my breathing enough to form words. "Oscar…how? What are you?"

"My father—he knows many secret things." When he began speaking, I had to turn away. I couldn't stand the sight of the thin mouth-line puckering up and crinkling like a claymation character come to life. It hurt my head and it hurt my heart. I stared up into the lights and listened as he went on. "He has been alive a long time. He has learned things. Learned how to make many wonderful things with his hands and how to command the—" He faltered for a moment, searching for the right word. "—the world behind us. He knows how to speak with things. They come from outside and dwell in—in dark places."

I could hear his wooden arms clittering and clacking as he moved slowly around the chair. "He wanted family. He built bodies, invited things from outside to dwell in them to be his sons." Here his voice dropped, and a dismayed chill crept into his voice. "They did not want to be that. They wanted real bodies to live in. Alive. Skin and sweat and blood. Father tricked them. He tricked them into his false bodies, and they were very angry with him. They are big, like him, tall and strong.

"They made trouble. They—what is the word?—threatened him. Demanded real bodies. Demanded bodies to—to do things with. Awful things. He let them into the woods at sunset. They made little trying to hide. They were not afraid in their tall, strong bodies. They took a girl and dragged her into the night. They were nearly caught by the people. Father worked so fast to cover up what my brothers did. The people knew something bad happened to the girl, but did not ever find her."

I thought of Lisa Miles, the girl who'd disappeared a decade earlier, and shivered. I tried to imagine Oscar's brothers. Tall gaunt creatures, puppets like him but cruel and vicious, skulking through the shadows. I strained against the straps at my wrists, sweat slicking my arms and forehead.

"Where are they now? Your brothers?"

"Father did not want them to lead people here. He tricked them again—they are not so smart as they are hungry. He told them a girl was in the cellar for them—a plaything. They did not question but hurried fast downstairs. There, Father locked them tight and there they stayed for many years. They hate him. Some-times they cry out and howl at night. They hate me too. Because I am not like them."

When he said that I forced myself to look at him. He stood at the side of the dentist's chair, his wooden arms crossed over his wide chest. I wondered what was beneath the t-shirt he wore, what his body was built from. Could he feel pain? He seemed to feel emotion. The features that made up his face were far less sophisti-cated than his arms but somehow, I could read sadness and regret in the tilt of his misshapen head. In spite of everything, I felt sorry for him. This pathetic, bizarre abomination was all alone in the world, friendless and unloved by his family. Then I remembered that he'd led me here so that his father could use me for God only knew what. I squashed my pity and narrowed my eyes at him.

"Oscar." My voice was harsh and commanding. "Look at me. What did your dad do to me? What am I here for?"

He made a choked, gargling sound, a sound of distress, and turned away from me. "I'm sorry. I did not want to have you hurt. I should not have asked him. I was just so alone. I came to this body freely, want to be in the light of this world. I want to laugh and be among others. It was dark where I was—so dark and cold—I thought this would be better."

Panic was starting to flood my body, making my arms twitch in their restraints and my feet kick at the chair. "What does that mean? What are you sorry for? What is he doing?"

"I asked for a sister. For games and reading and walking with. Father wanted to make this happen and wanted to try something new. Wanted his daughter to be a real body—of skin and blood, not of wax and wood. He thought he might invite in something—something like me to live where you once did inside. Inside of you."

"What?" I felt my chest tighten as my breath began whistling in and out. "NO. You can't…"

"I know. He knows. It did not work. He could not make it so. He could not cast you out just as he could not cast my brothers from the false bodies."

For a moment I felt hopeful. "Okay, so then he'll let me go. Right?"

He was quiet for what felt like a full minute before he answered. "Oh no, Leslie. I'm so sorry for this. So sorry for you. Please do not hate me."

"What do you mean?"

"You have been stinged. You see us as we are. They cannot find us in the house. He says you could find your way back and bring them. You could bring them and show them. If they came and you showed them, they might take Father and me apart from each other."

"I don't understand—" I said, even though I thought maybe I had some idea.

"He will not let you ever leave. When he wakes back up he will come here to you and…"

"Shut up!" I pulled and struggled against the straps and strained as hard as I could against the belt around my waist. "Don't say another word. Just help me, please. Oscar you've got to help me."

He stood still, his back to me, making unhappy sputtering sounds. He rocked from foot to foot and pressed his hands to the sides of his head. I kept saying his name, my voice rising. I begged him to unstrap me and let me go. I lied and told him he could come and live with me and my family. I promised him anything he wanted, even said I'd marry him so long as he cut me loose. Every second that passed, I imagined Mr. Lunnge awakening and heading down the musty hallway to silence me forever.

Finally Oscar turned around, his strange, doughy face a mask of conflict. "You must run and run fast. You will not be safe till you are free of the woods and then you must still even watch after that. He will always want to catch you back. Go nowhere alone." As he said this his softly rattling fingers began working at the strap that held my right wrist down. In a moment, it was loose, and I yanked my arm free feeling pins and needles tingle backwards from my wiggling fingertips. Oscar hurried to the other side of the chair and began undoing the other restraint as I used my free hand to unbuckle the belt around my waist. In a moment I was totally free of the dentist's chair. I slid the tubes from my arm and thigh and dropped them to the floor. I jumped to my feet and sprinted for the door. Oscar waddled after me. I turned to glance at the rest of his body, my curiosity unwilling to be denied.

His legs were, if anything, more elaborately designed than his arms and hands. There were round wheels and counterbalances suspended between wires at the knee that were constantly spinning while long strips of rubber expanded and contracted with each step. For a moment my fear was overwhelmed again with wonder at the magic that dwelt within this house. That part of me quickly grew faint beneath the louder voice of terror though, and I pulled the door open and scurried out into the black hallway.

Night had fallen outside. The only light I had to navigate by was from the room behind me. It leaked into the hallway, just bright enough to keep me from running into the wall straight ahead. I crept forward at a slant to the impenetrable darkness of the kitchen doorway and let myself be swallowed by it. With out-stretched arms, I shuffled along, feeling for obstacles, and trying to re-build the layout of the room in my mind. I was pretty sure the big, cluttered table was to my left with the counter and cabinets to my right. Not a drop of moonlight or starshine made its way past the dirty window to help me navigate. I didn't even know for sure if my eyes were open or closed. I was listing to the left, trying to gently bump into the table so I could feel my way around it and from there guess my way to the door. I was beginning to think I'd gotten myself turned around when light suddenly filled the room, shocking in its brightness, blinding me.

I screamed and shoved my fists into my eyes, rubbing to clear away the stinging brilliance. I was more confused than ever and the unreality, shock and terror of everything I'd seen that day finally overwhelmed me. I'd handled everything very resourcefully up till then, I think, but after all, I was still just a little girl. A little girl who'd found herself threatened and experimented on, surrounded by monsters and alchemy. I'd held up as long as I could, but in that flash of light I finally crumpled to the floor, crying and wheezing, curling into a ball and hoping that whatever happened to me would be quick and painless. Heavy footsteps thudded against the wooden floor and a soft, scolding voice called to me from across the room.

"Leslie, tsk, tsk. How'd you get out?"

I crawled away from that voice, dragging myself along the floor. My eyelids had opened to slits and vague shapes were beginning to come into focus. I pushed with my feet, shoving my butt along until I bumped up against a wall.

My eyes adjusted quickly and as the room became clearer, I realized I wasn't in the kitchen at all. This was a room I hadn't yet been in, high ceilinged and paneled with uneven, gray wood planks. It was empty except for a large cage shoved against the wall across from the doorway. The cage was empty except for a stained, limp-eared stuffed bunny. It stared up at the ceiling with unseeing blue-button eyes, slumped against the wire bars.

"Leslie, come over here to me now please." A thick wooden door was set into the wall behind Mr. Lunnge and his voice was answered with the sounds of barking, bleating and a horrendous pounding from the other side of it. Something in there sounded like it wanted to get out very badly. Several somethings.

I had no idea how I'd wound up in that room, but I wasn't surprised to find that the house had turned me around somehow. My blood ran cold at the sounds of those—things—pawing and howling at the cellar door. I shrank back against the wall, pleading with Mr. Lunnge. "Please, please let me go! I promise I won't tell anybody what happened!"

He stepped forward, grinning, one hand behind his back. He wasn't hurrying. "Sweetie, you're going to stay right here with us."

"Please don't kill me." I stood up against the wall and began scooting to the left.

Mr. Lunnge chuckled as if I'd just asked him some absurdly darling question. "Kill you? Is that what Oscar told you I was going to do?" He stopped where he was and laughed long and loud. The sounds behind the cellar grew and his laughter mixed with them like a nightmare harmony. I still hear that noise in my nightmares.

With all the ruckus going on, and me distracting him, Mr. Lunnge didn't notice Oscar sneak into the room behind him. He had an old brass ring of keys in his mechanical hand. He skulked along the wall opposite me, holding one wooden finger up to his face to shush me as he crept towards the cellar.

Mr. Lunnge, meanwhile, took another few steps towards me, still chuckling like the friendliest uncle in the world. He took his hand out from behind his back. Grasped in his fingers was an ancient, metal syringe with a thick, rust-eaten needle at the end.

"Honey, I'm not going to kill you. That would be awful, wouldn't it?" I think he thought his tone was comforting. "You're just going to live here with us. Forever. In there." He pointed to the cage in the corner. "I'll keep you fed and dry and you can play with Mr. Bunnyface." His mouth still smiled but his eyes darkened behind his thick glasses. "Of course, I'll have to remove your tongue to make sure you stay quiet. Maybe your entire lower jaw but that's no big deal. Is it?"

He was only three steps away now. He raised the syringe and flicked the needle-tip with his other hand. A few nasty droplets of dark liquid popped into the air. "This will only hurt for a little bit." He reached out for me, his fingertips brushing the front of my gown when a loud, creaking and banging filled the room and all at once everything went insane.

Oscar's voice called out, very quiet but audible. "Run Leslie! Now!"

The terrible noises from behind the door rose to a deafening crescendo and Mr. Lunnge, his arm still outstretched to me turned and looked over his shoulder. I looked too, and my mouth fell open. I only hesitated a moment before I broke into a run but what I saw coming out of the darkness of that cellar will never leave me. Time slowed and that two or three seconds seemed to go on endlessly.

Three tall, spindle-legged things clothed in tattered rags came shambling into the room, all sharing the same stiff, scissoring stride. As crude as Oscar's assembly was, these creatures had been put together with an even less aesthetic sensibility, though their construction was just as intricate. There was no way, even with the use of magic, these would ever have passed for human. They were all as tall as Mr. Lunnge himself, maybe a bit taller, with long, thin arms carved from what looked like raw tree limbs. The hands at the ends of these were wide with only two long, curved fingers like talons and an opposable curved and jointed thumb. They clattered like dry branches blowing against each other in a constant wind. There was so much more—bands and belts that hung from their barrel-like bodies, the seemingly impossible motion of their jointless legs, but I really only saw them for a moment and there was one feature that stood out above all the others. Their heads.

I almost laughed at the black absurdity of it and maybe I even did—it was so loud in there and so long ago, it's possible I ran out of that room laughing like a crazy person. It was the site of those brightly colored heads, swiveling on some recessed ball and socket hidden by their rags. If one thing could be said for Oscar's father, it's that he had a fierce sense of whimsy.

They looked like they'd come from some long-ago carousel that had perhaps stopped spinning around the time of the moon landing, three jolly, wooden animal heads. There was a tiger, a gorilla and a hippo, each with a big, friendly, tooth-baring smile. Though the paint was peeling, the colors were still very vibrant. They would have been almost cute if not for the fact that Oscar's father had dug the original eyes out, leaving gaping black holes from which issued an otherworldly green glow that misted and condensed in the air.

Suddenly Mr. Lunnge's squealing, terrified voice rose in wordless outcry and time went back to normal. The things converged on him, wrapping their long arms around his body. One of them—the one with the gorilla head—turned and fixed me with a passing glance. My eyes locked with the glowing holes beneath its brow before it turned back to its more pressing matter. That was it. My dismissal. My notice to vacate the premises, immediately if I knew what was good for me.

I shot out of the room and into the dark hallway, now considerably less dark since Mr. Lunnge had turned on some of the lights. I ran straight ahead. Where there should've been a doorway into the room where I'd been held captive, there was only a patch of solid wall. I hurried down to the end of the hall where there was a different closed door. I turned the knob and shoved against it crashing into the kitchen. From there, I could look through the hallway across the room—the one I thought I'd just come out of—and see into the room with the dentist's chair. I felt a wave of vertigo surge between my ears, and my knees buckled.

I managed to grab onto the wall behind me and steadied myself. After a moment the dizziness passed, and I turned to the door that led out of the house. I was certain it would be locked, or stuck, or magically sealed but when I turned the knob, it rotated easily and when I pulled, the door swung inwards with a rusty squeak. A soft, wet breeze blew in from outside stirring my hair and I ran out into the night.

I won't bore you with my trip back home through the black woods. To be honest, I don't remember much about that part. I think I was in shock, and I just sort of wandered aimlessly till I came to a place where the trees thinned, and I could see a streetlight shining down onto wet pavement. I'd found my way to the back end of Skipping Cricket Road which cut through the woods along the river for a while before crossing Main Street near the Sunoco station. That was only four or five blocks from my house.

Shortly before I got to Main Street, I had a thought that gnawed and nagged at me. What was I going to tell my parents? It hadn't occurred to me until I'd stepped out onto the road, that I'd left my clothes somewhere back at Oscar's house. All I had on now was that filthy nightgown. Did I tell them the truth? Some of the truth? Did I make up a story? Call the cops and lead them to Oscar's house? The idea of returning to that place, even if I could find it, made my stomach cramp. Of course, I couldn't tell the whole truth because no one would believe that. Even half the truth would only lead to more questions. As I've mentioned, though, I was a resourceful girl, and I finally concocted a story I thought might work.

When I walked into the yard there was a police car sitting in the driveway. I went inside and everyone exploded around me with hugs, tears, anger, and laughter. It was an emotional free-for-all. When the shock of my sudden appearance had subsided, the questions started. The story I told, and which I'm sure no one ever really believed, was that me and a couple of girls from school, who I didn't know very well, had decided to go skinny dipping down at the river. I said those girls stole my clothes and ran off with them, as a joke. Knowing that I was sometimes picked on, I thought my parents, and Will, would buy this story, and I also thought it might get me some sympathy.

I said I'd lost track of time wandering the woods, trying to find my clothes, before deciding to just come home. Luckily, I told them, I'd discovered this dirty shirt hanging out of someone's garbage and was able to put it on before I got out onto the main streets. Nothing anyone said could shake me from my story, flimsy as it was. I told them I couldn't remember the girls' names, that they were a couple years older and that I wasn't a snitch anyway.

With much rolling of eyes everyone gradually began to leave till only my family remained. I knew I'd be punished but that was okay. Anything would be okay after the horror of Oscar Lunnge and his house. As it turned out, they were so relieved to have me home safe, that I was only grounded for two weeks, an easy sentence considering the hell I must've put them through.

The Sunday after my punishment ended, I got into the car after church with my parents as Will made his way across the street to Deleary Park. I watched him go with dismay, not wanting him to set foot in that park. Will was older, though, and really only went there to talk to girls. There would be little reason for him to go near the woods and hopefully nothing would be bold enough to venture out into the daylight. My mom turned and gave me a funny look. "Aren't you going over to the park with your brother? You haven't seen your friends in two weeks."

"Nope. I'll see them at school." I shook my head looking out at the little playground. It no longer felt safe to me, especially now that Oscar's brothers had been freed. After that I never went to Deleary Park again.

There is one other thing.

After almost twenty-two years away, I moved back to Pierce Township a few months ago to help my mother. She can't do as much for herself as she used to and neither Will nor I could stand to see her put in a home. A couple of weeks ago, as we sat watching game shows, she asked if I'd heard about the missing girl.

"No," I said, "I haven't. What happened?"

"Her eighth-grade class was helping pick up trash in that empty lot across from the church. It used to be that park you and your brother played at all the time. Her friends said one minute she was shoving paper cups into a garbage bag back by the trees, and the next minute she was gone. I hope they find her, she's just a little thing."

Since then, I've wondered about my decision not to talk about what happened to me. How many other girls might there have been? There's no way of knowing how many. Teenage girls disappear every year, their pictures taped to convenience store windows and nailed to telephone poles. Some of them are runaways and some are victims of human monsters, but what about the ones in Pierce Township? What about this eighth-grade girl my mother brought up?

I've driven by that spot at least once a day since she told me. I can't stop thinking about it, wondering if maybe that little girl met a strange but nice little chubby boy back by the hedge who invited her to come see his room. I hope she'd be smarter than that. I hope that she'd turn and run in the other direction and tell her parents. It's a pretty weak hope. After all, I didn't run from him.

I went with him. And I never told.

LILY'S PRAYERS

Dan found Lily's diary under her pillow with little flowers and butterflies on the cover. He felt a twinge of guilt as he sat on her bed and flipped through the pages, but he wanted to know what kinds of things she found important enough to write down and hide. It couldn't be that exciting. She was only eight years old.

He stopped at a random page and read. *"Thursday, Aug 4: We made popsicle stick birdhouses. I painted mine white. Maybe a bluebird will live in it."* Dan smiled. The next several entries were all similar. He was ready to slip the notebook back where he'd found it when he came across something quite different.

It was a drawing. A mad cluster of red scribbles. Long stick-like arms reached out from the edges and at its center a yawning black mouth filled with long, sharp teeth that spiraled endlessly inward. She had drawn herself into the picture, smiling, wearing her striped shirt and purple shorts. She was holding one of the thing's crooked hands. Beneath it she'd written, *"God loves me."*

Dan looked out into the living room. All was quiet. He looked back at the drawing and frowned. Something about the dark scrawls of wax made him uneasy. It was like a scab come to life. Kids drew all sorts of strange things; monsters, fairies, unicorns. They carried on long conversations with imaginary friends. Had parties with stuffed animals and dolls. Held funerals for dead birds. They were weird, and you couldn't take anything they did too seriously. Still, the reference to God was new. They weren't a religious family. They didn't even own a bible. He knew that she'd picked up the habit of saying her prayers at night from her cousins, but he'd always thought it was just so she could keep the lights on a little longer. He'd never stopped to wonder who she was praying to.

He shook his head. No big deal. He continued flipping through the diary. The next few pages were more observations and doodles. Then he turned to the entry for Saturday, September 9th.

"When I said my prayers last night God talked back! He said Mommy and Daddy are bad and don't love me. He says they do nasty stuff to each other. When he told me what, I said, nobody would ever do that. God said if I snuck into their closet before they went to bed I'd catch them. So I did. Diary, God was right! I won't tell you what they did but it was horrible! It looked like fighting and sounded like it hurt Mommy. Daddy kept saying to keep quiet. I told God I was sorry I didn't believe him. He said it was okay, but they might decide to do that thing to me. God said I might have to do something that seems bad so they wouldn't. He said I might have to hurt them."

Below this she'd drawn a picture of her face, blue with a huge drooping frown. Dan's mind reeled as he pictured his eight-year-old daughter spying on Charlotte and him in the bedroom. He felt sick. Worse, he felt guilty. He wanted to put the diary aside, but of course, he couldn't.

"Tuesday, September 12th: God told me Mommy put poison in my sandwich. I threw it away at school. I'm really hungry".

"Thursday, September 14th: God says Mommy and Daddy are dead and that theyr ghosts. He said if I don't do something theyr going to make me ghosts like them."

"Sunday, September 17th: All my dolls were gone when I came home from school Friday. God says Mommy and Daddy cooked them up into the spaghetti we ate. God said theyll cook me next. He said I should kill them before they kill me."

Dan looked around the room. He never really noticed Lily's things but he knew that her dolls were usually posed around the big dollhouse in the corner. The dollhouse was there, but the dolls weren't. He read on.

"Wednesday, September 20th: I put the knife back in the kitchen. I told God I couldn't do it. I can't hurt Mommy and Daddy. God said he understood. He just needs me to pray for him to do it."

The sound of the front door opening was very loud in the silent house. Dan's chest tightened.

He turned the page, standing as he read.

"God says he will take Mommy and Daddy to heaven. I asked where that was and guess what he told me Diary?"

"Lily?"

"Right under my bed!"

Dan suddenly wanted out of the room. He tried to move but couldn't. His right foot seemed stuck to the floor. He looked down. Long, slim fingers were curled around his ankle. They were attached to a hand that that had snaked out from beneath the bed. Before he had a chance to scream, his foot was yanked out from under him. He crashed to the floor pounding his fists and kicking his free leg. Another arm, thin but powerfully muscled, slithered out from beneath the comforter and grabbed his flailing foot. Then another arm grabbed at his armpit. Another came out and covered his mouth. They all began pulling at once, dragging him into the darkness under Lily's bed. In those last moments before he was swallowed up, Dan looked to the bedroom doorway and saw his daughter watching.

She looked relieved.

CELAENO

Calvin pulled into the driveway and parked behind a battered old Dodge pickup. He stepped into the heavy August heat and began to sweat immediately, his glasses fogging over. He wiped them clear with the bottom of his t-shirt and looked around the yard.

There was a slovenly row of tall bushes lining the driveway on the left. On the other side was a large uneven lawn that looked like it hadn't been mowed in weeks. It was more yellow than green and there were balding patches scattered across it. In the upper right corner up near the house was a thick, gnarled tree, its roots clutching the soil like long, arthritic fingers. It had no leaves and many of its limbs hung broken and dry near the top. It didn't seem to know it was dead.

The house itself was one of the ten-thousand or more identical homes that made up the sprawling Northwoods subdivision. It was little more than a wooden box set down on a cement slab and wrapped in cheap, yellow siding. The windows were old. They didn't lock properly anymore and could be opened easily from the outside. There was no basement. The garage was too small for either his or Celia's car to fit in. At the house inspection the contractor took them into the cramped attic to show them that there was no insulation, and then showed them a long crack that cut across the peeling plaster of the ceiling.

Calvin and Celia thanked him for his time and bought the house anyway. They didn't explain that the mortgage their credit and income had secured was only enough to get them a place like this. Celia, seven months pregnant, desperately wanted a house and she wanted to be able to move in quickly.

"Hello. Anybody in here?" Calvin stepped inside, crossed the empty living room, and peeked into the narrow kitchen. There was a hammer and a grout scraper lying discarded on the grimy floor where someone had been pulling up old tile.

The stove had been pulled out, exposing an ugly gash in the wall and three cockroaches on their backs. As Calvin watched, one of them twitched its thin black legs weakly as it tried to right itself. He wrinkled his nose and stepped back into the living room. "Hey." He called out. "Nick?" Nick was the young carpenter who'd been hired to make the repairs they'd asked for in their contract. The pickup in the driveway belonged to him.

Calvin walked down the hallway past the coat-closet and the furnace-room to where the bedrooms and bathroom were. He could see from the hallway that they were all empty. He stepped into the master bedroom, a ceiling fan slowly stirring the stale air. Sunshine spilled through the naked windows filling the room with golden warmth.

Calvin adjusted his glasses on his face and smiled. Despite his misgivings about sinking their money and time into a house that was not in great shape, he thought that they could be very happy here. Then he thought of Elaine and his smile faltered. His chest tightened and his head began to buzz with guilt.

With effort, he pushed the thought away. He would be ending the thing with Elaine in a day or so and no one would ever find out about it. He and Celia would have a beautiful life together enjoying their new family and their new home. He forced the muscles of his face to make a smile. It wasn't too big of a smile, nothing ostentatious. He didn't want to overdo it. It was just a small, satisfied grin. The longer he kept it there on his face, the more real it became. After a few seconds he pretended to be okay again.

Then someone who had been hiding quietly in the shadows of the hallway strode forward and struck Calvin at the base of his skull with something heavy, knocking him unconscious to the floor.

***

Calvin slowly realized that he was awake. His eyes were squeezed tightly shut. His head felt like someone had been setting fireworks off inside of it. The further into consciousness he climbed, the more stunning the pain became.

With a grimace he tried to rub the back of his neck and realized that he couldn't move his arm. His eyelids flew open with panic, and he jerked his head around to find out what was wrong. A swift bolt of agony shot through his skull and a tiny whimper spilled out of his mouth. He closed his eyes, trying to will his head to stop pounding. That's when he heard a raspy, man's voice from somewhere above him.

"You awake over there?" Whoever it was sounded weary, almost disinterested.

Calvin tried to ask, "Where am I?" but all that came out was a moan.

"Y'alright? I imagine you're head hurts pretty bad. I'm sorry 'bout that."

A wave of dizziness swept through Calvin as he tried to turn his body towards the sound of the voice. He opened his eyes again and the first thing he saw was filthy, warped linoleum that looked like it had once been an avocado color but had faded to a moldy gray green. He was lying on the floor.

As he struggled to lift his head, he realized why his arms didn't work. They had been tightly bound at the wrists, stretched above his head. He tried to move his legs and discovered, with a sinking feeling, that he was also bound at the ankles. He could move his legs up and down at the knees, but he couldn't get them underneath him to stand up.

Calvin's heart began pounding in time with his head. Fear and bile bubbled up from his stomach and into the back of his throat. He could see a pair of legs a few feet away. He could also see the scarred wooden legs of the chair that the man was sitting on. Calvin couldn't raise his head far enough to see any more of the man except for the barest glimpse of what looked like a blue work shirt.

"Wh—" Calvin coughed as he tried to speak. "Who are you?"

"Reason you can't move your arms and legs is 'cause I've got 'em duct taped together. I hate to do that, but I can't have you gettin' up." The man's tone was as casual as if he was discussing the weather.

Calvin strained against the tape wrapped around his wrists and ankles. He rolled to his side so he could face his captor. "Why? Why are you doing this? Who are you?"

The man in the chair didn't say anything for a long time. He sat there, occasionally taking a drink of something (at least that's what it sounded like he was doing). After a few minutes of silence, the man spoke. "I'm your neighbor. Well, I'dve been your neighbor if you'd had a chance to move in." There was a pause as the man took another drink. "As for why I'm doin' this—well, I'm not sure if I'm gonna tell you that. I guess I ought to, considerin' how unpleasant it's gonna be for you."

Calvin swallowed hard. His heart was racing, and his arms and legs ached to be free. His glasses slid down his sweaty nose and came to rest against the tip. It was maddening. He was desperate to adjust them, but he couldn't get his forearms close enough to his face to do it. They were just a little too stubby, a little too thick.

"What?" He was on his side, trying to lean as far back as possible without toppling over onto his back. "Unpleasant? Unpleasant how?" He wanted to sound tough, aggressive, but his words spilled out in a nasally whine. "What are you going to do to me?"

The man in the chair breathed a heavy sigh. Calvin heard a lighter being flicked and a quick intake of breath. The smell of cigarette smoke wafted across the room. "I'm gonna tell you right now, sir, that you won't believe me. You won't understand why I'm doin' this, but I've been livin' like this too goddam long and I just can't stand another fuckin' day of it." His voice cracked on the last word and Calvin realized the man was crying.

"You gotta understand, first off, that I know this is all m'own fault. I know that I done wrong, and I guess I always knew that shit like that can come back on you. Karma and whatnot. But I never would have believed that any person deserves the kind of punishment I been takin' for these last few months." The man uttered a rueful laugh. "Shit, I still don't zactly believe it. I usually think that I'm just a crazy lunatic, locked up somewhere, and this is all just in my head. I go on thinkin' that till she comes back at night and then I know it's all real. That's when I know. I'll never be able to enjoy another day of my life…" The man's words became choked with sobs, "Not another sunny day or blue sky. Not another song or steak dinner. Nothin'."

Suddenly something whizzed through the air and shattered against the wall across from where the man was sitting. Calvin guessed that he'd thrown the cup he'd been drinking from. The man stood up from his chair and began pacing. Calvin watched the dirty boots sticking out underneath the cuffs of the man's jeans as they circled the room.

"Ah Christ. Ah fuck me, fuck!" The man slammed his fist against the wall of the kitchen and began weeping bitterly.

Calvin's terror was immense, his thoughts racing wildly inside his sore head. He was clearly at the mercy of a psychopath who was going to hurt him and hurt him *bad*.

Oh God, Calvin's mind screamed, *you're going to die! You're going to die! He's going to torture you and murder you and you are going to be dead.* He began to flop around on the floor like a fish on the shore, screaming.

The man in the kitchen stopped crying with an alarming suddenness. He clomped over and swung a hard kick into Calvin's side. "You gonna need to keep y'mouth shut now, friend." His voice was low and cold. "I feel sorry for you, I really do. I wish it didn't have to be like this, but I've already made up m'mind and this is gonna happen. I am not gonna have you yellin' y'head off and somebody maybe hearin' you." Calvin heard the man plop back down into his wooden chair. "Do that again and I'll tape up your mouth along with your arms and legs. I only didn't gag ya 'cause I feel so sorry for you, but I will in a heartbeat if you make me."

Calvin groaned. His ribs ached and his back throbbed. He closed his eyes, his panic replaced with a weariness that pulled him further into the floor. His head slumped against the faded tile and exhaustion numbed his fear. No one spoke for what seemed like a very long time. The only sounds were the ones that came from the man lighting another cigarette and the occasional creak of his chair. Calvin was beginning to sink into a black daze when the man started talking again.

"You know what? Fuck her." The man chuckled. "Do I deserve this shit? No. Do you deserve this shit? *Hell* no. Did that carpenter deserve what happened to him? Nope. Even though he did seem to be a massive prick."

Suddenly Calvin was wide awake again. He moved his head from right to left as far as he could, but it was tough lying on his chest that way on the floor. "Nick? What'd you do to him?" His voice came out in a husky croak.

The man didn't even seem to hear him. "Look. Yes, it was bad. Me and Melissa'd been married goin' on thirteen years this comin' January. That's a long time, right? We had our ups and downs. We had times where we'd fight, sometimes, real bad. But things was alright for the most part, even if we never did have any kids." Calvin heard the man light up yet another cigarette. There was the sound of a deep drag and then a long exhale. "She had a hysterectomy in '03. Cervical cancer. But it didn't seem to matter. We got along 'bout as well as anybody else. She worked at the retirement home, cleanin' rooms, and I went through a bunch of jobs. That's probably the thing that pissed her off the most before the other shit started up. I couldn't seem to hold down a job." He made a disgusted grunt. "I'm a fuckin' loser."

The man's voice began to waver again. "If I hadn't lost the job at the fastener place I'dve never ended up at Boynton's and if I'dve never worked at Boynton's I'd never have gone through that goddamned drive-thru in the first fuckin place." The man paused in his story to take a few shaky breaths and then smoked in silence for a little bit.

Calvin felt the need to shift his body. He was stiffening up and aching. He stretched out as quietly as he could, curling and uncurling his fingers. He moved his tethered wrists to the right and felt something sharp tear into the soft underside of his forearm.

He looked up towards his hands. The room was full of shadows, and it was hard to see around his arms, but it seemed like a corner of linoleum had curled up some and was now sticking up above the floor. Calvin wondered if maybe he could use that small point to saw through the duct tape binding his wrists. To position his arms above the sharp tile-edge he would need to scoot his body backwards across the floor a few inches. He didn't want to do this while the man was quiet though. He wanted that constant patter of the man's story to cover up the sounds of him swishing around on the floor.

"So, what happened at the drive-thru?" Calvin held his breath, waiting to see if his prodding would bring more words instead of more violence.

"What? Why do you care?"

"Well," Calvin stammered trying to think quickly. His brain was still very muddled. "I mean. If you're going to do something to me, I think I deserve to know why."

The man was quiet for a moment. He stood up and stretched, his joints popping. He moved towards Calvin and Calvin braced himself for another kick but instead of stopping the man stepped over Calvin's body and went out of the kitchen entirely. His heavy steps moved off into the depths of the house. Calvin listened for a few seconds and then, when the man didn't return immediately, he began shimmying against the kitchen floor hunching his body backwards.

A moment later Calvin heard the muffled flush of a toilet and the clatter of a seat being dropped and then the pounding steps of the man as he came back. Calvin hoped that his change in position wasn't noticed.

The man walked up behind him and stopped. "Its two-thirty. We gonna have to get started soon. She'll be back not long after dark and I want to have this shit done with by then."

"Look," Calvin decided to try to reason with the man.

"Whatever it is you think you need to do—you don't have to do it. It's all in your head. You don't need to hurt me." Sweat began to bead under his hairline as the seconds ticked by. "Nobody ever has to know this ever happened. You can cut me loose, I'll go about my business, you go about yours and I don't speak a word of this to anyone." Calvin hoped it wasn't obvious he was lying about this. "I don't even know your name. I swear I won't tell anybody about this, Mister. Please let me go. Please." Even with his hands and feet bound, begging for his life, Calvin hated the wheedling tone of his voice.

The man laughed, a short, sad sound. "Son, you tellin' somebody about this is just about the last thing I'm worried about." He stepped over Calvin and returned to his creaking chair. "Listen, it's like I said. I hate to have to do this, but I do."

Calvin, momentarily forgetting the man's threat of gagging him shouted. "*Why*? What do you have to do to me? What exactly are you going to do?" As soon as he realized he'd been yelling he braced himself for another kick, but the man didn't stand up.

"Well, I was getting to that when I had t'piss." Calvin heard the flick of the lighter as the man lit up again. "You need to hear this anyway. Somebody does. I feel like this is sorta' like my confession. I hafta' leave this with somebody before I cross over."

As the man began his story Calvin pulled his wrists taut and gently but firmly began sawing the duct tape back and forth on the sharp corner of tile. He had to keep reminding himself not to become panicked or too zealous lest the man notice he was up to something.

The man, for the moment, did not seem to notice Calvin at all. He had retreated into the telling of his story.

"I started working at Boynton's third shift, stockin' shelves. It was a shit job and my manager was an almighty asshole but it was work and that's all I needed to keep Melissa off m'back. I worked from eight at night till four in the mornin'.

"It was the damnedest, stupidest thing. After I'd left work one day, I realized I wanted a soda. Workin' at a grocery store you'dve thought I could' grabbed one there, but I didn't. I was gonna stop at a gas station t'get me one when I saw the all—night drive-thru at the corner. I figured, great, I won't even have to get out of the car.

"The first time I met Chrissy I didn't really think nothin' about her at all. She was cute enough, I guess, but she wasn't nothin' special. Kinda' chunky but not too bad and she had a hell of a rack on her."

Calvin wasn't sure, but he thought maybe the tape was beginning to give a little bit. The sticky threads seemed to be separating. He didn't know what he would do if he managed to free his arms, since his legs would still be taped together, but he would certainly be a lot better off than he was now. He continued to work the tape across the sharp tile as the man kept talking.

"The first few times, we were all business. 'Need a Coke,' I'd say, 'dollar-seventeen', she'd reply, and that was it. After a week or so, though, we got to bein' friendly. She was usually workin' the drive-thru alone when I came along. At some point it got to be, if I didn't see her car in the lot, I'd just drive on past, disappointed.

"We started flirtin' after a couple'a weeks. She was mighty bored, sittin' in there so late. She said sometimes she didn't see nobody come along all night.

"Well, then I started stopping just to talk. I'd park out front, go in and sit with her. At first it was just for fifteen minutes or so, but pretty soon fifteen minutes turned into a half-hour. Then an hour. Before I knew it, I was in there talkin' with her for nearly two damn hours at a clip. Melissa didn't get up for work till nine and she was a heavy sleeper. She never even noticed I wasn't in the bed with her.

"Me and Chrissy talked about stupid shit. TV. Sports. She loved NASCAR and I thought it was the dumbest thing on the planet, but she got me turned around, little by little, and I started watchin' it when I could catch it."

The man breathed a long, quavering sigh. "Wasn't too long 'fore we started talkin' bout real stuff. I talked a bit about Melissa, but not too much. Somethin' inside me said not to bring her up. Chrissy talked about the boyfriends she kept havin' who'd treat her okay for a while before takin' off. I'd sympathize with her when she'd get down on herself. Try to make her feel better. That's when we started talkin' about sex."

Calvin felt the dent he'd been wearing into the tape begin to tear. His heartbeat, already pounding hard and fast, quickened within his chest. It seemed as though he might actually get his hands free.

"We talked about what positions we liked." The man droned on, drowning in a sea of memories. Calvin was only half-listening, but a part of him knew exactly where this was going. This story was familiar to him, though the players and circumstances were different. "Really we was just jokin' about it. I said I liked it doggy style, even though I hardly ever got to do that, and Chrissy said she liked to be on top. We got to jokin' about how we should try both of 'em out with each other and see which one really was better. It got to be that we weren't really kiddin' around anymore.

"You gotta understand, I loved Melissa. I didn't want this to happen, not really. A part of me did. My dick sure wanted it to happen, but the rest of me was feelin horribly guilty.

"I got to thinkin' about it all the time while I was home by m'self. I'd catch myself, thinkin' about Chrissy, and then Melissa'd come home, and we'd have dinner together and watch TV, and on the inside I just felt real dark and sad. I wanted those thoughts y to go away.

"I told myself it wasn't ever gonna be anything more than talk. I promised myself that. Then, at four in the mornin, when I rolled up into the drive-thru and seen her sittin' there waitin' for me, smiling,' I forgot that misery. Forgot how it felt, layin on the bed, sick of myself, wishin' I was somebody else."

The man crossed and uncrossed his legs a few times, shifting in his chair with an uncomfortable grunt before going on. "I started to bargain with m'self. 'Well, maybe just a hand-job. That ain't so bad. Then one morning we found ourselves fuckin'.

"I don't even remember the conversation that led up to it. There wasn't no kissin' or nothin' I remember that. One minute we was talkin' and the next minute I was on the stool behind the counter with m'jeans down around my ankles and she was on top of me. I didn't even see her shorts come off.

"When I climbed into bed with Melissa, I thought sure she'd wake up and know immediately what I'd done. She'd smell Chrissy all over me or find one of her hairs or she'd just be able to look into my eyes and know.

"But that didn't happen. She might've never figured it out if we hadn't got ourselves good and caught." The man slammed his fist hard against his thigh. "I felt like the lowest piece of worm-shit to ever dirty up the world. Even worm-shit was too clean for me. I felt like I was just this jelly of guilt and shame, and my heart was broken. I kept lookin' at pictures of Melissa and my chest felt like it was splittin' in half. I hated myself. I don't know why people do this to themselves."

Calvin, still sawing away at the duct tape, found himself thinking of the situation with Elaine. He found himself sympathizing just the tiniest bit with the man, in spite of everything.

"I swore I wasn't gonna do it again. I wasn't never gonna go back to that drive-thru s'long as I lived and that would be that. I made a firm decision, and it lasted me all the way through my shift that night.

"Then, as I was drivin' home, I saw the lights on in the drive-thru and my dick popped up and said, 'aw, hell, y'already done it once you might as well do it again'. I disagreed with my dick, but I did decide to pull through just to get my soda. I wouldn't stop. I'd tell Chrissy that Melissa was suspicious, and I couldn't do it again.

"When I got in there it wasn't Chrissy workin, it was the other guy. He got me my Coke and gave me a wink when he handed it to me.

"The next night I didn't even think twice. Chrissy was workin. She had on this shirt with a real deep v-neck and when I pulled up she put her hands on my open window and leaned over. Her tits just about fell out of her shirt right into my face and next thing you know we were at it again.

"This went on for two weeks. Every day was gonna be the last. Every day I decided to break things off or not even go see her anymore, and then every morning at four I couldn't wait to pull up and do it all over again. Got to be so we got careless. We got thinkin' that no other customers were gonna come through. Of course, that was complete bullshit.

"She was goin down on me once when a guy on his way to work pulled through. She popped up from behind the counter to get him his cigarettes and acted like nothin' was goin' on, but I could see he knew exactly what was goin' on. Shit like that happened three or four times. We still didn't care. We never thought it would catch up to us.

"It caught up hard and now it's still catchin' up to me and I'm sorry to say, it'll be catchin' up to you very soon. That ain't y'fault but it's the way it is."

Calvin's blood froze as the man's words sunk in. He had dug a sizeable tear out of the tape and was now trying to widen it.

"Melissa didn't find out till Chrissy showed up here, cryin'. Turns out they had cameras in that little drive-thru and sometimes the owner checked the tapes to see what his employees were up to in the wee hours of the mornin'. He knew the whole time. The first time he actually was gonna let it go, she told me, but after a couple of weeks of it goin' on almost every night he got mighty pissed.

"Anyways, he fired her that morning and she didn't know what to do. It never occurred to me that she had her own real life. That she was an entire person of her own and that there might be consequences that weren't entirely mine to deal with.

"She panicked and decided to look me up. Melissa worked every day except Tuesday, and wouldn't you know it, that was the day Chrissy decided to stop by. Naturally, Melissa wanted to know who this crying woman was, and it all just came out.

"There were a lot of tears from all three of us. Some scream-ing from Melissa. She called Chrissy a lot of names. Mainly *whore*. She said *whore* a lot. I yelled at Chrissy. Asked her why she would come here. She knew I was married, I said. She just said she'd gotten fired, she was maybe gonna lose her place and her whole world was comin' down. She didn't know where else to turn. Even then, I didn't want to admit that I didn't care about that stuff. In my mind the only person really affected by all this shit was me. I know, I'm an asshole. Nobody else knows that better than me.

"Chrissy finally left. She ended up comin' back twice more to beg for a place to stay. She got kicked out of her apartment. Of course, she couldn't stay here. Me'n Melissa—I wanted to work it out. I loved her. Boy, it might not seem like it but I never stopped loving her. It was nothin' t'do with her and everything to do with me. Me just letting my selfish prick call the shots for both of us."

There was a long pause then. The only sounds were the gentle creaking of the man's wooden chair and his breathing. Calvin's arms were filled with a deep ache from the constant, tight move-ment of trying to undo the duct tape. He was almost through the it now. He had severed enough of the tiny threads that he'd created some slack. Another couple of minutes and he'd have his arms free. He couldn't work on it, though, while the man was silent and so he waited patiently for the story to continue.

"Poor Melissa." The man sighed. "She tried to make it work for a couple of months, but she just couldn't get to where she could feel normal and still live with me. Maybe if we'd had kids it would've been different. Maybe they would've kept us together. Who knows?

"She moved out and went to stay with her sister. She never even told Chloe why we were separated. Just said we weren't getting' along. Melissa had too much pride. She never would tell nobody what'd happened between us. She never wanted to look like a victim to nobody.

"Six months ago, she took a bunch of pills and killed herself."

A lump suddenly formed in Calvin's throat. He thought about Celia, imagined her finding out about him and Elaine. He tried to picture what that might be like. Tears stung his eyes as the image of Celia dumping a pills out onto a plate and tossing them into her mouth, handful after handful, assaulted his mind. He vowed to himself that if he survived this ordeal, he would break things off with Elaine immediately. No more putting it off. He would never let his wife feel the confusion, pain, and rage that this man's wife had.

"Not long after that, *she* showed up." The man's voice was an icy whisper.

"At first, I thought it was just a big owl sittin' in the tree out back. I kept hearin' what I thought were the neighbor kids hollerin' and playin' outside but I realized that couldn't be right because it was always after midnight.

"I lost my job at Boynton's, and I sleep most of the day now. Most nights I can't get to sleep 'cause I been out cold all day, so I'm up watchin' TV and smoking cigarettes and just tryin' not to think. I finally happened to look out the window one night to try and figure out who was makin' all that goddam noise and I saw her.

"Like I said, I thought she was an owl. A humongous one. She was perched in the tree out back. I seen her shadow against the moon. Looked like she was as big as a kindygardener. Round at the top, kinda feathery outline, and I could just make out her eyes. Big, round eyes.

"When I seen it I thought, *holy shit I oughtta take a picture of that*. I went to get my phone and when I come back she was gone.

"The next night I heard the noises again and I went to the window. I could see her shape out there in the tree. Weird thing was, the sounds were clearer. They sounded like singing. Like a beautiful lady singin' a beautiful song.

"It sorta' hypnotized me, I guess. I went to the back door and opened it and just stood there listenin'. I started to understand the words. It was sayin, 'open up and let me care for you; ask me to come in.' It was like what you'd think a songbird would sound like if it could speak English. Not one of those obnoxious parrots but a canary or somethin' like that.

"I think I thought I was dreaming, otherwise I would've known something was terribly wrong with that. I would never have said, 'come in and take care of me,' if I'dve thought that it was real. But I *did* say it and it wasn't even two seconds later that she shot through the door like a bolt of lightning and hit me in my chest."

Suddenly Calvin felt the tension between his wrists go completely slack. The underside of the tape had snapped. All he had to do was peel it off and he'd have his arms free.

The problem was what he would do once he tipped the man off to his sudden lack of confinement. As the man droned on about his guilt-induced delusions, Calvin lay there motionless trying to think of a way to use this opportunity as a means to escape.

"She wasn't no owl." He twisted in his squeaking chair to lean against the table. "She kinda had some features that you might say were *owl-like*, but really she was a thing all to herself.

"She's like a woman. If you look at her from certain angles, she's kinda pretty, but from other angles she is like some disgusting old hag with loose jowls and wrinkled skin. See, she changes. Not like she transforms but it just depends from second to second how you're lookin' at her. At least, her human features change. The rest of her is always the same. A little under five feet tall and covered with gray-black feathers. She's got wings. No arms. Just dirty, foul-smelling wings."

The man's words were coming faster now, and his quavering voice had risen in pitch to a whine. "She's got tits in the front and they're big and round and maybe you think that sounds good. Maybe sometimes it even *looks* good. Maybe that's part of what makes it so bad. Maybe sometimes you catch y'self checkin' 'em out even though you know what they're really like up close. Long, chapped leathery nipples, black veins criss-crossin' em like spider webs. The smell.

"Everything about her has a smell. Like a gas-station bathroom where somebody went in and shit all over the place—not just in the toilet but all over the walls and the floor and then, instead of cleaning it up, they just piled a bunch of bags of garbage in there and closed it off for a couple of months. That's the way she smells."

"That's very descriptive." Calvin heard himself reply. His addled brain was having trouble coming up with a plan that didn't end with the man pinning him to the floor before he could untie his legs. He didn't want to push the man into whatever gruesome act of torture he had planned, but Calvin also didn't want to waste this chance to outsmart his captor. He tried to slow his racing thoughts down to a flow that he could manage.

The man made a, *hmmph*, sound, and went on. "Her legs are these little stumpy thighs that end in scaly, clawed toes like a chicken but fleshier. Thicker. I don't even want to tell you about the place between those legs. I won't. I won't say out loud what it's like. Jesus, no I won't." His voice cracked with emotion and a few desperate sobs escaped his lips.

"On the front, her face, tits, belly and legs are like a person. On her back, from top to tail she's all feathers. She's a monster, I guess. I never heard of nothin' like her though she said I should'a heard of her. She asked me if I knew who she was. She said she was famous. I wasn't even able to answer her. I couldn't even say real words. I thought I'd finally snapped and gone crazy." He uttered a thin, high-pitched little giggle then, an utterly unhinged sound.

"She told me her name was Celaeno. She said that men had wrote poems about her but that she'd been around long before people had started writing poems. She told me that her and other things like her and other things besides came into being around the same time that people decided that there were such things as right and wrong.

"When she busted through the door she'd knocked me to the ground. After she'd told me who she was she crawled up on top of me and started using those sharp nails on her feet to rip my clothes off. She cut my legs and belly up pretty bad in the process and there was blood running everywhere. In a beautiful chirping voice she said, 'Timmy, you like fucking so much, I'm gonna give you some fuckin' you won't ever forget.' And that's just what she done." The man's voice choked up again with tears and he was unable to speak for a moment. He began to make strange, keening, humming sounds and Calvin thought that this might be the time to make his move but after a few seconds the man got himself back under control.

"Oh Lord. Oh dear Jesus when she does it…" Calvin heard the man tapping his fingers rapidly against the table. "I watched my kid brother die from Leukemia when I was fourteen and he was eleven. I got the living shit kicked out of me by a group of assholes one night behind Murphy's Pub so bad I wound up in the hospital for two days and almost lost my right eye. I went through all that shit with Melissa and Chrissy, and I tell you, boy, all'a that put together didn't count for half as bad as what she did to me on that floor. What she's done to me every night for the past three months." The man seemed like he was going to start weeping again but he kept it together with some effort. Calvin still hadn't been able to see the man from the knees up. At least now he knew the man's name was Timmy.

"The worst thing about it is that part of me kinda likes it. Not really though, not the real me. She presses down against me, presses her chest on mine and starts…wrigglin' around. Like a worm or a bug. Then she scootches down towards my—she scoots down and climbs on top and she—she starts ridin' me like some kind of wild turkey makin' these awful squalling, moaning sounds.

"I can't explain what it feels like. It just goes on, and on, and on, for what seems like hours until finally you…finish. But it don't feel good. It hurts. It hurts your body first of all, but worse, it hurts your mind and your heart. Makes you feel like every person you've ever loved has decided to come in and use you as their own personal human toilet because that's what you are." He paused for a beat. "At least, that's as close as I can get to what it feels like."

Calvin realized he'd been holding his breath through most of Timmy's story. He let it out in a rush blowing tiny tumbleweeds of dust across the dirty floor. "Timmy, I don't think you deserve that. No matter what you've done."

Suddenly Timmy stood up from his chair. "What?

You don't know me, you fat fuck." He stomped over to where Calvin lay. "You don't know shit about me 'cept what I've told you. You think I'm just some dumb redneck psycho who's gonna tear your guts out of your fat belly?"

Calvin sputtered, terrified at the way Timmy was screaming. "No! No that's not what I think at all!"

"You think I'm so bugshit crazy that I don't know about you getting' the tape off'a your wrists?"

Calvin's heart seemed to shoot like a pinball from his chest up to the middle of his throat. "I…I…"

Timmy chuckled. "Yeah, you didn't think I knew that, did'ja?"

Suddenly Calvin felt rough, strong hands grasp him by his upper arms as he was lifted off the floor and flipped over onto his back. He found himself looking up at his captor for the first time. Timmy's face was a gaunt block of jutting cheekbones and looming, shadowed brows. A thin parchment of pale, dry skin had been stretched tightly over it, topped with a drift of fine, wheat-colored hair. He was tall and scrawny, drowning in his blue work-shirt.

Skinny as he was, Timmy was alarmingly strong. It felt like Calvin's arms were being squeezed between vice grips. His heart sank as the will to escape drained out of him, replaced with a feeling of calm resignation that cooled his blood. He didn't even try to struggle.

Timmy leaned his face in close to Calvin's. His lips were chapped. His breath was hot and foul. "Well guess what shithead? You've seen one too many movies. I ain't gonna do none of that shit to you."

Calvin blinked stupidly. "What?"

"I said I ain't gonna cut you up. I'm not gonna kill you."

Calvin's brain was suddenly backpedaling. "What? I mean. That's great." He looked up into the stern face hanging above him. "Then what are you going to do?"

Timmy let go of Calvin's arms, dropping him gracelessly to the floor on his back. The tall, thin man turned around and reached out to a shelf between the counter and the doorway. He grabbed a shiny roll of duct tape and a pair of scissors. When Calvin saw what Timmy had, he started kicking and bucking on the floor, waving his arms, trying to find any available purchase with which to pull himself up and away. His frenzied flailings were no good, though, and Timmy squatted down onto his meaty chest. Calvin's head smacked against the floor as Timmy hit him hard across the face with his huge open palm.

Calvin tried to retaliate by swinging his fists through the air in Timmy's direction. He connected one glancing blow off his captor's shoulder, but all he really managed to do was allow Timmy to grab each of his wrists, pulling them together and holding them tight against his chest under one hooked elbow while he cut a long swatch of tape from the roll.

"I should gouge your fuckin' eyes out for pullin' that shit," Timmy wrapped the tape around Calvin's wrists several times as Calvin struggled to pull away. After a few moments Calvin's wrists were bound again.

Timmy stood up leaving Calvin on his back to stare up into the small, spare kitchen. He could see the old wooden table and chair where Timmy had been sitting and he could see out the doorway into the hallway beyond. He could also see the body of Nick the carpenter propped up in the opposite corner by the doorway. His bare chest was streaked with drying blood that oozed from ragged, crusting wounds. Calvin's eyes widened and he began to whimper.

Timmy set the tape and scissors back on the shelf and made his way over to the table. He plopped down in his squeaking chair with a sigh and grabbed up his pack of cigarettes. "Jesus boy, won't you cut that shit out? It ain't helpin' nobody, least of all you." He popped a cigarette between his lips and lit it, dragging on it with a grimace. "Besides you can't be that upset to see that kid dead. That's the kind of asshole that'd smile and wave at you after fuckin' your wife."

Calvin watched Timmy sit and smoke for a moment and then spoke. "Mr.—Timmy—what are you going to do with me? Please, don't hurt me. I've got a baby on the way—a wife—please. Please let me go."

Timmy looked at Calvin with sad, pitying eyes. "Partner, I can't do that. In fact, after I get done this cigarette I b'lieve we gonna have to get started. This is gonna take a little while."

"What?" Calvin lifted his feet and slammed them to the floor in frustration. "What goddamit, what? What are you going to do? Tell me right now!"

"Well, I'm gonna do to you what Celaeno does to me most every night." Calvin's eyes grew wide with shock and disgust. When Timmy saw his captive's expression he laughed darkly. "Wait, now wait. I ain't gonna fuck you. There's something she does that's even worse."

Timmy leaned back in his chair and looked up at the ceiling, letting smoke drift out of his open mouth. "See, this whole thing with Celaeno is more'n some monster hauntin' me—I can't die. Bet you don't believe that but it's true. I've tried to kill myself seven times since she come to me and every time I wake up, like I passed out drunk, and I'm still alive. Pills, gun, slit wrists. None of it took. I cannot die.

"You might think that sounds pretty great except here's the crux of the thing. She won't let me eat. I go down to the store to buy some food, I bring it back here then she shows up and takes it all away. She swallows it all whole and I can't do nothin' about it. I can't fight her. She does this thing where she—she sticks somethin' in me, like a stinger, and it paralyzes me. It's how she keeps me still when I try to fight her off when—'cept I don't fight that much no more. No use.

"If I try to go out and sneak food while she's away during the day I just vomit it back up or I can't even swallow it. Can't choke it down. It just sticks in my throat like a big, dry ball of dirt. I haven't eaten since she got here." His eyes welled up with tears. "Well, I haven't eaten anything 'cept what she feeds me."

"What does she feed you?" Calvin asked, unable to help himself.

"Sometimes you hear on the news about somebody just up and disappearing. They say that police are lookin' for a missin' man whose family ain't seen him in days. Sometimes they find those guys. But sometimes they don't find 'em. Some of the ones they don't find are the ones that Celaeno brings back here.

"It don't happen every night. Sometimes she just comes in and fucks me and makes me talk about all the bad things I've done and she puts pictures in my head—pictures of Melissa. Melissa takin' those pills one by one. In her little room at her sister's place, the TV on in the background playin' *Wheel of Fortune*." His voice started to crack and melt. "She's cryin'. Oh my God, Melissa's cryin' so bad and she looks so hurt so lost and she's just eatin' them pills and washin' 'em down with gin or vodka or somethin'. I can't stand it when she shows me that." He rubbed his hand across his face, looking out into the hallway at nothing.

"Then, other nights, she brings home strange men. Dead. She drags 'em in through the back door and she's singin' in the most beautiful voice, like birds singin' and chirpin' but its words—awful disgusting words. She kills these guys and brings 'em to my house and she lays 'em in front of me. Then she stings me—paralyzes me—and lays me down on the floor." He took two gulping swallows, his Adam's apple going up and down. "Then she starts to feed me."

Calvin was terrified, but part of him was fascinated by this tale of madness. Before he even knew he was going to speak, he opened his mouth and whispered. "How?"

Timmy fetched a heavy sigh. "Like a mama bird feeds her young. She starts to eat the dead man. She tears into his body with her sharp little needle teeth. She rips and pulls and gouges and slurps, and she chews it and swallows, and down it goes into her disgusting gullet. Then she hops over to where I'm layin. She hops over and squats on my chest." Timmy's eyes shone with tears. "Then she—she puts her mouth over my open mouth like we're gonna kiss. Then her body starts humpin' and hiccupin' and gagging like a cat getting' ready to herk up a hairball and she regurgitates the dead man's flesh into my mouth. Wet, and slimy and all squished up and chunky she spits it into my mouth and all I can do is swallow it.

"I can't even describe the taste of it to you. You've had vomit in your mouth before, you know what that's like. This isn't like that. It's like a bunch of raw meat that's been sittin' out on your kitchen counter for a week and you dump in some old, chunky sour milk and some blood and you mix it all together and then drink it. It's like that except a thousand times worse." He dragged the back of his hand across his dry lips. "On top of that, it's a person you're eating. You're like a cannibal on a semi-liquid diet and the fucked up part is I never throw *that* up. Nope. No problem keeping that shit down. Yeah, I gag and clench up and every little bit of me wants to reject it but it just slides down my throat like melted ice cream and my hunger pangs actually get better because I haven't eaten anything else in days. I try to go down the street and get me a burger I can't even swallow a bite of it but this—this stuff goes down and stays down. She does this till there's nothin' left. I don't know how she does it but she grinds up the bones, gristle, meat, and skin and barfs it into me and there's not shit I can do about it. After I'm fed she fucks me for good measure and all I can do is pray to die—even if I wake up in hell it would be better than this. Then at some point, I wake up in the morning and she's gone again till dark."

Calvin's gorge had risen, and his lunch threatened to come spewing forth." Jesus Christ…"

Timmy shrugged. "Yeah. You never get used to it. Never. And what with me not bein' able to die, I foresee a long, long life of this. I can't stand it." He looked Calvin square in the eyes. His face was slack with deeply shadowed lines drawn from the corners of his nose to the corners of his mouth. His eyes had lost any hint of pity and were as lifeless as two tarnished silver dollars. "But I found a way out."

Calvin's body tensed with fear. "Timmy?"

"I been prayin' and prayin' and prayin'. For forgiveness, for death, for it all just to end. For any way out. After months of prayin' I think somebody, somewhere finally felt sorry for me. Three nights ago, I had a dream."

Timmy stood up and walked over to the counter behind Calvin. Calvin heard him open a drawer and the shimmering hasp of something sharp being pulled from inside.

"In this dream, Melissa was sittin' at this very table. She had her bottle of pills in front of her and she talked to me while she took 'em. She said that if I wanted out, I would have to become Celaeno. I would have to become the harpy, she said. I asked her how I could do that. Do you know what she told me?"

Calvin's pulse was racing, his heart thudding in his chest. The sound of his blood in his ears was like the roar of the ocean. "Timmy—Timmy come on now."

"She told me, all I'd have to do would be to find somebody else who was guilty of what I done. In my dream, she told me to check the house across the street. Your house. Then she said to find somebody else, kill him, and piece by piece I'd have to eat him." He stepped back away from the counter. "Then, just like what Celaeno does to me, I would swallow it and then puke it back up into the guilty guy. That's you."

"Timmy no. Timmy, I'm—"

"I don't wanna hear your story tubby. This deal is done. She told me to find you and I found you."

"Maybe she meant Nick! The carpenter!"

Timmy shook his head. "Nope. You the one she meant for me to take. You must've done somethin'. I'll become Celaeno and you'll take my place. It's the only way."

Timmy walked over to Nick's body. Calvin saw that he held a gleaming butcher's knife in his hand. Timmy leaned over and grasped the top of Nick's head turning it to the side. He grabbed the edge of Nick's earlobe between his thumb and forefinger and, with one movement, sliced it off.

Turning to face Calvin, Timmy held up the small lump of flesh, turning it this way and that, examining it as if it were some kind of exotic insect. Then, hesitantly, he put it into his mouth and began to chew it.

Immediately Timmy's expression changed from one of dark despair to eye-rolling pleasure. He worked the morsel around in his mouth, He opened his eyes and grinned at Calvin.

"Boy, I haven't been able to chew and swallow my own food for months. You don't know how sad it's gonna make me to bring it back up but it's gotta be done. We'll do this bite by bite." He swung a leg over Calvin, straddling him, and dropped down, pinning his captive's bound arms. Calvin grunted as Timmy's weight, slight though it was, crashed down onto him.

Timmy dropped the butcher knife to the floor beside him and began rocking back and forth. His eyes rolled up to the whites as his body started to convulse. Gagging and choking sounds began to work their way up to his open mouth from the depths of his digestive tract. He leaned forward, slipping his fingers between Calvin's clenched lips. Timmy yanked and tore, trying to pry open Calvin's mouth. His nails scraped against the soft pink meat of Calvin's gums drawing blood. Without meaning to Calvin opened his mouth to cry out and Timmy was able to get his fingers in and behind Calvin's teeth. Timmy yanked Calvin's mouth open and leaned forward. Calvin's body strained and heaved as he tried to pull his face away, but Timmy was too strong. Timmy's face dipped towards Calvin's open mouth.

At that moment the sound of someone pounding on a door came from beyond the kitchen. Timmy sat up, still holding Calvin's mouth open.

Calvin tried to scream for help. He drummed his feet against the floor and did his best to holler but with his lips unable to open and close all that came out was a reedy, breathy, "yeeeeahyeegh yeeeahhhyeeya!" There was no way anyone would hear that. On the other side of the pounding came a stern voice.

"Police! Open up, please."

Timmy's eyes widened with wounded terror, his lips peeling back in a terrible grimace. He looked over his shoulder and out the kitchen doorway, neither answering nor getting up off of Calvin.

The pounding came again. Harder this time. "This is the police! Open the door right now!"

Timmy looked frantically down into Calvin's eyes. Tears began to roll down into the hollows of his grizzled cheeks. He leaned over slowly and picked the butcher knife up from where he'd dropped it. Calvin tensed in anticipation of being stabbed or slashed with it. He thought of Celia and knew she meant everything to him. *I love you Celia*, He tried to send the thought out to her, *I'm so sorry*.

Then came the sounds of the front door crashing in and heavy footsteps thudding across the room. From just outside of the kitchen doorway Calvin saw the cop speaking to Timmy, his gun clutched in his hands. Two more officers were standing just behind him, their guns drawn. As well.

"Sir, put the weapon down slowly. Put your hands behind your head and kneel face-down on the floor."

Timmy just sat there, straddling Calvin's chest, the knife clutched in his hand. He made no move to put it down. He stared up at the policeman, a look of curiosity dawning on his face.

"Sir! I said put the weapon down." Calvin watched him point the gun at Timmy.

Timmy continued to ignore the order to put down his knife. He turned and looked at Calvin. A small, hopeful smile twitched at the corner of his mouth. "I hope this works." He whispered.

"I'm not going to tell you again. Put the knife—" Before the officer could finish his demand Timmy stood up abruptly, raising the knife over his head and charged forward. There were two loud but un-dramatic cracks as the cop's gun went off and Timmy collapsed in a heap on the ground, the knife clattering to the floor. As Calvin watched Timmy turned his head slowly towards him and smiled, a thin drizzle of blood and saliva oozing from the corner of his mouth and pooling on the tile.

"I think it worked." Timmy looked up at the ceiling and closed his eyes. He did not move again.

***

It was a month after his ordeal in Timmy's kitchen, and Calvin found himself looking out his front window. It was sometime in the dark hours between midnight and dawn. He was looking to the now-abandoned house across the street. It was built in the exact same style as his. Its yard was equally shabby, its driveway and sidewalk just as warped with weeds growing up through the cracks. He had never thought about it or noticed it before the day he woke up inside of it, but now he thought about it every day.

He found out later, that an electric company worker, reading meters, had seen Timmy creeping around Calvin's house that day and then had heard what he thought was screaming a little while later and called the police. When the lone officer arrived, he'd found Calvin's house empty, but there was a trail of blood spatters that had led from Calvin's doorway to the house across the street. This was how Calvin had been rescued.

Calvin often wondered if the blood trail had been from him or from Nick. It didn't seem like it should matter, but somehow, to him, it did. He felt a heavy blanket of guilt every time he thought of the young carpenter.

He tried not to picture Nick's body slumped in the corner of the dirty little kitchen. His death had saved Calvin's life. No matter what Timmy said, Calvin knew that in the end, when Timmy realized his plan hadn't changed anything, he would certainly have murdered Calvin there on the tile of his kitchen floor. Perhaps he would have gone on to kill others. It was possible that Nick's death had saved many lives.

Celia was asleep in their bedroom, snoring softly on her side, her pregnant belly pushing over onto Calvin's side. He'd gotten up to pee and found himself drawn to the front window as he so often was these days.

As he looked out into the silent shadows that draped the street, he thought about Elaine again. *Tomorrow.* He told himself. *This time I'm really going to end it. For sure tomorrow. No more putting it off.* He felt his chest tighten with remorse.

Then he heard the sound.

It was very faint, like a radio somewhere off down the street. It was some kind of music, but he couldn't make out the words. He leaned his forehead up against the glass of the window and strained to hear it better. It was singing. Something about the sound of it chilled him deep inside and he shivered. He turned to look in the direction that it was coming from and that's when he saw the shape in the old, dead tree in his front yard.

He stepped hastily back from the window, nearly tripping over his own feet, a strangled little gasp popping out of his mouth. He had never actually seen an owl in real life, but he'd seen hundreds of them on TV and at the zoo. It perched on one of the hanging, twisted limbs.

He started to go back to the window to check again and then suddenly decided against it. It was just a night-bird looking for food, and the singing was just someone's car radio. He told himself he didn't hear it anymore, even though he knew that he did.

Calvin backed away from the window and went back to his bed. He lay down next to his wife and put his hand on her warm belly.

Tomorrow. I promise. I'll fix it tomorrow.

FROM NEXT DOOR

Lynn woke to Pepper's tongue on her face. The dog needed out. With a groan, she sat up, glancing at the clock on the stand; 2:45 a.m. Beside her, Abbie pretended to sleep, ignoring the situation. The dog never bothered her. It was frustrating.

"Okay, okay, I'm coming." Lynn stood and followed Pepper out into the house. She didn't need any lights, she'd made this trip a thousand times. She opened the back door and watched the dog run out into the moonlight. A breeze blew in and she shivered, willing Pepper to hurry.

Instead, the dog stood in the middle of the yard, facing the neighbor's house. She laid her ears back and growled deep in her throat. Lynn leaned out to see what had her riled up.

Standing at the fence between their houses was a shadowy figure. A short, female shape in a housecoat that Lynn recognized. It was Mrs. Rafkin, from next door. Except it wasn't. Couldn't be. Mrs. Rafkin had passed away three weeks earlier. Lynn and Abbie had gone to the service, bringing a small but lovely bouquet for the family.

Lynn squinted. She rubbed her eyes. The figure remained. She couldn't see Mrs. Rafkin's face, but her shape was unmistakable. She'd hung laundry on a line out there every day, chatting with the girls as they tinkered in their flower garden or played with Pepper.

Don't be stupid. She chided herself. It's just a weird shadow, or a bush. Except there were no bushes along the fence and nothing she could think of that would cast such an odd shadow. It could only be a person, but obviously not the deceased Mrs. Rafkin. She considered calling out, then thought better of it. She whispered hoarsely out the door.

"Pepper, come on." The dog whined and trotted back inside. Lynn lingered a moment longer, straining to see the details of the person's face. As she watched, the figure raised its hand and waved to her, very slowly. A chill slid down her naked back and her heartbeat quickened. She slammed the door and took a step back. She was breathing heavy. She locked up and hurried back to the bedroom, shutting the door behind her. She climbed into bed and scootched as close to Abbie as she could.

Abbie raised her head. "You're freezing."

"Did Mrs. Rafkin have a sister? A twin maybe?"

"What?" Abbie flipped around to face Lynn. "Why?"

Suddenly, Pepper whined, scratching to be let in. Lynn whimpered. "Can you please let her in?"

Abbie sighed, throwing the covers aside. "You're being weird." She stood, walking around the corner of the bed, and then stopped abruptly. "Oh never mind. She's right…" She looked up at the door, where the scratching continued from the other side. "…here." She looked to Lynn. "Why did you ask about Mrs. Rafkin?"

Then a low, gravelly voice called from outside the door. "Girrrrrls…" The knob turned, and the door opened.

BLOOD ORANGES

"So, what's that tattoo all about?" Lawrence pointed to the inside of Megan's forearm. She stopped arranging onions and turned her arm outwards, looking down at the drawing inked into her pale skin.

It was a human arm, hand outstretched and grasping as it disappeared into a field of lush, red flowers. She chuckled self-consciously and shrugged.

Lawrence grinned. "Does it mean anything?"

Megan kept her back to him as she hid rough looking onions behind fresh ones. A memory surfaced. Smashing open her seven-year-old brother's piggy bank and taking the nine dollars to go buy a single Vicodin from a guy up the street. When her mother confronted her, Megan had screamed at her to go fuck herself. Not long after that her last real friend, Sam, told her they couldn't hang out anymore because she'd become sloppy and mean and intolerable. She started going to meetings. A hard and painful year went by and at the end of it she felt like a better person. A sober person anyway. People were still avoiding her, including her family, but she was proud. She celebrated by getting the tattoo. She'd wanted to save up to get another one on the other arm. A companion piece that showed a girl climbing *out* of the poppies, triumphant. Rescued. She'd promised herself after holding down a job for a year (and staying sober the whole time) she would do it.

"Nope, I just thought it was pretty." A small silence fell between them and Lawrence fidgeted, leaning against his push broom. After a few moments he spoke again.

"So, you got any big plans this weekend?"

Megan shook her head. "No, not really. Just sitting in my apartment watching movies. By myself. As usual. How 'bout you?"

Lawrence suddenly turned shy. "You're gonna laugh."

"Maybe. Tell me anyway."

The young bag boy looked around the store as if someone other than Megan might hear. "Well, d'you know anything about that old building behind the store?"

"Yeah. It used to be a doctor's office or a medical testing lab or something. We used to try and break in there back in the day."

"Yeah, and now they keep that shit closed up *tight*." Lawrence dropped his voice to a whisper. "Cause it's *haunted*."

Megan burst into giggles, drawing strange looks from a customer across the aisle. Lawrence nodded, his expression showing he'd expected as much.

"Yeah, I said you'd laugh. It's true though. There's *lots* of stories about that place."

Megan leaned against her cart. "I know the one about the ghostly security guard with the flashlight." She considered, cocking her eyes to the ceiling. "And the weird noises."

Lawrence shrugged. "You forgot about the evil hippies."

"*Evil hippies?*"

"Yeah, like the Manson family. Hangin' out, getting' high. Killin' people."

She shook her head, her short shaggy hair bouncing. "So what's that got to do with your weekend plans?"

Lawrence pulled his phone from his pocket. "I'm gonna bust in there and get a ghost on tape."

He was suddenly cut off by a voice calling over the speaker system. "Lawrence, please come to the courtesy desk—Lawrence."

"Dammit. I gotta go. Smoke at midnight?"

Megan waved her hand at him. "Yeah. Get going." She pushed the little gray handcart through a pair of swinging metal doors at the far end of the produce department and into a small prep room. A stocky young man with black hair and a beard to match stood at one of the tables peeling and slicing his way through a pile of huge, red oranges. He didn't look up when Megan walked in. She stepped to one of the stainless-steel sinks to wash the stink of onions from her hands.

"Hey Gil."

He raised one hand without turning around. "Hey."

She hung the sprayer back on its hook and turned to watch what he was doing. He spun an orange expertly against the blade of his knife, the skin peeling away in one long, curled strip. He split the naked fruit down the middle and sliced it into wedges. He set each wedge carefully on a sample tray and licked his fingers after the last one had been placed.

"You done with that cart?" He asked over his shoulder.

"Kind of late for samples, isn't it?" It was nearly ten and the store was all but empty of customers.

He lifted the tray carefully and set it on the cart. He adjusted his heavy-framed glasses and shrugged. "I'm here another hour. I'm bored. Might as well." He picked up an orange slice and offered it to her. "Want one?"

She shook her head and made a face. "Ugh. No, thanks. I told you I hate oranges." Gil's expression went slack, and Megan realized her tone had been harsh. "But, I mean, they do look really pretty. I've never seen oranges like that."

Gil smiled. "They're specially bred blood oranges."

"Oh?" She was already bored. Gil was nice enough, but more enthusiastic about his job than Megan felt was normal.

"Yes." He popped the slice into his mouth, sucking the juice out with a wet, kissing sound before chewing and swallowing it. "Most blood oranges are smaller than the common sweet orange, and usually only the flesh gets really red. But these…" he looked affectionately at the tray of fruit. "These are a subspecies that was deliberately mutated by growers in Sicily. The seeds were sent here to be…"

Megan held up her hand. "You know what? That's awesome, but I've got to get some of that corn shucked and wrapped before my next break. And you wanted to get those samples out there."

He nodded. "Yeah, you're right." He turned and pushed the cart out through the swinging doors, calling over his shoulder as he went. "Seeya."

Later, on the bench outside the store, Megan told Lawrence about Gil's blood oranges, rolling her eyes and sighing heavily. Lawrence shook his head.

"You might think he's boring, but that chick sure don't." He pointed to a small hatchback huddled in a corner of the parking lot near the fence. Gil was behind the wheel and a young woman with long, slender legs and very short workout shorts was climbing into the passenger seat beside him. Her bright smile was apparent, even at that distance.

Megan squinted, nonplussed. "That's not his girlfriend is it?"

Lawrence chuckled. "Naw. Your boy's a player. I see him with different girls all the time." He dragged on his cigarette and sat back. "He gonna hit that ass *tonight*."

Megan cuffed him absently on the arm. "Don't be crude." She watched as the little car pulled away and drove off into the night. She almost told Lawrence about the scene she'd witnessed earlier, between Gil and the girl he was with. She'd seen them as she passed through the produce department on her way to break. They were standing close together, the woman bent forward, leaning on the sample cart. Her mouth was open, and Gil slowly and delicately slipped one of the orange slices between her lips. Her tongue had peeked out and grazed her fingertips while her eyelids slid shut. The ecstasy on the woman's face as she chewed and swallowed the fruit was, in Megan's opinion, a huge over-reaction, and more than a little gross.

But for whatever reason, instead of telling Lawrence, Megan simply wrinkled her nose and tossed her cigarette to the ground. "She looks like a slut." She stood and stretched. "Seena later man, I'm out." She went back to the prep room and worked there till the end of her shift.

Later, as she drove home alone to her apartment, Megan found it unsettling that Gil, the know-it-all fruit guy, was with someone that night (many nights, if Lawrence was to be believed) and she wasn't. She was pretty. She was interesting. She could play the violin. She was well read. She had nice boobs. How could someone like Gil be doing better than her?

Stop it. She took a breath.

That was the old Megan talking. She had her meetings now, and sobriety. She was better than that. She said the serenity prayer and it seemed to comfort her some.

When she stepped into her tiny apartment, she was greeted by the sour smell of dirty dishes—the smell of the careless. It was dark inside. Humps of dirty clothes littered the floor. "Welcome home, sweetie." She sighed as she plopped onto the couch in front of the TV. The hours passed slowly and quietly. She found herself imagining what was going on between Gil and his date. Did his beard tickle when they kissed? Was he slipping off her shorts, running his grubby little hands along her long, smooth thighs? Did their mingled tongues taste of citrus? She realized with dismay that she was imagining her own face on the girl's body and that her hand had strayed down the front of her pants. For a moment she loathed herself and thought to stop, but then, realizing it was all she had, she kept going until she finished. It didn't take very long, and eventually she fell asleep.

***

"In local news, police still have no leads on a missing Connorsville woman. Twenty-one-year-old Heather Aiken was last seen leaving Forever Fitness on Muncie avenue last Thursday at around 6pm. Aiken's mother reported the disappearance Monday when she stopped by her daughter's apartment after not hearing from her all weekend and discovering several days' worth of mail in the mailbox. Police, using a GPS locator, found her cell phone discarded at the side of a wooded trail in Whitewater State Park. A widespread manhunt has been launched, but so far no clues have been uncovered. If you have any information about Heather Aiken's whereabouts, you're urged to call Crimestoppers at …"

When a photo of the missing girl appeared on the TV screen in the break room, Lawrence began choking on the stale donut he'd been eating, spitting wet bits of pastry onto the table in front of him. Megan sat up, concerned, and whacked him on the back.

"Hey! Hey man, you okay?" *Whack, whack.*

The bag boy took a swig from his soda bottle and sputtered. He looked at her with wide, haunted eyes. "Did you see who that was?"

Megan glanced at the TV. The girl's picture was still showing. She was pretty, in a blonde, ordinary way. Something about her smile was uncomfortably familiar. "I don't know. Maybe. Who is she?"

Lawrence pointed to the screen and spoke in a harsh whisper. "That's the chick that left with Gil the other night, man."

Megan looked again. The story had already changed, but now that he'd said it, she thought he might be right. That had been almost a week ago, and she'd only seen the girl for a second, but she remembered that smile. She also remembered the way that girl had eaten an orange slice right out of his hand. She'd called the girl a slut. Her stomach churned. "You sure?"

"Yeah." His expression was miserable. "I was checkin' her out in the store for a while before we went on break. Dude, that was *her*."

Suddenly, a voice came from the doorway behind them. "You guys saw us?"

Lawrence and Megan both turned to find Gil watching them. "Naw, man, we was just smokin' out on the bench." Lawrence's voice sounded very loud in the little room. "Still, she was pretty hot. That your girlfriend?"

"Nope. She's a friend of a friend. She just needed a ride home."

"This chick on the news looked dead on her man. *Dead*. On her." Lawrence looked down at his hands, fidgeting. "Maybe your friend oughtta check on their friend."

Gil's expression remained blank. "She's fine."

Megan felt a dull ache begin to throb at her temples. She wanted a Vicodin. Her body yearned for a dark room, some low music, her pills and a glass of vodka to wash them down with. The walls seemed to shrink and the conversation had become overbearing. She needed to get away. She stood from the table and pulled her apron over her head.

"Well fellas, I'm gonna get back to work."

Before she could get out the door, Gil fixed her with his tiny eyes, reverse-magnified behind thick lenses. "Hey Meg, I've got a bunch of those orange slices set out on the sample tray. Could you wheel it out to the floor?"

She gave him a lame thumbs up and headed to the prep room. She found the tray all ready with the beautiful red slices arranged in concentric circles, like seductive little smiles. Beads of moisture clung to the scarlet rind and the flesh was swollen with juice. Megan's throat convulsed with the taste of bile. A painful morning vomiting up what felt like gallons of orange juice not so long ago had robbed them of their appeal. Her headache intensified.

She pushed the cart out the swinging doors and left it next to a display piled high with bags of mandarins and tangelos. A bit later, as she was tossing old, bruised apples into a box, she saw a young mother with a little boy of about five or six, standing by the cart. The woman looked around as if to ask permission to take a slice.

"Those're free samples, ma'am." Megan called. The woman smiled and thanked her, picking up a slice for herself and one for her son. She popped it into her mouth and worked her lips around it. Her face melted with almost erotic delectation. She pulled a tissue from her purse and wrapped the rind in it. She grabbed one more slice, then two, and began pushing her cart down the aisle. Megan was amused to see the little boy look at the orange slice, sniff it, and drop it to the floor. *Kid's got good taste*, she thought, turning back to her work.

She forgot all about the woman and her son until the next afternoon. The Channel 11 News van was parked in front of Brindle's Supermarket with a cameraman and reporter standing at the ready. They ignored Megan as she strolled past on her way into the store. It was Lawrence's night off, so she went to the front desk and confronted the night manager.

"Heidi. What's up with the news people out there?"

"Some kid got left here last night. His mom just walked off into the ozone. He said one minute she was holding his hand, the next minute she wasn't. He went over to look at the candy rack and when he turned around she was gone." Heidi popped her eyes at Megan to emphasize the point. "Like, *gone*, gone. She hasn't answered her cell, didn't call any of her family. Nobody's seen her since. Pretty messed up."

Megan felt cold. "Heidi, I think I saw them last night."

Heidi nodded. "Yeah, a few people did. Cops'll probably come and get a statement from you."

Megan drifted back to the produce department in a daze. A throbbing had awakened beneath her temples and her ears felt full of cotton. She remembered the little boy's mother, her face orgasmic as she enjoyed her orange slice. She thought of the way the boy had tossed his aside, wanting nothing to do with it. Then she tried to imagine the woman dropping her son's hand and just walking away from him, disappearing into the night.

At the back of the department she saw Gil, rolling stickers onto bell peppers with the labeler. He saw her looking and waved. She felt herself wave back and thought of the other missing girl from the news. Two plainclothes policemen drifted through the store, speaking to all the employees. When they asked her if she'd seen the woman and her son, Megan lied and said no. Somehow she was uncomfortable with Gil knowing she'd seen or spoken to them. An ugly, uneasy feeling prickled along the back of her neck. At quitting time she hurried home, glad to be away from the police, the produce department and Gil.

Later, in her dreams, two missing women became one female shade, wafting through the store in gym shorts, holding onto a faceless little boy, blood colored footprints trailing behind them. They would turn and smile at her, revealing bright red orange peels staring out from their eye sockets like twin suns.

***

Lawrence continued to insist that Gil was involved in the first girl's disappearance and probably the second one too. He said he believed Gil was sprinkling ground up rufies onto the oranges or something similar. "I swear to God. I would'a told the cops to check his ass out."

Megan told him she didn't want to hear any more about it. She had to work with Gil, and it was all stupid anyway. He couldn't hurt anybody.

"He's harmless." Her mouth went dry when she said this, but she held that line fiercely.

Lawrence wouldn't drop it though. He claimed to have seen Gil hanging around the building next door. Creeping in the shadows. He said he was going to watch the produce clerk closely. Catch him in the act. As the weeks passed, Megan began taking fewer breaks with the bag boy. Instead, she stayed in the prep room by herself, munching on chips from the vending machine till her fifteen minutes were up. Sometimes Gil would join her delivering unwanted sermons on the cultivation of fruits and vegetables. It seemed she had no escape. She kept getting headaches. She'd go home and tumble into bed, her skull buzzing with pain.

Then another girl disappeared.

Her name was Melissa and it happened on a night that Megan called off work, which she'd begun doing more and more frequently. Brindle's Supermarket wasn't mentioned in the news, but the last place anyone had seen the pretty college freshman was the little ice cream stand across the street. People often stopped there after grocery shopping.

Megan's headaches got worse.

One night, she heard her name squawked out of the intercom. "Megan, please report to the upstairs office. Megan to the upstairs office." The Upstairs office belonged to the store manager, Mr.

Keele. He almost never stayed in the store that late . Megan couldn't imagine why he would call her up there.

She looked to Gil who was wrapping tomatoes in little styrofoam trays. "Wonder what's up."

He glanced at her, then looked back at his hands. "Hmmmm. Dunno. Better go see."

She made her way to the front of the store, wiping her hands on her apron. Lawrence lounged at the end of a checkout lane. He waved as she passed and mouthed the words, "Sorry, man."

She walked up the steps and entered the office. Sitting behind a cluttered desk was Mr. Keele.

"Megan, have a seat." He gestured to the plastic chair in front of the desk. Megan nodded and sat wordlessly. Mr. Keele cleared his throat and continued. "Megan. This is probably the hardest job a manager has to do…" He talked about dedication to one's job. Staying focused. Being on time. Being at work when one was scheduled. During this speech, Megan just stared down at her tattoo. The arm outstretched, reaching for help from beneath a sea of red flowers. She thought of what it meant. Thought about the companion piece she was going to get on the other arm after holding down a job for a year, sober.

So much for that.

When she came down out of the office, she refused to look at anyone. She took her apron off and dropped it, right there on the floor in front of the customer service desk. She turned and started for the door. Lawrence came up behind her, putting his hand gently on her arm.

"Hey man, you okay?"

She pulled away from him and snapped. "Get the fuck off of me." His hand dropped, and she shuffled out of the store, alone.

Megan stopped doing laundry and quickly ran out of clean clothes. After a while, she wore dirty ones or none at all. It didn't matter much. She was barely leaving the apartment. She had not found a new job yet and the end of the month was fast approaching. She didn't care. Her headaches continued and it took most of her energy to keep from giving them the medicine she knew they so badly wanted. Lawrence kept texting her, wanting to know how she was, if she needed anything, and if she wanted to get together. She didn't want to hear from him or hang out. She deleted them as soon as she got them and after a while they stopped coming.

Then, one night, her phone started buzzing. It had been a week since she'd received a text or call from anyone. She looked at the clock. It was two-thirty in the morning. She'd been lying awake, her eyes shut, her head pounding mercilessly as she tried to force her way into sleep. She let the phone go for a while, listening to it vibrate amongst the water bottles and soda cans that littered the nightstand. It wasn't long before the sound became a needle, burrowing into her brain. Finally she sat up and grabbed for it, knocking a drift of garbage to the floor. Its glowing screen hurt her eyes in the dark. When she read the messages her anger melted immediately to cold curiosity. For the time being, her headache was forgotten.

"I did it!!!!!! Im in the building. Imma get my ghost footage. You should come down here and help me. Miss you girl. Imma wait 4 you. Hit me back pls"

"just heard somethin. A ghost? Excited. Text dont call"

Fuckn shit its Gil n here wit me. WTF?? You awake?"

"I dont know how he got in dis place it locked"

"Let hisself in w/ a key. He got a girl wit him"

As Megan read, the phone suddenly buzzed in her hand and played a sound like tinkling bells. It meant a picture message had come through. She looked at what Lawrence sent and shuddered. The resolution wasn't good and there was a bad glare from some unseen light, but she could make out two people walking down a narrow hallway together. Their backs were to her, but one was obviously a thin woman or girl, the other was a squat, male shape. The details were nearly lost, but Gil's denim jacket was recognizable. A chill slid down her spine. She tossed her sweaty sheet aside and swung her feet over the edge of the bed. She typed out a response, wishing her thumbs weren't so fat.

"GET OUT OF THERE! CALL THE POLICE! LAWRENCE! I'M SERIOUS!" She hit send and waited, her nerves jangling wildly. A minute later, he texted her back.

"Fuk dat! I just turned 18. I will go2 jail for real for trespass. DONT CALL NO COPS! Imma bust him! He aint shit. Look at this"

The bell chimed and another photo popped onto the screen. Lawrence had zoomed in on Gil and his companion. The girl had skinny legs. She seemed very young, a teenager maybe. Gil was pulling her along with one hand. In the other, he clasped something that glinted in the light. Megan couldn't be sure, but thought it might've been a knife.

The pounding in her head came back and it was hard to think clearly. What if nothing horrible was going on? What if there was no knife and Gil was just making out with some girlfriend? She didn't want to get everyone in a panic—involve cops—over a misunderstanding. Her thumbs worked madly, and she had to retype several words as she sent him another text.

"I'm coming. Let me in. Will figure it out 2gether."

A moment later her phone buzzed. *"YES! Plan! See You Soon!* ☻ "

Megan sat there a while longer, trying to gather her thoughts. She had to get dressed. All she had on was a dirty t-shirt. She tossed her phone on the bed and went to her dresser. Nothing was clean except some socks and underwear. She forewent both, pulling a pair of jeans off the floor and up over her bare hips. She slid her feet into some flip-flops and grabbed her car keys. As she stepped out the door she looked back at her little apartment. It was a wreck. There were paper plates, bowls and cups lying everywhere. DVD's scattered around the TV. Clothes draped over nearly every surface. Books. Papers. It hurt. This was her. This was who she'd become. Who she'd always been, with or without the pills. She tried to imagine it cleaned up, herself sitting in it, smiling. Maybe there'd be someone with her. She couldn't quite do it. With a sigh she closed the door and left.

She pulled into Brindle's and parked at the back of the lot. There was a fence around the building, but long ago kids had torn a corner loose on the side where it bordered the grocery store. There were only five other cars on the lot, four of which belonged to store employees. Megan never understood why they stayed open 24 hours anymore. People shopping late at night would rather go to one of the big, well-lit superstores. This place was honestly a little spooky.

She hurried to the hole in the fence and dropped to the ground. She came through on the other side and stood up. The building loomed above her, a mute box of brick, four stories tall. There were windows that went around the top two floors, but the bottom two were blank, except for graffiti. She knew from past experience that there were two doors around back. She crept through the heavy shadows and tall grass, around the corner to the rear of the building. Broken glass, beer bottles, mounds of cigarette butts and countless condoms littered the rocky courtyard. There was a bitter stab of nostalgia, and Megan smiled in spite of herself. She walked up to the nearest door and found it wedged open with a brick revealing a thin line of deep black. She approached cautiously and whispered into the opening.

"Lawrence? Hey. Where are you?" There was no answer. She reached into her pocket, intending to text him, and realized she didn't have her phone. For a moment she considered going back to look for it in the car, but remembered that she'd tossed it on the bed when she put on her pants. It suddenly occurred to her that she hadn't brought *anything* useful. All she had was a tiny LED pen-light on her keychain. She held it up and pressed the button. The bright blue beam was woefully small, but it was the best she had. With a deep breath, she pulled open the door and stepped inside. "Lawrence?" Megan continued to whisper his name every minute or so as she headed, nearly blind, down the hallway. She listened for footsteps or voices, but heard nothing. Not even the rustling of rodents. The place was silent.

She slid one hand along the wall next to her and eventually rounded a bend into a wider space. Shining the little light around revealed a small lobby. There were two moldering vinyl couches and a set of elevators. Megan swung the tiny blue beam across the silent doors and discovered a stairwell rising up into a dark passage.

"Lawrence?" Her whisper echoed and faded. There was no answer. Both her heart and her head were pounding. She slipped into the stairwell, swallowed by the gloom. Step by step she made her way up, the only sounds her clanging footfalls. She reached the first landing and tried the door. It was locked. She looked around, unsure whether or not to go on. She had nearly decided to leave when she heard a noise from somewhere above. Just a momentary voice, not even a word, just a sound, there one moment, then lost to the dark. But real. She licked her lips, uncertain, and started up the steps to the third floor.

She reached the next landing and stopped. Thin white light shined from somewhere nearby. The door was ajar. Something was propping it open. A foot shoved between the door and the wall. It dangled at the end of its ankle, limp and lifeless. Megan recognized the red Adidas with the loose, white laces.

"Oh my God, Lawrence!" She dropped to the floor and pushed the door away from his body. She climbed into the hallway and was nearly blinded by the sudden presence of fluorescent ceiling lights. She patted her hands along his torso until her fingers found the warm, red, sticky mess at his side. His shirt was ripped, the flesh beneath spongy and raw. He didn't move. His chest was still. The pain in her skull pressed against the back of her eyes and she squeezed them shut until it subsided a little. She looked at Lawrence's face. His eyes were open and dazed. She pushed her fingers beneath his jaw, trying to find a pulse. She felt nothing. She didn't need to. She knew by looking at him that he was dead. Tears began streaming down her cheeks and soon she was rocking and sobbing, clutching at the dead boy. This went on for what felt like hours, but eventually Megan became still. An idea struck her.

His phone.

She didn't want to, but she reached into the hip pocket closest to her. All she found was spare change and a small baggie of pot. She tossed it to the floor and checked the other. It was empty. She couldn't face trying to turn him over to search his back pockets and it was unlikely he'd put his phone there anyway. She scrambled around the hallway on her hands and knees, looking for it. After a few minutes, she was sure whoever had killed him had also taken the phone. She stood and gazed down at him one last time. He'd been her friend. Her *only* friend.

I'm so sorry Lawrence.

Megan walked on past the body. Doors lined the hallway, one every six feet or so and she read the nameplates that hadn't completely faded. *Sequencing. Extractions. UV. Composting.* Then, near the end of the hallway, they just became *Lab A, Lab B, Lab C.* She wondered what had gone on here, before the doors had been locked up and the lights turned out for good.

But the third-floor lights were on.

What was going on here now?

She reached the end of the hallway and stopped. Another passage crossed the one she was in, creating a "T". The ceiling lights were off again heading in either direction, but down the left-hand side there was a bright glow illuminating the walls. It wasn't fluorescent. In fact, it didn't seem manmade at all. It was like thousands of candles were burning down that way. Except even that wasn't quite right.

Megan turned, squinting into the light, afraid but unable to turn back. She moved forward into the hallway for another twenty feet before it suddenly opened into a wide, white room. A set of three steps led up to a platform that abutted the wall. In the center of the platform was an open door from which the light spilled like a golden mist. There was a smell. Fermentation and rot. It filled her nostrils and brought tears to her eyes. Her head had never hurt this bad. There were also sounds. Footsteps shuffling about beyond the door and a strange fluttering sound. It was like a wet umbrella being opened and closed. It was accompanied by interruptions in the luminescent flow, like someone passing a hand over a lamp. She stood at the bottom step and called out.

"Who's in there?"

"Come on in Megan. It's okay." She knew the voice. It was dreadfully expected. "I won't hurt you."

Of course not. You're harmless. Megan giggled as she went up the steps and through the door.

Whatever she might've been expecting to see in that room, this wasn't it. Her mind felt wobbly as she opened her mouth and screamed.

A high-ceilinged chamber opened up before her. There was a platform with three steps that led down to an aisle that ran in a square path around the room. In the center of the chamber was a huge open space and littered across this were the bodies of dead women.

Dozens. Dozens of dozens, perhaps. It was hard to say. Many had decayed to the point where they were barely recognizable as human. The stench bloomed around her, rich and intense as she tried to count them. They sprawled head to foot and stacked upon one another like firewood. This was bad enough, but it was the thing clinging to the far wall that *really* upset her.

A huge, glowing plant. Thick vines and tendrils radiated out from a greenish brown nexus like stiff tentacles, some of them seventy feet long. Large, spade-shaped leaves, green and splendid, sprouted all along these, swaying gently. Massive pink and white flowers had blossomed along the thicker vines, their petals opening and closing. It was from deep within their swollen pistols that the light was emanating. The tendrils would move and twist and the flowers would turn with them, shining like beautiful, awful search-lights. Darker appendages, almost black, split into smaller, grasping tongues of fibrous plant flesh. They snaked over the pile of bodies on the floor and Megan realized that many of them had found their way into the dead women's bodies, shoving down their throats and between their thighs. She thought of the door in the hallway marked *compost*, and dry heaved violently. She could hear the soft slitherings as the roots (and this is what the darker vines surely were) pulled out of one spot and sought to suck the nutrients from fresher sources. She looked again to the wall-climbing tendrils, drawn by the glow of the flowers, and noticed the clusters of fat red oranges dangling amidst the leaves.

Specially mutated by growers in Sicily.

"Megan?"

She turned to the voice. Gil was kneeling on the floor next to a naked girl. She couldn't have been more than fifteen or sixteen years old and was very skinny. Her lips and cheeks were sticky with red juice and pulp. She was smiling, her eyes searching the ceiling with dreamlike wonder. "Those are *horses Daddy!*" She whispered. The excitement and longing in her voice broke Megan's heart and cut short her squalling. Sudden anger flared within her. She began trembling, her fists clenching and unclenching, and when she found her voice, it rumbled like a summer storm.

"WHAT ARE YOU DOING?"

Gil looked up at her, nonplussed. He blinked behind his glasses. In his hand was a half-eaten blood orange. It hadn't been peeled, just bitten into, skin and all, like an apple. He raised it to his lips and took a chunk out of it, chewing with obvious pleasure.

"Fertilizing and cultivating this miraculous citrus sinesis. The only one of its kind."

"What?"

He gestured to the thing that seethed against the wall. It seemed to watch and listen to them. "When I busted in here a couple of years ago it was almost dead. It'd been living off of a security guard, a guy in a lab coat—probably a scientist—and maybe one or two others. They were so far gone it was impossible to tell for sure. Its fruit was withered and dry. But I was hungry, and it was still beautiful. Nothing like it anywhere else in this world. I was scared, but *so hungry*. I ate one of the oranges and a little while after that the voice started. It was low and soothing, like my mother's. It called me friend. It said, 'I need you. I need your help.'"

Megan looked at the bodies on the floor nearest to her. Horror blossomed in her chest as she recognized the woman who'd left her son behind at Brindle's. She lay face down, her head resting between another woman's feet. A thick root was shoved deep in her rectum, turning and rooting somewhere within her guts. Its movement caused the woman's hips to rise and fall slowly in a nightmare mime of intercourse. Megan's heart climbed up her throat and choked her. She looked for the other girl, Heather, but couldn't find her. Without her gym shorts, she was indistinguishable from the other pretty, dead girls. With a sob, Megan gazed across the crop of bodies to the heart of the plant. All the flowers had turned and focused on her and Gil. They were spot lit, the stars of the show, and it was waiting.

"Gil, please…" She could think of nothing else to say.

"It takes care of me. I was homeless when it found me, Meg. I was nobody. I ate out of garbage cans and shit in doorways. Now I'm special. I take care of it, feed it, protect it, and it takes care of everything else. Tells me *everything*. What to do, how to do it. I don't have to think much at all. I just eat these." He held the orange out to her. Juice dribbled down his fingers and pattered on the floor. He took another bite and patted the teenage girl's belly. "And *they* don't feel anything. They come along, easy as you'd want. They just have a few bites and they come back to me, ready to do whatever they're told. They let me…do things. Whatever I want Megan, before they lay down. If they just eat the fruit."

"Gil, this is wrong." Her words felt weightless as they left her mouth.

"It's easy."

She shook her head, trying to clear it of pain and confusion. Her brain felt heavy. "You tried to get me to eat those things. You tried to make me…" she pointed to the woman at her feet. "Like that."

Gil did not look at the woman. His eyes remained on Megan. "I tried to get you to eat the oranges, yeah, but not to make food out of you." He stood and took a step towards her. "I want to be your friend."

Her eyes widened and a laugh burbled up her throat. "Are you kidding?"

Gil's face was calm and solemn. "No. I need help. A *friend*. It wants me to have one and I thought…" he looked down at his feet, suddenly shy. "I just really liked you is all."

When he said this, the monstrous flowers began opening and closing rapidly, causing light to strobe against the dark walls. Was it blinking or applauding? Megan couldn't tell. Gil took another step in her direction, and she found herself wanting to meet him. She looked down at the tattoo on her arm. Taking her pills, drowning in those sweet, red poppies, had been like lying down on cool sheets, swaddled and cared for. She'd lost all her friends, and her family had nearly given up on her, but so what? It had been so hard and so painful trying to escape their grip. She'd tried and tried and had nothing to show for it but a filthy apartment and unwashed jeans.

Suddenly Gil was right in front of her. He held the orange out to her, and she took it from him. The knife he'd used to kill Lawrence lay beside the dream struck teenage girl. Megan knew she could overpower him easily. He was shorter than she was, and he seemed weak.

But she didn't make a move against him because the fruit was in her hand. She was Eve in the Garden. Minutes passed. Juice dripped into her palm and tears dripped down her cheeks. She looked up at Gil, who smiled at her, and she realized with dismay that she didn't know what she was going to do.

TWO EXTRA PRESENTS

It was Christmas Eve.

Drew worked hard to stay awake. He waited through his parents' wine-fuzzed murmuring. He waited through the somnolent ticking of the kitty-cat clock on the wall. He was sure hours had passed. His eyes were heavy. His blankets were warm, and his belly was full of cookies and hot-chocolate. He'd nearly fallen asleep when, finally, he was rewarded for his patience. Downstairs in the dark, he could hear something moving around. This was the big moment, what he'd planned for all year.

Santa.

He hopped out of bed, grabbing his camera from the nightstand. Down the hall to the staircase, swish-swish, in his footie-pajamas. From below, He could hear footsteps wandering around the living room. It sounded like Santa was trying to be quiet.

He reached the bottom and crept around the corner. A shadowy figure was slurping up the cookies and milk they'd left out. Drew raised his camera and pressed the shutter. There was a flash and the figure spun around.

It was not Santa.

Drew didn't know what it was.

It was tall and scaly, like a lizard, with two long, thin arms that hung from its rounded shoulders. Each hand had three fingers that were tipped with long, curved talons. Its head was the size and shape of a large pumpkin with one moist, glaring eye rolling in a loose socket. In place of a mouth it had a raw, round hole gaping below its eye, ringed with luminous fronds, like a sea anemone, that twitched and pawed at the air. Hunched over, its hands brushing the ground, it regarded Drew with cold curiosity.

With a strange sense of detachment, Drew realized the basement door was open. No one had really spent much time down there. They'd only lived in the house for a couple of weeks, but his mother had warned his father to keep the door shut because Drew might fall into the old well that was down there. His father kept forgetting, though, and Drew suspected that's where this visitor had come from. A dweller in the rank, lightless depths beneath the house.

The thing made a slobbering sound as it shambled towards him, its arms held out greedily. Drew was too scared to scream as it reached for him. Its tentacles stretched out and caressed his cheeks. He closed his eyes and waited for the end …but it never came.

Suddenly, someone else was with them.

The creature was thrown violently across the room, making a horrible squealing noise. A loud voice cried out, "Ho, ho, ho!" and there was a flash of light that blinded Drew. Upstairs, his mother screamed, "What was that?" Then everything went quiet. When his eyes cleared, he found himself alone in the room. He stood and looked around, noticing, as only a child could, that there were two extra presents under the tree.

He smiled. "Thanks Santa!" And with a yawn, Drew closed the basement door and went back to bed.

LAST NIGHT AT THE RED CARPET INN

Sirens wailed in the night, sounding like the end of the world as first one, then two police cars sped past followed by an ambulance. Red and blue lights danced and spun, reflected in the big front office window and then were gone. Charlie barely registered their passage. So long as they weren't pulling into the courtyard, he didn't much care.

The desk phone buzzed, and he winced. He hated the angry, impatient tone of it. He looked at the switchboard. Room 220. With a grunt, he pushed the button next to the blinking red light and hoisted the receiver to his ear. "Front desk."

"Hey," the voice was low and rough. Charlie vaguely remembered handing the room 220 key to a middle-aged man who'd been in the company of a young blonde girl in short shorts and a whisper-thin tank top. "Hey, somebody in here lookin' at us. Somebody in the bathroom."

This didn't surprise Charlie in the least. He was barely interested. "Okay. Do you want me to call the police?"

There was a long pause and then the deep, whispering voice spoke again. "Nah, nah. Never mind, I think I'm just—" there was an obscene, gurgling giggle, "—just a little too high. Youknowwhat'msayin?"

Charlie set the phone back in the cradle without answering. He did know what the man was saying. Most people who stayed overnight at the Red Carpet were a little too high. If they weren't, then they were coming down from being too high or getting ready to get too high. That was one of the few reasons anyone would ever hand over fifty dollars to stay in one of the motel's small, poorly lit, sticky, smelly rooms.

Sometimes someone got so high they forgot to wake up. Not just when the sun came up, but ever again. They'd miss the checkout time and after a couple hours of not answering their phone, Valentina, the day manager, would let herself into the room to find them stiffening on the bed. Calls would be made. Cops and paramedics would show up. Sometimes there was half-hearted CPR performed. More often, there wasn't. Then the body was strapped to a gurney, loaded into the back of an ambulance, and hauled away. No wailing sirens or lights for them. Some paperwork was filled out, maybe a few questions asked and answered, and that was it. Charlie always found it horribly depressing to think that those people had spent their last night on Earth at the Red Carpet Inn.

After the call from room 220, there was a lull where the only sounds were from the occasional traffic out on St. Xavier Boulevard, the muffled noise of a TV blasting from a nearby room and Charlie's own fingers clicking away at his laptop. He found himself yawning and was just deciding to get a cup of coffee when a man walked past the office.

Charlie looked up and watched as the silent figure made his way out beneath the courtyard archway to the gravelly shoulder of the boulevard. The man stood there a moment, his head turning back and forth as he watched the headlights coming and going. After a minute or two, he turned and shuffled away along the roadside. Soon he was out of sight.

The guy had been Dacey's "date" for the night. The two of them had sauntered past the office, arm in arm and giggling, nearly four hours earlier. Most of them didn't spend that much time with her, they didn't need very long. The thought brought an unwelcome twinge of jealousy. Charlie knew it was stupid. He was well aware of what she did, but knowing didn't chase away the churlish little pinprick of spite he felt every time he saw her with a date.

They were never Johns, always *dates*. "Johns," she'd told him once, "are who escorts fuck. I'm just tryin' to have a good time with some nice, generous guys." She'd considered a moment then. "I mean, I guess technically they *are* Johns, but I don't like that word. Sounds unsanitary. Reminds me of toilets."

He felt like an idiot for having a crush on a prostitute. He was like one of those guys at the strip club who took flowers and jewelry to a particular dancer, week after week, because they thought maybe they could woo her away to a normal life. Pathetic, sad, suckers. She would never be interested in a guy like him, a dork with no money who worked the night desk at a sleazy motel. She was sweet as could be to him, but Charlie knew they would never be anything but friends. Acquaintances, really.

As if his thoughts had summoned her, Dacey walked into the office, the bell above the door tinkling as she passed. She had a short, battered trench coat with wide lapels wrapped tightly around her petite frame. It stopped well up on her thighs and Charlie was certain she was naked underneath. She often came in to talk after her dates left and was usually in some state of undress. A few times she'd even breezed in wearing only a bra and panties (and shoes, she didn't walk the grounds without shoes). She was never self-conscious about it so for her to have the coat closed so tightly could only mean she was wearing nothing else. Charlie's pulse quickened, and his mouth went dry.

"Hey Dace, how's your night been?" He snapped his laptop shut and watched as she plopped into the chair next to the gumball machine.

Normally she lounged, one foot hoisted up onto the empty chair beside her, but tonight she sat up straight, her knees kept together. She looked over at Charlie as if she just realized he was in the room. She blinked slowly, once, before favoring him with a weary smile.

"Hey Charlie Brown, how you doin'?" She sounded weird. Her voice was low and syrupy. It held a melancholy and distracted tone that he'd never heard from her before.

"What's up Dacey? Everything cool?" He stood up and leaned on the desk, hoping he sounded casual and only mildly interested.

Dacey flapped her hand at him dismissively. "Fine, fine." Her eyes were dreamy. "I'm just—worn out. Long night." She smiled again, her red lips glistening, and leaned back, relaxing a little. She was still clutching her coat shut with one hand. She peered out the office window, into the courtyard and to the street beyond. After a moment, she looked over at Charlie. "Is he still around or did he take off?"

Charlie nodded toward the window. "Nah, he left a couple of minutes ago. Walked out to the Boulevard and just wandered off." He looked out at the road, not wanting to stare at her. "He somebody you know?"

Dacey shook her head, spilling a lock of hair across her forehead. "Nope. Met him over at the Taco Bell tonight, got talkin' and we walked here together." She tucked her hair behind her ear, saying no more, and gazed with Charlie, out into the night.

She was acting peculiar. Normally after a date, her mood was buoyant because the deed done, and she was good and high. She would bounce in, chatty and loud, firing jokes and banter at him like a late-night talk show host.

Occasionally she was angry, ranting about how some low life had tried to do something she'd made it clear she wasn't going to do. Like the time she'd broken a guy's nose with her shoe and chased him out into the courtyard when he wouldn't take *no* for an answer. After her rage had subsided, she couldn't stop laughing about it, regaling Charlie with the story ("You can put it in my ass if you want," she'd told him, "but don't try to put it back in my mouth afterwards.").

Another time she'd come into the office wide eyed and shaken after a small, shaggy man with a hillbilly drawl had put a knife to her throat. In the end, all he'd wanted was to steal her little furry boots, but for a moment she'd thought he was going to kill her. Even then, she talked with an animated buzz about how it felt, thinking she was going to die at the hands of some no-name gutter dweller. In fact, Charlie could not recall a time she'd ever been quiet, contemplative, and lethargic the way she was now, and it made him vaguely anxious.

He tapped on the front desk to get her attention. "Hey." She didn't respond at first, keeping her eyes out on the street. He spoke a little louder. "Dacey. Hey." She finally turned to him, eyebrows raised. Charlie wasn't sure he wanted an answer to the question he was about to ask but went on anyway. "Did that guy—" he rolled his eyes, trying to think of how to ask. She'd told him plenty of stories about her dates, sometimes in gory, technicolor detail, but Charlie didn't feel comfortable asking about her business himself. Somehow it seemed rude and intrusive.

He struggled a moment longer, wishing he had a cup of water. "Did that guy—I mean, was he—did he do anything weird? Did he hurt you or anything?"

Dacey kept smiling but it became stranger than it already was, sadder. "Well, yeah, he *was* a weirdo. He took forever, for one thing. Jesus, I hate when it takes so long to finish, and he wanted something…extra." Her eyelids dropped in that slow double-blink again. "Never had a guy ask me for that before, but I guess I pulled it off. He finished. *Finally*. And he paid me."

She glanced quickly down into the dark depths of her jacket, frowning, and sighed. She looked back up at Charlie, her head tilted, and she grinned a crooked, dirty-joke kind of grin. "Toss me a cigarette, bitch, and I'll tell you all about it."

A glimmer of her normal self had returned, but Charlie's heart still fluttered with disquiet. He took a cigarette from the crinkled pack next to his laptop and flipped it to her underhand. She caught it delicately in her palm and popped it between her lips. She cocked one eyebrow at him.

"Lighter?"

Charlie reached into his hip pocket and pulled out the lighter. He came around the desk and placed it into her outstretched hand. "I'm not throwing lighters around the office." He said it playfully but his concern for her had gone up a notch. Up close, she looked drained and dreadfully pale, her cheeks hollow and gaunt. She lit her smoke, pretending not to notice him noticing her appearance.

Charlie grabbed the empty chair and dragged it to the center of the office plopping into it across from her. She sucked smoke into her lungs and then exhaled it melodramatically to the ceiling. "Oh, daaahling, that tastes so good." She adjusted herself in the chair, scootching her butt back into it. A silence spun out between them while she smoked, and he waited. When she hadn't said anything for a while he cleared his throat.

"So, you were saying?"

Dacey shook her head and tapped ash to the floor. "No. I decided I don't wanna talk about it after all."

Charlie's eyes dropped to the floor. "Oh."

"You know," she looked around at the office as if it she was seeing it for the first time and deciding how best to redecorate it. "This was my last one. My last night turning tricks here." She ground her cigarette out against the scratched metal top of the gumball machine and let the butt drop to the ratty carpet. "I can't do it anymore." There was a bitter edge to her voice, more regret than resolve. "I've been whoring for four years now off and on, almost five. That's a long fuckin time. It's like dog years. Every year you're in it feels more like seven." Her voice was bitter. "I'm 26 but I feel like I'm 70."

Just then the desk phone buzzed, and Charlie made a disgusted face but didn't move to answer it. It kept going and Dacey looked at the desk. "Don't you have to get that?"

Charlie leaned forward. He could smell the perfume she always wore. It was a cheap one that reminded him of dark, sweaty dance—clubs but on her it was sweet and feminine. "Eh, fuck 'em. It can't be anything important." The phone buzzed three more times and then went dead. "See?"

He hoped what she was saying was true. That she was really going to give up on the life that brought her to the Red Carpet Inn over and over again. Even if meant Charlie would never see her again, he'd be happy to know she was living a different kind of life. He knew, though, that people had a lot of trouble leaving their struggles behind, especially when they seemed as alone in the world as Dacey did.

Charlie tried not to sound so cautiously optimistic. "Holy shit, that's great! I'm excited for you." He smiled at her, knowing that he *was* genuinely excited, and *was* optimistic about her chances, even if only cautiously. "What are you going to do instead? You have somewhere to go?"

Dacey shrugged. She looked past Charlie and bit her lip. Suddenly, she was struggling with tears. "I don't know. I don't know where I'm gonna go actually and that scares me. I don't think I can leave just yet. I'm sort of, stuck here till something comes along that'll get me out." Her eyes went dark, and her mouth hardened. "But it's fine. I'm out. Even if It's all that fucker's fault, I'd already been thinking about quitting for a while. I was on the fence about it and then he comes along and that is *that*. There's no way I can keep doing it after *that*."

Charlie leaned forward in his chair, afraid to hear the answer but unable not to ask. "Fuck, Dacey—what did he *do* to you? Seriously, you can tell me. We can call somebody, or I can drive up the Boulevard, try to find him. I'm not just gonna let somebody hurt you—make you feel like this."

Dacey's eyes settled back on Charlie's and her expression softened. She smiled wistfully and sighed. "You're such a sweetheart. You always have been. You never treated me like a whore. Never were creepy or some white-knight type who wants to save me. You've just always been a friend to me. I appreciate it, Charlie."

A lump formed in Charlie's throat. "Dacey—"

"And you're so fuckin cute too. I've gotta be honest, I always hoped you'd ask me out. Not—you know, like for sex, but just to go to a movie or something. I've always liked you." Her smile turned sly then. "Course, I'dve fucked your brains out if you *had* asked me for the other kind of date. You wouldn't have known what hit you."

"I've always liked you too." He hadn't meant to blurt it out like that, but it happened before he could stop. "I've been wanting to ask you out forever."

"Why didn't you?"

Charlie felt his face flush. "Well, um, because…"

"Because I fuck guys for money." She looked down at the floor. "I get that. Believe me, I do."

"No, that's not why. Not really." Charlie shrugged and crossed his arms. "I don't care so much about that, people are people. Everybody's got their own shit. I live with my sister and her husband and their kids. I sleep in their attic. This is the only job I can find. I mean, I *guess* it is, I'm too lazy to try and look for another one. I just mean that I don't have any issue with what you do."

"Then why?"

Charlie's face broke into an unexpected grin, and he chuckled. "I think I was worried you'd laugh at me. Think I was creeping on you or just a geek or, I don't know. I didn't think you liked me that way. I was too scared that you'd say no." He paused for a moment. "And I was kind of worried about how I'd introduce you to my mom. So, I guess part of it *was* because of what you do, but not because it bothers me personally."

Dacey kicked his ankle impishly. "Charlie Brown, you thought about introducing me to your mother?"

Charlie sputtered. "I mean—ahh, you know. I just thought if— I don't know. It's no big deal."

Dacey burst into giggles, sounding the most like herself since coming into the office. "It's okay, sweetie. That makes me feel good. Makes me feel like an actual woman for once and not just some plaything."

Charlie looked up at her and they locked eyes. Something passed between them—a heat, a breath, a magnetized silence that held them together. His heart was pounding in his chest, and he wondered if hers was doing the same. Then the screaming started from somewhere beyond the office and the moment was over.

Charlie looked over his shoulder out the door. "What the hell is that?" He jumped to his feet and stepped to the door, opening it. A woman was shrieking madly just across the courtyard. It sounded like Ana, one of the two housekeepers on the night shift. Charlie turned to Dacey who hadn't moved from her seat and didn't look at all surprised to hear such wailing in the night. "You wanna come with me, see what that's all about?"

She grimaced. "No, I'm good. I think I'll just wait here."

"Okay. I'll be back in a few. Hopefully." Charlie shoved out the door and jogged across the battered pavement. A few windows lit up along the motel's two floors as people opened their curtains to see what the commotion was about. Most stayed dark.

Charlie could see Ana now, crumpled to her knees in front of a room, the door thrown wide open, spilling sick yellow light out onto the walk. She was sobbing. Sudden panic flooded his system as he realized which room it was, and he broke into a run.

Ana heard Charlie's footsteps pounding the concrete and looked up at him. She had vomit all down the front of her scrubs. She began babbling in a mixture of English and Spanish, all of it choked with tears and none of which he could decipher. He began shushing her, hoping to calm her while his own fear was growing like a black tumor wrapped around his heart and lungs.

Before he even stepped into the room Charlie could see blood splattering the wall above the bed. It dripped down over the headboard and congealed in a thick, red pool on the pillow. He took a deep breath as he approached the doorway, trying to prepare himself for whatever lay inside.

Oh Dacey. Christ, what did you do in here?

He stepped into the room. Two rumpled hundred-dollar bills lay curled up on the nightstand and red, wet handprints stained the wall in a merry pattern above the TV. Charlie felt his gorge rise as a hot, foul odor wormed into his nostrils and down his throat. He could still hear Ana weeping outside.

He took a step forward, his shoe squelching in a viscous puddle of blood and tissue. Hot bile worked its way up his esophagus, the ghost of vomit yet to come. He swallowed hard, his eyes squeezed shut against the spell of dizziness that swam behind them, and somehow managed to keep himself together for the time being.

He took another step, then another, and came around the corner of the bed. There, on the floor in front of the dresser, was a thick puddle of blood. A red swath that led from the main room to the bathroom. Charlie's gaze followed it along the carpet, over the tile where it turned shiny beneath the sallow lights to the body propped up against the mirror. The legs hung over the edge of the sink, arms dangling limp at its sides. Its torso had been opened wide, spilling a dark rainbow of fluids and entrails, like the limp fronds of dead sea creatures.

Before crumpling to the floor in a black swoon, Charlie had time to wonder how he'd just been talking with Dacey back in the front office when she'd also been here, split down the middle and emptied of her guts at the same time.

****

Back in the front office a detective named Reynolds leaned against the desk watching through the window as Dacey's body, wrapped in a shiny black bag and strapped to a gurney, was hoisted into the back of an ambulance. Charlie did not watch. He heard the doors to the ambulance slam shut and a moment later the rev of the engine as they pulled out onto the boulevard. There were no sirens for her. No lights.

Valentina had come in and she and Charlie both gave statements, telling everything they knew about Dacey. She'd kept a room at the Red Carpet, paying a weekly rate, for the past nine months or so. She was a prostitute, somewhat classier and more in-demand than some of the others that hung around the motel. Neither of them knew where she'd come from. Charlie said he thought she'd mentioned once that her mother had died when she was a little girl, but he wasn't totally sure.

Detective Reynolds asked about the man she'd been with that night. Charlie described him as best he could, but in truth, he hadn't looked closely at him. He didn't like seeing her with guys. He didn't tell Reynolds that, only saying that the man was plain and of average build. He told the detective that the man had wandered off down St. Xavier Boulevard into the dark. The police took statements and then they were gone. Dacey's killer was gone. Dacey was gone. The motel felt like an abandoned ruin.

Charlie did not mention the conversation he'd had with Dacey in the office. He really hadn't had time to process that yet. He tried to tell himself that he'd dreamed the whole thing after losing consciousness in her room.

That seemed okay until he went back to the office and found the cigarette she'd smoked, still lying on the floor next to her chair. When he kneeled to pick it up, the smell of her perfume swept up at him like a ghost, warm and sad and over-sweet. He'd cried then, sitting on the floor next to the empty chair until he heard Valentina's footsteps coming back across the courtyard. When she came in through the glass door, he was sitting quietly in the chair, holding the butt of Dacey's cigarette in his closed fist.

The sun had been up for some time and traffic out on the Boulevard waxed and waned. Valentina's eyes were haunted. She walked behind the desk and grabbed the coffeepot. "You want some?"

"Nope."

Valentina nodded. "Yeah, you probably wanna get home. Get some rest. Try to forget about all of this." She sighed. "Dacey was a nice girl. What a goddam shame."

Charlie bit his lower lip, fighting back more tears. After the night he'd just had and the things he'd seen, it felt like he'd never sleep again. Valentina walked around the desk and patted him on the shoulder. "You take tonight off. Tomorrow too, if you need it. I can cover it, or I'll get Deon to come in."

Charlie laughed then, a dark and jagged sound. "Actually Valentina, I think this was my last night at the Red Carpet Inn. Sorry to leave you hanging, but I can't do it anymore. I really can't."

Valentina said nothing, just looked at him for a moment before turning and taking the coffeepot back to the restroom behind the office to fill it. Charlie left before she came back out.

He got in his beat up little car and idled beneath the archway that overhung the courtyard, trying to decide which way to turn. Home was to the right. Sleepless nights, empty days, bad dreams. Dacey's killer had turned left and walked up the Boulevard. On a whim, Charlie pulled out and headed in the same direction. He didn't know if he expected to find the guy but at that moment, looking for him was the only idea that made sense. For the choices Dacey never got to make and the what-if's he'd never be able to answer.

As he cruised down the Boulevard, a figure walking towards him along the sidewalk caught his eye. A pretty, young girl in jeans and ankle-high, fur-lined boots. She had on a short trench coat over a blood-red tank top. As he passed, she looked right through the window at him and smiled. She brushed a wayward lock of blonde hair behind her ear and blew him a kiss. Then she was gone, and Charlie drove into the stream of morning traffic, sunlight stinging his eyes.

THE BLESSED RESURRECTION

*"It's these quiet towns you gotta watch out fer. That's always
where shit goes the wrongest."*
—Highwayman's Proverb

A pair of human heads mounted on wooden poles greeted the riders as they approached the town from the east. Indians, by the look of them. One had a strip of hair running down the center of its split and blistered scalp. The other had no hair and precious little skin. It looked like a shriveled pumpkin, rotted black and full of holes that crawled with burrowing insects. Its lower jaw had fallen into the dry scrub below. A cloud of flies buzzed around them, landing long enough to get a taste before flitting away. Spooked, the horses began to whinny and toss their heads. Above them, shrieking crows wheeled and circled. The three riders had to rein their mounts up a good distance back from the grisly discovery, and even then the skittish animals pawed at the ground, chuffing nervously.

Jake slipped out of his saddle and dropped to the ground. He grabbed his flat-brimmed hat and put it on as he walked towards the decomposing heads. His belt and spurs jangled loudly, and his shadow stretched out long to the east. The sun was low on the horizon, a shimmering orange ball sinking into the hard clay and a ghostly moon was waiting in the wings. Night would soon fall.

He stepped up to the head on the right, the one with the scant line of hair, and took a good long look at it. He wrinkled his nose at the hot smell of decay. The eyes were long gone, and the mouth hung open on desiccated tendons. He spat tobacco juice to the ground, rested his hands on his belt and looked up at the sky, contemplating the scavengers cawing overhead. He looked to the assemblage of low buildings fifty yards ahead. The town of Cottonwood, named for the trees that marked its eastern perimeter. It seemed mighty quiet. He didn't like the way this trip was turning out. Not one bit.

"Hm." He looked over his shoulder at his friends and pointed at the heads. "Them are new."

"What you think that's about?" Dakota "Cody" Warren, still sitting astride his palomino, sounded nervous.

Jake turned and squinted up at Cody, the youngest of the three companions. "Well, I don't rightly know." He spat another squirt of tobacco juice into the dry grass. "Let's go ask somebody."

Cody looked off across the grassy heath towards the town, the corners of his mouth turned down. He pushed his Stetson up on his forehead, chasing the shadows from his face. "I don't know. This don't exactly holler, 'hey come on in and sit a spell,' if you know what I mean."

Byron Webber was the old man of the group. He chuckled as he crawled carefully out of the saddle. "What you worried about, sonny? You think they gonna spike y'head out here too? Make you lucky number three?" He leaned back pushing his fists into the small of his back and grimaced. He pulled his canteen from his saddle-pack and took a long drink. When he was done, he wiped his white mustache dry and patted his horse affectionately on the rump.

"I don't know." Cody slid from his saddle, stumbling as his feet hit the ground. "I reckon maybe they're tryin' to let folks know they ain't welcome."

Jake walked back over to where Cody, Byron and the horses stood. He rubbed the muzzle of his horse, Foxy, and spat the remains of his chaw to the ground. "Well. Redskins are decidedly not welcome no more. That seems clear. Seein' as how none of us are of that persuasion, though, I think we'll head on in and say, 'how'do?' If they seem less than welcoming, well then we'll ride back to that creek we camped at last night and figure out how best to handle the situation."

"And what if 'less than welcoming' means, 'cut yer head off and put it on a spike'? What then?" Cody stuck out his chin defiantly.

Jake patted the Colt revolver tied down at his right hip and grinned viciously. "Well, sir, they're gonna have to get close. Ain't they?"

The three men laughed until, one by one, their eyes strayed back to the things staked in the ground. Their laughter dried up, leaving the hoarse cries of the circling crows and the manic buzzing of flies the only sounds under the red sky.

***

Despite all the tugging, coaxing and cursing, Jake, Cody and Byron could not lead their horses past the Indian heads into the town proper. They walked the uneasy animals back to a copse of tall saguaro a couple hundred yards back and tied their leads to the cacti. The horses calmed down after a few minutes and began cropping the low, yellow grass at their feet. With the fading sun in their eyes, the three men turned and headed into town on foot.

Cottonwood was silent. There was no one out on the street. No harried businessmen closing up shop at the Denver National Bank or McCardle's Mercantile. No clerks standing on the porch of Burkett and Sons Hay and Feed filling the barrels outside with oats and grain. No ladies wilting beneath rough-spun bonnets and no old men leaning against support posts, loafing. Aside from a few dry tumbleweeds kicked along the street by a low breeze, everything was still.

As the trio walked along the wide avenue they noticed the windows in most of the buildings were busted out. Jagged shards of glass poked from their wooden frames. Cody was fidgety and kept looking over his shoulder at the deserted street, his eyes darting back and forth. "I'm gonna be honest with you boys. I do not like this." He pulled his britches up and adjusted his gun-belt. "I don't want ya'll thinkin' I'm yella. I came to do a job and I aim to do it, but somethin' ain't right here. All this quiet, these busted windows? Them injun's heads back there? Somethin' ugly's happened here. I can't say what, but I'd bet a nickel it's why we ain't heard from Farley in so long."

"Well, we'll know soon enough." Jake turned to Byron. "You got the papers?" Byron patted his front pocket and Jake nodded. "Alright then. Let's head over to the Sunset."

The three men headed down the center of Main Street, the click and clack of their boots very loud in the heavy silence. The sun had all but disappeared into the west and shadows filled the town. None of them spoke of it, but they all shared an uneasy feeling of being watched. It was as if the empty buildings had come to life and were just biding their time, waiting for the right moment to reveal themselves.

They turned onto a shorter, narrower street, passing the jailhouse. At the corner was a water pump. Fat drops swelled at the lip of the spigot and fell into the basin below with a hollow, "drip, drip." Ahead of them at the end of the street, across from one another, were the tallest and most important buildings in Cottonwood: the church and the saloon. The church was a squat brick building with a steeply pitched roof and a white, wooden belfry jutting up from the top like a finger pointing to heaven. It was all clean and pious lines with wide, well-swept steps leading up to its arched door. A hitching post out front was festooned with the tattered remains of thick tie-ropes that swung slowly in the breeze. Curiously, the broken windows on either side of the entrance had been boarded up from the inside with tightly packed cedar planks.

Directly across the street, three hundred feet away, was the church's dark opposite. A tall, crooked building stained the color of dried blood. Its hitching rail had been snapped in the middle and left in two pieces. A sign hanging above the door stated that it was the "Sunset Saloon, Hotel and Postal Depot." This was the place where the three companions had expected to find Farley Applewaite, the town's post-master. Like everything else, the building was unnaturally quiet. There was none of the usual grinding piano. No voices raised in revelry, or saloon girls singing drunkenly. With darkness almost upon them, the Sunset Saloon should've been revving up to full swing, but not even a single oil lamp seemed to burn within.

"That don't seem right. Not at all." In his slightly tremulous voice Cody was echoing Jake's thoughts. Something was wrong in Cottonwood.

They took another ten or twelve steps when Cody put his hand up for Jake and Byron to stop. "Hold up a second, fellas." He cocked his head, his face drawn in concentration. The breeze picked up a hair, stirring some wind-chimes into discordant tinkling and brushing the brims of the men's hats. "Y'all hear that?"

"What? Them wind chimes?" Jake pulled his tobacco pouch out of his coal-gray duster and shoved a plug into his cheek. "What of it?"

"No. Listen." Cody leaned forward, straining to hear. "It's somebody singin' I think."

Jake cupped his hand behind his ear. "Oh yeah. Sounds like a kid."

Suddenly Byron joined his voice to the other in a low, tuneless whisper.

"Work, for the night is coming,
Under the sunset skies;
While their bright tints are glowing,
Work, for daylight flies.
Work till the last beam fadeth,
Fadeth to shine no more;
Work, while the night is darkening,
When man's work is o'er..."

The singing faded away. Byron wet his lips and went silent. He realized that his companions were looking at him with raised eyebrows and his gaze went to the ground. He kicked at the hard packed dirt and spoke softly. "It was my granny's favorite hymn." He looked back up at them, daring them to laugh and, of course, neither one did. Jake nodded and looked towards the church.

"Probably comin' from in there." He shot another splash of tobacco juice to the dirt and jerked his head towards the boarded up church. "Maybe whoever that is can explain what the hell's goin' on around here."

Cody's eyes were wide. "You think it's a good idea to just walk on in?"

Jake looked at the boy sidelong. "It's a church. They welcome everybody." He started towards the steps, Byron at his heels. Cody hung back a moment, looking over his shoulder at the silent buildings behind them. After a moment, he hitched up his belt and followed.

The toe of Jake's boot had just brushed the top of the first step when the church door suddenly crashed open with a sound of rattling chains. Two figures stepped out into the fading daylight. A man and a small girl.

"That was lovely Tasha! Your voice has never been so beautiful. Praise be to God." The man's voice boomed, bouncing off the false fronts of the buildings along Main Street. He was short and stocky in a round-collared, white shirt and a low crowned, flat-brimmed hat. The three companions knew him immediately. He was the town preacher, Humbert Loftus. They'd seen him come to the depot in the saloon many times to pick up his mail, wearing a self-righteous smirk on his round, sweaty face. Farley always joked that the man could bore the dead back to life and then to death again with all his Jesus-jumping and plate passing.

At the moment he was looking off into the distance, mouth split in a wide, exalted grin, his eyes sparkling. "Rejoice, for soon you will be touched by the very hand of Christ our Lord, Amen little sister, Hallelujah!" He didn't notice the men at the foot of the steps.

The girl, whom the preacher gripped firmly by the elbow, did notice them and her dull, dazed eyes lit up for a moment with an odd mixture of terror and hope. She was no more than seven or eight, a tiny thing in a cotton shift, hair like corn silk flying in the breeze. Like most young'uns she wore no shoes and there was something peculiar about her feet. She stood on her right and kept her left off the ground, held up almost beneath her skirt. She glanced up at the preacher who continued to shout into the night as if to a full congregation, and then back at the three men. She said nothing.

Jake made a loud throat-clearing sound and the preacher shut his mouth abruptly with a clicking of teeth. His gaze fell upon the men and, for a moment, a look of utter contempt twisted his features. Then it was gone, replaced by a welcoming smile. "Look Tasha, we've got visitors." He turned towards the men, roughly dragging the little girl to his side. She hopped on her right foot, trying not to fall, crying out when her left foot scraped against the ground. "Gentlemen, it pleases my heart to welcome y'all to our fair town. The book of Hebrews tells us to show hospitality to strangers, for by so doing, some people have shown hospitality to angels without knowing it." He inclined his head towards them, burying his eyes in shadow.

Jake spat on the ground and looked from the preacher to the girl. He glanced over his shoulder at Byron and Cody and was bolstered by the steely look in their eyes. Something about this scene stunk like a carcass at the side of a trail, and they all knew it. He turned back and touched the brim of his hat. "Rev'rend, we're obliged but pardon me for sayin', we're not angels nor are we strangers. We've been to Cottonwood many times over the last couple years. We're pony-boys for Russell, Majors and Waddell. Mr. Applewaite over to the depot is our contact." His eyes flicked to the little girl. "Sweetheart, you okay?"

"No. They're gonna eat me." Her voice was low and impassive. She yanked at her arm, making a half-hearted attempt to free herself from the preacher's grasp, but she seemed tired, weak. After a moment, she gave up and went limp. The preacher, his eyes trained on the men, gave her a violent, bone rattling shake, his smile never wavering.

"You'll have to forgive her fellas, she's got a big night ahead of her. It's to be expected that she'd be a little … apprehensive. She's the last of my flock. All the rest have reaped their reward."

Jake felt his heart pounding. What the hell is going on here? His hand fell to his hip, settling on the butt of his Colt, and he heard the jingle of his companions' gun belts as they followed his lead. The preacher didn't seem particularly concerned. He just kept smiling, his gaze cast heavenward. Night was nearly upon them, and the sky faded from a deep, velvet purple at the horizon up into black where stars were beginning to blossom high above.

"Rev'rend," Jake spoke slowly and deliberately. "We've noticed Cottonwood seems a bit—empty—at the moment. You think you could give us an idea why? We got some important documents we need to get to Mr. Applewaite."

Loftus chuckled good-naturedly. "This town may appear empty, but it is truly far from it lads." He stepped forward, sliding the girl along with him. She grimaced as her left foot touched the ground, but she didn't cry out. "You three gentlemen are very fortunate. Beloved of God. Tonight you will bear witness to His most powerful miracle—His most sacred and loving gift."

"He gonna turn my water into wine?" Byron snorted.

The preacher fixed the older man with a grave scowl. "No sir. Tonight, when full dark is upon us, you will witness the majesty and awe of the blessed resurrection. Not much longer now."

Loftus continued towards the men, the girl hopping at his side. Jake slid his gun from its holster and pointed it at the preacher. Loftus stopped, only a few feet away from them, and cocked his head quizzically. "Why do you draw your weapon?"

Jake spat another brown stream of tobacco juice. "Well, sir, I've still got a few questions and I believe, for the moment, that's as close as I want you to get to me and mine here."

Loftus nodded. "Fair enough. In the eyes of mortal man, the glory of God can be frightening. You may want to let me finish with the girl here, though, before you ask any more questions. The hour groweth late and we need to get inside the church quickly."

"See, now, that's one of my questions. What, exactly, are you doing with that kid?" He motioned towards the girl with the barrel of his gun. "She looks hurt." Jake looked the preacher dead in the eyes. "Did you do somethin' to her?"

"He hurt you honey?" Byron called from over Jake's shoulder.

The girl brushed a long tangle of hair behind her ear and looked wearily down at the men. When she spoke, her voice was hardly more than a whisper. If the town hadn't been grave silent they wouldn't have heard her at all. "My foot." She lowered her left foot gingerly until her toes brushed the ground. She winced and picked it up again.

The preacher smiled down at her with fatherly warmth. "Not your foot, Tasha, your ankle." He looked out at the three riders and explained. "Two nights ago as we were heading up to the belfry to watch God's children from the safety of the roof, she slipped and fell. Poor thing broke her ankle, very badly I'm afraid. Well beyond my skill to heal. It's bothering her something awful." He patted the girl gently on the head. "That's when I realized how selfish I'd been to hold her back. She alone amongst the townsfolk had not received the blessing. In my loneliness, I kept her here so she could gather food and supplies for me while they slept. I was wrong to do so. I had denied her God's heavenly mercy." His eyes fell. "So, the Lord pushed her from the ladder as a sign to me. Hard as it was, I realized I must send her to meet her brothers and sisters and reap the blessing as it has been handed down unto them." His eyelids slipped shut and his face seemed to glow in the dark with the light of his righteous ecstasy. "They will take of her communion, just like Jesus told his disciples on the mount." He opened his eyes and smiled placidly down at them. "Amen."

As the preacher finished, Jake felt Cody tug at his sleeve. "Jake, I think I hear somethin' movin' around in the saloon." His voice was low and nervous.

Jake barely heard this. He waved his free hand dismissively back at Cody. "Can't you see I'm in the middle of somethin' here?" His attention returned to the preacher. "What does that mean, exactly?"

"It means," Loftus regarded Jake as a teacher might regard a dull student, "that I will nail her hands to that hitching post, arms outstretched as Christ's were on the holy cross, and when the blessed awake they will cluster round her, a loving family reaching their arms out to enfold her, and they will bestow upon her their gift." He looked down at her with love. "Of course, to receive the Lord's mightiest miracle, she must first shed her old, sinful life. Only then will she be reborn."

Jake's eyes went wide. "You're gonna crucify her? Are you out of your goddamned mind?" He trained the barrel of his gun on the preacher's forehead and pulled the hammer back with a click.

Loftus's eyes darkened and he pointed a furious finger at Jake. "How dare you blaspheme on these hallowed grounds? You're as bad as those red savages. You're worse. A white man should know better!"

Jake felt Cody tapping at his shoulder. "Somebody's just come out of the saloon, Jake." Jake spared a glance back at the dark building behind them. Sure enough, buried in the shadows beneath the overhang, just outside the door, a figure stood. Jake couldn't tell if the person was young or old, a man or a woman. He could only see a pale, white hand poking out from a tall, gently swaying silhouette.

"Hey!" Jake's voice was flat and sharp. "Hey you! Come here!" The person didn't respond. They just watched silently from the gloom.

Loftus chuckled warmly. "Ah, God be praised. The blessed are coming out to join us."

Jake turned back to the preacher but spoke over his shoulder to Cody. "Go on over there and talk to that—whoever. See if you can find out anything useful." He spat. "But be careful. Don't let 'em get the drop on you."

Cody pulled his gun from its holster. "Alright. If they make a move, they're gonna get blown straight to heaven."

"They've been to Heaven. God sent them back here." The preacher's voice was gentle. "Go receive the Word."

Cody shot a worried glance at the round-faced preacher and then turned and headed for the saloon. Loftus watched him, panting like a man watching a woman slowly undress.

Jake's eyes remained on the preacher. He could hear Cody's jangling spurs as he crossed the street. Could hear him call out to the person at the saloon. "Hey fella. You hear me?" Jake heard the wind sigh along the boardwalk as it picked up sharply, dragging a chill from the desert night, and a dry, sour smell. He heard Byron's uneven, old man's breathing beside him and he heard a sound like a stack of wood crashing somewhere out in the town behind him. But his eyes never left Loftus. He stared into the pale blue eyes buried in that pink, sweaty face and he could almost grasp what was going on.

Above them, the sky was a deep blue-black. The sun was long gone, and the moon peered down, cold and bright. Something was about to happen. Jake could feel it. He still didn't know what, but he thought it best that they leave town before it did. He was about to call Cody back when the younger man's voice rose in a gobbling scream that reverberated back at them in a hundred shrill pieces. Three shots were fired, "BLAM BLAM BLAM!" but the screaming went on and on. As he and Byron spun around to see what was happening, Jake heard Loftus atop the steps, sighing contentedly.

"He that eateth My flesh and drinketh My blood hath everlasting life. God be praised."

The first thing they saw when they turned was Cody being viciously attacked by the person in front of the saloon. They'd tumbled out from the thick black shadows beneath the saloon's overhang and were grappling in the moonlit street.

The man was gaunt, his jacket hanging loose and tattered from a bony frame. Cody's hat had fallen to the ground and his assailant had one thin arm wrapped around the young rider's neck. As the entangled men swung around, Jake could see the man was biting Cody, digging into the soft hollow of his throat with clamping teeth. Cody grasped at the man's collar with one hand, trying to pull him loose. The other hand waved wildly in the air, gripping his six-shooter. The high pitched—ping!—of a renegade bullet ricocheted off the concrete steps of the church just a few feet from where they stood, and both men flinched (though neither the preacher nor his young captive seemed startled by the discharge).

This would have been enough all on its own, but there was also the problem of the people making their way, slowly but steadily, up the dark avenue behind them.

They were nearly silent as they lurched and shambled towards the church. If Cody hadn't gotten himself into a fight with the man at the saloon, the three riders would've never known they were coming. Jake watched, hypnotized for a moment by their jerking, dragging movement. They leaned this way and that, arms hanging limp or else held out in front of them, grasping at the air. Their feet shuffled listlessly, and they all seemed to have forgotten how to walk properly. But they advanced with a sense of obdurate purpose. Whatever it was they were after, they aimed to get.

"What's wrong with 'em?" Byron's voice showed only curiosity, but he pulled his gun just the same, holding it at his side.

"I don't know." Time slowed for Jake. The seconds ticked down to a dead halt, and he assessed their situation, breaking it down, piece by piece in his mind. It was a skill learned, not from his time spent as a postman, but in the years before, spent riding with his father, a cold and calculating Texas Ranger. His daddy had taught him how to shoot, how to track, and how to make ten seconds feel like thirty. To see everything at once and to make a plan. Jake knew the preacher and his small captive would hold for the moment. Cody's brawl with the haggard man seemed the most urgent. From the sound of it, things were not going Cody's way and the man might have the poor kid's throat out at any moment. But it was the advancing crowd of ungainly townsfolk that bothered Jake the most. As he'd watched the procession making its way towards them, he'd seen a man crawl slowly through the window of the leather shop four doors down, and a woman in only a camisole and stockings tumbling from a shadowy doorway near the corner. For whatever reason, it looked like they'd all been hiding inside the buildings, waiting till dark to come out. It was unsettling. More than that. It was wrong. Very wrong. This whole trip had gone rotten shockingly fast.

All this went through Jake's head in a space of seconds, and he decided on a plan of direct, simple actions. He turned to Byron. "Get the girl and the preacher into the church and shut the door. I'm gonna go get Cody. I'll shout when we're ready to come in."

Hearing himself mentioned, Loftus cried out indignantly. "You will not TOUCH us! This girl was meant to join the returned. You will not deny the will of God!"

Jake fixed the preacher with a cold eye, his gun still pointed at the man's head. "You wanna talk about the will of God? I'll be more than happy to introduce you to Him, preacher, and you two can discuss it all you want. Do not doubt it." He spat tobacco juice, glinting in the moonlight as it fell. "Now you get your ass in that church, and you shut your mouth."

Byron started up the steps, his pistol held out in front of him. He turned and spared one last look at the parade of shambling townspeople and shivered. "Somethin' really bad about this, Jake."

"I know. Don't much matter. We're leaving." Jake strode across the street to where Cody and the man from the saloon continued to grapple. Cody was making all sorts of yelps and grunts, but the man remained silent. Cody's gun went off again and Jake saw his attacker's body jerk backward. Looked like the boy'd finally made a shot that mattered. But Jake saw the man continuing to stay on his feet, clinging to Cody's neck. What in the blue hell is going on here? He hurried, taking aim at the man's back, looking for an opportunity to pull the trigger.

Jake was a hard man. He'd had plenty of guns pointed at him, bullets fired in his direction, and he'd fired his fair share back, but whatever was happening in this town scared him green. It had only been ten years or so since the Donner's ill-fated attempt to cross the Sierra Nevada and the story had spread like an August brushfire. Yellow journalists from Boston to San Francisco did everything they could to dig up more stories of people losing their humanity in isolated places, committing unspeakable acts, giving in to madness. Those stories came back to him as he watched the crowd slinking through the streets. It seemed this lonely town at the edge of the desert had spoiled under the Arizona sky.

"Cody, get out from under him!" Jake was only three steps away from the tussle now and was trying to find a shot. He glanced back down the road at the approaching crowd. He saw the man who'd crawled out of the window was now creeping along on his elbows. There was something horribly wrong about the way he moved but Jake couldn't tell yet what it was. He had more pressing business.

At the sound of Jake's voice, the man from the saloon lifted his dripping face from the hollow of Cody's throat. In the silvery moonlight, the gore streaking his lips, cheeks and chin was black. Jake could see the man's teeth shining through like gravestones in dark earth. Cody flopped, limp in the man's arms and Jake realized that the boy hadn't really been fighting. The man had been holding him up, spinning around in a frenzied waltz while he tore out Cody's throat with his teeth. Worse, Jake realized he recognized the man. It was the postmaster of Cottonwood, Farley Applewaite. His right eye was gone, along with most of the flesh around the gaping socket. Ragged chunks of chewed up tissue clung precariously to a ring of filmy white bone that seemed almost to glow.

Jake grunted in surprise and disgust, stopping suddenly. His mind reeled. He didn't understand how a man could be standing on his feet with a wound like that, much less hopping around mauling people like a mad cougar. Without a second thought, he raised his Colt and fired into Farley's chest. The shots rang loud, shattering the unnatural quiet. It felt like shooting off firecrackers at a funeral.

Farley staggered back a few steps as the bullets slammed into him, ripping smoking holes through his shabby vest. He opened his arms and dumped Cody to the ground with a heavy thud. Cody's neck, shoulder and throat were a wet, glistening ruin of gristle and blood. A shimmering pool began spreading across the dirt beneath his head. He blinked his eyes slowly, once. With what looked like great effort, he stared up at Jake, mouth agape. Air whistled through the hole in his throat with a reedy hiss. He reached out a hand and then let it drop. His eyes closed and this time they stayed shut.

Jake glanced back at Farley and was shocked to find the man stumbling forward despite the lead slugs lodged in his chest. A quick look to his right showed the loping, crawling throng of silent townspeople had closed an unsettling amount of distance in just these last few seconds. He was desperately sure that he needed to be somewhere else before they reached him. He didn't have time to think or feel. He only had time to act.

"Shit." With his teeth clenched, Jake fired the last three chambered rounds into Farley's face as the man staggered into grabbing distance. The one-eyed former postmaster flew backwards, his feet flying out from under him, and hit the dirt on his back. He didn't move again.

Jake spared one moment to look down at Cody. He shook his head sadly. The boy had been a fool, that was certain, but he'd always had their backs. He talked yellow sometimes, but he'd gone to his death fighting. That was some comfort to Jake. As he turned and headed back to the church, it occurred to him how strange it was the way corpses could keep twitching well after they'd died. As he hurried away through the awful stillness, he could hear Cody's fingers dancing and drumming against the hard packed earth.

Twelve bounding steps brought Jake to the church door. He spun around to look again at the mob limping its way up the avenue. Under the light of the full moon, they were painted in shades of blue, black, and gray, and as they drew nearer, Jake was able to pick out injuries similar to Farley's. Gouged flesh with hints of bone shining through, heads tilted at grotesque, impossible angles, missing limbs. It looked as if the whole town had been run through some huge, hellish meat grinder. His gaze flitted from one broken, jerking soul to the next, along the ground at their dragging feet, until he found the man who'd pulled himself through the window of the leather shop. He was slithering along on his belly like a huge rattlesnake. Jake watched with a mixture of awe and cold, paralyzing horror as the man hauled his top half through the shadows that skirted the dark buildings, his bottom half, hips, legs, feet and all, entirely nonexistent. Instead, a tangled mess of thin, ropy entrails hung behind him like useless ribbons, sliding silently along. Even though it couldn't be real, couldn't be true, Jake knew it was. That man was dead, or had been recently before deciding to get back up again. Jake looked across the motley congregation and knew they were all dead. Walking, crawling and biting, but dead.

Holy God above in heaven save and preserve us… the ever-loving-blessed resurrection. That cracked preacher was right. But it wasn't some beautiful rebirth, but rather a return to the ragged flesh and bones from which their natural lives had fled. Animated with the fetid breath of some dark unlife they rose, driven to walk again. Driven by what? Jake was afraid he knew the answer to that.

He that eateth My flesh and drinketh My blood hath everlasting life.

He began pounding on the church door. "It's Jake! Let me in." He grabbed the door handle, but it was locked tight. He shoved against the door. It didn't budge. He turned to face the oncoming townsfolk, stumbling and silent. The nearest one, an old lady clutching a parasol, her throat a shredded ruin of flapping skin and stringy sinew, had almost reached the church steps. More made their way around the corner at the far end of the street. He turned and slammed his fist against the door again. "Let me IN Goddamnit!" He dug three bullets out of his belt with one hand and unholstered his Colt with the other. He flicked the cylinder open and loaded it with nimble fingers. He snapped it shut and spun it, hoping a round was in the chamber. The old, dead woman was clumsily staggering up the steps towards him, only a few steps away. Aside from the scuffling of her feet she made no sound. Jake pointed the gun at her vacuous face and pulled the trigger.

Click.

"Oh hell." Her hands reached out, dry, flaking fingers scrabbling madly in the air just inches from his chest. "Sorry ma'am." He squeezed two more times before the gun finally spit fire. The back of the old woman's head exploded outwards in a wet, black spray of blood and brains, her lifeless body dropping to the ground with a thud. Jake grimaced out at the gathering crowd. At the sound of gunfire their heads all turned, slowly, on stiff necks to look at him. He aimed at the nearest one, a young boy in overalls who was missing most of his arm from the elbow down. The boy looked up at Jake and his mouth yawned wide, black tongue wiggling, wormlike. Jake put a round between his eyes, knocking him to the ground.

Jake spun around, beating on the door and shouting to be let in. He was about to shoot the lock, a desperate and senseless plan, when the sound of rattling chains came from behind the heavy wood. A moment later, the door swung inward a few inches and the barrel of Byron's gun sprung from the darkness.

"You alright? Where's Cody?" The old man's wide eyes peered out above the gun.

"No, I'm not alright!" Jake shoved through the door, pushing Byron out of the way and slamming it shut as three dead people clambered up the steps behind him with a dreamy slowness. He leaned back against it, breathing hard. A moment later, he felt their hands tapping on the other side of the door. He pulled his hat from his head and wiped his face with his wrist. "And Cody's dead."

The lines in Byron's face deepened as the corners of his mouth drew down. In the faint candle glow that wavered behind him he looked as if he was made of stone. "Shot?"

"Nope." With his back still to the door, Jake reached up and turned the bolt.

Byron removed his hat and bowed his head. "What a pity. He was a good kid." He looked up, his eyes shining within the shadows that crossed his face. "How'd it happen, Jake?"

Jake stood and faced the door. There were two heavy chains threaded through the lower door handle and wrapped around a thick wooden post that stood to the side of the door. A heavy padlock lay open on the floor. Jake bent, picked it up, and began dragging the chains through the handle, securing the door. He spoke over his shoulder to Byron. "Farley Applewaite tore his throat out. With his teeth."

"What?"

"I said…" Jake pulled the chains as tight as they would go across the door and slapped the padlock on them. He turned and crossed the candlelit narthex, speaking as he passed. "That Farley Applewaite ripped Cody's throat out with his ever-loving teeth." Without stopping, Jake moved with purpose into the nave.

Loftus stood leaning against the back row of pews, his face solemn with smug piety, his arms crossed. As Jake approached, the preacher raised the index finger of his right hand as if to point to heaven. "Only too late do you now understand the power of the Lord our God."

"Understand this." Without slowing, Jake swung a powerful right hook at the preacher's face. Loftus, whatever he was expecting, wasn't expecting that. Jake's fist connected with Loftus's jaw just below the corner of his mouth. The preacher cried out, his hands flying into the air like startled birds, and his hat flipped over the back of the pew. He went to the ground with a crash and covered his face, moaning and cringing. Jake pulled his booted foot back as he prepared to kick Loftus's ribs until he heard them crack. "You were gonna hang that little girl up out there for bait like a worm on a hook, you sonofabitch. You were gonna let them eat her alive!" His foot came forward and slammed into the soft, plump padding of Loftus's side. The preacher howled in pain and called out to his god.

"Jesus, save me! Save me from this agent of Lucifer!"

"Jesus ain't here Rev'rend." Jake landed another kick. "He ain't anywhere in this town." And another. "How'd you manage?" He pulled his leg back and kicked Loftus again. The preacher's screams turned into sobbing moans and grunts. "Huh? How'd you manage to survive when all the rest…" Jake stopped kicking and hunkered down near Loftus's face, his hands dangling between his bent knees. "How many of those monsters out there belong to you?"

Loftus was wheezing, each breath sucked through clenched teeth. Even so, instead of answering, he began to sing. "Rescue the perishing, care for the dying, snatch them in pity from sin and the grave…" He took a wet breath, blood and spittle spraying from his lips. "Weep o'er the erring one, lift up the fallen, tell them of Jesus, the mighty to save."

Jake let Loftus finish the stanza and then drew his Colt from its holster. He pulled back the hammer and pressed the tip of the barrel against the preacher's temple. Sweat poured off the holy man, glistening in the flickering light of the candles. Byron and Tasha watched silently, the girl perched on a footstool, her bad leg held out to her side, while the dead kept a steady rhythm, pounding and clawing at the door of the church.

"That don't answer my question Rev'rend." Jake's voice was low, almost a whisper. He pushed the barrel harder against the preacher's head. Loftus's eyes had gone wide, and he seemed to hold his breath. "Now I've about done run out of patience with you. The minute that happens you're gonna get to meet your God face to face. But I'm willin' to give you one more chance here. How. Many. Are. Yours?" He tapped the barrel against Loftus's head to punctuate each word. Several long moments spun out, the ragged sound of the preacher's breath and the pounding of hands against the door the only noise to be heard. Finally, Loftus's face hardened, and he spoke.

"The lot of them. Good men, women and children who I helped to become the vessels of Christ—his living body and blood upon this Earth. I helped them by locking the doors and leaving them to receive the word, out there in the streets from their brothers and sisters who'd already been filled with the Holy Spirit." Loftus spat a tooth from his mouth to clatter against the floor. "You will be judged most harshly by He that sits on High for this. Make no mistake. You will burn in hell."

Jake nodded. "I have no doubt." He wiped his hand across his mouth, two days growth of beard rasping against his fingers.

Byron called out quietly from behind them. "Jake…they're getting more—agitated—out there. Sounds like the whole town's beatin' on the door. We need to get outta here. Pronto."

Jake stood back up and spat on the floor. "Get up."

The preacher pulled a childish, defiant face. "No thank you, sir. Yea, though I walk through the valley of the shadow of death I shall fear no evil. I fear you not, nor your bullets. The end of my life on Earth only means the beginning of my life in Heaven."

Jake flipped the pistol around in his hand, butt first. "I ain't gonna shoot you Rev'rend. I'm just gonna keep beatin' on you till you do what I say. I won't work you over hard enough to kill ya, but you sure will be hurtin' somethin' awful." For a moment, it seemed as if Loftus still was not going to budge. His eyes were blazing pits of hatred and his mouth was set hard. Then Jake jerked forward, bringing the butt of the pistol towards the preacher's face and Loftus let forth a high pitched whimper and flinched, throwing his hands over his head. Jake stopped short of hitting him. He didn't need to. He wasn't a gambling man, but it was clear. The preacher had shown his hand. He might not be afraid of dying, but he was afraid of pain. A few seconds later, he took his hands from his face and spoke.

"Alright. As you say." With much grunting and groaning, Loftus pushed himself into a sitting position. He leaned against the back of the pew and took a few deep breaths. "I will try to forgive you these barbaric trespasses."

Jake ignored the remark and looked back to the entryway where Byron and Tasha waited. The clamor from outside had risen to a mad pitch, the door shaking in its jamb, rattling against the bolt and chains. How many? The question still remained unanswered. Cottonwood was small. Accounting for the farmers who lived on the outskirts of town, their families and farm-hands, a few soldiers from Fort Defiance (they often came to indulge in a bit of gambling followed by some good-natured whoring) and probably a couple of drifters and vagrants, there might've been three hundred in all. Give or take. If three hundred people, even dead ones, wanted to get at you through a church door, sooner or later they were going to.

"How'd you get away?" Jake spoke over his shoulder as Loftus slowly stood.

"I am the instrument of God. He was saving me for the purpose of helping his blessed flock. I prayed for strength and guidance and…"

With lightning speed, Jake spun around and backhanded the preacher across his pasty pink face. Loftus shrieked and clutched at his stinging cheeks, his eyes full of reproach and fear. Jake held a finger up in warning. "No more holy rolling. Got me?" The preacher nodded, his hands still plastered to his face. Jake shoved his Colt back in its holster and turned away. "Good. Now tell me what you did to get away before they had a chance to chew on you."

With a sullen expression, and still rubbing his wounded face, Loftus gestured with his head to the church behind him. "I climbed up into the belfry. Being newly reborn, they're confused and disoriented. They had trouble understanding that I was there to shepherd them. They were closing in, blocking the front door so the belfry was the only place I could go. I scrambled up the ladder, expecting that they were right behind me, but when I chanced a look down I saw them on the ground just sort of—pawing—harmlessly at the rungs." He shrugged. "It seems that when receiving the gift of resurrection, one trades a certain level of—dexterity and thought. They were unable to follow me up." The preacher bent at the waist and picked up his hat, placing it back upon his head. "Eventually they made their way out of the church, and I was able to come down and secure the doors. Later that day, I discovered Tasha asleep behind the pulpit, undiscovered. She'd come in to pray and find shelter. Together we formed a routine, me sleeping during the daylight hours, she gathering supplies from the abandoned buildings, and at night, when the blessed awoke to walk the town, we watched quietly from the rooftop." His eyes narrowed. "They had no idea we were in here, our silence buying us their indifference. Now, thanks to your thickheaded gun-blasting, they are aware of us. God does work in mysterious ways."

Jake held his hand up for Loftus to stop. "Enough. I found out what I needed to know. Now shut your flapping gums for awhile and sit tight." Loftus crossed his arms, leaning against the pew. Byron was pressed up against the door. The pounding from the other side was constant and the heavy wood seemed looser in its frame. Jake strode into the narthex and laid his hand flat against the door, feeling the insistence of the dead outside vibrating against his palm. There was a smell now. A wisp of rotten meat that crept under the door like smoke.

The older man's eyes were filled with concern, but no fear. Jake found a moment to be grateful that he'd brought Byron on this trip with him. The man was solid. His white mustache twitched, and his eyebrows went up. "So?"

Jake dug the remainder of his chaw from his cheek and dropped it onto the floor with a splat. "We're goin' up the belfry and out to the roof. Sounds like they only come out after sundown so, we'll just stay up there till mornin' and wait for 'em to go back into their holes." His eyes blazed. "Then we'll climb back down, chop us up some barrels and whatever else we can find, for kindling, and set this hell on Earth to burn. Once that's going good and hot, the four of us will hightail it outta here, well before dusk."

"All of us are goin'?"

Jake nodded, his eyes grim. "I know. It's gonna be rough going, but I couldn't leave nobody out here without a horse and some water. Even that fat, crazy bastard."

Before Byron had a chance to respond there was a great surge of pressure against the door and the bolt gave way with a horrible, wooden, SNAP! The door pressed inward against the chains and moonlight spilled through the sudden four inch gap on a wave of stench. Immediately, a wriggling forest of pale, bloody fingers filled the gap, groping and grasping. Jake and Byron both let out cries of surprise and disgust. They shoved their weight hard against the door, trying to close it again, but against the mass of the entire town, it budged only a little. Behind them, Loftus cackled from his spot against the pew.

"Might as well try arm wrestling the Holy Ghost you faithless apostates. Ha!"

"We get outta this, I'm gonna shoot him if you don't." Byron panted.

"We'll draw cards for the privilege." As he pressed his hands against the door with all his might, Jake felt something brush softly against his thigh. He looked down, startled, to find that Tasha had hopped her way across the room to add her weight to the door. Somehow, the bravery of her effort touched Jake deeply. It must have cost her quite a bit of pain to get over there. I'm getting her out of here if it's the last thing I do. And on the heels of that. If I can't get her out, at the very least I can give her a better end than being eaten alive by her family and friends. He wondered which corpses out there were her mother and father. Her brothers and sisters.

It quickly became clear that holding the door was a futile effort. The gap had widened and now whole arms were snaking their way through, swiping at Jake, Byron and Tasha. Behind them, the sound of Loftus's footsteps leading deeper into the church prompted Jake to turn around, pressing his back against the door. He watched as the preacher started up a thin wooden ladder at the back of the pulpit. He was heading up to the belfry. Jake itched to grab his pistol and put a bullet in the preacher's back, but he knew he needed to conserve his ammunition. He tossed his hat to the floor and spun back around.

"The time has come for us to take our leave." He looked down at Tasha. "Sweetheart, you ready?"

The little girl's voice was flat and emotionless. "I'm ready."

"Good." Jake glanced over his shoulder. Loftus's feet were disappearing up the shaft that led to the belfry. "Byron, you're gonna let go first. Run back there fast as you can and get up that ladder quick. Make sure our friend the Rev'rend don't get any funny ideas about tryin to trap us down here. You have my permission to break his jaw if he gives you any guff."

"Got it. What about you two?"

"Soon's you're up inside the shaft, give a holler and we'll be along lickety split. We can't afford to all get hung up at the bottom of the ladder."

"You wanna give me a count 'o three?"

Jake shook his head. "No, dammit, just go."

Without another word, Byron let go of the door and hurried into the church. Jake could hear his boots clacking down the center aisle. A moment later, Byron's voice rang out from the pulpit as he shouted up at Loftus. "Hey! You stay put or I'll blow your cock off." This surprised a laugh out of Jake, and it seemed to lift his spirits some. *Maybe we'll get out of this after all.*

He looked down at the little girl. Her face was soft, with chubby cheeks and a cute, upturned nose. It was the face of any well-cared for child. Pretty and unremarkable, but her eyes were hard and cold. The eyes of a gunfighter or an old soldier who's seen a hundred battles. He tried to imagine what it must've been like for her. Watching the dead come back to life to hunt the living. Finding safety in the church only to have her pastor try and crucify her. She'd come through all of that still standing and fighting to survive. She was strong. He felt a wave of admiration for her and resolved, again, that he would see her safely out of this town. A moment later, Byron's muffled voice came from somewhere behind and above them.

"I'm up!"

"Alright girl. It's time." Jake licked his lips. His tongue was dry and rough. "I'm gonna grab you up and put you on my back. You gotta hold tight around my neck. Try not to choke me though, okay?"

"Yessir." Her voice was quiet but steady.

"I'm afraid it might hurt your ankle some, getting tossed around. I'm sorry for that. I'll try to be careful, but we're in a hurry."

Tasha looked him in the eye then. Hers were hard, yes, but somewhere way down in those deep blue irises was the faintest glimmer of fear. It was held in check but it was there and Jake felt better for it. It meant she wasn't just a hollowed out husk running on nothing but spite and instinct. She wanted to live. She held his gaze for a few moments and then nodded, strands of straw-colored hair falling into her face. She swept them back behind her ears. "It's okay. I'll be just fine."

Jake didn't need any further encouragement. He jumped back from the door and, with one fluid motion, swept Tasha into his arms. He flung her over his right shoulder, trying to be mindful of her ankle, and she wrapped her arms around his neck trying not to squeeze him too hard. The moment their weight left the door it bulged inward against the chain. The gap was now nearly a foot wide and dead townspeople pushed their vacuous faces into it, their teeth clicking together as they worked their hungry jaws. The chain pulled tight and the door handle around which it was wrapped creaked ominously. It wouldn't hold much longer.

Jake hurried down the center aisle of the church. He stepped up onto the pulpit and reached the ladder against the back wall in two long strides. He looked up the dark belfry shaft. A tiny triangle of moonlight fell across it at the top, but he couldn't see Byron or Loftus. It suddenly occurred to him that the shaft might be too small for him to climb with Tasha hanging on his back. Shit. He thought. This is gonna be tight.

He put his booted foot on the bottom rung and hoisted himself and Tasha up onto the ladder. His head pushed into the darkness of the shaft, and Jake knew immediately that, no matter how tightly Tasha flattened herself against him, they were not going to go up together. The space was horribly narrow, like an upright coffin. He had no idea how the thick preacher had managed to scramble up it so nimbly. Dismay filled him and he climbed back down, quick as he could, stepping to the floor. He pulled Tasha around and sat her in the crook of his arm.

"Well kid. That ain't gonna work. Is it?"

She looked across the church. It sounded as if the door was being battered to splinters. She looked back into Jake's eyes and shook her head.

"You're gonna have to climb." Jake knew how slowly the going would be, and seconds were precious now as the slavering dead tore their way into the church. "I'll be right behind you, helpin' you along." When she replied, her voice was so low he wasn't sure what she'd even said at first. "What?" He asked.

"I said, leave me." Her eyes flicked back to the door. They were almost in. At any moment, the handle would snap off or the door would simply crumble beneath their weight and they'd come spilling into the narthex.

Jake laughed, a high pitched, lunatic sound. He took her chin in his hand and turned her face to his. He got close enough to feel the whisper of her breath on his sweaty brow. "Girlie, you listen to me. The single, most important reason I've got right now, for trying to live through this hell, is to get you out of this God-forsaken place. You hear me?" The girl's eyes glistened at the corners, but no tears fell. She leaned forward and kissed him softly on the cheek, and then nodded her head. He touched his thumb to the tip of her nose and gave her what he hoped was a reassuring smile. "Alright, upsy-daisy."

Jake took the girl under her arms and lifted her as far above his head as he could. She grabbed onto the ladder and began hauling herself up. Jake took a few moments to load his revolver. He was surely going to need it. Six shots were barely a drop in the bucket against a town full of walking corpses, but they might buy ten or twelve seconds. That could mean the difference between life and… whatever that was at the door.

He turned to the ladder and climbed onto the first rung. Tasha's bad foot dangled just above his head. He reached up and boosted her rump another three rungs. "Keep goin' girl. We gotta move." Tasha put her good foot down and slid her hands up the ladder, grabbing the rung above her head and pulling herself along. Jake was able to move up a little bit, and when her foot was in front of him again they repeated the process. Twice more and Tasha's head finally disappeared up into the shaft. Two more after that and Jake would be in the tight darkness behind her. He was shoving her upward when a loud metal SNAP! and a horrendous wooden crash filled the church. A mad scraping and shuffling followed, like a hundred brooms clacking together as they swept across the floor.

The dead had finally gotten in.

Jake's heart began hammering in his chest. He was still only four rungs up from the floor of the pulpit. He watched as the first corpses stumbled into the nave, behind the last row of pews. An old man in an apron, his face smeared with gore from the tip of his chin to the middle of his cheeks, was the first to lurch into the aisle. His spectacles hung askew on his head, the lenses cracked, and his arms hung limp at his sides as he staggered forward. Behind him was a little girl, about the same size and age as Tasha, her hair tied up in a pretty pink bonnet. Her eyes were both gone and a huge, red slit across the front of her dress leaked greasy coils of intestines that flapped against her waist as she walked. Her arms were outstretched, hands curled into claws. A shadowy, moving mass undulated behind her, shoving forward. Gray faces streaked with red swam out of the darkness, teeth bared. Voiceless, they came for him.

Jake looked up at Tasha. She'd only gone another four rungs. He shouted up the shaft. "Byron!" A moment later, the old man's voice came back, sounding hollow and far away.

"Jake? You okay?"

For the first time all night, Jake felt real panic. He tried to lick his lips, his tongue still spitless and harsh. "No! Try to reach down and grab the girl, she needs help up. Fast!" The old, dead man was now halfway down the aisle, thirty feet from where Jake hung on the ladder.

"What about the preacher? He's liable to…"

"FUCK HIM!" Jake drew his pistol and fired at the approaching dead thing. His bullet carried off most of the top of its head and the creature dropped to the floor. The little dead girl had somehow wandered up into one of the pews and couldn't seem to navigate her way back out. But four or five other former citizens of Cottonwood had filled the aisleway and were shambling steadily on.

Above him, Jake heard a wooden clattering in the belfry shaft and Byron's voice calling out. "Come on, girl, reach for my hand. Just reach!" Jake took his eyes off the advancing dead folks to look up into the shaft. He watched as Tasha's bare feet, dangling in midair, disappeared into the darkness like magic. When he looked back, the corpses had nearly reached the pulpit, a stinking procession of rotten, walking meat.

"God-damn." He fired at the nearest one, which had begun clambering up onto the platform. His aim was off, and he hit its shoulder. It slowed not at all. Jake gritted his teeth and fired again, this time hitting it just below its cloudy, right eye. It fell to the floor and four more of its kind trampled over it in their single-minded desire for warm flesh. Their twitching fingers found the edge of the platform and their mouths dropped open with anticipation. Jake holstered his gun and started up the ladder. He hated turning his back on them, but he knew to wait any longer would be suicide. His face disappeared into the black of the shaft and he breathed a sigh of relief, never having been so happy to be swallowed up by darkness.

Then a hand closed around his ankle, yanking his foot from the ladder.

Jake screamed and let go of the rung. He surely would've fallen if not for the tightness of the shaft. He fell backwards, one foot still on the ladder, his shoulders bumping up against the wooden wall behind him. He hung there for a moment, not moving, and it was long enough for him to regain his senses. He reached out and grasped the ladder tightly with both hands.

He tried to look down and see the thing that had a hold of him, but his body was in the way. For being dead, its grip was like iron. It tugged and pulled at him, trying to dislodge him from the safety of the shaft. Very carefully he let go with his right hand and snaked it down to his thigh. He pulled his gun free, transferring it to his left hand and grabbing back onto the ladder with the other. He was not so good with his left hand. He wasn't a professional gunfighter, and he'd only ever had need of one pistol. He'd honed his skills with his right hand to where he was quick and accurate. With his left he'd be lucky to hit the side of a barn. Still, he didn't know how long he'd last in a standoff with the thing trying to drag him down. And who could say it might not eventually figure out how to climb up?

He held the gun down along his leg. He began to say a quick prayer, asking that he somehow manage not to shoot himself in the foot and then thought better of it. God didn't seem interested in the living and breathing of Cottonwood anymore. Jake thought it wiser to trust to luck. With eyes tightly shut and breath held, he pointed the gun and fired.

A sudden, stinging heat raced across Jake's ankle and he thought, Dammit! Missed! But the fingers wrapped around his ankle came loose and a sound like a bag of dry kindling being dropped to the ground drifted up from below. Without needing any further prodding, Jake holstered his gun, pulled his leg out of the reach of grasping hands, and hurried up the ladder, squirming through the dark. A few seconds later, his head passed through a trapdoor in the middle of a platform and the space above him was lightened by squares of dark, velvety blue. He smiled at the sight as if he hadn't seen a night sky in years. The ladder ended, and he found himself standing on the platform. Above him was a large, rounded silhouette which could only be the bell, but he saw no sign of his companions.

"Byron? Tasha?" The corners of his mouth turned down. "Rev'rend? Y'all up here?"

"Out here, Sonny." Byron's voice came from somewhere above. "Be careful. It's tight around that bell."

"How the hell do I get out of here?"

"Walk forward, there's a set of steps. Bring you right up into the bell chamber."

Jake came forward and, sure enough, there was a small rise of stairs. He climbed them and found himself pressing up against the fat body of the bell, the butt of his Colt clanging against the metal. He turned and hugged the bell and followed its curve until he came to the open side of the belfry. Suddenly he could feel a cool breeze caressing his face and neck. A moment later he was climbing, carefully, out onto the roof of the church. The sky opened above him, vast and dark, dotted with stars, and it felt like rebirth. He gulped the fresh air, free of the stench of corpses, and, more than ever before, felt how alive he was.

A few feet away, Byron sat with the heels of his boots dug in between the roof planks, his arms wrapped around Tasha. His gun was out and pointed casually at the preacher who sat cross legged a few feet away, scowling and muttering to himself. Jake made his way over to the old man and the young girl. He sat and tugged his chaw pouch from the pocket of his coat, stuffed a plug into his cheek, and looked out over the top of the small town.

The moon had moved across the sky, but not very much. It hung, pale and bloated, looking down on Jake's little group with indifference. Less than an hour had gone by since they'd come upon Loftus and Tasha but it felt like a year had passed. It seemed that most of the dead folks had formed a mob at the front of the church, all of them trying mindlessly to squeeze through the door. A few still lumbered in the street, wandering aimlessly, tottering about on unsteady feet. Jake couldn't see around the corner, where the water pump, drip, dripped into its wooden basin, and there was no way to know what, if anything, waited there. Jake spat out into space, the juice falling into the shadows of the alley between the church and the building next to it. He had a question for the preacher.

"Hey. Those things ever leave town? Our horses are tied up at some cactus out by them Indian heads you popped into the ground."

Loftus looked up slowly. His eyes gleamed in the shadows beneath his hat brim and his mouth crimped with distaste. "That was no work of mine."

Jake snorted, disbelieving. "If not you, Rev'rend, then who?"

Loftus tilted his head towards the scrubby plain to the east. "The same red savages that brought them here when they still sat atop living shoulders. They were of the Godless tribe who had to be run off of Royston Mulroney's land because they wouldn't leave." His lip curled with contempt. "They rode in and dropped them off, four of them, sick and in need of help at my very doorstep. Being good, decent Christians, we brought them in and tried to do for them what we could. Alas, their conditions worsened and in their final throes they became violent, nipping and biting at the hands of their caretakers. Mamie Liston nearly lost a finger. I had been preaching to them and I think, in the end, they repented of their heathen ways. It was the best I could do. They died just at sunup, and we placed their bodies in two hastily crafted pine boxes and leaned them against the back of the church." Hatred simmered in the set of his expression. "Their beastly brethren rode into town later that day, searching high and low till they found them. They took the bodies out of their boxes and dragged them to the edge of town. I made protests to the sheriff, but he, being a coward, stated that we should let the redskins have their own to bury as they saw fit."

At that moment a night bird shrieked as it passed overhead, its shadow a huge black ghost that crawled across the church roof. Tasha looked up in wonder, her face genuinely childlike for the first time since Jake had made her acquaintance. He glanced up just in time to see the dark shape disappear beyond the steeple that topped the belfry. He spat again and eyed the preacher.

"So, you're sayin' it was their kinsmen that did that to 'em?"

Loftus nodded. "They took the bodies, just before sunset, and performed some devil's ritual. They screamed and whooped and each man of them dragged a bone knife across their chest, drawing blood that they wiped on the grass. Then they pulled out axes and removed the heads from the bodies. They drove those stakes into the ground and mounted the heads like demon trophies, two at the eastern end of town, two at the western end. Then they set the bodies afire and rode away. It's a wonder they didn't burn the whole town down."

Byron chuckled drily in the dark. "Not a wonder. A shame."

Loftus smiled ferociously at the old man. "But they didn't. God had other plans for us, and that night the blessed resurrection began. Three days later, all of the meek had fallen and risen, drawing each other, one by one into the light of God's mercy."

Jake nodded thoughtfully. "Amen and hallelujah, we know." Below him the sounds of dead people banging about inside the church, trying to find warm prey, rose from the depths of the belfry shaft. "So, like I was saying, do they ever try to get out of town?"

"They are the chosen of God, his lambs, his children. They will not pass by those heathen abominations. They bar their way as the angel Gabriel barred Adam and Eve from paradise with his flaming sword. They..."

Jake held up his hand. "Alright, alright, I got it. They don't go past the Indian heads. At least we don't have to worry that there's any stumbling around out in the desert, waitin' for us."

Loftus stood carefully, leaning over and keeping one hand against the roof. "May I come over and offer you the comfort of prayer?" He started towards Jake, moving slowly. "So, you may repent of your sins, lest God judge your defiance of his will harshly."

Jake responded coldly. "Don't talk to me again Rev'rend, lest I decide to chuck you off this roof. I've had my fill o' you." He shot tobacco juice onto the roof planks.

Loftus held up his finger. "If I may, one last thing."

Jake turned to the preacher, looking up at him with an exasperated grunt. "What?"

"God forgive you." Before Byron or Jake had time to react, Loftus had covered the short distance between himself and the exhausted postman, scrabbling across the roof with wicked speed. He raised an object above his head and swung it. He was aiming for Jake's head, but at the last moment, he stumbled on the plank and the hammer he'd concealed in his sleeve slammed into Jake's shoulder instead. Jake cried out and rolled down the steep roof. He slid over the edge, his gun flying from his hand, and landed hard on his side in the shadows beside the church. At almost the same time, his Colt hit the ground nearby and went off with a loud, Bang!

On the ground, Jake moaned, feeling snaps and cracks in his side as he rolled onto his back. He looked up to the roof in time to see Tasha jump from Byron's lap and scream. She instantly lost her balance as her bad ankle buckled and went tumbling past the laughing figure of Humbert Loftus. As she flew over the edge, she grabbed on to the gutter, slowing her fall, but the weight of her dangling body was too much for her tiny fingers and she dropped to the ground. Loftus hunched over, clinging to the roof like a spider, and made his way past the stunned Byron, climbing into the bell chamber.

Byron scooted down the slope of the roof on his butt as quickly as he dared, and peered over the edge. The darkness between the church and the next building was thick and to Jake the old man's face seemed to glow.

"Jake? You alright?"

A growing crowd of dead folks, having given up on finding live meat in the church, suddenly seemed interested in the alley. They stumbled down from the church steps, much too close, their stink sweeping along ahead of them. They'd be on top of Jake and Tasha in seconds.

Jake tried to call out to Byron, but he couldn't get his breath. He wanted to tell him to stay on the roof till morning. Leave them to their fate on the ground, and save himself, but all that came out was a dry wheeze. Byron waited a moment and then, with a grumbled curse, began easing himself over the edge of the roof. His knees went over, and he slid backwards, gripping the gutter tightly, until he was supported on his elbows. With a groan, he stretched his arms out, dangled over the edge, and dropped.

The old man landed hard, but he kept his feet. He scurried over to Jake and Tasha, his eyes full of fear. The girl was sitting up, clenching her teeth and rocking back and forth, trying to be quiet. Beside her, Jake had caught his breath and was trying to get up onto his knees, but he was in great pain. He squeezed his eyes shut and trembled with the effort. Byron stepped over to him and hunkered down, drawing his gun.

"Where's it hurt?"

"My side. I think I broke some ribs." Jake slid back to the ground and rolled onto his back, breathing hard. He opened his eyes and looked at Byron. "Take her and get the—ooh, GOD!—hell out of here." His eyes flicked to the front of the alley. A small dead boy, dressed in his Sunday best, head tilted crazily where his neck had been eaten mostly away, was only yards from them now and closing. Behind him the silhouettes of walking corpses were gathering. Byron took aim at the boy and pulled the hammer back. Before he could fire, Jake reached out and touched him.

"The head. You gotta get 'im in the head."

Byron nodded, raised his hand a few inches, and shot. The boy's head exploded, gray and black mush flying in all directions. The old man holstered his weapon and stood over Jake, leaning forward.

"Come on, hoss, I ain't leavin without ye." He grabbed two handfuls of Jake's duster and pulled him to a sitting position. Jake cried out in agony, but he managed to steady himself with his hands. The dead had completely blocked their escape, climbing towards them over the dry shrubbery that fronted the church, silent except for the swishing of their feet. The street could no longer be seen through the growing horde. Jake watched their slow but steady approach, drained of hope.

"I don't think you're leavin' at all." He climbed gingerly to his feet, letting Byron help him. Every time he moved it felt like he was being stabbed. He winced and reached down for Tasha's hand. The little girl tried to stand and take his, but her left leg was even worse than before. She wouldn't be able to run, and Jake didn't think he'd be able to pick her up. "None of us are." He sighed, knowing what must be done. "You're gonna have to do for us with the shots you got left. I'd do it m'self, but I lost my gun."

Byron slapped him across the face. Jake recoiled, hissing with pain, and held his hand to his stinging cheek. The old man scowled at him. "Don't get yella' on me, son. Don't you do it." The dead woman in the camisole and an old man whose shopkeeper's apron was shredded and bloody, were at the head of the procession and almost near enough to touch. Jake could smell them. Byron jerked his head to the building next to them as he blasted the woman's still pretty head off. "We can get in there through the side door, buy a couple'a minutes."

"You're gonna have to carry her, I don't think I can."

Byron stepped around Jake and bent over, sweeping Tasha into his arms. He handed his gun to the younger man. "Cover me."

Jake turned and fired, putting a bullet through the eye of the blood spattered shopkeeper. The dead man fell to the ground, harmless, but there were dozens more right behind him, crawling into the alley. Jake looked into their slack, vacuous faces. For a moment, he considered throwing himself into the crowd to divert attention away from Byron and Tasha, allowing the resurrected to devour him. Then he thought about waking back up. Walking the streets of Cottonwood, driven by hunger, till his body fell apart, piece by piece. What then? Would his dust be swept along, still feeling the urge to feed? It was a thought that threatened to open deep, black holes in his mind that could lead only to madness. He decided, instead, to run.

He blew the head off of the nearest corpse and turned in time to see Byron kick open the door of the building beside the church. Jake stumbled along, every step a painful jab in his side, and followed his friends into the dark. He slammed the door behind him and bolted it. The only sounds were their collective breathing and the scraping of the dead outside as they pressed against the building. Moonlight spilled through the windows and front door, sparkling on the broken glass. This was not going to be a safe place for long.

The three survivors looked around the room. The walls were lined with recessed shelves, and three low tables were spaced out across the floor. Tasha's eyes gleamed in the darkness.

"This was Mr. Connington's store. He was the shoemaker." She took a hand from Byron's shoulder and pointed at the front counter. "He always had a jar of candy up there. It's gone now." She wrapped her arms around Byron's neck and said no more.

Jake surveyed the back of the store. Time was fleeting. "Do you think there's a way up to the roof?" The sounds of shuffling footsteps grew louder outside.

Byron's mustache twitched. "I don't know. I don't see any stairs or anything. We could

maybe…" Suddenly he was screaming. No one had seen, nor heard, the dead man who'd crawled up onto the table behind the old man until it reached out and grabbed his shoulder. Tasha squealed as the thing stretched its dry, flaking jaws and sank its teeth into the wrinkled flesh of Byron's neck. Blood squirted in a jet, spraying Tasha in the face. She fell to the floor as Byron flailed at the creature clinging to his back. It dug its fingers into his shirt and held on, tearing out hunks of meat, chewing loudly.

Tasha used the table to pull herself up, balancing on her good foot. She hop-stepped over to Jake's side, frantically trying to wipe Byron's hot blood from her face and hair.

Jake waved the six-shooter, unable to place a good shot. The seconds spun out and Byron's blood gushed. His screams were growing quieter, his struggling weaker. The dead thing bit off his ear and he barely seemed to notice. Finally, Jake sprung forward to physically beat the creature, but the old man stumbled backwards, holding his hands out. His knees buckled, and he spilled both himself and his attacker to the floor. When he spoke, his voice was low and hoarse.

"Do for me…"

Jake shook his head violently. "Don't do that!" He didn't know he was shouting. Outside, the living dead had crept around the front of the building. They trudged slowly onward, reaching towards the empty windows. Their shadows climbed the outside walls, chased by the moonlight.

Byron pressed himself against the dead man beneath his back, trying to hold it down. His eyelids fluttered. It seemed to take a lot out of him to speak, and he could barely be heard under the pounding at the side door. "I'm a goner…do for me…and then…do for this sonofabitch." His wound was no longer gushing but trickling instead, slow and sticky. He made a great effort to look up into Jake's eyes. "Please. Don't let me … get back up."

Jake's eyes narrowed. He stepped forward and pointed the gun. He looked down at the torn and bloody old man and the abomination writhing beneath him. He spoke through gritted teeth. "Goodnight old hoss." He fired two rounds and everything inside the shoemaker's shop became still for a moment.

Then Tasha shrieked.

Dead hands were reaching in through the window, tearing gray flesh from scrabbling fingers as they raked across the broken glass. Jake stepped over to her and held out his arm, like a gentleman asking a lady for a dance.

"Grab my arm. You're gonna have to hop as fast as you can."

The little girl looked up into his face, terrified, and nodded. She linked her arm through his and they started across the store to the door at the far end, near the counter. Behind them, the door they'd come in began to splinter under the weight of hungry corpses. Jake threw open the front door and stepped out.

It was a nightmare parody of what the town must've been like before the resurrection. Townsfolk bustling in the street, coming in and out of shops, drunks and gamblers swaying in front of the saloon. But instead of fresh, ruddy faces, squinting in the sun as they went about their business, it was gray faces, slack and yawning under the pale moon. They dragged themselves along, slowly but surely, intent on pulling Jake and Tasha into their fold, welcoming them with teeth and dry tongues. A line of them was wrapped around the shop, choking the alley as they followed the leaders to where they'd seen the living disappear. Another throng had pressed themselves against the false-front of the little store, while others just shambled and jerked in random directions. When the postman and the little girl burst through the door, they all stopped and turned, their jaws working greedily.

Jake was hurting, and he knew that Tasha's leg was in bad shape, but a glimmer of hope had blossomed within him, small but bright. Whatever else these dead folks might be, fast they weren't. Even limping, if he and the girl moved quickly, they could outpace the things. If what Loftus had said about them being unable to go past the severed Indian heads was true, then they just had to make it around the corner and up the street. He hurried along, dragging the girl with him. He barely dared to hope that the next street wouldn't be overrun.

As they burst out onto the street, a voice, very much alive and familiar, called out from behind and above Jake and Tasha. "Ho there! Where's the old man? Did he accept God's grace and submit to His will?"

Jake knew it was foolish. He knew it was a waste of time and ammo. But every ounce of anger and grief pulled at him, inexorably turning his body and pointing the gun in his hand at the roof of the church. Humbert Loftus was standing near the belfry, his hands held to the sky, triumphant. Jake should have missed. He was too far away. It was dark, and he was beaten and distracted. But when he pulled the trigger, the preacher's right leg jerked and spilled him down the sloped roof. He bounced off the gutter and rolled over the edge and into the sea of ghouls swarming the shadows beside the church. Jake looked down at Tasha and was surprised to see a ghost of a smile on her lips. He grinned back at her. It felt unnatural on his face, but he enjoyed the moment nonetheless. Then he looked over his shoulder at the ever advancing army of dead townsfolk and decided it was time for them to move on.

As the postman and the little girl made their escape, another night bird cried out from above. Jake thought it was probably laughing at what it was seeing; a race through the dark streets of Cottonwood, between the crippled and the dead, all of them limping and shambling along desperately. Even at their hampered pace, though, the living were outdistancing their pursuers. They quickly reached the water pump, and Jake held his breath as they turned the corner, afraid of what might be waiting there.

Nothing was.

It was just an empty street that led past a few silent buildings, across a grassy heath to where the two spiked Indian heads stood watch. Jake's side burned with pain, his legs tired and weak, but his heart was suddenly lighter. He pushed himself harder, yanking Tasha forward, no longer trying to be gentle. Behind them and around the corner, the sound of hundreds of shuffling feet grew a little fainter, like voices whispering. Just another fifty yards now.

Suddenly the screeching ping of a ricocheted bullet struck the ground at Jake's foot. He spun around wildly, his eyes wide. Standing not far behind them, leaning on the water pump, was the Reverend Humbert Loftus. He was pointing a familiar Colt revolver at them.

"Found your gun on the ground back there." His voice was high and reedy. "God helps those who help themselves." He took a limping step forward and fired again. The shot hit the toe of Jake's boot and he fell to the ground, pulling Tasha with him.

So close. He grimaced, furious at the thought. We almost made it Goddamnit.

The preacher staggered towards them like a drunkard, waving the gun and cackling. "You thought you could challenge the will of the Almighty? Fool!" He pulled the trigger again, but this time the shot went wild. He didn't seem to notice. "Still, He will welcome you into his flock. 'Bless them, Father, for they know not what they do.'"

Loftus didn't see the figure come lumbering out of the shadows until it reached out and grabbed him by the arm. The preacher spun just as the creature sank its teeth into his shoulder. He uttered a horrible scream and collapsed to the ground, the gun falling from his hand. The thing crouched over him, and Jake and Tasha could hear the sounds of it ripping cloth and flesh, even over Loftus's cries. Jake got slowly up, helping Tasha to her feet. Ahead, at the street corner, the first of the resurrected mob was arriving. Jake started to turn, ready to make for the barrier, when the dead man who'd pulled Loftus to the ground looked up at him.

It was Cody. Or rather, what had once been Cody. Gore dripped from his lower jaw as he locked eyes with Jake for a moment. Then he dipped his head back to the preacher, digging in to the fat of his neck. Jake touched the brim of his hat, issuing silent thanks to what had once been his friend, and then hurried on. They covered the ground fast and soon they were passing the Indian heads. It didn't surprise Jake at all to see a green, misty glow shining from their empty eye sockets.

The horses were where they'd left them, calm and quiet, knowing nothing of the horrors that had befallen their riders. Jake untied their leads from the cactus. He pushed Tasha up onto Foxy's saddle and then climbed on behind her, wincing at the pain in his side. He took a look back at Cottonwood. He could see the dead. A huge crowd, had fallen upon the preacher, bringing their shepherd into the flock. When Tasha turned to see, he tried to keep her from it.

"Hey, you don't wanna see that."

Her eyes were steely. "Yes, I do."

So, he let her get an eyeful. When he thought she'd seen enough, he grabbed the other horse's reins. He put the spurs to Foxy and gave a shout. The horses took off at a run and the post-man and the little girl rode on towards the east and dawn.

PUBLICATION HISTORY

"Permanent Residents" first appeared in "Daylight Dims: Vol 2" Edited by J.W. Zulauf & Kristopher Mallory ©2014 *Stealth Fiction*

"Blood Oranges" first appeared in "Twisted Yarns" Edited by Gloria Bobrowicz ©2015 *Sirens Call Publications*

"The Other House" first appeared in "Final Masquerade" Edited by Stacey Turner ©2016 *Lycan Valley Press*

"The Visitor" first appeared in, "Midnight Movie: Creature Feature" Edited by T.W. Brown © 2011, *May December Publications*

"Simulacrum" first appeared in, "Best Served Cold vol.1: An Eye for an Eye" Edited by Christopher Ficco © 2011, Runewright LLC publi*shing*

"Fishing Hole" first appeared in, "Indiana Science Fiction Anthology 2011" Edited by James Ward Kirk © 2011, *James Ward Kirk, An Angels & Demons & Ghosts Publication*

"Flood Photos" first appeared in, "Evolutionary Blueprint" Edited by Joe Jablonski © 2011, *Static Movement*

"Late Night Laundry" first appeared in, "Daily Flash 2012: 366 Days of Flash Fiction" © 2011, *Daily Flash Publications, an imprint of Pill Hill Press*